Think Zombie

By Jason Ernest

ISBN 978 1490 403 595

Published in the United Kingdom

First Published, 2013

Contents

1.   Outbreak

Mary was sitting on the edge of the bath. She noticed that the toilet roll had nearly run out. For a split second she started to rise to get a new one from the cupboard in the hallway. She stopped, trembling at the mere thought that she might have willingly walked into the horror unfolding in her home. She put her hand over her mouth as she was engulfed by uncontrollable sobbing. The bang at the bathroom door brought her to her senses. She was less than an arm's length away from it, about as far as was practical in the tiny room. Mary stared at the lock in which all of her hopes for survival were vested, a flimsy mechanism being called upon to perform a task way beyond its duty. Mary's self-delusion reassured her that it would hold, despite the screws already starting to give from nothing more than daily use. It would barely cause the imminent onslaught to stumble.

'Help me…' came a weak, decaying voice. 'I'm your brother.' Mary couldn't believe that her instinct for survival, magnified by the carnage beyond the door, had left no question in her mind that it was staying locked. Of course she felt deep shame that it was a victim of the horror behind it, and not the monster that was cannibalising her family, although her relief adequately compensated for the guilt. Mary quite easily referred to the perpetrator in her mind as a monster, despite the fact that only minutes earlier it had been her daughter, Kate.

Kate had returned home from university for the Christmas holiday the previous day. Mary had been so looking forward to seeing her daughter again after nearly ten weeks away. There was so much for them to catch up on. Mary couldn't understand what could have just happened. Why on earth would Kate bite clean through her granddad's cheek, and plunge her fingers into his eye sockets? Why had she torn away a chunk of flesh leaving a hole in the side of his face exposing his teeth and tongue?

Mary felt complete failure at not having spotted any signs of Kate's unhappiness, or whatever it was. She thought back over the regular phone conversations that they'd had over the previous weeks. Kate had been worrying about her coursework, maybe going out too much, and asking for money. Nothing at all unusual for a student. If anything she'd seemed a lot happier recently. She was always talking about the group of new friends she'd met, signalling to Mary she'd finally moved on from pining for her pre-university way of life. She wanted to talk about how well they all got on and the ideas that they were having. Mary had occasionally wondered about Laura, a friend that Kate had made in her first couple of weeks and whom she'd seemed very close to, but no longer mentioned. She had even talked about bringing Laura over to visit during the holidays, but Mary knew that it wasn't unusual for those early college friendships to quickly fade. However, Kate had moved on to talking about all sorts of things with such exuberant optimism, about how they could change the world, what was so right and wrong with politics, religion, government and everything else, and the new philosophy that could sort things out.

Mary so wanted to believe that Kate and her friends would change the world. She wanted to believe that they'd be the first of so many groups before them who'd also believed in their own limitless potential. Even if Mary wasn't quite convinced, she'd persuaded Kate that she was. Mary had lived the bit of life that comes later, and had to suppress her cynicism, if only to enjoy believing in Kate's dreams with her. It had been fun while it had lasted, and Kate had become so enthusiastic about the ideas that she'd been telling her mother about in the last few days, that Mary was even starting to believe that Kate and her friends might really change the world.

When they'd last spoken the night before, Kate had still been trying to tell her mum all about their ideas. She'd talked of virtually nothing else, and they'd only just managed to make arrangements for the following day. Kate was so excited, almost euphoric, but she'd run out of change for the payphone. Having already queued for nearly an hour to use one of the half a dozen or so such phones provided in halls, and the queue behind her now even longer than when she'd first arrived, it would have to wait.

Kate had got home in the early hours. She'd arrived in town late the previous afternoon but had wanted to meet up with her friends immediately, aching to catch up and share news. When she got home, Mary was in bed. 'Mum!' she'd shouted. 'Mum, mum, where are you? Are you in bed? Get up. I've got loads to tell you.' Mary was fast asleep and alone in the house, her husband having left when Kate was nine, and hadn't heard the door go. She began to emerge from her deep slumber as Kate thumped up the stairs. Mary was just awake enough not to suffer fright-induced shock as Kate burst into her room, like a five year old on Christmas Morning. She began talking incessantly but Mary didn't take it in. She was exhausted having worked a twelve hour shift at the supermarket the day before in order to get the next day off. They had the family coming over for a special lunch. Kate carried on talking. Mary gave some bleary indication of being over the moon to see her, briefly hugged and kissed her, but soon fell fast asleep, content in the knowledge that Kate seemed happy almost to the point of ecstasy without having acquired a stench of alcohol.

When Mary awoke later that morning, she had no idea how long Kate had stayed talking to her, but presumed she'd gone off to her own bed quite soon after. Kate was in the living room of their three bedroomed semi, talking on the phone as if she was commentating on the Grand National. 'Morning,' said Mary. Kate carried on talking.

As Mary sat on the edge of the bath going over these events, she recalled that everything in the house had seemed untouched that morning, whilst she'd been getting ready for the visitors who'd be arriving at around 11.00am. It wasn't until they arrived that she noticed there was now silence from the living room. The family had all arrived together as Mary's brother Jack and his wife Annette, had collected granddad. The usual family greetings took place, Mary stressing she was nearly ready. The two young children, Paul and Dick, had made their way straight to the living room ahead of the adults. 'You be good!' shouted Annette. 'Don't go annoying Kate.'

'I'm not sure where she is,' said Mary. 'She was on the phone in there, but I think she must have gone upstairs.'

'Hi Kate,' they heard the boys say.

'Where's my dinner?' said granddad, and they all laughed covering up the noise from the living room.

'Come on through and sit down,' said Mary, helping granddad. The living room was a long through room with the entrance door in the middle. To the right of the door were the seats, television, and brick effect fireplace. A further space was available to the left which had a dining table and sideboard. As the troupe of three adults entered the room, they all looked over to the settee on the right where Kate was sitting.

'Kate, come and say hello to your granddad,' said Mary. Kate was sat upright leaning forward with her shoulders slightly raised. Her long, straight hair hung over the sides of her face, and her head was slightly bowed forward. She stood straight up, stopped for a second, and then quickly started walking towards them all.

Mary and Annette took a sharp intake of breath. Kate didn't look normal. She was bearing her teeth, her lips and nostrils flaring, her eyes wide, and her breathing heavy, almost growling, whilst seeming to grin. Mary and Annette didn't even notice at first that Kate's hands were covered in blood, though they couldn't miss the smattering around her mouth. Granddad couldn't see properly and held up his hands to greet Kate. Jack was still in the hall hanging up the coats. Moments later, Kate was tearing at granddad's face. Annette screamed, frozen to the spot. Granddad fell to the floor, trying to grasp at Kate to pull her away, his frail arms failing even to make contact. Kate didn't fall all the way down to the floor with him. She'd bent halfway as he fell and then stood bolt upright, her teeth tearing the flesh from his face. It was then that everyone saw through the hole in granddad's face, drawing them to stare at the old man as he choked for the last time.

Nothing was ever going to be normal after this. No one had any reference point with which to gauge Kate's devouring of granddad, having never happened at a family gathering before. Kate chewed on the flesh in her mouth. Mary stepped forward, her mother's instinct guiding her to comfort Kate, as if somehow a victim, whilst trying to illicit the rational explanation every parent believes exists for their children's actions. As Mary approached Kate, her attention was finally distracted by the corpses of Paul and Dick lying in a heap by the table to the left of the room, like two dolls cast aside by a bored child. Both their throats were ripped open, drenching them in blood. Moments before, the boys had run straight up to Kate to say hello as she sat on the settee, oblivious to her new demonic persona. In doing so, they'd positioned themselves perfectly to each side for her to grab their throats and crush the life silently out of them. Her wrenching had thrust the corpses to the other end of the room, before she'd slumped back down to taste the morsels as the next victims approached.

Mary turned to the bodies of the boys. 'Oh God,' she barely whispered. Annette's screaming caught Kate's attention. She was slightly taller than Annette, making it relatively easy for her to grab hold of Annette's long brown hair with her left hand. Annette started to raise her arms, but was far too slow as Kate rapidly thumped the back of her head into the wall, as if trying to shatter a walnut. Annette was out cold after the second hit, her whole body going limp as blood gushing from her split scalp decorated the wall.

Jack got to the living room. He lost a moment staring in disbelief at what was happening. He grabbed Kate's arms. Kate let go of Annette, her body slumping to the floor. As Jack leant forward pushing Kate away, she grabbed at his head by the ears, and pulled him towards her. His own weight carried him over, and he fell forwards onto Kate as she fell back onto the floor. Jack put his arms out to break the fall, leaving his face at the mercy of Kate's crazed, chewing frenzy. By the time they'd hit the ground it was already impossible for him to see through the blood as Kate bit through his flesh, swallowing mouthfuls.

Mary looked up from where she was kneeling by the corpses of her two nephews, consumed by terror. She ran out of the room, leaving Kate feeding on Jack like a shark with a toddler in a paddling pool. Mary ran up the stairs eager to get to the phone in her bedroom. She ran into the room. The phone wasn't there. She felt cold as she remembered she'd taken it down to the kitchen. She could get out though, if Kate was still eating Jack in the living room. She rushed to the top of the stairs, but her way was blocked. Annette had come round and was at the bottom, but Kate launched herself onto her back to begin devouring her dessert. Mary was trapped. She ran to the bathroom and locked herself in.

Mary now sat in the bathroom, hearing her dying brother pleading for help without any idea of what to do next. The normal response of rushing to the aid of a family member offered no hint of a solution. Suddenly, Jack screamed. The door jolted, straining the hinges and lock as the bodies on the other side bashed against it amid noises of slaughter. Silence followed. 'Jack?' said Mary. She knew silence would have probably been the better option, but her desire to do something overwhelmed her, alerting the basic instincts of the monster. The door flew open, the lock smashing easily. Kate was covered in blood, as if emerging from a vat of the stuff. 'Kate,' said Mary hoping to appeal to the daughter lost somewhere in this beast. She'd hardly finished her utterance before Kate dived at her.

A short time later, the glass front door to Kate's home smashed as she ran into it. After killing her family, she'd continue to wander round the house looking for flesh, visiting each room several times before noticing a world outside. There was still food in the house; she'd taken no more than a few bites from any of the corpses, but living meat and the kill was so much more satisfying. The glass front door was the obvious route of exit. Kate had bounced off it three times by walking straight into it, before running with enough force to overcome her invisible assailant. Neighbours peeped through their curtains. Three of them called the police as Kate proceeded to indulge in her new habit, starting with a man out walking his dog.

***

Kate's friend Laura had also returned home at the same time. Her first few hours back were nothing like as eventful as Kate's had been. She was feeling a little disappointed that the plans she'd discussed with Kate earlier in the term hadn't come to fruition, and how much they'd drifted apart. She was aware that part of her disappointment may have been her ego being knocked by Kate deserting her for her new friends. Laura didn't like them, and her misgivings were motivated by far more than her loss. However hard she tried to convince herself that it was just her jealousy teasing her, she couldn't shake the uneasy feeling she got from these new friends, and especially about what they were saying. She was resolved though, to accepting it as one of those things, and as she relaxed at home after her first night back, she had no idea how soon her resolution would be hurled into disarray, reconfiguring her life beyond recognition.

2.   Spreading

'This is the six o clock news.'

The newsreader read out the daily greeting with the kind of enhanced solemnity that indicated something particularly grim had happened that day, whilst hiding an enthusiasm at reporting something different to the dreary squabbling of politicians. 'Tonight, a young woman in Linderford murders fourteen people including her own family before being shot by police.' This headline confirmed that the introduction had been apt, but barely hinted at the true horror. The newsreader continued listing the other headlines. It was a heavy news day. The second item, 'Airliner plummets killing all on board, cause unknown' would normally have been a major story. The newsreader finished with an apology for postponement of that night's special report.

The newsreader then returned to the real meat of that day's news. After slaying her family, Kate had spent the next twenty minutes eating people on the street. The man walking his dog had been an easy victim. Kate had simply rushed up to him and bitten into his neck severing his jugular vein, and then gnawed at him oblivious to the blood rebounding out of her mouth and off her face. Although not frail, the man had been in his sixties and was simply too slow to respond. As his knees had bent and he fell backwards, his dog, a black Labrador had jumped at Kate, but she deftly grabbed its nose with one hand and lower jaw with the other, before snapping the poor animal's face apart. A steady stream of food had then made its way to Kate, not sure whether they were assisting Kate in helping an injured passerby or preventing a mugging.

Kate, devoid of reason, had simply fed on the writhing bodies as they'd piled up on the pavement until the police car arrived. There were by now several bodies lying over the full width of the pavement, plus a dog. Blood flowed freely, still trickling along the gutter halfway down the street.

'My God,' said WPC Kent as the police car approached in full Christmas tree mode. She slowed down.

'Pull up there,' said PC Trimble. He was a young policeman with less than a year in the force. WPC Kent stopped the car. Her seventeen years of experience told her, 'if you don't recognise it as a familiar situation, play safe'. She had every intention of returning home to her husband and daughter that evening. PC Trimble could see that only Kate was moving. The blood covering her was starting to darken as it attempted to coagulate.

'There's only the one of them,' said PC Trimble who was already jumping out of the car. He felt pretty confident he could handle this, being a second row forward for the Force rugby team, and there'd been no reports of firearms, although the ongoing updates had seemed bizarre.

'No, wait!' WPC Kent spoke softly but meaningfully whilst leaning slightly over to PC Trimble, still engrossed in assessing the situation. It was too late. He was out of the car and her half attempt to grab hold of his body armour was never going to stop him. She stayed in the car and radioed in a commentary, a subconscious decision for survival. Evolution had favoured WPC Kent, but the childless PC Trimble's genes were about to leave the pool.

Kate devoured the PC, his attempts at reason and futile swipes with his regulation big stick failing to save him. Meanwhile, WPC Kent made the call that resulted in Kate being shot dead fifteen minutes later. It wasn't without incident. The arriving vehicles and bodies had simply signalled 'dinnertime' to Kate. Fortunately WPC Kent's description of the scene had meant that the marksmen were briefed to kill and dispatched her immediately as she rushed towards them.

The news report had related the whole story as best it could, though facts were still muddled. The team on the scene were only able to film large blue plastic police tents erected over the

9

bodies and blood. Kate's home was encircled by the obligatory blue and white plastic tape, though this seemed pointless as there were further cordons at each end of the street. One neighbour had managed to get some early shots of blood and gore with a video camera, which the news reporter routinely warned contained disturbing images, before every viewer watched them.

The neighbour had been quick off the mark in getting the video cassette to the television station. He was hopeful that he would get paid for it by the show that showed video clips of people falling over and children hurting themselves, having failed to get any payments so far for the obviously posed videos of his children falling over and hurting themselves. He would have to try and claim his reward later from the news team. There were no shots of the actual deeds, but an ample level of shock and revulsion was still conveyed by the aftermath.

The report was padded out with snippets of interviews with anyone who had the vaguest of connections with Kate.

'She seemed pretty normal.'

'An ordinary girl, just like everyone else.'

'A mate of mine says he chatted her up at a club one night.'

'She was always part of the gang. They weren't a bad lot or anything. Maybe she just got in with the wrong crowd.'

'I was at junior school with her. I can't really remember her doing anything like this back then, but I can't be sure, man. It was a long time ago.'

The news reporter interviewing the willing respondents struggled to maintain interest, as she captured the banal and relentless wisdom from neighbours and acquaintances desperate to exploit their fifteen minutes of fame without having to resort to divulging their most sordid secrets on a daytime television show.

In order to show their extended coverage of what was already being called 'The Linderford Massacre', despite lack of adequate material, the channel had had to cancel an item on a new philosophy that loads of people had been contacting them about. Such a dull story would never have normally made the news had it not been for the number of calls. As it was, the journalists had become particularly enthusiastic about this story, and were quite upset that it had to make way for a real life horror flick.

To fill some more time, the news team concocted a background story suggesting that Kate was severely depressed, based on little more than a suggestion from someone who'd seen her at the supermarket. However, as the television news entered its last five minutes, the depression angle suddenly became superfluous.

'I've just been told that we're receiving reports of a similar incident in Chesborough.' The newsreader said 'similar' with emphasis and paused, his face conveying the genuine shock that he now felt. Having delivered such extraordinary news, he felt he couldn't just sit in silence, aware of the anticipation among the millions of viewers. He started adlibbing as words failed to appear on the autocue. 'I say similar incident, but at the moment I can't be sure exactly what that means. I strongly doubt it can be that similar. These events are so rare. I can't actually remember the last zombie rampage...' He stopped suddenly, pausing to realise that he had just called the Linderford Massacre by the not-to-be-used-outside-the-news-team name, 'zombie rampage'. 'I mean, the Linderford Massacre. The chances of two in one day... well!' He stumbled on as best he could.

The main significance of this late breaking news turned out to be the national coining of the term 'zombies', along with 'zombie rampage'. From this point on, the term zombie would be used by everyone to refer to the perpetrators of the rampages. Those involved were not zombies in the traditional sense, having not risen from the dead as described by Voodoo legend. They were though, a close enough fit to the fictional zombie-type that had developed, appearing to have replaced their humanity and reason with boundless savagery.

As it turned out, the event being reported from Chesborough was indeed similar. Another young girl had started by devouring her boyfriend. The commotion from their flat had caused some of the neighbours to come and see what the problem was. Sally had simply growled from behind the door as the neighbours had shouted to see what was up, eventually agreeing to force their way in. The numbers present meant that a couple of people managed to avoid a zombie welcome and stay outside, pulling the door shut. The opaque security door saved them from being compelled to watch Sally munching, though the screams got through. A similar scene to Kate's demise had then resulted, but this time involving a single police marksman, apparently due to resources being stretched in the area.

Throughout the night, details of an increasing number of similar events emerged, and filtered through the media to an intrigued, but increasingly terrified public. To those who hadn't experienced a zombie rampage first hand, it still seemed like a remote event that couldn't possibly happen to them. However that soon changed. By eleven o clock that night, it seemed hundreds of events were being reported. It was becoming clear that several had been in Chesborough, with descriptions coming in that made it sound like a human abattoir. Although initially hyperbole, the attacks there continued to increase and the exaggeration very quickly became reality. Chesborough was the first place to achieve the single identity of absolute carnage as opposed to being several individual attacks. The concentration of calls for help in this tiny town had made it flicker up as zombie ground zero among the authorities, and was the place that national officialdom chose to disperse its resources in the hope of, if not containing the plague, quickly coming up with some answers and an effective defence. The town was cordoned off by midnight. In contrast to Chesborough, the rest of the attacks appeared to be pretty randomly dispersed around the country.

By the early hours, virtually everyone in the country lived within forty miles of a rampage. Those who lived close enough to one to directly feel its gory effects, were contacting friends and relatives in far flung places. The first hand experiences they conveyed made it increasingly real, making the whole country feel that they were all a part of this danger. It was only a matter of time before reality would catch up as the mood moved towards hysteria. As it happened, this was appropriate as the rate at which the attacks were spreading suggested that zombies would soon be on the streets everywhere and complete societal collapse was not far off. Everyone was presuming that 'they' would do something about it, despite little evidence so far.

***

Like just about everybody else, Laura had watched the reports of the attacks on the news. It was an extra struggle for her to make sense of the situation, not only because she personally knew Kate, but because she could have been there. The initial strike of horror she felt was replaced with relief that she'd escaped this fate to be followed up with shame at such a selfish thought. Laura pondered for a moment whether there was some sort of connection to Kate's new friends, but knew this was probably just a reaction to their part in the demise of her friendship. As Laura tried to make sense of this maelstrom of emotions, the reports of the attacks in Chesborough, her university town, appeared on the television. She felt herself being inexorably sucked into the centre of these events, as she grabbed the phone to try and contact her friend, Luke.

3.   The Goode Things

The following morning, national panic was evident. The newspaper headlines declared 'Zombie Rampages', 'Britain Blood Bath', and other splashes ensuring that the panic was not diminished through lack of rhetorical fuel. More telling though was how hard it was to get hold of one of these newspapers, as the invisible machinery that normally ensured their daily ubiquity struggled. The delay in newspaper reporting meant only a handful of incidents were covered, although the number had escalated way beyond any reasonable estimate. There didn't even seem much point in counting anymore. Anyone living near other people was going to be attacked by, or become a zombie very soon. It was difficult to tell which was preferable.

The television, with its more immediate response, didn't fail to convey the horror. Plenty of channels had maps showing the locations of outbreaks using various symbols, from simple black dots to red splodges to caricatures of zombies and their victims. These maps had quickly become a splurge of colour in the barely perceptible shape of the United Kingdom, as if the weather reporter had enjoyed a particularly exotic curry and too many beers the night before.

Shane, like so many others, was fixated by the pictures from his television, the flickering screen hypnotically seducing him. For many of the other people engaged in similar activity, it was a novelty to be spending the morning in front of the television. Some were able to witness the unfolding massacre right outside their front doors, whilst others were watching the television to ascertain if it was safe to venture out. It was like watching travel reports after a night of heavy snowfall, to decide whether or not they could get away with taking the day off. The added element of mutilation and death convinced most people that they could.

Watching television like this was nothing new for Shane. He did it every day. The reporting of national carnage and the change to the schedules did offer some slight alternative to his normal routine, but only marginally so.

'Oi!' shouted Shane, struggling to lift his head. His bulk was slumped so that he was virtually on his back on the couch, only his generous backside preventing him from sliding off. Calling his wife was an effort, but far less than doing something for himself. 'Oi!' he called again, a term he may have used simply because he couldn't recall her name.

His wife appeared at the door. Though not particularly thin or well kempt, when compared to the stained shell suit engulfing the couch, she appeared quite passable. It was hard to pin ages on either of them, the spirit of hopelessness they'd chosen as their lifestyle suggesting something way beyond their twenty-something years. Shane was quite happy with his lot, but his wife was just enduring a stunned existence, unable to comprehend how the dreams of marriage she and so many others had believed in, had failed to deliver.

Today, she appeared substantially more numb than normal, almost glazed, looking past Shane and out beyond their front window, through the closed curtains in defiance of the daylight outside.

'Lager,' grunted Shane; as it was such a special day he felt entitled to make an early start on his daily intake of alcohol, though there wasn't much in it. With that, his communication with 'Oi' was complete. He felt satisfied at his ability to simply demand his supplies be brought to him. In fact, he hadn't moved from his couch in several months, as evidenced by the sores on his legs and the stench of toilet functions.

Shane's disability did not concern him, having achieved it through his own idleness and gorging, the associated entitlements he received being more than adequate compensation. He was easily able to sustain this state whilst the woman brought him an endless supply of processed fat and sugar. A simpler solution would have been to have sent her on a world cruise, but the system would never allow such a thing. It was a system with a life of its own, that no one seemed to really want or understand, but affected everything and everyone. Ensuring rights for Shane regardless of reality, he would have had more chance of reading The Odyssey in the original Homeric Greek than understanding the consequences of his decisions within it.

The woman, shuffled out of the room without any response. It may have been that the news had left her distraught. Or it may have been the lack of response from Shane the night before as she'd tried to tell him all about the exciting things her friends had been talking about, his undisguised contempt and ignorance finally breaking her will. Shane couldn't care less as long as she brought back lager.

Shane flicked through the four television channels, feeling that so few being provided must be an abuse of his rights. Virtually all of the shows that morning were taken up with viewer phone-ins, each competing to get the most gruesome first-hand zombie experience. He eventually alighted on The Goode Things, and was intrigued enough to have his attention held for longer than a few seconds.

The Goode Things was a daily morning show that already comprised of phone-ins on issues of the day, so they were adept at sifting out the I'll-say-anything-to-be-on-television types, from the people who might occasionally be worth listening to. The normally cheerful presenter, Martin Goode, had lost much of his humour that morning, and resembled more closely than ever the host of a competing show on the other channel, who coincidentally looked like an angry version of Martin. Shane often played the game of flicking between the two channels to create his own mini show of 'happy Martin, angry Martin, happy Martin, angry Martin'.

The angry Martin show was in the best tradition of Hogarth's Bedlam with society's unfortunates being dragged on to air the multiple embarrassments that constituted their lives. This ranged from questionable parentage to various crime-fuelled addictive pastimes, motivated by a belief that being subsequently recognised on the streets somehow counted as their longed-for celebrity status. Shane was hoping to appear soon having found someone to complete the application form for him.

Martin Goode's show that morning, virtually high art compared to the alternative, was a curious blend with a queer aura of solemn excitement. The outbreak of zombie rampages had enlivened the mundane lives of the majority of the population, many worrying that they may have somehow wished this event into existence. Many chose to focus on the mantra that it was bringing people together and creating a stronger community spirit, and if any occasion ever called for it, this one did.

The show was a harrowing combination of witness reports, terrified members of the public expressing their fears and feelings, and various pictures and videos. Containment of the zombies had collapsed during the night as police resources had become stretched beyond their limits. The pictures and videos showed that the perpetrators were not normal. It wasn't just the blood and eating people. Their expressions revealed empty eyes behind which all reason and empathy seemed to have vanished. The zombies appeared almost physically disfigured, all expression drained, so that that their gnashing as they sensed flesh, was all the more terrifying. They were the worst of all worlds, unreasoning animals left with only human hate to drive them.

Martin Goode's usual panel of people was reduced to just him and show regular, Claire Sherman. Claire was someone who prided herself on knowing how to think properly. She knew the right view to support or attack, the right words to use and the right people to know. Claire had been on the panel the previous day, and had been able to fully empathise with the caller from a hell hole of an estate struggling to pay her bills. The caller was at her wits ends as she described her 'slob' of a husband and hopeless life. She was looking for anything that would give her something to live for, her desperation an invitation to exploiters of the vulnerable. Claire understood, explaining that she'd also experienced difficulties when she'd found it hard to cope with paying her children's school fees, until her parents had stepped in. Claire had even offered to help, but abruptly turned when the caller had tried to suggest that it was Claire's elite cabal and their ideas, hopelessly divorced from reality, that trapped her in her torment. Martin had finally hit the cut switch after Claire accused the caller of being a 'ranting extremist fascist'. None of these regular episodes troubled Claire in the slightest, who could effortlessly doublethink away the conflict between her views and lifestyle. She probably wouldn't even recall the incident any longer, let alone the caller's name.

Martin with his likeable demeanour and controversial but ultimately non-threatening style had risen rapidly. He liked Claire as, like a comfort blanket, she represented the ethos that had dominated his time as a student a few years earlier in the eighties. It was the trendy way of thinking that everyone subscribed to regardless of any real beliefs, an essential badge of compliance to show their radicalism and independence. Comment couldn't be valid, music couldn't be good, comedy couldn't be funny, if it didn't fit the rules. This hegemony dominated youth culture as it began its march with its ageing converts into the adult world.

Shane had flipped over to The Goode Things just as the show's jolly opening theme music was finishing and the camera swept through the audience. A couple of the audience members appeared in a daze, far more than usual, but given the circumstances they'd have had to have endured to reach the studio for their reward of the split second of fame delivered by the camera sweep, it was not surprising.

'Only one topic today,' said Martin, taking an intake of breath and raising his eyebrows in Claire's direction, beckoning her to respond. Ordinarily, she wouldn't accept any such subjugation by a man, but she did like being on television so much, and was keen to remain in the small circle of friends who comprised the panels on Martin's show. She limited her discontent to a slight delay and an easy-to-miss look of contempt at Martin before replying. Martin didn't miss it and quite liked it.

'Zombies,' replied Claire. She waited for Martin to comment, always keen to take the opposite stance to others. Martin for once, felt relaxed in the belief that he'd get his thinking right today, and that they would both be in agreement.

'Do we call in the army now?' said Martin, aware that the police couldn't cope.

'What?' exclaimed Claire. 'What kind of a fascist are you?' she continued, always keen to personalise her attacks.

'I…' stammered Martin, utterly perplexed.

'The army, and the police, are the problem,' announced Claire. 'They're attacking these zombies without any idea of their issues. Their behaviour has obviously been caused by state oppression.' Claire was immediately into full flow and on message. Aware that the Government in power was not to the extreme left, she knew instantly that everything was their fault, and with her powerful intellect, would be able to rationalise exactly why she was right later on if need be.

'What about people being killed?' replied Martin.

'They're collateral, Martin,' came back Claire, not missing a beat. 'If you use that kind of excuse to justify state sponsored brutality, you're virtually living in a dictatorship already.'

'What about the human rights of the victims?' asked Martin, hoping to meet Claire on her own ground.

'What about zombie rights?' snapped back Claire.

Martin was confused. Surely Claire, his guru, couldn't be wrong, and yet she seemed to be talking absolute rubbish. Not for the first time, Martin was struggling to hold it together through the internal ravages of his cognitive dissonance, though it had never been this bad. He was saved by news coming into his earpiece and the need to move on to callers.

'We're getting reports that the Government is already assembling a specialist task force to tackle the problem,' said Martin, having to suppress any cynicism.

Oddly enough, it was Government obsession with presentation and spin that had led to such immediate and decisive action. The governing party were desperate to avert attention from another corruption debacle involving a senior minister acting more equally than the people. He'd been accepting, among other things, holidays, cash and girls from a major Government contractor, Karpitem, the winners of yet another large, pointless Government contract signed off by the minister. Once again, those involved were caught out when the minister and his associates forgot that what they were doing was illegal. As a result of this pending political disaster, the Government were looking for anything that would divert attention. This time, they didn't even have to manufacture a problem, though many within the party were still asking later that day whether it was really ethical to instigate mass slaughter to benefit their own political ends.

'Well, let's wish them all the very best of luck and let's hope they can get to the bottom of this,' said Martin, cutting off Claire's guaranteed hostility. 'We've got a caller. Hello Amanda.'

'Hi Martin. I know that what is happening is terrible, but I'd love to tell you about something that is keeping my spirits and hopes high. It's called the new…'

'Yes. Thanks Amanda,' said Martin covering the flicking of a cut-off switch. 'We'll save that for another day.' They'd been getting many callers like Amanda, and had succeeded in filtering virtually all of them out, though they were struggling with some of their staff becoming inordinately engrossed. 'Next caller is Bill,' continued Martin moving on.

'Hello Martin. I was going to ask what the Government are doing about this, but it sounds like they've got the Zombie Squad on the case.' This caller had the honour of coining the name for the specially convened group that they themselves would be using by the end of the day. Sadly, Bill would be devoured three hours later.

Martin briefly discussed the name, the Zombie Squad, with Claire who saw the squad as another attempt to impose authoritarian control, but all this was soon forgotten after the next caller.

'Go ahead, Laura. I understand you knew the girl from the first attack.'

'I…' Silence followed with some weeping in the background.

'This must be very difficult for you Laura. It's okay. Don't feel you have to say anything. We'll go to the next caller.'

'No wait,' said Laura, realising the opportunity she'd been desperate for was about to slip away. 'I've been trying to talk to the police, but I can't get through. You've got to listen to me.'

'Okay,' replied Martin, inquisitively stretching the 'o' of 'okay'. 'Carry on. Take your time.'

'I didn't just know Kate. I knew some of the others in Chesborough.' The panel were suddenly highly attentive, the studio silent. Chesborough had been the second place that attacks had broken out. It had been established as the hotbed of zombie rampages during the night, though other places were now catching up. Laura's voice indicated that 'the others' meant zombies. Martin was desperate to ask Laura how she knew them all, but remained silent in case he spooked her. He could be getting the best story of the day. This was even better than being the first to publicly name a celebrity suspected of paedophilia. Laura continued, 'Kate knew them as well. We were all at Chesborough Uni together.' Martin and Claire looked at each other realising that Laura had made a connection between the first outbreaks.

Martin had to ask a question. 'If this is true, why haven't the authorities found out yet?'

'Because anyone who could tell them is [beep] dead,' came an emotional reply down the phone line. The time delay had worked effectively.

'Ok Laura, I realise that this is very distressing,' Martin offered sympathetically. Given the extraordinary circumstances, and the valid defence that any information Laura might provide could be of public benefit, she hadn't been immediately cut off as the beep insertion would normally have required. 'Is there anything else you want to say Laura?' The amplified telephone call filled the studio with weeping.

'I... I... I...,' said Laura, as she struggled to speak but was caught up in sobs and involuntary gulps of breathing. Laura was desperate to tell them how close a friend Kate had been, but how they'd become more distant over the last week or so because Laura didn't want to hear about the new philosophy that Kate was increasingly obsessed with. Laura was normally strong, but this was the first time she'd experienced how a waited for opportunity could cause her emotions to overwhelm her.

'We'll leave it there then Laura. Stay on the line, we'll talk to you some more off-air. Claire?' Martin realised he'd already been gifted plenty of information to grab audience share with Laura's revelation, as well as feeling a tinge of genuine sympathy. Nonetheless, the off air conversation would be a thinly disguised 'thanks for that, now sod off'. For the next few minutes, Martin and Claire, along with the audience and various telephone callers believed they were having a meaningful conversation, as they endlessly repeated the same details. Eventually a caller moved them forward.

'What if it's something they catch?'

'What do you mean by that? That they go out and find a zombie?' replied Martin missing the point.

'No, not like that. Something that they've all caught, like a cold or some kind of a virus.'

'How would that explain people committing these rampages?' retorted Martin, immediately realising the answer as he said it.

'It turns them into zombies and once infected, they go on a rampage,' replied the caller. Hands were rapidly lifted to mouths to cover involuntarily expletives. No more explanation was needed. In this morning of madness, something actually made total sense. It was already clear that the zombies were acting under the same influence. It was inconceivable that so many similar acts all happening at the same time was merely coincidence. Although a virus now seemed obvious, it had needed someone to say it above the noise of the relentless reports of attacks.

For a brief second, the suggestion of a virus offered relief. If what was happening could be explained, then it could be understood, just as people need a God to explain what they do not understand in a random and cruel world. The relief was short-lived though.

'If it's a virus it might be contagious!' Martin paused looking directly into Claire's face. 'It could get worse! It could affect any one of us!' Claire said nothing, allowing a low growling to be heard above the silence. Martin and Claire's expressions, already in shock, deepened in intensity, and their eyes slowly rotated to gaze out into the audience. The video editor switched to a shot of the audience. One of the members was rocking on his seat, in short, rapid movements. He was sat on his hands, as if his bum had pinned them to the seat. His head was slightly down but rising up slowly.

Its eyes were wide, the grin inane and the saliva flowing. The zombie released a hissing snarl through its clenched teeth, spraying phlegm over the audience members in front. The audience was only about fifty in total sat on four rows, and the few covered in the spray were more disgusted by their shower, than affected by the terror that they should have felt. The zombie jumped up and ran at Claire. It was impossible to tell if this was because she looked tastiest, or because of some latent feelings lingering from the zombie's recently dissolved consciousness.

The show ended unusually that day as mass hysteria broke out and camera's were knocked over, as the screaming audience began to run around irrationally, suddenly incapable of finding the exit. The studio control room managed to switch on the jolly theme music, a comical accompaniment to the ensuing chaos, rather like 'Benny Hill does the Chainsaw Massacre'. Unfortunately the shot being broadcast was from a camera that had been knocked over, so that all the viewers could see were the bottom half of legs moving up and down their screens, as if running around a vertical wall. Splatters of blood sprayed sideways across the picture as the zombie gorged, before a body fell onto the camera completely obscuring the shot, followed by silence once the theme music had subsided.

Shane found it all very amusing, and spat food all over his generously stained shell suit as he laughed.

'Oi!' he shouted, calling his wife. She didn't come. 'Oi,' he called again, louder and more unpleasantly. She appeared in the doorway. He strained to turn his head round, stretching the copious flab on his neck to look at her, and then looked back to the television to see if they'd returned to shots of the chaos. He found himself double taking, or as best he could. For a second he was confused as he found himself looking at the same thing that he'd just seen on television. Shane struggled to understand, but managed to grasp that he ought to be panicking.

He tried to manifest the terror that now kicked in, trying to shift, but all he managed to do was trigger oscillations of flab. He whimpered, consigned to his fate and consumed with his own self pity, devoid of the slightest tinge of unselfish emotion or concern for his wife. She lunged forward at him screaming, teeth bared. It was as if years of abuse, insults, being downtrodden and shattered dreams, exploded out of her in one sudden flash. She tore away the shell suit on Shane's front, and ripped a hole through his skin. Her hands burrowed rapidly away at his torso, like a child trying to dig sand out of a hole on the beach. Shane cried and wailed. Initially neglecting his head ensured that he would endure the full pain of Oi's excavations. There was nothing he could do as he wished his death would come quicker to end this horrific ordeal.

The children were playing on their video games upstairs, the beginnings of Shane and Oi's state funded tribe, its further growth only stalled by morbid obesity ceasing their father's carnal exploits. The two children continued to play their game, oblivious to their father's fate and that they were next on the menu.

4. The Zombie Squad

Around mid morning, the core members of the Zombie Squad, the group convened by the British Government, met for the first time. The setting was a rural location, around forty miles to the North West of London, a nameless place, known only as Location Three. A few single storey prefabricated buildings and a large corrugated barn was all that stood above ground. The tracks to and around them could barely be described as roads. These meagre facilities were set behind fencing topped with barbed wire that stood a half a mile away from the buildings at their closest point. The prefabs were only occasionally used by a couple of guards, a token presence merely to prevent Location Three from appearing completely derelict. The main security was located in the underground complex supported by assorted state-of-the-art electronic surveillance. Continual satellite imaging of the whole area across the full electromagnetic spectrum meant that a single detached operator at a desk was far more effective than any number of guards. No vehicles could be seen parked anywhere, as they drove straight in or out of the barn without pause to access the main entrance to the underground area.

Location Three provided a working environment supposedly insulated from all knowable dangers that were likely to threaten those based within it. It was the most secure facility available with Location One being a scaled down version of Location Three used for anything from planning strategies against striking workers to middle management Government meetings, and Location Two being nothing more than a pseudo-secret administration facility. Their real purpose was to act as cover for Location Three, demoting it in the perceived pecking order. Location Three was barely adequate for what the Zombie Squad would have to deal with.

However apt a choice, the seriousness of the situation was in no way appreciated when Location Three had been selected as the base the night before at the emergency top level meeting headed by the Prime Minister. The response was based on what the media was going to make of it all, with decisions as to how they responded coming a poor second. This approach had come to serve pretty well as a governmental approach to policy, with action effectively only ever occurring as an unintentional consequence of presentation. Any Government that didn't follow this approach quite simply found themselves voted out. Fortuitously, in this instance the scale of the story, and associated fear of accusations of ineffectiveness from the media mob, had led to about the best option being taken.

The meeting was due to convene at 11.00 am. Some minutes before, the key members of the Zombie Squad were already assembled in Location Three's main conference room, along with their own people and various support staff provided to them, in all around thirty in total. The important business of stocking up on tea, coffee and biscuits was taking place, as there was every expectation that this meeting might actually start on time. Indeed everyone was seated and ready to start on cue as, just before 11.00 am, a couple of people had sat down to avoid the chit-chat. This had caused a panic among the others who for once, were desperate not to be seen to be holding things up.

'Welcome, everyone,' said a lady in her fifties in a business-like fashion. This was Harriet Tomes, a career civil servant who was the key liaison to the Government. Harriet was the archetypal civil servant, not too glamorous, though not quite frumpy, a consummate diplomat and observer of etiquette, convention and the done way. She exuded an air of being able to get things done, though like most before here, her actual ability was little more substantial than the draft of a butterfly's wings. Although she was unable to make little happen, it was not made to happen in the correct way ensuring that everyone was content and that no boats were rocked. Fortunately, by the end of the meeting the escalating severity of the zombie crisis would ensure that the prospect of yet another 'Harriet debacle' would be snatched from her hands.

Harriet had a reputation for being the 'go to' person for such things as whitewashes or implementing policies based on questionable political ideology, and the rapid promotions she was invariably rewarded with ensured that she was never around when her seeds of chaos had blossomed into full grown fiascos. It really should have been a simpler task to spot that investigations into election fraud, thousands of illegal migrants 'vanishing' and the cost of new systems costing more than the taxes they collected, were all preceded by the same woman being the boss of elections, borders and the national revenue.

Along with Harriet, another three people were sat around the table. Behind them seated along the walls were the rest of the participants, their junior ranking to the main players obvious. The table that they were sat at was a long thin classic conference table. Although it could amply take a dozen people on each side, the group had sensibly opted to gather at one end with Harriet at the head. The room was just wide enough to allow adequate room for anyone to pass in front of those at the edges. For an underground bunker the room was well lit, with around six landscape paintings along the walls failing to disguise the fact there were no windows and the closest daylight was several storeys above them.

'For the sake of time,' continued Harriet, 'I'll briefly introduce everyone.' They were all content with this; it would be sometime before egos got in the way too much.

Harriet went around the table, introducing the main members of the group, finishing with a cover all of the others. There was General Adam Spelling, the military man. He was of a similar age to Harriet having spent his whole working life in the army, the latest son of a successful military family, though the premature death of his eldest son in a recent war threatened to end this. He was clean-shaven with a long thin face. Although announced as being there for his expertise, no one doubted that his ability to command military resources was just as important, if not the real reason, and Location Three was a military installation.

Dr Javed Hussain was the Government scientific officer, not dissimilar at a distance to General Spelling, though of a darker complexion and portraying the native south asian characteristics of his parents.

Ian Milton was sat on the corner next to Harriet. He was the youngest person present by at least ten years. Ian was appointed as the cabinet's special advisor. A few eyes darted around the room, almost unnoticeably, to see who else was aware that he was the party political man, there to not only ensure that the ruling Government was not harmed in any way, but also that every benefit for the Party could be extracted from events. Ian noticed those who had clocked him, being politically astute if little else.

This was a man whose rise was assured. It wasn't a question of intellect, for his was barely sufficient, just enough to ensure that, along with the essential right family connections, he had got onto the escalator of political success. He was now well on his way to being another identikit politician; he didn't even know if his chosen party was to the left or right. Ian's route was increasingly the only one, and ensured that those on it were disproportionately divorced from the life of the voters that they relied on. The field upon which Ian and many others like him played their games may have been representative democracy at some point, but was now no better than offering up a choice of a Labrador, a Poodle and a Jack Russell to a population of cats.

'Well, we all know the reason, we're here,' said Harriet. 'We're the Extraordinary Response Squad to the Multiple Psychotic Massacres. May I thank you all for agreeing to be part of it at such short notice.'

'What's our brief?' asked General Spelling, keen to start forming some kind of clarity and purpose for his being there and delivering on the stereotype of man-of-action.

'Quite,' replied Harriet thankful for the cue. 'It's pretty short but broad, as is often the case in these situations.' She smiled having expressed her experience.

'I have a copy here direct from the Prime Minister,' interrupted Ian Milton.

'How nice,' replied Harriet, desperate to remain diplomatic, but struggling to resist reacting to the youngster, the manner he'd developed as a toady to his house master at one of the country's best public schools still escaping. She quickly recovered. 'Maybe you could read it to us all.' Ian complied.

'The brief for the Extraordinary Response Squad to the Multiple Psychotic Massacres is to ensure damage to the nation as a result of the massacres is minimised, by taking any legal actions utilising standard resources. This will include maintaining appropriate data, identifying causes, predicting events and acting to repair, limit or prevent damage.'

'Thank you, Ian,' Harriet said with a 'now-shut-up' smile. Despite this, the two were very similar, their similarities being the key to their success. 'I know that you're all aware of the terms and conditions of your appointments, and that we're all going to be together for the foreseeable future. So to bring you up to date…'

Harriet began her litany of facts with the caveat that it was an ever-changing situation and this was the best information that they had. This was received by most people as meaning that they couldn't be sure about anything other than something really bad was happening. Ian Milton wondered what the food was like and how he should describe the meeting in his diary that evening, as he day-dreamed about his stellar political career.

There had been several hundred zombie attacks, possibly thousands, though it was fast becoming impossible to get reliable information. These attacks were displayed on a map of the UK as dots, similar to those being used on television shows, if not exact copies. There appeared to be a slightly higher concentration in the North West and far fewer in the extremities of the North and South of the country, but that was about it. Next there was a graph showing how the number of attacks had been increasing over the last few hours.

'I'm sure all of us can see that the frequency of attacks is exponential,' pointed out Harriet, as she trailed the pointer along the upwards curving line.

'So what's the prediction?' asked Adam. Harriet hesitated. She didn't want to answer this question, but knew that she had to respond.

'Dr Hussain will explain,' she said as she sat down.

Javed took a breath, knowing he was theorising from a basis of little fact. 'The data for attacks so far is not comprehensive, and there could be errors with what we've got,' he began, building up a sense of anticipation as he spoke with a light Pakistani accent adding a certain mystery to his words. 'However in the last two hours we have seen roughly a doubling in the number of attacks, which the earlier figures do not conflict with. On that basis, by midnight tonight we could have several thousand attacks on our hands.'

The room was aghast as everyone seemed to recoil in shock at once.

'What about midnight tomorrow?' asked the General calmly, feeling that same twinge of excitement he'd experienced when he first confidently directed troops in battle. His stomach churned slightly though, as this time the enemy had not been carefully selected by his masters on the basis of their massively inferior militarily ability and posturing dictator sat atop massive natural resources.

'Well, we really don't know if the prediction is correct, and it's really just a notional figure.' Javed laughed nervously as he spoke, partly because he was embarrassed that the science he loved could be providing such ridiculous results, partly because they might be right. The General gestured at Javed to continue. 'Anything from ten thousand to millions.'

'That's nearly everyone!' exclaimed Ian Milton. 'How the hell am I meant to spin that for the Party?'

'Well you won't have to worry then will you,' commented Adam dryly. The mood lightened slightly.

'This really is theoretical. I'm sure it's not going to be everyone,' said Harriet, in some way managing to provide a little relief that a few non-flesh eaters would remain.

'I'm afraid we're wasting time,' said Harriet. 'It comes down to what we know and what we're going to do.' She continued with her update calling on various assistants for information as she went on. The situation was quantified as far as possible, slowly draining the emotion from the group as deaths and massacres became data and statistics. As well as the home situation, there was international concern. Though not on the same level, there were some similar foreign reports, and the cessation of international flights was inevitable.

Harriet's report lasted twenty minutes. As she finished, a support officer entered the room and handed her a piece of paper. It only took around ten seconds for her to read as she'd been expecting it, but the suspense seemed to drag out this brief pause indefinitely, heightened by the intensity of her expression.

'Well I didn't want to mention this until I got some confirmation. Apparently a young lady called a television station today suggesting that some of the victims were known to each other and had recently been in physical contact. Our preliminary enquiries appear to show that this checkouts.' Harriet looked around the table at the Zombie Squad members, using the opportunity to see how quick each was to catch on. Ian Milton looked around quizzically as if he were the only child in the playground unaware of the joke being played on him.

'I take it then, that given the severity of the symptoms,' General Spelling began, 'a plan of quarantine is the only option.' Harriet nodded slowly but solemnly. The General and Harriet stared knowingly at each other for a second. 'Although I never thought I'd see it in my lifetime, I presume the order sanctioning martial law is on its way,' continued the General. Harriet's eyes closed as she nodded once to the General's enquiry. He continued, 'I'll set things in motion.' Although the Government were still in charge of the country, and Harriet was still, technically at least, the senior member of the Zombie Squad, the imposition of martial law would naturally elevate

Adam's standing and many would be unable to not see him as the senior person. Harriet frowned, but had no choice other than to accept it. The General leant back and whispered no more than a few sentences to one of his support staff, who promptly left the room to implement a myriad of planning that had already begun prior to the meeting.

'What are you doing?' asked Ian Milton. 'What's changed? I'll have to clear this with the PM.'

'Do you really not get it?' asked Dr Javed Hussain. 'This evidence suggests that the rampages are being caused by some form of contact. It is impossible to be sure at this stage, but it suggests some kind of disease, a virus or the like. As this is about the only information we have so far, the only option open to us is to prevent any unnecessary contact between people who haven't already been exposed to each other.' Javed, with his sharp analytical mind, had perfectly and coherently summed up the situation. Ian was still confused whilst looking for the political motivation, but he decided to shut up for now. Javed continued, 'We're going to need more information, but at least we have something to follow up. I suggest we get on with it.'

'I'll let you know when the PM's approval comes through,' Adam said to Ian, who mistook this for deference to his sense of self-importance.

'And the young lady who made the call?' asked Adam. Harriet looked uneasy.

'We have a recording of the show,' she began, 'but we've drawn a blank in trying to trace her.' Adam cringed at the familiarity. There was nothing more to add. Harriet moved on. 'We'll convene again in ninety minutes.' The formal meeting disintegrated to be replaced by scattered conversations.

5. The Motorway

Derek Hammond wasn't sure if he would make it to the next services or have to pull over to the side of the motorway. He'd suddenly become aware of a heavy vibration in the Rontel car he was driving. It was only about two years old. It had been one of the last built before the collapse of the weary monolith of a manufacturer that had limped along for nearly two decades after fatally wounding itself during industrial turbulence a couple of decades earlier. He wished that he'd listened to his friends' advice, but it was such a bargain. Now it looked as if he was going to be stuck on the hard shoulder of the M6 on this drizzly day, waiting for another motor recovery operative to yet again question his purchase.

In the split second it took to notice the problem, he was aware that he couldn't identify its source, or which particular component was about to join the others in the scrap yard, and that it may have been coming from outside. He looked over to his left out of the passenger door window. Always apprehensive of his car's foibles, he was travelling steadily along the slow lane of the motorway oblivious to the impatient motorists hurtling past, giving him a clear view to the side. At first he wasn't sure if he was seeing correctly through the drizzle. There were three military helicopters flying alongside past his vehicle, barely off the ground. These were not the kind of tiny day-to-day helicopters used by police forces or company executives. Two of them appeared to be not too dissimilar to tanks with rotor blades and side-mounted gun turrets.

A few seconds behind these, and somewhat higher was a twin bladed Chinook, its back doors open, allowing Derek to see that it was full of troops eagerly grouped at the edge of the craft, waiting for the ground to buzz close enough for them to jump out. The vibration and noise had quickly increased and was triggering secondary rattles throughout Derek's car. He looked into his rear view mirror, but couldn't make out what was behind through the blurred image. Other drivers were also staring over, captivated by the impromptu demonstration of military hardware, their attention drawn away en masse from the motorway.

Cars were beginning to veer, brake lights were flashing sporadically, and a car strayed too far and bumped the side of Derek's Rontel. He quickly applied his brakes, his immediate thought along with his automatic reaction for his own safety being the cost of the inevitable damage. He caught the eye of the driver of the estate car that had hit him who was also slowing, and was just about to start mentally noting the make, colour, model and number plate when he felt a sharp click to his neck, and that was the last thing he was ever aware of.

The driver of the large articulated truck behind Derek had not only been more interested in the trio of helicopters, unaware that the cars in front of him were slowing down, but had also been unconsciously accelerating before hitting the back of Derek's care with significant force. The back of Derek's car was thrown up slightly and over to the right, confusing its traction as it tried to cope with its own momentum. The Rontel swerved to the left, rolling as it did so. Behind it the truck driver, in a panic swerved to the right, jack knifing his lorry in the process. What followed was mechanical carnage, a metallic metaphor of the zombie rampages. With so many drivers beguiled by the helicopters, like little boys at a toy shop window, dozens of cars were now rear-ending, swerving, skidding, crumpling and rolling all over the motorway. A similar single lapse of concentration and unfortunate clipping of vehicles on the other side of the carriageway meant that the whole road was soon playing host to a multitude of twirling, spinning, slamming vehicles.

'This is road block leader eighty one. We appear to have a road incident involving multiple vehicle crashes. Several injuries, fatalities and probable fire risk. Is civilian support available?' The pilot of the helicopter that was relaying details of the unfolding pile-ups was correct in his predictions.

'Negative eighty one,' came the reply. 'Priority is quarantine. Dispatch troops and set up road blocks away from the incident. Stay in the area to provide air support.'

The large twin-rotored Chinook dropped off a couple of dozen troops a short distance from the side of the motorway. They ran through the down draft, a couple stumbling and falling over as they attempted to swing their rifles from side to side, still not used to manoeuvring in their bio chem suits. Whether or not they provided any protection from the unknown cause of the zombies, they definitely added an increased level of menace. The helicopter rapidly pulled up, leaning over as it twizzled around, heading away to drop off a similar consignment of goods at the next venue. All around the country, similar road blocks were being set up. This was just a small part of the huge effort now being undertaken to enforce total and immediate quarantine. No one was to move between any major population centres from this point forward.

The M6 incident was a particularly nasty affair, but it wouldn't even make the newspapers. The fear created by the zombie crisis meant that extreme measures were in order and concerns were focussed elsewhere. This in no way lessened what was happening on the M6. As troops ran over fields brandishing guns to broadcast the we-mean-business message, the crash site took on a semblance of Hell's scrapyard. The initial impacts had created a cacophony of thumping metal and splintering glass, but even as the Chinook vanished into the distance, there were still screeches of tyres and clangs of car meeting car. The fires started quickly, with various plumes of black smoke, at first looking no more threatening than the discharges of heavily clumped together factories. Very quickly though, the screaming and bloodied semi-injured, some dragging with them the unconscious and seriously injured, defined the real scenario.

There were calls from the injured, but cutting deep into the soul were the screams and pleading of those wanting help to free their companions from the cars that were gradually being consumed by the growing inferno. It had been the assumption of the victims that the troops had been dropped off to help them, but they were quite wrong. The troops quickly distanced themselves some way away from the massive bonfire, and set about blocking the road and turning traffic around. A few victims became exasperated at the nonchalance of the troops and ran at them, not quite knowing what they were going to do. However a couple of shots were fired into the air by the already over-excited troops, fearful not only of mob justice, but also of the zombie rampages. The shots signalled a mood switch as a cold realisation chilled the whole scene. Things were very different now. The screaming momentarily subsided only to be replaced by the roaring and heat-induced fracturing sounds coming from the blaze, which drowned out the shrieking of those roasting within. The only salvation was that there wasn't also a zombie rampage in the middle of it all.

The intention had been to simply block the road and send traffic back. In most areas it was a pretty routine affair. In times of crisis the vast majority of the public are surprisingly compliant, a fact well known by many world leaders throughout history. Even if they weren't, a tiny minority of the troops relished the opportunity to invoke the shoot to kill orders. However, by exuding an atmosphere of blood lust, they inadvertently reduced their chances of doing so legitimately to virtually nil.

All around the country, major cities to small towns, were resonating to the columns of tanks and troop vehicles, signalling that the repeated quarantine requests on the television and radio were deadly serious. As it turned out, the only major incident directly caused by the initial imposition was the M6 crash. In total, around one hundred people were killed, mainly by the fire. However this event was hardly distinguishable from the various zombie rampage episodes that were breaking out at an increasing rate.

The majority of people had heard the message within two hours of the order to impose quarantine and martial law emanating from Location Three. Most complied and stayed indoors. Those that weren't happy at this stripping away of their rights, also stayed indoors to find out more from the television and radio, and to telephone people they knew to rebelliously declare that they weren't going to stay inside. Most of the few who were left on the streets unaware of the turmoil, wondered why the streets were so empty, and so went inside to find out what was going on.

Alongside the orderly clearing of streets, there were still the zombie rampages. These seemed to act as magnets for every flavour of civil unrest; looting, arson, mugging, rape, murder. Although all such instances were classed as zombie rampages, it was impossible to tell if some might have been opportunist disorder. Given that the real events tended to be centred on one individual eating others rapidly trying to get away, it was pretty certain that the reports of zombies making off with electrical goods, alcohol and other consumer goodies were not in fact zombie related. One cornered criminal even claimed, 'I can't help it, I'm a zombie,' adding another excuse to his list of favourites such as ADHD and E numbers.

No one cared too much at this stage though. The plummet to base and savage tendencies by the looters and criminals didn't exactly separate them from the zombies. For those troops at the sharp end, this was the realisation of every video shooting game they'd ever played. The best that they'd previously ever hoped for was to be shooting poorly armed soldiers, maybe even gangsters or drug-runners, but to be re-enacting the fantasy worlds of haunted houses and post apocalyptic worlds was a truly unexpected thrill. Thanks to such games, they were all well-drilled in shooting the heads off their quarry.

Britain gradually became an eerie world of empty streets and locked doors, peppered with street crime explosions. These incidents were complemented by the real rampages, an increasing number of homes erupting in frenzies, smashing windows and crashing doors, often kicked through as the inhabitants were suddenly faced with potential death by mutilation. Although the troops, along with the now ubiquitously armed police, were adept at targeting the zombies, this wasn't always so. A few non-zombified individuals still succumbed to an errant bullet as they ran into the fresh air, blood drenched by geysers gushing from their ripped flesh. They enjoyed a brief moment of relief at having escaped the seemingly inescapable, only to crash to the ground lifeless, courtesy of their newly acquired hole in the head. The zombie rampages were actually a better deterrent for the criminal and looting sprees than the police and military, as the gung-ho wrong doers with their whooping and nihilism started to attract zombies seeking fresh blood. The zombies were more than eager, and able to rip the head from a miscreant mistakenly thinking the threat they were facing was a peer after the loot that they were carrying. Societal collapse was rapid and escalating.

***

Laura was watching the decline through her television and window. She was still trying to contact someone in authority, but her calls kept getting cut and it wouldn't be long before the whole phone network was no longer effective. She lamented her efforts to get through to the right people, frustrated by a mix of the overwhelming demand that the attacks were putting on them, along with having to try and engage with the bureaucratic machine as she answered page after page of questions only to find it was the script for a different anticipated scenario. It seemed the only constant anymore was the stripping of humanity. Even her call to The Goode Things had failed her, so she thought. She had felt like an animal pleading from a zoo cage. She knew that she may have got the whole thing wrong and was aware that her theory was outlandish, or that they already knew about it, but she at least expected someone to want to hear what she had to say, if only to dismiss her ideas. All she wanted was to speak to a person that she could reason with, but she couldn't penetrate through the automata tasked with preventing this from happening, as she remained data stuck in a process. She couldn't understand how everyone seemed to be so consistent in their compliance, regardless of what she said or however she tried to reach through to the real person she was speaking to. The demoralisation she felt made her want to give up trying. Most would have. But Laura wasn't the type to be consumed by the beast without a fight. She knew that desperate measures might be called for, maybe even putting herself in extreme danger and risking her life, especially now that quarantine had kicked in and the phones were failing. The fact she would probably die anyway if she did nothing, made her choice easier.

6.   The Promotion

The Zombie Squad were once again gathering in the conference room at Location Three, the previous hour and a half seeming to pass in an instant. They assembled around one end of the conference table as before. The initial excitement of being at the centre of a national crisis was now replaced by nervous apprehension at being caught out for not having managed to complete their given tasks, despite having made quite reasonable progress. Harriet Tomes had not yet taken her seat at the head, displaying an uncertainty as to what her next move should be.

'Sorry I'm late.' The door to the room was briskly opened as General Adam Spelling marched through to take his seat. A couple of people from Whitehall looked puzzled as they checked their watches, unaccustomed to such a statement from someone who was seven seconds late. Two equally confident, though younger support officers in green military jumpers and complementary attire sat behind him. They were both clutching neat stacks of folders that they would hand to the General, appearing to predict what he would need next.

'Harriet,' continued the General, 'I believe you have an important announcement to make regarding the Squad before we continue.' For a second Harriet did not react, shocked that she might have to announce the obvious and already fully accepted fact that the General was now in charge. The General gave Harriet a subtle indication, highlighting the so far unnoticed new face at the table. Harriet quickly recovered as she realised that the General would never have been so crass.

'Oh yes, thank you General,' started Harriet. 'As you'll see we have a new member to the Squad.' Everyone turned to look at a rather portly chap in his sixties with a grey beard. 'This is Doctor Bob Davis, an expert in contagious diseases from

London University.' Bob tipped his head forward slightly to look over his steel rimmed rectangular spectacles and gave a brief expression of hello.

Bob was there at Adam's request. The pair had met when they were far younger and at relatively early stages in their careers. Adam had just been promoted to the rank of Captain and had been sent on a semi-covert mission with a squad to extract Bob and his colleagues from a small African country where the local troubles had suddenly escalated into full blown civil war. Bob was there as part of a research team gathering crucial information into a newly identified virus that was threatening to spread. Although backed by his own Government, the local regime were not so keen on, or even aware of Bob's presence, and as there was significant involvement of pharmaceutical companies, capture of Bob and his cohorts could have been very embarrassing.

Initially the extraction went to plan. Having located Bob and his team, a trek of several miles was then required to reach the pickup point. Along the way the ad-hoc expedition encountered a small village. Being somewhat exhausted, they decided to take a short break, encouraged by the inhabitants' hospitality. If they had just carried on walking straight through the village, it would have probably remained a place of little significance to any of them. However, their brief sojourn and Bob's team's discussions with the villagers in the local tongue, exposed them to certain information that would change everything.

Local militia were in the area and it was a certainty that the village was soon to fall victim to one of their sadistic frenzies. The scientists and military men had all witnessed firsthand exactly what these blood crazed sub humans could do. Even the stomachs of the most hardened men churned at the impending fate of the children they were playing with whilst they relaxed. The troops knew that they could easily protect the village, being better armed, trained and having the element of surprise, but Adam was under strict instructions not to get involved. Adam knew that the risk to his group was virtually negligible, and that he could still complete their mission if they were to extend the hand of humanity, but orders were orders. He had to decide, and in full knowledge that the real cost of his actions was probably his career, chose to stay and protect the villagers. The skirmish that followed could barely be described as that. Adam's well placed and concealed snipers took out the would be murderers and rapists in an instance, once they had wandered well into the apparently deserted village and congregated as a group in the centre to decide whether arson or pillage was their next step.

This ironically compassionate act of slaughter should have destroyed Adam's career, and indeed the ability to follow orders is a key necessity for any military commander. But so is humanity and adaptability. Whether Adam acted correctly or not, Bob could see that he was of the right stuff. Before they continued their trek, Adam who was resigned to his fate, was quickly briefed by Bob on a semi-accurate report that he would be claiming to have given Adam earlier. It regarded outbreaks of the infectious virus in the surrounding area, which Bob deemed harmful enough to require avoidance. This provided Adam with a valid reason for remaining in the village, the dispatching of the rogue militia being a necessary remedial action.

Bob's report saved Adam's career. The pair were also recipients of a big dose of luck, as successful careers require, when it turned out later that the virus really had spread to some of the areas that they would have been trekking through, filling the gaps in Bob's hastily concocted story. Adam had got away with and learnt from it, even though it meant he faced a couple of actions he was forced to take over the years that stung his morality. Bob admired Adam's actions, and Adam was deeply indebted to Bob's intervention, the two remaining lifelong friends.

'Obviously, we'd be lost without Doctor Bob given the nature of the current situation. Glad you could make it, Bob,' filled in Adam Spelling. 'Right, updates,' said the General, his sweeping the room as he said so, instantly recognising the fear and shrinking away indicating how poorly the group thought things were progressing.

'I'll start,' offered the General, allowing him to gain a fatherly respect. 'As you are all aware, I received written confirmation from the Prime Minister shortly after the last meeting that a state of Quarantine Alpha One had been approved, which brings with it automatic martial law.' A few heads nodded, mainly among the support staff sat to the edges of the room who had no idea that this was the highest level of quarantine that could be imposed. The General proceeded to explain what this had meant.

The plan had been enacted through a communications and physical enforcement strategy. All major media broadcast channels had found themselves directly reporting to a military communication's officer. It was a set up that had politicians of all persuasions salivating. This ensured that the majority of media was in direct control of General Adam Spelling.

The message transmitted by this formidable communications weapon was stark and unequivocal. All civilian travel was cancelled. A twenty-four hour curfew was introduced. Violators risked detainment or being shot. Anyone unable to get home should make their way to the nearest hotel, all of which had been ordered to provide free hospitality. It was assumed that everyone would have adequate food and drink supplies to get them through at least forty eight hours, whilst plans to distribute rations were being put in place. Key workers, such as water and power, were expected to stay permanently at their places of work, with neither access in or out allowed. As it transpired, this didn't prevent reports of zombie attacks in these places.

The communications strategy was backed up with physical actions that could easily have been mistaken for invasion by some enormous and asset-rich enemy nation. In the initial stages, a few people yet to be corrected by the media machine did make this mistake. Along with military resources, a wide array of civilian public workers found themselves commandeered into the effort, to create a force resembling a rag-tag army of revolutionary citizens and renegade generals. Many of the police, fire officers and traffic wardens among others, found it a welcome change to the day-to-day tirade of abuse they endured from the large-enough-to-cause-daily-displeasure minority who amused themselves with authority-baiting between sporadic visits to benefits offices and narcotics suppliers.

Major transport routes were physically blocked along with the occupation of train stations and airports. Not only were most citizens now isolated from their immediate neighbours, Britain was cut off from the rest of the world. Permanent patrolling forces were deployed in well over four hundred conurbations, whilst only the most isolated members of the population escaped regular drive or fly-bys to check all was in order.

The General concluded his report after around five minutes. No mention was made of the M6 incident, and only statistics were given on the still increasing number of zombie rampages. It was nevertheless a horrific report.

'It all sounds very efficient, General, given there are so many different agencies involved,' said Bob Davis with a hint of a smile. The General knew the real question was 'How have you managed this so well, compared to the traditional debacle associated with any kind of national crisis?' The General was sorely tempted to inform the group that martial law afforded him many benefits that meant he could get the job done. One example was the contractor whom General Spelling may well have had called in and had shot if time had permitted. Barely had the previous meeting disbanded than Adam Spelling received a call from a rather demanding fellow by the name of Ken Green. Ken was the owner of Clean Out, a contractor who specialised in the disposal of infected animals. Ken had the previous year narrowly avoided being blacklisted from Government work, which he felt gave him the right to demand extortionate contracts from public officers. His demands were rarely ignored, many Government departments having learnt that career-wrecking media stories of their failure to protect the public were likely to appear very soon after refusing Ken's requests.

Unfortunately, during the previous outbreak of a particularly nasty pig flu, an investigative journalist had caught Ken transporting lorry loads of pig carcasses on a journey of over two hundred miles to a depot some twenty miles from the routes start point. The lorries were uncovered as their specially manufactured covers had been left at the depot, the existence of which had secured Ken the contract in the first place. Fortunately for Ken, accusations against him could not be substantiated in the face of his defence of human error. Ken was well aware that the days of striking off those who had failed the public, such as the Delorean accountants leading to several years of reasonable ethics in public sector contracting, were now over. Fortunately, General Spelling was driven by a belief in responsibility and morality. Ken Green suddenly found himself the cowering bully who had made the nearly, literally fatal error of mistaking the General for the kind of administrator he usually squeezed cash out of.

'All agencies and individuals concerned have worked together very effectively and have been most co-operative,' said Adam returning a mischievous smile to Bob.

'Unfortunately, although we've executed Quarantine Alpha One to plan, the core problem still exists.' The very mild sense of self-congratulation that had crept into the room was burst like a soap bubble. 'Javed. Perhaps you could update us.'

A large flat panel folded down from the ceiling on the wave of a remote control from Javed. He had chosen to show some television reports of killings as he spoke. Only a couple of people not yet exposed to these images flinched in horror.

'The number of zombie rampages is continuing to increase,' began Javed, 'as we predicted. Each is centred on an individual. At the moment, we haven't identified any particular triggering or excluding factors in the victims.' Nervous looks were exchanged around the room. 'We're still gathering witness statements, but have only been able to eliminate depression, anxiety or similar. In fact, it almost seems that the zombies are of quite the opposite state of mind before they turn. We have also established that just before the turn, they appear to become uncommunicative for a period from a few seconds to half an hour.'

'Uncommunicative?' enquired Bob Davis, eager to cut to the point.

'Yes. They cease to respond to any stimulus, er, such as people talking to them. They almost retract into their own world.' General Spelling leant forward suddenly raising his right finger.

'Tell me Javed, what is the average death toll per individual rampage?' asked the General. Javed looked stunned for a second as he was taken off script, but none the less happy to oblige.

'Around four.' The General was pleased with Javed. 'This figure is based on the information from two hundred and eight attacks. In eight of these there have been zero fatalities. The most for one attack is thirty three.'

'Do we have any Zombies in captivity?' asked Adam.

Ian Milton, the young policy advisor sat up ready to speak exuding an air of aloofness. He cut off Javed, saying, 'I know the answer to that. I was told just five minutes ago by the Prime Minister.' He then sat back, failing to provide the salient fact that would have originated from Javed in any case.

'Well?' said a now slightly agitated General. Ian looked surprised before catching on.

'None,' said Ian.

'Thank you Ian,' replied the General, unimpressed. A knock at the door ended the embarrassment.

'Urgent message for Ian Milton,' came the voice from the door. The room breathed out with relief. Ian exited, but he was back within seconds before much had moved on.

'I've just had a report from Number Ten.' The sombre look of Ian suggested other than just more name-dropping. 'The Prime Minister's wife has just gone on a… zombie rampage.' There was a momentary pause to take in the shock.

'The Prime Minster?' asked Harriet, aware that this was her boss.

'He's not dead,' Ian paused again, continuing his fragmented update, 'but he is critical. Oh, and his wife has been shot. She took six people with her, including two Ministers.'

'There goes another specimen,' commented the jocular Bob Davis. General Adam Spelling almost smiled perceptibly at his friend's black humour. The General allowed the room to murmur for a minute whilst he and Harriet swiftly debriefed Ian. The conversation around the rest of the room varied, with much of it centring on the celebrity magazine reports of the Prime Minister's wife and her obsession with alternative therapies, philosophies, and dubious friends. The General sat back at the head of the table, the meeting quickly coming to order.

'It appears the situation has dramatically escalated. The Prime Minister is out of action. The senior politicians who would ordinarily step in have to be considered infected. Therefore, I am exercising the power I have to impose Martial Government.' Harriet Tomes, Javed Hussain and Bob Davis all looked downwards to the table as if their own death sentences had been announced, whilst accepting the necessity.

'We now control the country,' said the General, though in truth it was him. He was now Martial Governor of the UK. 'Let's get on with it.' The meeting dispersed.

7. The Incarceration

Beyond Location Three, the country was in turmoil. The rate of the spread was unprecedented. The curfew and quarantine order imposed as part of martial law had enabled some vague form of control to be maintained, but it was scarcely discernible from anarchy. The zombie rampages were still breaking out and escalating. Every part of all major cities had heard at least one volley of gunfire enforcing a summary execution of a zombie feasting on family, friends, neighbours or pets. The additional outbreaks of looting, murder, rape and other opportunist criminal activity further exposed the martial forces increasing powerlessness.

Communication was severely limited. The phone network had just about ceased working as it ran out of people to keep it going. The media was barely still broadcasting, reducing to automated messages, as the facilities succumbed to a similar fate to The Goode Things.

People are resourceful though, and were developing all kinds of Heath Robinsonesque ways to exchange information. This ranged from digging out walkie talkies and CB radios, to holding placards up at windows along with newly evolving semaphore type languages. Additional information and ideas to the official broadcasts were still able to work their way around the diminishing non-zombie and non-eaten population. It was as if society was evolving a new nervous system in response to this potentially extinction-level event, a tiny hope for this floundering beast.

Inevitably, conspiracy theories abounded from the almost mandatory 'Government experiment gone wrong', to 'Alien Virus', through to 'It's all a hoax to keep us inside'. The last of these was struggling a bit though. Alongside the theories numerous preachers, evangelists, cults and even mainstream religions were prophesising damnation and imminent Armageddon. Their spread was severely limited by the curfews and collapsing communication network, but they were still introducing their infection into the system.

The soothsayers had all leapt upon the back of this ideal sales opportunity to boost membership or create a new movement, as more and more people were prepared to buy in, given the hopelessness of the current situation. It is after all, no coincidence that most religions emerge or evolve during periods of extreme human crisis. A contingent environment is a far greater midwife to spiritual epiphany and enlightenment than a charismatic leader. There are always plenty of new messiahs lying in wait when the time is right. One example was the New Philosophy, a particular success story. More and more people were talking about it as the new hope and it was able to be quickly passed on.

Meanwhile, people were barricading themselves inside. They were assisted by Central Communications at Location Three finding that information films on turning household furniture into makeshift barricades were proving particularly popular, rehashed relics originally intended for a nuclear attack during the recently ended Cold War era.

By the end of the day, 'Day One Proper' as many referred to the first day after Kate's initial Rampage, Britain had transformed, the rate being truly terrifying.

At Location Three, day two brought an early start for most who felt themselves lucky if they had got three hours sleep. The General had asked Javed Hussain and Bob Davis to join him in his office. Up above on the surface, it was still pitch black, an irrelevance to the three men.

'At the moment, I would say that you two are the most important people in the complex,' said Adam Spelling. He was speaking honestly. From anyone else, Bob would have suspected a charm offensive. Javed felt flattered. Adam paused. 'Do you have adequate resources?'

'We're a bit limited here,' said Javed before optimistically concluding, 'but we've still got access to some other key scientific institutions. Obviously, we can't travel, but as long as we can talk.' Adam managed a slight smile and exhalation of relief. Having secured his initial objectives, longer term strategy was his priority. News had filtered in overnight of various ministers and their associates rampaging. The democratic infrastructure was carnage.

'We have a briefing prepared for you,' said Bob reassuringly. The General picked up his coffee and leant back in his chair.

'Please, continue,' said Adam. Javed described the profile they'd compiled. The rate of outbreaks indicated that within eight to ten days, half of the population would be zombies or victims. This succinctly summed up the scale. Alongside this, a pretty good description of the effects of infection were beginning to emerge, carefully qualified by Javed.

The total time from infection to zombification seemed to vary from under an hour to a few days. Transmission appeared to involve direct exposure to the infected, and this possibly had to be before the carrier had turned. It appeared that exposure needed to be for an extended period of at least several minutes. Just prior to zombification the victim would enter a trance-like state. Javed added that the specific mechanism hadn't yet been identified, although they naturally and fairly assumed that it was some kind of virus or germ. General Spelling was suitably impressed by Javed's work in its own right, confirmed by Bob's nods.

'Would there be any reason not to make public the information about the trance state?' asked Adam. 'At least they'd have a warning. And we'd appear to be getting somewhere.'

'None at all,' replied Bob, supportive of Adam's suggestion. The information would be released soon after the meeting concluded, broadcast for the last few operational hours of the television and radio channels.

'There is something else,' said Javed. 'Some anomalies.' The General tilted his head and grimaced slightly. Javed raised his eyes to towards Bob. Bob picked up on Javed's unease and took the lead.

'Javed has done an incredible job putting together these figures,' said Bob dismissing the crucial role he had played. He paused. 'As would be expected, we can't account for every single infection. However, there are two problems. The first is that statistically, the number we can account for does seem to be too low.' The General said nothing. Bob appeared uneasy. He was not keen on the level of uncertainty he was reporting on.

'The second is a worrying possibility that keeps coming back that some of the zombies appear to have been infected without contact through any of the known sources,' concluded Bob.

'If that was happening, it would account for the numbers,' said Javed. The General felt uneasy. He looked to his friend Bob.

'We'll keep looking. Maybe there's something we're missing,' Bob offered, though his tone leaked a hint of doubt.

'Where's it come from?' asked Adam as he explored another line of inquiry, like a fictional detective. Javed had a kind of answer for him.

'We can't say where it came from,' began Javed, 'but we are quite confident we can say where it hasn't come from.' The General awaited enlightenment. 'We've found absolutely nothing like it whatsoever in any animal species. We have attempted to infect animals with various samples from human zombies, but there's absolutely no effect, as well as no recorded examples of anything like this in the archive.' The General was intrigued by this finding, as were Bob and Javed. They could sense the significance of this finding, but felt as if they were still some considerable distance from the insight it offered.

Before anyone could comment, there was an urgent rapping at the door. 'Come,' said the General. A young man sharply opened the door, marched in briskly and saluted. Everyone recognised him as one of the two members of support staff who had sat close to the General at the previous meeting.

'General,' he said as he thrust a piece of paper forward at the seated General. 'There's been an outbreak in Brazil.' If this announcement had come a few minutes earlier, there may well have been shock. Now, nothing was shocking. The latest information seemed to allow for outbreaks anytime anywhere. The General took the paper and stood slowly, reading as he did so. He frowned slightly.

'This came in thirty five minutes ago?' He looked up from the paper to the messenger, his frown intensifying.

'Yes sir,' began the messenger whose fate relied on how he responded in the next few seconds. 'I brought it straight to you when I saw it had come in. The operators hadn't notified anybody.' The General understood.

'Take me to them. Now!' His response reassured the messenger that he had acted correctly. The General moved with authority relishing the chance to tackle a simple and practical diversion. The messenger took the cue to lead the way and marched off apace. Javed and Bob followed, having to half-run to keep up with the pair ahead of them. They could barely make out the rapid update the General was receiving.

Less than five minutes earlier, the messenger, Colonel Stephen Shelley, one of the General's trusted deputies, had entered communication room thirty-four on his rounds. This particular room was occupied by two of Location Three's staff, Alistair and Kalpana. The pair were monitoring various phones, screens and printers which formed part of the hub connecting them to the rest of the World from British Embassies to lower-level secret service channels and some mainstream media.

The Colonel's checking tended to consist of a quick head in the door seeking a verbal reassurance. He would spend longer with staff, were it not for the extraordinary circumstances. The Colonel had poked his head into communication room thirty-four briefly and sounded a brief 'hello' before ducking back out. At first he'd thought that all was well. Alistair and Kalpana were deep in conversation. The Colonel had presumed they were discussing important operational matters and didn't want to disturb them further. However, before he'd continued, something had tingled his senses. It was worth a second check.

He'd stepped back and took a couple of steps into the room. He stood and looked around, his gaze passing over the animated pair several times as he surveyed the screens, keyboards, printers and stone-cold coffee in the two cups by the conversationalists. His scrutiny finally fixed on Alistair and Kalpana, astounded at their complete failure to acknowledge in anyway that he had entered the room. This particular pair already tested his patience at the best of times. Alistair for his dumbness that he tried to hide behind outlandish stories of his exploits that a ten year old would struggle to believe, and Kalpana for her faux over-friendliness that barely made up for the threat of the knife she would plunge straight into your back to give her career even half a step up. Colonel Shelley was already aware of the flashing urgent communiqué on the screen to the right of the pair intermittently illuminating the dull room.

'What's going on?' The pair carried on talking. Colonel Shelley felt an anger well up rapidly inside. 'Look!' he exclaimed as he grabbed the back of Kalpana's swivel chair and jerked it round so that she could see the flashing screen. Her long black hair swished around up off her shoulders, and she couldn't help but look at the screen. 'You as well,' the Colonel snapped at Alistair.

'We were just talking,' said Alistair, totally oblivious to the seriousness of his and Kalpana's predicament, a look of almost childish nonchalance over his face. The Colonel desperately wanted to tackle the miserable pair in the room, but the flashing message was of a greater priority.

'This is over thirty minutes old!' he exclaimed exasperated. 'Jesus, have you seen what it says?' The Colonel had quickly scanned the message and was now acquainted with the basic facts of the Brazilian rampage. The printer by the screen was already rasping out the message. 'What on earth have you been doing?' asked the Colonel, partially to himself and rhetorically to the inept pair.

'She's been telling me about this great new thing, some kind of philosophy or other,' answered Alistair unnecessarily. 'It's great. Kalpana knows all about it. You should listen,' continued Alistair, the events of the last few seconds appearing to have completely passed him by. Colonel Stephen Shelley took no notice as he grabbed the piece of paper before it had not quite finished being ejected, leaving some ripped remains behind ready to clog it up the next time it was used.

'Guard!' he shouted down the corridor as he marched off. 'Secure this room and the occupants.' A young soldier ran past the Colonel, raised his gun and stood astride the door, excited to be experiencing some real action having missed out on the zombie shooting with his colleagues. He looked into the room disappointed to see that Alistair and Kalpana had no intention of offering any resistance, and were quite content to be allowed to continue with their conversation.

A few minutes later, the General arrived at the room with Colonel Stephen Shelley and the two scientists trailing behind. The guard stepped aside in perfect synchronisation with the General. Adam stood astride the doorway, hands on hips, staring into the room. There were three people there.

'Milton! What are you doing here?' Ian Milton looked round at the General. He was sat on a chair pulled up close between Alistair and Kalpana, the three of them huddled together. Ian Milton barely made an effort to look at the General, his head straining round but his whole body still eager to remain where it was, like a kitten momentarily distracted from gorging on a plate of cream with its siblings.

'Oh, General,' replied Milton. 'I've been with them all morning. I've just got back from the loo. I was bursting.' The General looked over to his colleagues, firstly to Colonel Stephen Shelley then the two scientists. It was obvious to them all that Ian Milton was complicit in this dereliction of duty.

'Can you explain why this was ignored?' demanded Adam Spelling, holding up the crumpled Brazilian memo in his shaking fist. He awaited some plausible explanation.

'It's the New Philosophy,' said Milton, confirming his implication. 'Kalpana's been telling us all about it. It sounds fantastic. Why don't...' The General had heard enough.

'Lock them up,' the General instructed to the soldier who had been guarding the room and the two colleagues that had joined him. Such summary and harsh action was in no way the norm for the General. However these weren't normal circumstances. In any case, judgement hadn't been passed, merely action to fix the intolerable weaknesses. The General stepped well away from the door to the other side of the corridor as Alistair, Kalpana and Ian were dragged from the room off to Location Three's cells, only concerned with continuing their previous conversation. He really didn't care who Ian Milton was shouting that he knew in Government, as most that he named had been eaten by the Prime Minister's wife.

After a minute or so, the final echoes of the party of soldiers and captives ceased to bounce around the non-descript corridor. The walls were entirely flat and textureless. It was like standing inside a rectangular steel pipe, apart from the occasional light recessed into the ceiling, set flush to the surface and failing to break up the monotony.

The General broke the silence. 'Who are these New Philosophers?' No one spoke. He was now leaning back against the wall, his legs straight and his feet an uncomfortable distance in front of him, straining his knees to bend in the direction they weren't intended to.

'It rings a bell, but that's it,' confessed Bob. Javed shrugged his shoulders.

'Suppose we'd better let Harriet know about Milton,' said Adam. They knew she would protest no more than the minimum. Location Three's omnipresent background hum prevented complete silence.

***

Meanwhile, Laura was barricaded in her home, one of the 'lucky ones'. She was alone. The difference between Laura and the others hiding away was that she didn't have the added fear of not knowing if she may turn into a zombie at any moment. She'd moved on from the initial terror of this new world, and was now focussed on her task. Wallowing was futile. She was aware that time was running out. She may have been safe from turning, but had no idea how long her defences may hold. She'd been watching the zombies and the quarantine enforcers passing by for several hours. This was where her only hope lay. She had as good a feel as she was going to get for when a low point of zombie activity would coincide with a passing patrol. The next opportunity may be the last. She would have to take it.

8. The Tupelo Star

Charles Lampton felt a tinge of guilt as he stared out at the ocean. The rough swell forced him to clutch tighter at the ship's railing as he felt himself jolted. The Tupelo Star began to rise up in the expanding sea, rolling slightly over and causing the deck Charles was stood on to ascend quickly. The sea dropped rapidly downwards and out of his sight, presenting him with a momentary view of nothing but continuous grey, afternoon sky. Charles's stomach turned over for a second as the seas once again reminded him that continual caution was a necessity to prevent being lost forever should he fall into these waters. Even if he were found, the extreme cold would have frozen him to death in moments. The Tupelo Star came crashing back into the waters, dousing Charles as the cutting wind snatched the spray, stinging his face as if he'd been caught by a discharge from some unseen hunter's shotgun hiding in the undulating swell.

He had taken some time out to reflect on the news that they'd been hearing on board. Realising that he was one of the lucky ones to escape the zombie horror that had probably consumed some of his family and friends, he was experiencing feelings of unworthiness.

He'd always found the front of the ship as good place as any to be alone. He was always struck by the irony that there was virtually no privacy on board any of the scientific mission ships that he'd spent most of his working life on, yet they were as remote and isolated from other human life as possible, this one being somewhere in the South Atlantic. Even aircraft would take several hours to reach them, ensuring the ship existed in solitude whilst condemning its occupants to virtually inescapable and unremitting closeness. Normally, communication beyond the steel hull would be limited to intermittent radio contact, the occasional exchange of crackly voices when conditions allowed. However, this voyage had been enhanced by the testing of new equipment that had allowed greatly improved communications for all on the ship, even video link ups. It was the 1990s' state of the art kit. As well as demonstrating the technical advancements, these extra information tentacles seemed to have had at least as big a social and psychological effect, lifting spirits on board, and bringing all sorts of extra, as yet unknown, enhancements.

The waves crashed against the bow, their sound part of the inescapable backdrop that Charles Lampton and his crew had lived with for the last four months. It may have been summer there, but there had hardly been any let up in the energetic churning of the seas. Charles felt the guilt again as he contemplated his good fortune.

Most of the crew were single and had only left behind occasional relationships, their lifestyles reflecting the choice that they had made to spend months away from home on scientific missions. Charles, like most of the rest of the crew, didn't know how to cope with the unfamiliar blend of feelings that he was having. They knew that they were probably directly affected by the carnage back in Britain. They could relate to the people and places described and had family and friends there. However, it still had that feeling of distant unreality, like a war zone on the news in a far away, foreign country. These reports had the facts, reported deaths, even the occasional rhetorical conversation took place, but it was not like day-to-day life. The reality for most westerners viewing the news of conflicts in the Middle East was not much more real than if it were a conflict in Narnia.

Charles knew he should feel an emotive connection with the zombie crisis back in the Northern Hemisphere, but he couldn't. Every time he tried to rationalise his confusion he merely ended up at the conclusion that his apathy was a result of his gratitude at being safe. He no longer felt any of his previous loathing towards his fellow crewmates and their ship's prolonged isolation, but an almost evangelical gratitude at their good fortune.

The ship hit a huge wave. Charles held tighter, his knees bending. The noise from the crash of the wave intermingled with the patter of the spray against the deck, quickly subsiding to reveal a screaming from the other end of the ship. Charles could hear the scream, but took a few seconds to comprehend what he was hearing above the ongoing confusion of the crashing and buffeting waters. He looked back along the ship, upwards at the two higher decks and their front facing windows. The ship, though not an ocean liner, was not insubstantial. A loud crack, like a gunshot, yanked at Charles's attention. It was a door that had slammed back, around thirty metres away. He was trying to rationalise what he was seeing. The door had been left open and unlatched to be caught by the violent wind which had made good its perpetual, aggressive promise, and slammed the door back against the wall of the deck. Faint reverberations were still resounding around the ship as it resonated from the almighty thump.

Charles looked down to the deck just ahead of him. His reasoning misdirected him a few times, unable to cope with the unrealism of the situation. Had the two colleagues that he could see fallen over? They didn't seem to be trying to get back up. Were they drunk? They hadn't been drinking earlier, and their movements didn't suggest this. Were they fighting? He took a couple of steps forward firmly grasping the ship's rail. Then he stopped before he could call to the two men. He was duty bound to intervene as a senior member of the ship's crew, but this was not a normal fight. In fact, this was not a fight. The blood that a split second earlier had momentarily convinced him that he was looking at an overheated scuffle, was not just the spatters of a split lip or broken nose. Mike Cotton who was on top of his victim, Ghazan, had blood all over his face. It was dripping in such quantities that it formed a continuous strand, like a huge lump of red snot, to the fountain on the neck of Ghazan. Mike stabbed his face again into Ghazan's neck. Ghazan's arms stiffened outwards in rigid pain as he lost his grip on the back of Mike's jacket, and his legs stiffened upwards. Ghazan's limbs shook for a second as the snarling man atop him continued to tear at his throat, before he collapsed lifeless against the deck.

Charles stood frozen in horror, as the chill of the wind cut at the exposed skin on his face. He'd seen enough pictures to know what this was. He felt betrayed by the luck that only moments earlier he had been celebrating. Mike stopped snarling. He was resting on his knees and hands astride Ghazan, every bit the devil dog stood over its kill. Ghazan's limbs were now slouched motionless on the deck, the upper half of his body raised up as Mike continued to grip at his throat with his teeth. Ghazan's head had fallen back, and as Mike released his grip, it made an almost inaudible thud against the deck as the sea continued its background symphony. Mike had not moved as Ghazan's body had slumped down.

Charles hoped he wouldn't be noticed by Mike. There was nowhere to run. He had no weapons. He knew he couldn't fight the zombie. He didn't want to die. Mike lifted his head back whilst remaining on all fours. His hair was dishevelled and waving in the wind creating all manner of styles as the blood dripped and blew about. It had grown quite long in the months at sea. The zombie looked to his right down towards the back of the boat, away from Charles. Charles felt relief, which only heightened his terror as the thing then looked to its left and fixed on Charles. Charles didn't know how much of his violent shaking was caused by the cold, and how much by his mortal fear.

It stood up. Reality was crashing in on Charles. He felt connections being made to the news coverage of the last few days as it became instantaneously real and he rapidly sketched in the missing emotions. He knew the zombies were meant to look inhuman, devoid of reason, like rabid animals, but all of this had been words without the understanding of experience. He now understood, like the child who finally grasped an understanding of adding fractions, despite reciting the rules meaninglessly for weeks previously. Zombie Mike stood up in one deft animal-like movement and began striding quickly towards Charles, slightly slouched forwards. His hands and face glistened a deep scarlet, his dark jumper merely shone black, sodden by the blood. Charles had no plan. He found himself calculating how long he had before he was dead. Four seconds, three seconds. Mike began to run. One second. Charles' fear overwhelmed him. He couldn't breathe as he felt his bladder about to release. His body felt like a cold stone block awaiting the imminent fatal blow.

The ship lurched. Charles was already holding the rail as tightly as he could and remained stuck firm to the deck. It was the best thing that he could have done, although he could do little else as the terror consumed him. The ship jolted Mike as it lurched. His legs were whipped to the side quicker than his upper body could follow, sweeping them away and causing him to fall over sideways. The lurching deck continued to play with him and rolled him backwards a few metres, just over the edge of the ship under the rail. Charles felt feeling return to his body as his heart beat violently within his chest, like an entrapped woodpecker desperately trying to escape. His luck had returned after its momentary desertion. His whole body pulsed with the warmth of relief, but as he looked down at the deck, settled back to cold.

Mike hadn't gone completely over. He was flailing wildly as his legs dangled, but was, fortuitously for him, pushed up against a railings post. It had caught under his armpit, and had stopped him from sliding along and off the edge of the ship. Survival instinct exploded in Charles. He was not an unfit man, and threw himself forwards to grab the railings above where the flailing Mike was balanced, ready for the offensive. The zombie, in its stupor of savagery, had not had the intelligence to make a grab for the railings post, but grabbed at Charles's right leg driven by the primeval urge to eat flesh. As it did so, it slipped back so that Charles' leg was almost out of its reach, but then it just managed to grasp the leg with its outstretched hands. If the zombie had managed to wrap itself right around the limb with both arms in order to begin its devouring, Charles's fate would probably have been decided in that instant. As it was, luck had cast Charles' fate into his own hands, as once again the devil played poker with him. Mike, with his full zombie strength, started pulling forwards along the leg, the nails of his right hand piercing through Charles's trousers into his skin, embedding his fingers within the flesh.

Charles had to act now or never. He saw Mike's head moving towards him, jaws agape ready to feed. The looming head suddenly appeared as a football passed to a well-placed striker in the dying seconds of a crucial tie. Charles kicked for goal with his free leg with all his might. Though right footed, his left leg did not fail him. Charles screamed as the backwardly projected Mike clung on and tore the flesh in his calf. Charles looked down at Mike's face. The savage intent was still there, despite the injuries Charles well-placed foot must have inflicted. It was impossible to tell through the blood-sodden face, whether it was a broken nose, smashed teeth, burst eyeball or a combination. Charles felt horror return. No man could have held on through such a violent strike he thought, though Charles's rather gentile life had protected him from exposure to the horrors of such pastimes as cage fighting. He kicked again, still hard but with less force than the first time. He again felt the pain in his right calf as the impact was directed through the zombie to its fingers embedded in Charles' flesh. Charles kicked again, and again, and again, not caring about the excruciating pain that was starting to leave his right leg numb. The numbness simply made it easier as the pain stopped distracting him. He could worry about the mutilation later and carried on kicking, until he realised he was kicking fresh air.

Charles looked down to the sea as he began to hyperventilate, and saw Mike bob in the water just to the side of the back of The Tupelo Star, before being sucked into the backwash. Even a zombie was no match for the icy Antarctic seas. Charles fell onto his left knee as the pain from losing almost a pound of flesh out of his calf kicked in. The torn and reddened trouser leg flapped in the wind, like the ragged flag of a vanquished fortification. The blood that had already gushed from his wound was frozen on the deck, though fresh liquid was still flowing onto it. Charles remembered the strawberry lollies that he had enjoyed as a child.

Charles began to sob as the adrenaline searched for another outlet. His immediate instinct of relief soon subsided though as he thought of calling for help. He needed help, but if he called, what the hell might he attract? If he went searching, what else might he find in the ship waiting to feed? He had no idea if Mike was the only one, or if the ship was crawling with zombies. The information they'd been receiving from home gave little clue. Maybe he should wait on the deck and hope any zombies killed each other before venturing into the confines of the ship? Maybe they had already done so and Mike had been the last one?

He stopped sobbing. He looked towards the door that Mike and Ghazan had crashed out of. Ghazan's body lay on the deck just in front a few metres ahead of Charles. Charles wanted to get to Ghazan to see if he could help, though it was clearly a pointless act to alleviate his own guilt at having survived, again. Charles knew he couldn't stay outside. He would certainly freeze or bleed to death. He had to get into the ship, and hope for the best. He convinced himself that everything was going to be okay.

Charles stood quietly just inside the open door. He had approached as carefully as he could. His right leg offered little support, and he'd found himself ironically treading on Ghazan's stomach as he'd clumsily tried to respectfully negotiate his way around the corpse. It had shown as much sign of life as a discarded cushion. Charles stopped, and listened. Now that he was inside the ship, he realised he was hopelessly without any form of a plan. He heard nothing out of the ordinary above the background noise of violent sea and groaning ship. He stepped carefully forward, intermittently dragging his savaged leg. He had to continue further into the ship. He remembered being forced into the House of Horrors as a child by his parents on a visit to the travelling funfair late one October, and the weeks of nightmares from the poorly painted pictures on the converted lorry trailer of people being mutilated and devoured by demons and monsters, with dangling eyeballs ripped from their sockets.

Some quarter of an hour passed before Charles began to feel any form of safety. As he'd made his way through the ship, he'd become aware of trails of blood, long thin streaks on the floor, finger marks along the wall. He found himself compelled to follow them, each time the intensity of the crimson decor increasing until he found the devoured source. Charles was now on a lower deck, away from the bodies, trying desperately and unsuccessfully to ignore their existence just above his head. He stopped. He'd not heard any movement, and given the ferocity of Mike's attack upon, was fairly sure that this was a good indicator that there were no more zombies. Whether or not this was a fair assessment, he'd convinced himself it was so, as he was aware that his heavy blood loss along with the pain and the cold were leading to his consciousness failing. He needed help, and possibly only had a few minutes to attract it.

'Hello!' shouted Charles. His call echoed around the ship, searching for survivors. There was no reply, but then again Charles knew from having watched many classic horror movies, there never was an instant reply. 'Hello!' he shouted again. The echo again reverberated, like darting ghosts rapidly investigating in a flash of haunting. Charles readied himself for death.

'Charles!' He heard a faint calling. As his mind drifted, he felt some relief at the call from the other side. He'd been expecting to be entering the 'tunnel' soon, maybe beckoned by a light at the end. He reawakened his senses with a start. Was the call from within the ship?

'Yes, it's me!' he shouted even louder with strength he had no idea he still had.

'Where's Mike?' came the reply.

'The sea!' shouted Charles. He heard clanking of a solid steel door being opened afar just before he passed out. The six crew who had made it to safety during Mike's rampage would soon be with him.

9. Atlantic Communication

Location Three received details of the Tupelo Star rampage around two hours after Charles passed out. Fortunately, the blessing of the new communications equipment had allowed this message to get through substantially faster than may otherwise have been expected. Its passage within Location Three had also been helped by news of the communications failure earlier that day involving Ian Milton, Kalpana and Alistair leading to the incarceration of all three. This had ensured that Location Three's staff were not going to allow anything to slip by for the next few hours at least.

General Adam Spelling was in the central communications room presiding over a direct link to the Tupelo Star within eight minutes of the information being received. The central communications room was a large room, around half the size of a tennis court and pretty much square. Its décor maintained the style of the rest of Location Three, plain grey steel walls with a ceiling emanating a fluorescent glow from several non-descript inset lights. The floor of one half of the room was raised to around knee height, with the entrance door being at the back of this platform. At the other end of the room, the wall was adorned with various screens, dominated in the centre by a single large panel, some four metres across. The room was straddled by long rows of continuous desks facing the screens, split down the middle by a centre access aisle along with side access. There were four rows in all, giving eight blocks. At each block sat three operators with their own cache of the very latest military communication tools including at least three monitor screens, headset, telephones, keyboard and so on. It was every bit the stereotype of the classic Cold War movie operations room, though heavily tinged in drabness. This was the communications centre where all information in and out of Location Three could be controlled, the cultural manifestation

65

of the Zombie Squad. There were various other smaller communications rooms around Location Three whose task it was to filter information or deal with that not deemed quite important enough for the centre stage. But the central communications room was where the power lay, if for no other reason than being able to create the greatest sense of theatre.

Adam Spelling was leaning over an operator sat towards the back of the room who had received the initial communiqué from the Tupelo Star. Adam had taken up this position when he arrived. The feed from the operator was now on the main screens at the front of the room for all to see, but Adam Spelling had become too engrossed to notice, and remained transfixed.

Adam's strategically nimble mind was already thirsting for the crucial information that this latest outbreak threatened to provide. Headlines on the large screen proclaimed the key facts along with live video feeds to the ship's communication systems. The pictures were suffering from bad reception, offering at best fuzzy images interspersed with screens of snowy static, at times hard to distinguish from the exterior shots from the Tupelo Star of the surrounding sea. The two scientists, Javed and Bob entered into the room, having come straight from some joint activity. They took a couple of steps in and stopped clumsily, centrally aligned with the large screen on the wall ahead. They were familiar with the room and would now scan the large screen as a matter of habit whenever they visited for the latest information. They stared straight forward, open-mouthed as they fought to make sense of the message, stopped as if they'd walked into an invisible concrete block. They read the headline, 'Outbreak in South Atlantic', and almost instantaneously took in the accompanying fact described in the lines below, that the ship had not docked for over three months. Both of them found themselves staring at the various video feeds, needing the images to make real the incredulity of what they were reading.

Bob looked around the room and quickly saw Adam Spelling. 'Adam!' called Bob. Adam turned his head looking up for a second, briefly acknowledging Bob and then looking straight back as if his head had been on a piece of elastic attached to the monitor in front of him. Bob made his way over as quickly as his portly frame would allow. Javed followed, slightly slower to react. Adam was leaning over the left shoulder of the operator. Bob took up the position to the right leaving Javed to hover behind.

'I came as soon as I could!' came a call from the door. It was Harriet Tomes, the senior Civil Servant. Although usurped as Zombie Squad leader by Adam Spelling, Harriet was still a figure of some importance and had been informed as a matter of urgency of the latest developments. She was rather out of breath, having run to the room, encouraged along by her awareness of Adam Spelling's reliance on the scientists and the need to maintain her profile.

'How are you getting on with the voice link,' Adam asked the operator with impatience.

'I've just about got it sir,' came the reply.

'You are sure that this is absolutely secure?'

'Yes sir,' replied the operator who was making every effort to comply with the General's demands. 'That's why it's taking so long. The data demands are stretching a link this poor to the limits.' The speakers to the side of the monitors were hissing ferociously like tortured snakes. 'It's coming through now,' said the operator just as the hiss began to subside.

'Hello,' came a faint, barely distinguishable voice.

'Hello,' replied Adam immediately, eager to grab hold of the delicate communication. 'This is General Adam Spelling, Martial Governor of the United Kingdom.'

'Yes sir,' came the hiss enveloped voice. A face could just be made out as the accompanying image to the voice on the monitor screen, though it added little. 'We've received your briefing and fully understand.'

'Now listen,' said Adam as he spoke with some confidence, reassured that they understood the new management arrangements for the homeland. 'What I am about to ask you, and your replies, must remain completely confidential. This is top secret. If anyone else contacts you, you must not say anything about this discussion. That goes for the whole crew.' The hissing continued for a few seconds in lieu of a reply. Bob and Javed looked at each other.

'We all understand,' replied the voice.

'Right. Can you confirm that you have not docked for the last three months,' asked Adam. There was a short pause.

'We can confirm that.'

'Have you had any contact with any other ships, or has anyone else come aboard during that time?' Again there was a pause after Adam's question.

'There's been no other contact.' Adam stood up straight. He had the answers he needed. He slowly turned his sombre gaze to Bob, who had something to say.

'Ask them if they've received any supplies, any airdrops or the like.' Adam duly acted asking the voice from the Tupelo Star the question. Maybe this would provide a clue. There was yet another pause.

'Nothing come aboard, sir,' was the reply. The mood of Bob and Javed darkened as they realised the implications of this response. Their earlier fears that the infection could be spread without any kind of contact were confirmed. Harriet had joined them during the exchange, and her mood dropped in sympathy, though she was desperate to know why. Adam directed the operator to end the communication.

'Has the link been closed?' Adam asked the operator.

'Yes sir,' he replied.

'And can you block all of their communications.'

'I think so,' said the operator clinically.

'Good. Do it,' said Adam as he turned to the scientists and Harriet. 'Unfortunately we may not be able to stop news of this rampage breaking out. There were some communications before our contact. What we can do though,' continued Adam, 'is manage it.' Adam knew that the infection being spread without contact added an extra dimension of terror to the situation, and the public finding out would be more disaster upon the current disaster. Even if control of the country was looking like it had already slipped away to the point of no return, he was still going to act as if it could be retrieved. The corners of Bob's mouth curled up in admiration of Adam's habit of being continually ahead of the game.

'We won't be able to explain the movements of the ship,' said Adam. 'If we say they docked, someone could check it out, even through this turmoil. We'll go with an airdrop, a top secret one with equipment for a military experiment.' Adam stopped for a second, his brain almost audibly whirring. 'Operator, can you do some jiggery pokery with the recording of that last transmission and insert one of the Tupelo Star's yes replies to my question about the airdrop.'

'It's done sir,' replied the operator routinely.

'Good man,' responded Adam. 'Make it top notch. We don't want it actually exposed as a cover up like half the rubbish we churn out to send the conspiracy theorists in circles.' Bob smiled as he recalled the many similar stories that Adam had told him, and probably only him.

10. Contact

Nigel and Simon both felt ambivalent. On the one hand they were happy not to be spending six months in a desert being shot at and bombed by the people they were told they were there to liberate. On the other hand, their home country was now a mess of murder, mayhem and suffering which made their intercontinental travels seem like a boyhood adventure. The initial excitement that came with action had been forced aside by distraught isolation at the realisation there was no home to return to.

The armoured personnel carrier they were looking out from the top of turned into yet another ravaged suburban street of semi-detached houses. As with most streets, smashed up and burnt out cars that had long since stopped smouldering, littered the kerbside. The odd one or two ruined the uniformity having been abandoned in the middle of the road, some on their roofs, some crushed together. Every one of them had a different story to tell though. The various blood stains across their bodywork gave few clues. Some had been attacked by zombies causing owners to swerve or inexplicably jump out and run. Some had been crashed as they were driven away at unmanageable speeds. Some had been torched by anarchistic mobs.

The scene was now so different to the recent orgy of mayhem. The desolation suggested that the place may have been devoid of human life for weeks. This was merely an illusion. Many of the houses did contain life. These were the people who had quickly realised that the zombies needed signs of life to attract them. Even the criminal element had deserted the zombie-owned streets. The strategy for survival was to become invisible. Evolution had weeded out those without the skill or intelligence to realise this, their houses ransacked and cleared of life.

Nigel and Simon heightened their awareness as their vehicle proceeded into the street, taking them along a path that they desperately wanted to run away from. Every turn threatened attack. If they were lucky, the zombies would be at the other end of the street and easily taken out. If not, the zombies could be on the vehicle within seconds. Although the zombies were still relatively easy to dispatch, a jammed gun, a shot not quite fully penetrating the brain, a second's lack of concentration, all provided the opportunity for the zombies. The vehicle slowed, having speeded up to take the corner. It looked quiet. The heavy churning diesel engine announced its arrival. One or two curtains almost perceptibly moved, the occupants desperation to reassure themselves there was still some remains of the Authorities intact momentarily destroying their invisibility.

'Zombie!' shouted Nigel, simultaneously lifting his gun and aiming just beyond a burnt out car around sixty metres ahead. A shot rang out. It was hopelessly off target and smashed the window of a house. Simon had pushed away his colleague's gun just as he'd squeezed the trigger, though given the awkwardness of their bright yellow bio chem suits, it was unlikely such a hastily taken shot would have been successful. The vehicle stopped.

'It's waving something!' shouted Simon. Nigel and Simon became agitated and looked around anxiously. They knew they were now in extreme danger. Zombies were attracted by noise, even from a gun intending to kill them.

A dirty rag appeared more clearly from behind the car. It was held by a young girl, about twenty years old. She was dishevelled and dirty, an increasingly common appearance for most of the population.

'I'm not a zombie!' shouted the girl by way of reassurance. Simon looked at Nigel relieved at the use of language. He could see that Nigel was eager to kill anything that presented the slightest suggestion of a threat or simply was not fully understood.

'We've got to help,' said Simon. 'Drive forward,' instructed Simon to the driver. The vehicle moved to within twenty metres

71

of the girl and she stepped out into the middle of the road. They stopped. The engine continued to idle, still loud, but not quite enough for their voices to be incoherent.

Nigel trained his gun on the girl. 'Why aren't you inside?' called Simon. His question came over as significantly more malevolent than intended from beneath the plastic of the bio chem suit, the cartoonish bright yellow offering little light relief. In lieu of knowing what was causing the plague, all precautions were employed for all known threats. Unfortunately, as insufficient numbers of army issue khaki suits were available, which as well as being more appropriately coloured were also far better suited to the movements of soldiering, this particular patrol had drawn the short straw and had been equipped with the ones they were now wearing. As well as being garish and awkward, they were far too fragile and already the soldiers were trying to ignore the rips and tears they'd acquired. The girl could barely make out a face through the single transparent rectangular panel at the front of the amorphous hood, depriving her of that vital link.

'I need to speak to whoever's in charge,' replied the girl. She was obviously tired, but composed. 'My name's Laura. I was a friend of Kate's, the first victim.' Laura thought how this sounded for a second. 'The first zombie. I've got some very important information that could help. I've been trying to get a message through to the Authorities, but they must just think I'm a loony.'

'There's a lot of them about,' said Nigel, bizarrely switching to effortless casual conversation, still muffled by the suit. 'They've been inundated with them. Too many to handle.' Nigel paused. 'Hang on. I heard you on The Goode Things the day after the first attack.'

'We'd better radio it in.' Simon ducked down into the vehicle to carry out his own command. Nigel continued to train his gun on Laura. She stood still, seemingly unthreatened and weary from the last few days. She'd grown tired of trying to convince people of what she knew, and her pathetic appearance in no way reflected the courage and altruism required to take the course of action she had chosen. Simon re-emerged. 'We're to await instructions,' said Simon with a sarcastic air. Nigel and Simon continued to look around nervously, whilst Laura stood motionless, subservient to the military vehicle in front of her, like a condemned prisoner accepting imminent execution.

A loud screaming growl rung out. Nigel and Simon rapidly looked backwards, forwards and sideways. The direction of the growl wasn't yet apparent, though its source was beyond dispute. Laura started shaking slightly and breathing more rapidly. She looked down at the ground a few metres in front trying to pretend she wasn't there, though she had no hope of fooling a zombie.

A second growl came from no particular direction, but this time as it tailed off, the direction focussed to the street corner ahead of them, directly behind Laura. A zombie came running round, barely distinguishable as a human being; it was filthy with dirt, scabbed blood and probably excrement. A few rags of clothes hung from it flapping like long knotted unkempt fur. It was running as best it could, but with a chimpanzee-like skip. It was probably carrying injuries from a futile attempt at self-defence by one of its meals. It was about six house widths away from Laura, closing too fast.

A shot rang out. Blood sprayed out in all directions from the zombie's head and it fell to the ground. Simon had been the first to react, and had extinguished the threat with a crack shot. The relief felt by Simon, Nigel and Laura was short-lived. As the echo of the shot quickly vanished a chorus of growling and screaming could be heard making its way towards the morsel stood in the street. The execution of the zombie seconds earlier would be inviting even more of them to the party. The engine of the military vehicle began revving.

'Hold on!' shouted Simon to the driver. He knew they couldn't leave Laura but was overcome with ambiguity. To save her, they would have to pick her up and she could have vital information. If they did that though, they might be exposing themselves to infection, given the shoddy state of their suits. She might become a zombie herself at any second. It was a dilemma. The desire to save a life where hope was almost non-existent was painfully strong. Two more zombies appeared from the direction of the previous one. Nigel and Simon took aim. They had to be careful as Laura was precariously close to the line of fire. Laura closed her eyes tightly. Shots rang out whistling past her head. She closed her eyes and bit her lip, thankful that the zombies were being picked off before they could savage her, terrified that any second she would be shot. These shots were not quite as true as the one that had killed the first zombie. They carried on limping. Nigel and Simon fired again. And again. This time, the zombies lay dead. Nigel and Simon breathed deep sighs of relief.

Their momentary relaxation was shattered, this time by a screaming growl that sounded like it was within an arm's length behind them. They quickly turned, half expecting to be immediately greeted by the teeth of a zombie clamping onto their faces. As they gathered their focus, they saw a zombie leap into the air and land against the back of the vehicle securing a grip on the roof to pull itself up. The vehicle was taller than a man, a fact that had saved the lives of Nigel and Simon.

'Mine,' said Nigel. He methodically, pointed his gun at the face of the zombie as it rose up above the roof line. As it released one of its hands to swipe at the muzzle, spitting and growling, Nigel fired. The top of its skull was shattered clean off by the ferocity of the close range shot, kicking it back off the vehicle. Its brain visibly fell from its skull as it crashed onto the ground, like the insides of runny boiled egg topped by the flick of a spoon.

Another shot. Simon had turned back to the front of the vehicle as more zombies had appeared. Another clean shot but there were now another two. He shot again and again. Nigel fired. He had assumed the rear guard. There were no more zombies there yet, but no time to relax. Over to Nigel's left he saw a zombie coming from the side passage of one of the houses. He fired twice at it to make sure and then continued scanning the rear and the sides. The training was kicking in. He barked an instruction to Simon to watch the right side. The vehicle began to move backwards. Laura stood still, as she watched her only hope, however slight, begin to fade. She wanted to cry.

'Cover me!' shouted Simon as he dropped straight down into the vehicle before Nigel had a chance to object to his almost impossible task. Simon pulled himself forward through a gap in the partition into the driver's cab. 'What are you doing?' asked Simon. The vehicle continued to trundle away. Simon looked out of the windscreen through the heavy metal grill that protected it. He could now see four zombies at an alarmingly close distance from Laura. He froze as four shots echoed. Three of the zombies lost their heads and fell down. A fourth staggered with a chest wound, and then collapsed as a fifth shot hit.

'We're getting out of here!' shouted the driver. Simon, despite, or maybe because of his military training, was not going to see a human being die in front of him if he could prevent it. He pulled his gun forward and forced the long muzzle hard upwards into the throat of the driver, threatening to tear his bio chem. suit. The driver spluttered but knew better than to struggle, having been on previous tours with Simon. There was a thump from the back of the vehicle, then another as zombies attached themselves. Two shots rang out removing the clinging zombies.

'We pick her up right now!' The driver began driving forwards slowly to pull up besides Laura. As Laura's salvation approached, zombies began appearing from all directions. Nigel's shots became continuous as he entered a trance-like state systematically annihilating them.

'Get in!' shouted Simon, having reached out with his left arm to fling open the door of the vehicle, whilst continuing to force the gun into the driver's neck. Laura looked up in shock for a second. She had fully expected to die. 'Move!' screamed Simon. Laura grabbed the door quickly pulling herself in and slammed the door shut, the vehicle accelerating as she did so. Nigel continued shooting for a few seconds before descending into the vehicle once it had reached sufficient speed for the zombies to bounce off or be crushed as they pointlessly threw themselves at it. They would have to find food elsewhere.

Simon removed his gun from the driver's throat and moved into the back of the vehicle. Laura sat rigidly in the passenger seat staring forwards. The driver looked over to her angrily, blaming her for the humiliation he had just endured. Laura felt naked as the only occupant of the vehicle not enveloped in a bulky yellow plastic suit.

Nigel was tightening the hatch in the roof of the vehicle. Simon slumped down, exhausted, in the back. Nigel looked at him quizzically, unaware of what had just happened in the cab, then poked his head into the front. He stared at Laura. 'What the hell have you brought her in here for?' he asked the driver.

'Ask him,' said the driver. Nigel was able to turn his head to see into the back without moving from the front. His face was strained with fury as he stared hard into Simon.

'What have you done? She could be one of them?' screamed Nigel.

'She's not,' said Simon unconvincingly, but lacking the energy to respond otherwise. Nigel tightened his grip on his gun that was pointing at Simon.

'You've killed us all!' screamed Nigel, his voice tinged with the real terror of a condemned man. He was all too aware of the inadequacy of the suits, or their potential pointlessness in the face of no real explanation as to the cause of the zombie plague. Although they'd been fed an official line, the men talked, and were all too well aware that no one really knew what was causing the problem. Nigel moved his gun away. Nigel glanced back over to Laura. Under the filth was a slim young girl with long black hair. It was difficult to distinguish any natural beauty under the circumstances, but Nigel could see she possessed the prettiness that any girl of such an age should, having not succumbed to excessive weight. He smiled sinisterly.

'Maybe he's done us a favour, eh?' said Nigel, addressing his comment to the driver. 'It has been a bit lonely in here, and no one knows we've got her. How could she have survived them zombies?' The driver and Nigel laughed at the vile suggestion now being inferred. Simon felt his body gripped with rage, but knew there was little point in unleashing any kind of opposition at this point. He felt his stomach turning over with sickness as once again he was confronted with the darkest behaviour male members of his species were capable of. Laura didn't react at all.

The radio crackled as a message came through. 'We have instructions directly from the Martial Government. You are to bring the girl in.' The mood changed immediately as they realised Simon's irresponsible, though deeply human actions, had saved them from endless debriefings and enquiries. The radio continued, 'She must be protected and is required unharmed. Contamination is not an issue as progress has been made.' The last part of this message was a total and calculated lie that worked to comfort the three soldiers exactly as intended.

A dialogue ensued as the potentially appalling results of the exchanges a few moments earlier were rapidly forgotten. The vehicle was to rendezvous with a helicopter that had already been dispatched, as they were currently well over a hundred miles away from Location Three. General Adam Spelling had received the news directly about Laura, and wanted her secured as soon as possible. The heightened alertness to messages of interest had yielded her some good fortune.

11. Helicopter Journey

Simon helped Laura into the back of the helicopter, despite struggling himself in his bio chem suit. Nigel sat and watched from inside having already got in and settled himself. He was unhappy that he had had not been allowed to bring his gun with him. Simon shouted for him to help Laura, but it was easy enough for him to ignore the request above the roar of the helicopter's engines. They were in a large open field surrounded by at least one hundred metres of open ground all around, and a good mile from the nearest dwellings. Even so, nowhere could be regarded as safe from sudden attack by zombies. Instant ability to get away was now one of life's essentials for survival. The armoured carrier that had brought the three of them to the rendezvous with the helicopter was already making its way from the field. The lone driver was eager to get back to the barracks as instructed, part relieved at the imminent respite from duty, and part terrified at being alone. Needs had dictated that Nigel and Simon escort the girl leaving the driver to his own devices as he began his lone journey.

As Laura settled herself, Simon leapt up into the helicopter, as it left the ground almost before he was in. The turn of their stomachs as they accelerated upwards triggered an overwhelming feeling of relief as they were literally dragged out from a nightmare. As the helicopter climbed they looked back out of the doors as the field shrunk to reveal itself as a single rectangle among a patchwork of many others. Simon recalled a similar view looking down from the window of an airliner as he'd left Britain for a week's holiday some six months earlier with a pal. He was kicked from his reminiscence by the sight of streaming dots making their way towards the field they had vacated seconds earlier. Some were even starting to cross the outer edges. The zombies had made good time, attracted by the whirring helicopter, but there was to be no feasting on this occasion. Simon felt himself falling from his state of relief as he envisaged what might have been back in the street, before catching himself in a net of relief that they'd escaped. He caught a glimpse of some of the swarming dots around the escaping driver and his vehicle. It looked like he was getting through, but Simon couldn't be sure. The helicopter leant back into a turn, the view of the fields dropping away to leave visible only a patch of random sky.

Simon familiarised himself with the helicopter. Nigel appeared to be already engrossed in animated conversation with the doorman. Simon realised that this was no normal helicopter. Nigel was talking to the doorman through an intercom. The doorman was behind a transparent panel that separated Simon, Nigel and Laura from the rest of the craft, leaving them with a feeling of being stranded. Nigel seemed unconcerned as he quite happily chatted. The doorman had a lot to say, his mouth moving so quickly it resembled watching a film on fast forward, the rest of his face covered by the fly-eyes visor of his green helmet. Nigel was leaning against the inside wall of the helicopter, opposite to where they'd entered. He had his finger fixed on the intercom button as he conversed, the doorman using a microphone and headset built into his helmet.

Simon wasn't going to get any response from Nigel. He looked over to Laura, not quite sure what to expect, looked briefly back at the transparent shield and then at Laura again. Laura knowingly shrugged her shoulders as they both accepted their enforced separation from the front of the craft. The screen was merely confirmation of what they'd suspected when Nigel and Simon had been told to leave their guns with the driver before boarding the helicopter, instructions they'd already received over their radios, but which had been reiterated to them via a loud hailer affixed to the outside of the helicopter.

Laura was leaning against the same wall as Nigel but with an appreciable gap between them. Her sense of threat had become sharply honed in the last few days. The three of them had about as much room in their partition of the helicopter as they'd had in the back of the personnel carrier. The doorman had far less space to himself, sharing it with the two pilots seated at the front of the craft; there had been some hasty changes to the helicopter to convert it into a travelling isolation chamber. Simon moved over to sit between Nigel and Laura and leant against the wall. He sat closer to Laura than Nigel, but consciously afforded a gap between the two of them, although she wouldn't have minded if he had sat closer. She was unaware of the extremes that Simon had gone to to save her, but it was as if she could sense it.

Laura turned and looked at Simon, briefly smiled, and then the pair of them looked out of the open door of the craft. They were low enough to see towns and countryside rushing by. Neither could stop themselves from imagining what horrors were still taking place below, and remembering how different it had been a few days earlier.

'How long till we get there?' asked Simon, snapping himself and Laura from their thoughts. Simon had no idea where 'there' was, but knew they wouldn't be flying around aimlessly. He didn't even know if they wanted to get 'there'. The end of the journey might be salvation, or equally, extermination having been labelled as infected cases. Nigel didn't respond. He just carried on conversing with the doorman, shouting above the engine's roar. Simon pulled on his arm, and as Nigel turned briefly, Simon repeated his request. Nigel turned back to carry on talking to the doorman. Simon waited for a few seconds for a response before giving up. He leant back turning to look forward and away from Nigel, accustomed to his colleague's casual ignorance.

'At least he's got something to talk about,' said Simon, half to himself, but enough at Laura for her to catch his sentiment. Laura wasn't quite sure if she'd heard right, but leant forward to look across Simon at Nigel at the animated doorman. The doorman was the most vocal, obvious from his twanging lip movements and jiving hands, Nigel the eager listener.

'What are they talking about?' Laura asked Simon, with an air of anxious inquisitiveness.

'No idea, but I'm not getting any sense out of him.' Simon gestured his head towards Nigel, the upper corner of his lip snarling on his last word. Laura leant forward. Something was nagging at her. She moved onto her hands and knees and crawled across the front of Simon, keeping close to him wary of the open helicopter door, and strained to listen to the conversation. Simon instinctively lifted his arms over Laura's back to grab her and keep her secure, but stopped at the last second for fear of misinterpretation. His arms hovered just above her. She was unaware of his presence, her own guard waiting to jump in and save her if need be.

Simon felt a vague warmth at Laura's lack of fear, cruelly shattered by her darting back to her sitting position, like a naughty child about to steal from her father's wallet. Simon just as quickly pulled his arms back before Laura noticed. Simon knew he'd not knowingly done anything wrong but was apprehensive. How was he to know that Laura would have welcomed the security of his embrace?

He stared straight out of the open door and made a futile effort to calculate their speed by estimating distances along the ground and counting seconds, to block out other thoughts. He didn't want to lose the warm feeling he'd had a few seconds ago, but it was too late. He felt Laura's arm moving and wondered if she might be about to strike him. Her hand took a firm hold of his wrist. For a second he was confused, before realising she was seeking his help. He looked over to her fearfully. For a second they looked at each other, Simon frozen by the alarm in Laura's face. Laura moved as close as she could to speak into Simon's ear. Her warm breath on his neck sent a tingle down his spine.

'We've got a problem,' said Laura. There was a pause. Simon didn't move, expecting and needing to hear more. 'I think the guy behind the screen is about to become a zombie.' Simon jerked sideways away from Laura to look at her. Although his reasoning told him that she couldn't know this, the slightest hint of being trapped with a zombie was enough to terrify anyone in these perverse times. Laura's face was pleading with Simon to trust her. He could feel her pleas, though she said nothing, and was desperately trying to make sense of what she had just said. Even though he was already starting to feel the first hints of a bond with her, he knew very little of Laura. She could be insane or about to become a zombie herself. The last few days had changed everybody in some way.

'The warning!' exclaimed Simon, his expression changing to one of excitement at his belief that he'd cracked the conundrum. He remembered the information they'd received, that zombies would go into a trance like state just before fully turning. With the sharpest of twists, he looked round to confirm his assumption and his trust in Laura. A stab of disappointment hit his gut as he watched the doorman continuing to talk to an enthralled Nigel. Simon looked back to Laura in search of explanation.

'Listen to what they're talking about,' said Laura in response. Simon obliged and tilted his whole body whilst looking ahead to eavesdrop on his colleague. After a few seconds he straightened up. It had been difficult for him to make much out, but he thought he'd picked up the general gist. He moved his mouth as close as he dare to Laura's ear and spoke.

'Something to do with the New Philosophers?'

'Exactly,' said Laura, stifling her desire to shout out her response to Simon's realisation.

'What's that mean?' asked Simon. 'I think a couple of the other lads have mentioned it only today.'

'Oh my God,' squeaked Laura in a rapid exhalation, emotion threatening to boil out. She recomposed herself, and added in a cool, calm voice, 'People have just started talking about the New Philosophy, and people have just started turning into zombies.' Laura delivered the killer fact, hitting Simon like a spear of ice down the centre of his spine. Although it made sense, and he didn't know why, he found himself wholeheartedly believing what Laura was telling him. This also meant that they could be about to be trapped hundreds of feet up in the air with a zombie. Although there was a screen between them, there was no knowing how effective it might be against the maniacal strength of a zombie. Simon continued to stare into Laura's face. Laura looked back, signs of relief breaking out in her expression as she realised Simon believed her. They continued to remain motionless, as not responding provided a vague comfort as opposed to having to make a decision on dealing with what appeared to be an impossible situation.

'What can we do?' asked Simon eventually. He spoke quietly and mechanically, unsure how to react, realising he needed Laura's help.

'I'm not sure?' replied Laura. 'If we land and can get out, we might be okay. But if he zombies in the air, I don't know what chance we've got.' Simon took in what Laura was saying.

'What about Nigel?' asked Simon, desperately collecting as much information as possible to delay making a decision.

'He's been taken in,' replied Laura, 'He's responding to the New Philosophy.' The terror on Simon's face increased, even though he didn't really understand what Laura meant. 'Don't worry,' she consoled, 'he won't change for ages yet.' Simon looked momentarily relieved and was now starting to trust Laura. He paused for a second, only for his face to be revisited again by terror.

'Can't he infect us?' asked Simon sharply.

'He can,' began Laura, 'if you listen to him.' Simon looked puzzled. 'Just don't listen to him,' said Laura, stating what she thought was the obvious.

'That won't be a problem,' replied Simon sarcastically. Simon and Laura smiled at the momentary relief. The seriousness of the situation soon returned.

'How soon before the doorman changes?' asked Simon. Laura didn't move but her eyes looked over towards the doorman. She looked back at Simon and shrugged. They continued discussing what was happening for several more minutes. Laura was having to almost shout to make herself heard above the motorised din, but Nigel was unaware. She was adamant that the doorman would soon change into a zombie as he continued to converse enthusiastically with Nigel. Simon realised that he had to do something. He turned towards the separation screen.

'Doorman!' shouted Simon. Nigel was still talking away. 'Doorman!' shouted Simon again. Simon began thumping on the separation screen with his fist. The doorman was no longer talking and his movements had slowed. Simon looked down at Nigel. Nigel was still talking away, pleading with the doorman to respond to him. The two-way conversation had ceased. Laura moved up to Simon's side. Simon continued to bang on the panel and shout at the doorman. The doorman gradually raised his right arm towards his visor. He clumsily pushed up the visor, his heavy gloves causing his hand to slip and fail to gain a grip. As the visor eventually locked back to reveal the doorman's face, he slumped down, sitting on his bottom with his arms at his side. Simon and Laura took sharp intakes of breath and moved closer to each other.

'What's wrong with you, mate?' asked Nigel as he screwed up his face inquisitively. The doorman's expression was fixed in a mildly euphoric state. He appeared to still be speaking slowly, but couldn't be heard as his clumsy hand had pushed the helmet microphone away from his mouth.

'We've got to land, now' said Laura to Simon forcefully. He looked down at Laura as she looked back at him, both of them beginning to be consumed by panic.

'Pilot!' screamed Simon as he began to hammer on the separation screen. He shouted three or four times but got little reaction. He looked over to the intercom. Nigel was slumped over it pathetically seeking reassurance from his zombifying friend. Simon squeezed his way between Nigel and the screen. 'Pilot! You've got to land,' shouted Nigel. There was no response. He tried again and again, eventually shouting, 'The doorman's a zombie!' He looked through the screen and saw the two pilots quickly look at each other, back into the craft at the now stupifying doorman and then back at each other. They triggered the intercom so that Simon could hear what they were saying.

'You're not a zombie are you, Roger?' asked one of the pilots as he turned round.

'I'm... not... a... zombie,' came the reply, faintly picked up by the pilot's microphone, just audible to Simon.

'There you go mate, he's not a zombie,' came the reply from the pilot to Simon. 'Are you okay Roger? You're sounding a bit strange,' continued the pilot, oblivious to his disastrous ignorance. Simon continued talking through the intercom.

'He's about to go into the change,' Simon began pleading. 'Look at him.'

'Hang on mate. I'm trying to talk to Location Three. There's a call coming through, but I'm having trouble.' The pilot's full attention was diverted to the gremlins in the communications system, away from the seemingly trivial conversation regarding the doorman. As the pilot toyed with the dials, Simon could see the doorman's expression becoming increasingly crazy and euphoric. The grin of a killer in waiting began to shape in the doorman's mouth. Simon raised himself slightly and looked down to Laura.

'Keep trying,' said Laura, her rapid breathing giving away her rising fear.

'You've got to trust me,' Simon pleaded down the intercom. 'He's going to change. We haven't got long. You've got to get us down.' Simon waited and listened. The pilot was still attempting to talk to Location Three and ignoring him. Simon tried again. 'For God's sake, he'll kill us all.' Simon looked at the doorman who had now progressed to the euphoric trance phase of the zombie state. 'Pilot. Ask him again if he's okay. Please, just ask him. Even if you don't believe us, you can see for yourself now. Remember the warning. Pilot! Pilot!' Simon was becoming increasingly frantic. He was thumping at the screen with the same desperation of a man at a shatterproof windscreen in a burning car.

'Can't make you out properly Location Three. Hope you can hear us. We're coming into land,' came the overheard message from the pilot who hadn't turned off the intercom to the cell at the rear of the helicopter.

'Thank God!' exclaimed Simon as he slumped back against the side of the helicopter alongside Nigel who had still not given up on his pointless efforts to gain a response from the doorman. Simon was breathing rapidly, but there was little else he could do now apart from wait for the satisfying bump of the helicopter's skids on the ground. The previous few seconds seemed to have passed Nigel by completely. Laura remained on all fours in front of the screen, closely observing the doorman.

'Simon,' said Laura with the kind of expressionless monotone voice that could only be associated with foreboding, 'how long before we touch down?' Simon, who had now flaked out, his head back, leant forwards to look over at Laura. She turned to look at him, mouth open, her dread manifest. Simon pulled himself forward onto his knees as he turned to look at the doorman through the screen.

'Come on mate. What's the problem? Talk to me,' continued the pointless pleadings of Nigel in the background. 'I want to hear more about the New Philosophy.' Nigel's voice seemed to Simon and Laura to drift into the distance as their full focus was dragged towards the doorman. There was no longer any euphoria within his expression. He was dribbling from the sides of his mouth. His eyes stretched wide open, the whites dominating the dark pupils and stark irises in the centre. His lower jaw was gradually dropping and his lips pulling back to bare his teeth. Simon and Laura knew the change was nearly complete. Their stomachs turned as the helicopter made a sudden drop and began its descent, triggering relief that they might just make it.

A mechanical click and whirr started, mingling with the drone of the helicopter, startling Laura and Simon.

'What's that?' asked Laura. Simon was already looking around eager to answer the question for himself.

'No! What are you doing?' shouted Simon. He banged at the screen as he passed alongside it to start stabbing at the intercom button. 'Pilot, what the hell are you doing? You can't trap us in here with that!' Simon was shouting hysterically.

'Procedure,' replied the pilot, still suicidally oblivious to the danger emerging just behind his head. There was a click as the pilot turned off the intercom.

'Pilot! No! Listen to me!' shouted Simon pointlessly for a couple of seconds. He stopped, aware that he needed to think quickly. The outside door was being automatically closed to contain them once the helicopter had landed, probably condemning all of the occupants to being the unwilling participants in the doorman zombie's inaugural feast.

Simon darted across the helicopter to the door space still available as it trundled over, moving so quickly that Laura thought for a second he had chosen to fling himself to his own death rather than face the zombie. He grabbed the sides of the diminishing space and looked out towards the ground.

'We're too high to jump,' he said as he continued to stare out, aware that the door would be fully shut way before they had reached a survivable height. He was trying to think quickly. Laura suddenly shrieked. The doorman was starting to hiss and spit and shake his head. Simon looked at Laura. 'Help me with this door.' They now had absolutely no concern for the pilots, who had not only put themselves beyond help, but probably everyone else.

Simon and Laura began pushing at the door as it continued to slowly slide across the opening. Simon put his back against the edge of the door and pushed on the other side of the opening with his boots, despite the edge cutting sharply into his back and making him yelp. It was all for nothing. Their efforts didn't even appear to slow it up for a second. Simon felt his body begin to crush and he knew he only had a split second to free himself. For a moment, he contemplated the insane gamble of throwing himself out, but he chose to stay with Laura, and sprung back into the chopper. As the door finished its journey to slot into the neat space, Simon and Laura fruitlessly tried to pull it back, just getting their fingers out of the remaining space in the nick of time.

They slumped down against the closed door, breathless and terrified. With that battle now lost, they became aware of a banging on the separation screen. It was coming from the other side. They both looked up to see the increasingly mobile zombie banging its fists against the screen, staring at them ravenously and eyeing them as a cure for its hunger. Simon and Laura didn't move.

'What's wrong mate?' said Nigel, accompanying his ridiculous question from the other side of the helicopter with a bang against the screen. The zombie turned and then bounded across to the other side with primate-like moves, and pushed itself up against where Nigel was located. Nigel was staring through at the doorman with a confused expression. He continued to ask questions as the zombie slobbered against the screen, the spittle dribbling down from the patch it created.

Suddenly the zombie leant back. Its whole body seemed to tauten, as if it had become a new being. It drew its right fist back and let rip into the separation screen with an almighty punch. Laura, Simon and Nigel all jumped back and froze. The zombie hardly paused before punching it again. As it drew its fist back, a smear of blood was left behind from its split knuckles. A third punch crashed home, but this time as well as leaving behind more blood, a crack appeared. The screen wasn't going to hold. It might not even last another couple of punches. Laura and Simon held each other tight, their worst expectations beginning to be realised. Nigel gazed idiotically at the cracked screen. He was still struggling to comprehend the obvious.

'What the hell is going on back there Roger?' shouted one of the pilots so loudly, that he could be faintly heard in the isolation compartment. The zombie, without any hesitation, scrambled away from the screen and then turned, stepped and finally leapt forwards into the cockpit, every bit an animal pouncing on its prey. Simon and Laura breathed a restrained sigh of relief, their sympathy for the pilots limited, as the zombie devoured them. Nigel continued to stare through to the front of the helicopter, increasingly incredulous as he watched the zombie start to tear at the pilots' flesh. The helicopter pitched violently forwards and sideways. Simon and Laura's relief was once again ripped from them as they realised the inevitable.

'We can't be that high up by now,' said Simon, attempting to reassure Laura, immediately realising he'd probably had the opposite effect. The helicopter lurched.

'Woah!' exclaimed Nigel with all the concern of someone who had slipped and slightly lost their balance on a piece of ice. The lurching continued. The longer it went on, the more likely death was imminent as their stomachs signalled rapid downwards acceleration. The confusion Laura and Simon experienced of needing to crash quickly whilst instinctively not wanting to, was brought to a sudden halt along with the helicopter, throwing the occupants forwards with a violent flick. The instance of deafening crashing and screeching as metal contorted and glass shattered seemed to last an unfeasibly long time. Nigel somehow maintained his balance, as he fell forwards against the screen whilst riding the careering vehicle like some kind of crazy rodeo ride. Simon was lifted clean off the floor through the air, to be stopped by his head thumping into the screen that separated the isolation compartment. Even this almighty force, which left Simon in a heap on the ground unconscious, failed to make any mark on the screen which the zombie had been able to split with its fist. Laura had held onto the helicopter for long enough to restrain herself, so that when she was finally catapulted into the air, Simon was in an ideal position to cushion her landing. The helicopter continued to bounce for a second rolling fully onto its side, before coming to a stop.

Laura and Nigel gradually started to move, initially coming to terms with the fact that they had survived the crash, before progressing on to check that they still had their limbs and could still move them relatively painlessly. Laura, realising she was substantially intact, ignored her bruises and cuts as she turned her attention to Simon's body lying motionless below her. She tore away the remains of his bio chem suit, to reveal standard army fatigues. The suit had already been rendered useless as it was torn apart like tissue paper as Simon was flung around the cabin.

'He's unconscious,' she said to Nigel, not really sure what he could do, but instinctively looking to the nearest available person for support. The heavy whirring of the helicopters engines had now dispersed, though there was still a more than adequate background of sound from the hisses and creaks of the dying vehicle. Nigel heard Laura but ignored her as he looked over his arms which he was holding up in front of himself in order to look right around them with astonishment, flabbergasted at his luck. He'd removed his own suit, his hood having been dislodged from his head during the landing, but seemed unconcerned at the potential exposure he now faced.

'Would you believe it?' said Nigel. 'I must be the luckiest man alive.' Laura wanted to point out to him that Simon needed help, but she just looked at him silently. She looked down to Simon and gently pushed him. He let out a slight groan. Before Laura could respond, her attention was taken by Nigel. 'Hey, look. There's the doorman,' he said. The now all too familiar feeling of overwhelming zombie-related horror once more consumed Laura. She tried to stop Nigel but was frozen. If she made a noise, she would attract the attention of the zombie. If she did nothing, Nigel was going to attract him anyway. She just waited.

'Hey, mate!' shouted Nigel, 'Look at this. I'm completely unhurt.' Nigel was oblivious to the potential insensitivity of his remark. He carried on shouting, and the zombie's attention was soon attracted. Nigel continued to call, unable it seemed to even remember the zombie's manic punching at the screen just before they had crashed, let alone that it had caused the crash.

The zombie was caught up among the bodies of the pilots. It managed to rip them clear, cracking a limb of one of them in doing so. The sounds from the front of the craft were now audible to the back, as the screen had cracked extensively from where the zombie had previously ruptured it with its punching. Laura flinched at the stomach churning sound of breaking bones. The zombie clambered through from the front, climbing with all the grace of a drunk attempting to ballet dance. Its face and hands were soaked in blood, its white, crazy eyes shining through and quickly pinpointing Nigel. Nigel fell silent as he remembered. He stumbled back slightly as the zombie ran forward, but it was stopped abruptly by its face smashing into the screen.

Laura shook Simon with small but vigorous movements, careful not to attract the attention of the zombie, whose attention was now solidly fixed on Nigel, as she looked back and forth between the two. Simon groaned again as he gradually began to come round. Laura placed her hand over Simon's mouth in mild panic. He opened his eyes, struggled slightly, but saw Laura. He relaxed a bit and her hand slipped away as she looked down at him.

Suddenly Laura and Simon were sprayed in shattered glass as the zombie dived clean through the screen headfirst, howling like a banshee and spraying blood in all directions as its nose, cheeks and lips were crushed and burst. Nigel screamed in terror, his behaviour finally appropriate. The zombie seemed to fly through the air, arms outstretched, straight at Nigel's head. Nigel fell backwards, putting his arms back instinctively to protect himself, leaving his neck and face exposed. The zombie wrapped its arms round Nigel's head as its face plunged into his neck. The zombie's horizontally lunging body dropped down onto Nigel as the pair fell to the ground in a writhing mass of screaming, snarling and feeding.

Simon stared in disbelief through his daze. 'Come on!' whispered Laura at Simon. She felt no attachment to Nigel and was already attempting to stand and climb, simultaneously making her way towards the jagged hole in the screen. She managed to grab a strap on the helicopter ceiling, now vertically to the side, and pull herself up, whilst yanking Simon sharply with her other hand by the shoulder of his jacket. The impolite tug ripped Simon from his daze. He looked up, quickly realised that Laura had found a route to potential survival, and started to make his way to his feet. Laura was already making her way through the hole, grasping at any available hand hold and kicking at anything her foot could make contact with, but she still didn't manage to completely avoid injury entirely from the edge of the shattered screen. Simon gave Laura a push, just as her flailing foot cracked into his eye. Laura was propelled through the hole landing headfirst and rolling head over heels on the other side. Simon fell back to his knees, somewhat dazed, but managed to stop himself from falling over with a hand to the helicopter's side. Nigel was now silent, but the gnawing of the zombie was still enthusiastic.

Laura had got back on her feet and turned round ready to help Simon through. Simon got fully to his feet, took a quick look back to be sure the zombie was still occupied, and then jumped at the hole in the screen whilst pulling himself up by the edges. Mortal fear masked the pain to his hands as the plasticky glass gouged through his palms. He fell down halfway through the hole onto the edge, which dug into his stomach, his jacket protecting him from serious injury. For a second he seemed stuck, like an over-optimistic, obese cat attempting to get through a cat flap. Laura without hesitation jumped onto her tiptoes to reach over the top of Simon, and grab the back of his jacket. Gripping tightly, she pulled him towards herself, falling over in the process and bringing Simon toppling through to land on top of her as the pair of them crumpled onto the floor.

Simon and Laura clambered to their feet. They were bruised and bleeding, but were fortunate no major veins or arteries had been severed, yet. They knew the zombie would soon take care of that if they didn't move, and could now fend for themselves. They climbed and crawled their way into the cockpit, ignoring the fact that they were stepping on the two pilots' corpses. One of the doors was now the floor as the helicopter lay on its side, so exit through this was not an option. Simon tried the other door. It unlatched, moved slightly then jammed. Simon pulled it back and forth but it merely rattled within its half inch of travel. He rammed upwards hard at it a couple of times with his shoulder but gained no extra give. He sank back down to look around the edges, running his hands over a couple of them. The twisting of the helicopter had wedged it fast. Laura was already looking around for another option.

'The windscreen,' said Laura as she pointed downwards. It was made from two separate sections with a metal boundary down the middle. The side that was now higher up was still intact, but the lower one was cracked and had come away from its surround on one of the upper corners. Simon crouched and looked at the ground. The side of the helicopter had driven its way into the mud and even if the windscreen could be displaced, there was barely a gap there. Laura looked at Simon and felt his doubt. 'What else can we do?' she said before he could speak. Laura began kicking and stamping at the windscreen. Simon leant over to look back into the helicopter. As he did so, the zombie dropped the body of Nigel. It stood motionless, its back to Simon. It slowly started to look around. It wanted new prey.

Simon quickly turned and began kicking. The sound was going to attract the zombie but it was their only chance. They only had seconds. The windscreen had been badly damaged, and although Laura's initial kicks had seemed hopeless, it gave quickly and in a frenzy of stamps was driven into the ground as it came away in one piece.

'Go!' said Simon, despite Laura already being on her knees and diving forwards. Simon looked back for a split second. The zombie had heard the noise. Though still in the very back of the helicopter, it was about to clamber through the hole. It was moving with less zeal than its earlier attack on Nigel, its hunger somewhat quelled. It still wanted to feed, but every second helped Laura and Simon's survival.

Simon dropped to his knees ready to escape but Laura was still only halfway through. She was grasping at the grass on the other side but making little progress. Simon pushed as best he could but to little effect. He pushed harder, desperate to get Laura through the tiny gap, and not just for her sake. He even fleetingly considered pulling her back into the helicopter, but shocked himself. He could hear the zombie climbing through the hole in the screen. He pushed harder at Laura, but it was pointless. Suddenly, he noticed that part of her top was caught on a rivet. He grabbed it and pulled hard backwards. Laura screamed believing the worst. Simon released her and Laura felt herself spring forwards further than she had previously. She tore at the grass in front whilst wriggling violently, and was out.

Simon could hear that the zombie was now through the hole in the separation screen. It could now easily dive at him and grab him. Simon knew that if he looked back he would lose a vital moment, sabotaging his own escape. The years of training at crawling under nets suddenly felt like the most purposeful thing he had ever done. His waist was larger than Laura's, but he was moving forwards. The grass was in his face, and he could see the close-up blades passing by his eyes and underneath him, raising his hopes. He heard the sound of the zombie treading on the pilots' corpses. He didn't even know if he had any time left now. He wasn't quite halfway through, and his buttocks had still yet to pass out of the helicopter. He expected to feel the zombie's teeth sinking into them at any second. He tried to crawl faster, but was already going flat out.

Laura had managed to stand up and had instinctively stepped away from the helicopter to a zone of some safety. She was still orientating, and had managed to focus on the inside of the helicopter through the remaining windscreen. She could see the zombie coming through the gap in the pilots' compartment. Her heart and lungs felt icy. She glanced down at Simon who was still pulling himself through the gap, but well within the grasp of the zombie which would effortlessly pull him back inside to devour. Laura lunged forwards and grabbed Simon's wrists pulling his hands away from the grass. Simon gasped as he lost his only means of freeing himself. She leant back, catching a glimpse of the zombie as she did so though the windscreen. It had seen Simon. The white discs on its face enlarged as it realised it had found more food. She started pushing herself backwards violently, her heels kicking and digging into the grass. The zombie dived down at Simon, but somehow Laura had found the strength she needed, and Simon's body slithered through the gap to freedom, like a new-born calf finally exiting its mother.

There was no time for relief. The zombie could quite easily follow through the hole. Simon and Laura got to their feet and began to run. They didn't know where to, just away from the helicopter, but they knew it would be hopeless unless they could find help or sanctuary quickly. They were breathing heavily and were confused. They had no idea where they were, but just ran as they looked around for some purpose.

'There!' shouted Simon, as he pointed to a barn type building and some prefabs. The buildings were about three hundred metres away, but might offer some help, or not. Given the breakdown of the country, there was a good chance that they might be running into a zombie-infested nest. However they had both grown to trust their instincts. A helicopter crash would have inevitably summoned more zombies, and the fact none had appeared yet gave them some hope.

A snarling growl came from behind them and they swiftly looked back. The zombie had broken free from the helicopter and had spotted them. It began to run. Laura and Simon had some fifty metres advantage, but these zombies could move. The distraught pair carried on running. Simon could see that there was a doorway, big enough for a vehicle but not much more, in the barn. 'Head for that door!' he shouted to Laura. It was some kind of a plan, but the chances of survival once inside were not much better than if they stopped running now. They both knew they were hoping beyond hope, but such was the human condition.

'Okay,' replied Laura, but as she spoke, they both saw the sliding door to the entrance began to move. It was going to lock them out before they got there.

'No!' screamed Simon in a futile attempt to hold onto their vanishing sanctuary. The door was clanking shut as they got to closer to the building. Laura glanced back. The zombie was some twenty metres behind them. The pair stopped and turned round, panting. 'Come on then,' said Simon as he resorted to his final plan. He assumed a wrestler-type pose, ready to pointlessly grapple with the zombie. Laura closed her eyes. 'You go,' said Simon softly to Laura, resigned to his fate. Laura opened her eyes to see the zombie about to complete its hunt and lunge at them both. She didn't move.

95

12. Entry

Laura and Simon were grasped by unreality. Were they still alive? Had they instantly been killed to find that the afterlife was exactly the same? They were both aware of a fading windy sound, the decaying echoes of a shot fired a few instances earlier. Simon was looking down at the zombie lying in front of them. Laura couldn't see properly as her eyes had been subjected to a splash of blood from the face of the zombie as a high-velocity bullet had ripped through its forehead. Laura and Simon were alive. They had been less than a breath away from death, but that didn't matter now as they had somehow survived the imminent devouring that they'd faced. They started to breathe again. The zombie's body twitched and convulsed for a second as it lay on its back, then stiffened arching upwards momentarily, before slumping dead.

The pair looked at each other. Once again, shared survival from a near-death experience had strengthened their bond. They felt like they could trust each more than many people who spend years together. They turned slowly, hesitating for a second as they came to face each other square on, before continuing, each now grasping the hand of the other as they looked back at the barn which they had been running towards. They couldn't see anyone. They waited.

'Do not move. You are under armed cover.' A threatening male voice rang out. They could just about make out that it was coming from the general direction of the barn through some kind of loud hailer or speaker. The echo died away. They had no intentions of moving. Though terrified, the authoritative dominance of the voice assured them that they were no longer in danger of zombie attack. 'Please raise your right hand if you understand us.' Laura and Simon compliantly did so, eager to confirm that they were lucid. After a second of holding their arms aloft, they allowed them to fall back to their sides. 'Please raise your arms if your name is read out,' continued the disembodied voice. A list of names were read out, among them Laura and Simon's, along with the roll-call of the recently deceased from the helicopter journey. Nigel's name was bizarrely read out after Laura and Simon had confirmed who they each were.

After they had identified themselves, there was a pause. They both turned and looked around whilst they awaited further instructions. There wasn't much to see apart from fields bounded by trees and hedges along with the barn and outbuildings ahead of them. 'What shall we do?' asked Laura.

'I don't know,' replied Simon.

'We can't just stand here,' said Laura. 'Let's go over to the building.' Laura began to walk forwards. Simon hesitated for a second then shrugged briefly and followed.

'Stop!' came the voice. They both stopped immediately. 'Await further instructions.' Laura and Simon both sighed, becoming exasperated after their very recent exhilaration. 'Proceed towards the barn,' came the voice a mere couple of seconds since instructing them to refrain from the same action.

'Bleeding typical,' muttered Simon under his breath.

They trudged through the grass. There was no noise and the silence of the countryside was stark once the final echoes of the voice had dispersed. There was no hum whatsoever from Location Three, such was the care taken not to give away its true motive. Simon looked up at the top edge of the roof, and could just make out what looked like a ventilation shaft cover. It was very small, far too small for a man, but just big enough to take an automatically controlled rifle, camera and loud speaker.

On reaching the barn, the doors that had moments earlier shut before them seeming to close off their last chance of survival, reopened. Inside they didn't notice much; a couple of vehicles and some bales of straw, which once they had walked past, realised were there to hide doors and various other out of place fittings. All the time, they were being remotely controlled by the voice that had greeted them after the execution of the zombie. Devoid of any experience or context through which to make sense of what was happening, they complied without question.

The large doors closed behind them. There was a second or two of darkness before a dull red light enabled them to at least move without too many collisions. From a trapdoor in the floor, a large box with a door on the side rose up. They dutifully stepped inside as instructed, glad to do so as the brighter light within beckoned. Once inside, the door closed behind them and they heard the click of a lock.

The rise of their stomachs signalled that the box was descending relatively slowly. After an elevator type ride of a couple of minutes, the movement eventually slowed, suddenly brought to a stop with a clunk. A couple of minutes passed, then the whole of the opposite side of the box slid away to reveal a wall with a door. They passed through this door to the room and found themselves in a room. They stepped inside, and the door behind them closed, almost seeming to vanish into the grey plain steel walls that were the only feature of the whole room apart from two chairs.

Laura stood, Simon sat. Simon was used to the assumed compliance without explanation having been a soldier for well over two years. It was obvious to him that he was in the system. They were at the place that the helicopter had been trying to reach just prior to the zombie attack. If there had been any intention to kill them, it would have happened by now. Simon's role was to do as he was told. There were two chairs and the two companions in the room, so he would sit and wait. He had no intention of instructing Laura to do the same. She was pacing throughout the small square space which only allowed her four steps in any one direction. Simon sat away from the centre allowing Laura room to move. The unoccupied chair was right next to his, and like his, was a basic thin tubular metal construction with a plastic seat and back, the sort found in community centres. Every now and then Simon could hear Laura huffing. She was clearly frustrated though they'd only been there about twenty minutes and she had happily complied with the instructions on reaching the barn. Twenty minutes was barely a wink of time to Simon compared to the monotony of much of his army experience.

Suddenly, the wall in front of them moved entirely sideways to reveal a transparent screen. Behind the screen was a similar room, but it went back about three times as far and had a door to the side at the back. There were two people seated a short distance away from the screen. It made Simon and Laura feel equal to their newly revealed observers in a strange sort of way. There were two other people stood directly behind the front two and to the back of the room a couple of armed soldiers. Laura and Simon felt fear. They had no idea who any of the people were, why they were there, what was going to happen or if they were the target of the guns.

'I'm General Adam Spelling,' said a man seated at the front. 'I'm the Martial Governor of the UK.' The enormity of what they had just heard failed to have any real effect on Laura and Simon. They both decided that no question they could ask was likely to yield any better information, if any, than they were likely to be told, and so decided to listen. 'You are safe here. We have no intention of harming you... quite the opposite. Your welfare is our concern.' Adam knew he had to gain their trust as quickly as possible.

'Why are we locked up then?' asked Laura unable to resist questioning the obvious contradiction. She pulled up the chair next to Simon and sat down, facing her inquisitors head on.

'We need to establish some facts,' said Adam.

'Sir, why are you talking to us?' asked Simon stressing the 'you'. He had now begun to comprehend the importance of the man sat in front of him, which clashed with his sense of order. If the most important man in the UK was talking to them, they were being treated as of some importance themselves, but why? Laura and Simon had quickly focussed on the person who could give them answers. They were all but ignoring the others in the room. Seated next to General Adam Spelling was Dr Bob Davis. He was leaning forward, hands on his chin, elbows resting on his knees in contrast to Adam who was sat upright. At this point, Bob was still in the mode of examining specimens. Dr Javed Hussain and Harriet Tomes stood behind Adam and Bob, Javed with his arms folded in the same zone as Bob. Harriet wasn't too sure what to do.

Adam continued. 'It's Laura whom we need to talk to,' said Adam. His manner was suddenly very relaxed and friendly as if he were about to discuss tales of an adventurous expedition with a returning friend. 'I heard the message come in about what you had to say, and I've also listened to your call to the television show, The Goode Things.' Adam's intrigue was apparent. 'In fact, I heard most of the transmission from the helicopter.' Adam looked momentarily mournful. The death of his men always hurt. 'You're lucky I was in the control room to hear the message come in.' Bizarrely, given the complete collapse of society along with the probable massacre of her family, Laura did feel lucky. The situation was very lucky for everyone. Information like Laura's could quite easily have got missed or lost in the chaos that was now Government, a hasty replacement for the previous chaos that was Government, even though her information was probably the most important piece of information available.

'I followed your whole flight in. We were able to turn on microphones throughout the helicopter. We heard you predict that the doorman, Roger, was going to turn before the recognised symptoms kicked in. I'm sorry we couldn't intervene more quickly when the pilots were ignoring you, but we were at least able to make sure you weren't the targets once you landed.' Laura and Simon didn't move or show any response, but both felt a chill in their stomachs run down along their thighs. They really were very lucky to be alive.

'Laura. Please tell us what you know.' Bob Davis spoke to Laura for the first time. He'd observed his specimen enough and was now engaging with a fellow human being.

'Why are we locked up?' asked Laura restating her previous question. To her it seemed a perfectly reasonable question given what she knew, but without this information, it was a completely ridiculous assertion. Even Simon turned to her and frowned slightly.

'As far as we know, you may be infected,' said Bob, mildly irritated at having to restate the fact.

'Do I sound like I'm infected?' replied Laura. This created curiosity for the interrogators.

'I think you're going to have explain that,' replied Adam.

'Well, if I was infected, you'd know about it,' Laura retorted. Laura's answer and sharpness was affected by her subconsciously presuming that the others must now know what she knows. 'Just like I knew that the guy in the helicopter was… infected. I'd be talking about it wouldn't I?' The room seemed to still. The moment lost some sense of time as the minds present struggled to process this unfamiliar paradigm. Bob broke the tension.

'So this is how you knew what was going to happen in the helicopter?' Bob spoke slowly but intently, as he looked straight at Laura, aware that his enquiry could make some progress towards the information he required.

Laura paused. She'd presumed that they must have discovered something about the zombies here in Location Three. Even though she was not really sure exactly where she was, she'd rightly assumed that this subterranean habitat had the best available resources, and General Adam Spelling had already revealed the power based there. An organisation like this, big enough to run the country, must know what she alone had already discovered? Then she realised that if she really believed they must know, she would not have had to take the risks she did to reach them.

Laura felt a fleeting tinge of delight. She really did know more than them, with all of their power and resources. The tension flushed back through her face though, as she contemplated the struggle that lay ahead to convince them of what she believed.

Laura wondered for a second if she had done the right thing. Her recent experiences had nearly crushed her, when she found that doing the right thing can be a very expensive personal option. Prior to starting her course, she'd secured a vacation work placement at a community charity on a particularly run down inner city estate, working with people who were homeless, many of whom had turned to alcohol. Laura had always excelled academically despite the struggles of her early family life. She could easily have chosen to pursue personal gain, but instead wanted to play a part in making the world a fairer place for everyone.

At first, she thought that she'd found the perfect placement, as the charity had just received substantial government funding and had a well connected boss. However, from the first day she'd struggled with the quirks of organisational life. Her supervisor, Sarah, had let off steam in the office after being chastised for not informing the boss that she was going to the toilet. This was insisted upon as the toilet was in a different building, and as was explained to Sarah yet again, nobody would know if anything had happened to her. Laura, having hardly sat down, listened to Sarah's frustration at the way common sense seemed to be ignored by other people who so easily become compliant parts of the machine. Laura's hopes that Sarah was someone like her were soon shattered when Laura found herself being berated an hour later for not letting Sarah know that she was going to the toilet. After all, 'nobody would know if anything had happened to her' Sarah explained devoid of irony.

It didn't get much better. Unfortunately, Laura's belief that the organisation's funding was for helping those struggling without a home, trapped in the temporary relief of drink-induced stupor, was even less than a secondary concern for the charity. Its priority turned out to be the engagement of consultants in producing vaguely relevant but ultimately pointless reports. There were plenty of candidates for this work, being drawn from the boss's network of friends and colleagues. They all enjoyed membership of various groups pursuing similar aims and purposes, not least of which was securing funding and promotion for each other. As a result, the substantial part of meetings to discuss how to help homeless alcoholics, was primarily focussed on the meeting participants' extra-curricular pursuits and activism. It never occurred to anybody to question Laura being at these meetings, however confused she was.

Having made the mistake of believing that the funding was really for the homeless, and after being aggressively chastised by the boss for suggesting to her that her dealings were a little dubious, she'd made the mistake of going directly to the Government department that was providing the funding. Laura was not one to keep her head down and toe the line allowing her soul to gradually decay. Unfortunately for Laura, the official she spoke to had been involved in the appointment of the charity's boss. As Laura's college was also receiving substantial funding from the same department, she eventually found herself lucky not to be thrown off her course. She was though, labelled as a troublemaker, as someone who simply could not understand that what she thought was self-indulgent exploitation, was part of a bigger plan that need not be questioned.

The whole experience had left Laura distraught, but despite all the clues to the contrary, she had convinced herself that it was a one off. She had concluded that the world was fundamentally good and that the truth would always come out. Of course, she was right, but it's often so long after events that nobody cares, and it's too late to affect the winners and losers. Fortunately, her laudable but erroneous conclusion had meant that she was still prepared to risk even her own life to do something about the zombie menace.

This time, Laura was going to be smarter. She was determined not to fall victim to her better than average intelligence, by stumbling along in a direct and clumsy way, oblivious to the necessities of packaging and presentation, or simply knowing when to say nothing.

She looked deeper into Bob's eyes as she considered her response. She realised she must answer simply, unemotionally, and above all, deferentially, despite Bob being more objective than most people. Self-satisfaction could not be allowed to endanger the little hope that the human race had.

'Yes. It is how I knew what was going to happen. If I was infected, I would be talking about it.' There was a pause as Bob considered why people would be talking about becoming zombies. His eyes beckoned for more. Laura tilted her head to gaze up to the right, and then to the left. She'd been so focussed on Bob, only now was she aware that the rest of the room had concentrated its attention on her, stares fixed, some mouths slightly ajar. She looked fully to her side at Simon, to be met head-on by a similar expression.

She was startled back slightly, as an icy cold blast wrenched through her whole body in reaction to the vaguely zombie-like state of Simon. 'Sorry,' he said quickly. Laura gave him a reassuring smile, which he returned as she took his hand and gently squeezed. He reciprocated.

'You only have to listen to what they're talking about,' began Laura. 'That guy in the helicopter, the people in Chesborough, it's all the same.' The observers were straining, anxious for her to conclude. 'They all talk about the New Philosophy.'

There was an audible gasp from someone in the observation room. Those at the front turned to see that Harriet had raised her hand to cover her mouth. Laura looked mildly surprised. She had been worried that she was going to struggle to get them to take her seriously, but Harriet's reaction seemed to indicate otherwise. Bob maintained his scientific demeanour.

'They mention the New Philosophy you say?' quizzed Bob, keen to avoid ambiguity.

'Yes,' said Laura, now more at ease as she felt the growing potential for acceptance.

Bob looked to Adam. He showed little expression, but Bob's face gave away that Laura's revelation had collided with some other information they held. The stillness of the room had given way to irritability among the occupants. Laura's comments had disturbed them, though they could not have achieved this in their own right. Laura was aware of this, but before she could continue, Adam knew he had to respond to the change of mood.

'I think we'll take a break,' said Adam, avoiding looking at Laura and turning at the same time to make his way out of the room. Bob was still looking at Laura, as he began to rise.

'Thank you Laura. We'll get back to you,' he said, as if he were addressing an auditionee for some minor role in a provincial drama production. Laura looked slightly bemused, unsure how to respond. She wasn't' sure if this was a good or bad response to what she had said, just a few words, and yet the whole mood had changed and people were leaving. The loss of communication was unsettling and upsetting, not helped by the wall moving back across the transparent screen.

Adam the Martial Governor of the UK, Bob the academic, Harriet the civil servant and Javed the government scientist walked out of the observation room, took a couple of steps across the corridor, and stood in a silent, pensive huddle. They exchanged expressions reflecting the implications of what they had just heard. Laura's comments would have not been that exceptional, if it were not for the preceding events in the control room.

Earlier that day, Adam's instinct had been nagging at him from the first moment he'd ordered Laura to be brought in, insisting that Laura could be of great importance. It was an exceptional circumstance, and he wouldn't even have been told about such a trivial matter ordinarily, being Martial Governor of the UK. However, the news of had reached Location Three shortly after Kalpana, Alistair and Ian had been sent to the cells for failing to pass on the information about the zombie outbreak in Brazil, and those in the control rooms were on extra high vigilance. The information about this event had transformed for a while, every action and operation in the communications rooms. If the message about Laura had come in either side of this short window, Adam may never have become aware of it. But it had, and once planted, it was always going to stir his instinct.

The failure of Kalpana and Alistair could well have been a major intersection along the path of destiny. It wasn't fate though. All outcomes in life are dependent on what has happened before, and therefore can always be explained after the fact by the tiniest of interventions, seemingly only explicable to the human mind as a mysterious force of fate casting its will. It was a reminder of how tiny chance events can have big effects in our lives, and how very often, all of our efforts to shape our own futures, maybe to reach the pinnacles of wealth and celebrity, can be utterly useless compared to the might of a lucky break. The hard worker struggling to get by alongside the lazy chancer living in luxury are merely the outcome of so many people in such a chaotic environment. It's the essential raw fuel for the evolutionary mechanism without which we wouldn't even exist. The irony is that gift of life comes inextricably entwined with the playing of cruel games and mocking parodies on the countless conscious beings through their temporary sojourns of existence.

Regardless of the reasons, Adam had found himself in the control room watching as Laura's flight had approached. Harriet, Bob and Javed had joined him, some of them slightly irritated at wasting their time on paying such close attention to what was probably just another attention-seeking wannabe, oblivious to their choice to stay close to power.

As they waited for the helicopter to reach Location Three, they had heard the events onboard preceding the crash landing and Laura and Simon's desperate flight from the jaws of the zombie doorman. As they had awaited the imminent arrival, communication problems with the pilots and Adam's increasing displeasure, had led to the controller suggesting that they might be able to access the microphone that had been installed in the isolation compartment.

'Do it,' said Adam. The sound from the isolation compartment was better than the connection the controller had to the pilots. This was probably helped by it being robust enough to block out a lot of the helicopter noise. Even so, it was not easy to make out what was being said. Adam and his four colleagues were simply pleased that they could hear voices, as although they could not make out what was being said, they were now assured that the helicopter was still on its way. Adam seemed to smile, but it was merely the release of tension and anxiety from his face.

Adam's attention was so taken up with his worry for the fate of the helicopter, he only realised an officer was stood to his side waiting to hand him a report once he was hit by the wave of relief at hearing voices on board. He took the report only half-interestedly, more concerned with the progress of the helicopter. The report was on the Tupelo Star's communications. It was an initial report that had been hurriedly put together. There wasn't much detail in it, just a list of what looked like computer data with occasional words among the new electronic letter delivery system it was trying out. Adam quickly flicked through the pages bound by soft brown cardboard, just long enough to establish there was nothing for him to worry about at this moment. The Tupelo Star had already yielded its crucial message he thought to himself, that the zombie infection seemed to have spread without contact. His arm just started to fall down to his side, when he wondered if the Tupelo Star events might have more to tell, and finished the movement of his arm with a swing to the side and up, arcing the report to Bob. 'Bob, would you mind?' he asked.

Bob obligingly took the report and quickly began consuming its contents. The rest of the group, distracted by the lack of activity on the helicopter, had noticed Adam preferring to give the report to Bob.

Bob had an ability to quickly glean the key facts from data, an ability that Adam was well aware of and which he knew was an invaluable weapon against anyone who might wish to bamboozle him. Bob was a powerful man here. After Bob had been flicking through the report for a few seconds, Adam glanced over to his side to catch up on his progress. Just as Adam began to look away, he paused to turn back to Bob for a second longer, surprised at how quickly he had become engrossed. Adam realised that the Tupelo Star may well be divulging further secrets. However, Adam's attention was snapped back to the activity in the room, and all thoughts of what might be in the Tupelo Star report quickly dispersed like the brief trace of smoke from a cap gun shot.

Adam's attention was taken by what was happening on the helicopter, and the heightened voices infused with rising panic echoing out of the loudspeakers in the room. Although muffled, the increased volume of the voices made it possible to make out the warnings that Laura was shouting. Her panic at the impending change of the doorman into a zombie had captured the interest of the group mesmerically. All except Bob, who was still intrigued by the report.

Bob had noticed a few, maybe three mentions of the New Philosophers. He saw this in the data connected to some written exchanges that had been part of the new technology. It was a like a letter but electronic and could be sent down wires. It could be printed out, or even read on a screen. Nobody was convinced that it would be adopted much outside of the academic world which had been using it for some time, and the Tupelo Star crew using it for trivial information, such as wacko new age ideas, would only really confirm to most people that it wouldn't ever catch on. Doing it over a radio link to a ship in the South Atlantic was a breakthrough approach though, and the ability to record the information for Bob's later digestion was unprecedented and hugely fortuitous. It had provided a trail of the crew's exploits for the keen-eyed Bob to uncover. They didn't have the full exchanges yet, just a log of opening communications, much of it computers speaking to computers, but the shreds of information hidden away were just enough for Bob to notice the strange reference among all of the technicalities.

The situation in the helicopter had yet to develop into the full zombie attack, and so the group were still paying enough attention to Bob to question why he thought the mentions of the New Philosophy might be significant. He'd acknowledged happily that he did not know why yet, and that they may well be of no significance, but he then put the whole weight of his character behind reminding them he was rather experienced and good at his job, and he had a feeling. Adam supported Bob.

Despite the lack of a substantiated case, the group noted Bob's observation. Bob used this kind of delivery sparingly, but thanks to his wise use on this occasion, the link that could so easily have been lost or written off as hindsight, was about to be made later that day when Laura would also raise the spectre of the New Philosophers in connection with the zombie plague.

Now, as they stood in the corridor outside the observation room, Bob's comments had come hurtling back to them, reactivated by Laura's mention of the New Philosophy. They stood and contemplated in the corridor, unsure of where this left them.

13. Revelation

Adam took a seat in the meeting room two doors up from the observation room where they had been questioning Laura and Simon. He settled back in his chair looking surprisingly relaxed given what he faced and his responsibility. He lifted his head and looked round once at the others as he took a deep breath. No one else had yet sat down, and their intentions weren't clear, so Adam lifted both of his outstretched arms, palms down, and lowered them gently as he exhaled. Everyone dutifully sat down.

No one had said a word since they'd left the observation room. They had simply followed Adam. There was a meeting room directly next door to the observation room, as equally well soundproofed as this one, but nevertheless it gave Adam an extra sense of security to be an extra space away from the captives. They all looked around for a moment, Adam, Bob, Harriet and Javed, still saying nothing. They were all well versed in diplomacy.

'So who are these people and what do we know?' continued Adam. Adam confirmed, 'The New Philosophers.'

In the following discussion, it became apparent that what was most shocking was how an event of such an unprecedented magnitude had occurred, with so little being known about the New Philosophers, or them even being mentioned, if indeed they were involved. They had a girl making claims of uncertain provenance that the New Philosophers were involved with creating the zombies, but she had made unprecedented predictions. There was also an association between the New Philosophers and an outbreak on the Tupelo Star, which had not had any physical contact with anyone or anything since way before the virus's believed incubation period.

They could all see that a connection between the cult of the New Philosophy and the zombie outbreak was likely. Yes, there was a lot of conjecture and assumption, but the gathered experience in the room could feel that they were right. Given the gravity of the situation, they were even prepared to admit this opinion, to each other at least, rather than, as usually happened in such matters of major importance, jump onto the fence to protect their positions. This was not the time to hide behind the commissioning of further reports and inquiries, maybe taking months or years, allowing demands for answers to die down. The difference this time was that a lot more could die. It wasn't that they were not going to look further, and Adam was already planning in his head whom would be tasked with this in the next few minutes. It was that given the rapid deterioration of their world, there were unlikely to be any repercussions, and this left them feeling oddly liberated.

Each of the occupants of the room was saved from the potential trauma of having to speak first by a knock at the door. Adam looked up to see that Javed was within an arms length of it. Adam nodded to Javed, who opened the door. Adam was unusually, too pensive to call out to the visitor with his usual authority. One of his close aides walked in hesitantly, not sure if Adam was there having not heard his voice. She carefully walked over to Adam with a report consisting of several sheets of paper, explaining as she did so.

'Sir, we have the information from the Tupelo Star communications you asked for.' The aide handed the report to the General who immediately started scanning it. He'd asked for this to be prepared just after Bob had highlighted the Tupelo Star references in the initial report, specifically asking that they have the full details of anything referring to the New Philosophy.

He flicked through the pages. Something was grabbing his attention. Adam got to the last page and let his hand drop down whilst clutching the report. He looked around at everyone in the room with a look of amazement. His hand was clutching the report tightly as it hung over the table. He was staring straight ahead, his mouth slightly agape. In the short time that they'd been confined to Location Three, no one had seen him like this, but from the expression of his long standing friend, Bob, he never had neither.

Bob was sat close to Adam, and raised his arm towards his friend to request the report. Adam didn't move. Bob looked around the room. The aide was standing to attention with a fixed forward stare, but couldn't help a quick glance at Bob as she wondered how her master the Martial Governor would now react.

'Adam,' said Bob gently, as if he were a hypnotist bringing round a subject. Adam didn't respond for a second. Bob just waited. He tried again. 'Adam.' He suddenly snapped to attention.

'Oh!' He looked around quickly, as he reoriented himself. He glanced at a couple of faces before fixing on Bob. He could see Bob was waiting for something, and looked down along Bob's arm to his finger which was now casually pointing towards the report. He looked at the report, and stopped for second.

'Oh yes, of course Bob.' He handed the report straight to Bob, before slipping back into thought. Bob flicked through unemotionally, making the occasional 'hmmm'. It took him a minute or so to glean the key message, as the rest of the room began to grow increasingly eager as to when they would find out what was so intriguing. As he finished, Bob held the report with both hands in front of him, looked forward with a tightened expression around his mouth, and let out a deep sigh. He looked towards Javed and Harriet, moving just his eyes to catch each of their gazes, and then moved his head to look at Adam, who was still pensive. Bob handed Javed the report. He flicked through it before handing it on to Harriet.

Harriet was the first to speak. 'It doesn't tell us much, does it?' She'd really intended to simply question the others on what they thought.

'You think so?' replied Bob. His response was neutral enough for Harriet to believe her thoughts may coincide with the majority. She was now cornered into having to give an opinion, but felt blind not knowing the direction to take.

'Well there's nothing obvious is there. No mention of zombies, or...' She searched around for other acceptable Government mantras, '... terrorists.' The room was reactionless. Harriet felt a bit braver. 'Someone did seem to spend a lot of time getting information on this New Philosophy.' The recent discussions had given Harriet some clue. 'But they were just talking about it,' she concluded.

'Did you notice anything else about the New Philosophy communications?' asked Bob.

'Like what?' Harriet replied, nervous that she might be exposed.

Adam spoke up. 'Who was making and receiving them?'

'Well, it wasn't always clear,' replied Harriet, sensing she was falling off a cliff of ignorance. She began to rapidly flick through the report that was still in her hands. Bob and Adam looked at each other as she searched and mumbled. Javed had managed to keep out of this, and intended it to stay that way. 'Oh yes,' mumbled Harriet, 'some have got names.' She mouthed the name to herself as she followed her finger up and down the pages.

'Mike Cotton?' said Harriet, as she looked up from the report. She wasn't sure of the significance, though she could hear the faint ringing of bells in her head. Javed took pity.

'He was the chap who went on the rampage,' said Javed leaning his head slightly towards Harriet, 'The zombie!'

'My God!' exclaimed Harriet. 'He was in on it with them. He was one of this New Philosopher cult all of the time!' She breathed out sharply. Harriet was in no doubt as to the nature of this New Philosophy problem. She shook her head, ignoring the silence of the others in the room who could only wish they possessed her certainty.

'That would explain it,' said Bob, heavily emphasising and pausing after the 'would', as he preferred to keep an open mind.

'Yes, it would,' added Harriet, eager to confirm any possible support. She stared at Bob, willing him to continue and confirm that she was right. Adam joined in with beckoning Bob, looking straight at him. Bob obliged.

'Our problem with the Tupelo Star has been the lack of physical contact, because we've been looking at this as some kind of infection.' Everyone waited. 'Some kind of cult could explain it.' Harriet nodded at Bob's reference to her own theorising and smiled slightly. 'The thing is though, all of our evidence so far has suggested an infection, something like a virus, due to the way that it has spread.' Bob paused for a second.

'Could be both,' offered Javed. Bob looked up at him. 'It could be a virus that they've used.' This was clearly plausible as it would fit with the spread that they had seen.

'Wouldn't you release it in many places at once?' asked Bob. He was aware that the spread seemed to suggest a single outbreak, setting aside the Tupelo Star.

'Maybe,' replied Javed, 'but the data we have doesn't exclude that possibility.'

'But it has been released in more than one place at once,' spluttered Harriet, suddenly animated. 'The Tupelo Star!'

Bob and Javed looked at each other, as Adam confirmed, 'She's right.' Bob looked unconvinced.

'And this Mike Cotton was behind it. He must be a New Philosopher,' added Harriet, seizing the moment.

Bob and Javed were pondering the same point. Javed spoke first. 'Then why was Mike the one that was infected and not the others?' he asked. Harriet looked pensive, then replied.

'A suicide mission!' There was some look of surprise around the table. Harriet persisted. 'They're not unheard of. Extremists carry them out all of the time. And if this is anything, it's extreme.' This could not really be argued with. 'Or he could even have just accidentally infected himself.'

'I wonder what their motive is?' said Bob to himself, but audible to all, as he accepted the New Philosophers involvement, 'and how come we know nothing about them?'

Adam stood up decisively. 'The report is clear.' He paused. 'The ship was receiving information about the New Philosophy, and as far as we can tell, it was to Mike Cotton, who then turned into one of these… things.'

'And we know that they'd had no physical contact with anyone else,' said Bob concluding the point.

'We've also just come from an interview with Laura who has identified the New Philosophy as somehow being implicated,' said Adam.

'It is odd though,' said Javed, 'that the reason she knew the helicopter doorman was going to turn was because he was one of them.' Bob was immediately taken with Javed's point. 'You'd have thought they might be a bit more subtle if they were spreading it, even if they are all on suicide missions.' This needed an answer and Harriet provided one.

'They could be some kind of doomsday cult. They've existed before. Why not now?'

'And now they've got serious weaponry,' offered Bob, his scientific objectivity allowing him to support any valid proposals.

'But why talk about it?' asked Javed, returning to the implication of his previous statement.

'Euphoria?' said Harriet. 'They're doing what they've been planning for ages.' It was all starting to fit together.

'I've just remembered,' said Bob, raising his head to arc a look across the wall opposite where he was sitting, 'where I have heard about this before.' He emphasised the 'have' and immediately gained everyone's attention. 'It wasn't long before we came here. With everything going on, it had slipped my mind.' Stares were intently fixed on Bob. 'I bumped into a student who had missed a tutorial as I was leaving my office. I asked him to step inside a minute to check everything was okay.

The thing was, whatever I asked him or said to him, he just wanted to talk about something else. He was going on and on about all of these obviously crazy ideas. Loads of stuff, all twaddle, but he was convinced. I remember now, he mentioned this New Philosophy. I was in quite a hurry and getting nowhere with him. I didn't have time to sort out where he'd been before, so I told him to sod off and we'd sort it out at the next tutorial.'

Bob looked around the table. The stares were still fixed. 'The thing is,' continued Bob, 'and it's only really just occurred to me now as odd.' He paused to gather his thoughts, whilst everyone else felt their anticipation rising to burst. 'It took me a few minutes to find something that I needed for the meeting before I could leave my office. As I came out, the student was talking to another young fella. At the time I thought that they were just friends, good friends, as it was quite an animated discussion.' Bob paused again. 'But thinking back, I overheard him telling this chap all of the same rubbish he'd been telling me a few moments earlier.' He paused. 'It was what I'd been listening to, plausible at first, but it didn't take much thought to see the holes. Thing was, this other chap was lapping it up and couldn't get enough.'

There was a silence, and Bob seemed to sink deeper into thought, grasping at some distant sense of the significance he felt existed for what he had witnessed.

'So they've been recruiting,' said Harriet with gusto, abruptly concluding everyone's pondering, like a stone thrown into a rippleless pool. 'And it's anyone, not just students. They even tried to get you,' she said looking at Bob.

'Anything else?' asked Adam inquisitively, not altogether sure of the relevance of what he'd just heard, but aware of the possibility. No one spoke. Adam decided to sum up the position. 'So, we are agreed that a cult that we know as the New Philosophers is probably connected with the zombie event. We think that they may have been recruiting people to their cause, or whatever it is. We don't know who they are, how they are connected, or why they doing it.'

'That's about the strength of it,' concurred Bob. 'But we've got something to work on at least.' There was the first feeling of any relief that there had been since the crisis began at this breakthrough, however meagre.

Javed had been leaning on his elbow with his hand embracing his chin between his thumb and fingers, his palm covering his mouth as he listened, his brow furrowed. 'How are they doing it?' he said. 'Even if we can find them or find out their motives, whatever they are using to create these zombies is out there now.'

Adam responded. 'Javed's right,' he asserted. 'We need to either find out how they're doing it ourselves, or,' he paused, 'find them and make them tell us.' He was slightly more forceful in pronouncing 'make', betraying the regularity of such methods. 'This is dangerous stuff. Right now, we need to find these New Philosophers.' Having given himself permission to act, he went to the door and beckoned in one his aides. A brief conversation took place in the room, until just enough information was imparted for the aide to instigate researching the New Philosophers. As the aide left the room, Adam sealed the instructions with the phrase, 'And let them know that this is my priority.'

Adam's mind now moved towards the more scientific end of the conundrum. 'What are our test results telling us about the zombies?' he asked. Since the Zombie Squad had convened, several zombies had been subjected to all manner of chopping up and testing, both dead and alive, or at least active killing machines. This testing was under Javed's instruction, with Bob taking oversight. He looked over to Javed who was uncomfortable with the question. Bob stepped in.

'Nothing,' said Bob boldly, not wanting to mislead or waste time on petty back covering.

'Nothing?' said Adam incredulously. Bob nodded, and turned to Javed, who also gave a nod. 'We have people turning into crazed cannibalistic killers, but our tests on them have found nothing?' Adam paused. 'Is the testing…' Adam began to ask, but was so laboured, that Bob saved him finishing by cutting in.

'Javed's doing an excellent job,' offered Bob. This was enough to reassure Adam.

Javed felt braver and became confident to fill in the details. 'We've tried to…' He stopped and then restarted. 'We've looked for toxins, bacteria and viruses, every technique we have; chemical, biological, NMR. We can't find anything.'

'What does this mean then?' asked Adam. The science was struggling as they entered the realm of speculation.

'It could be that they're using something beyond our science,' offered Bob. Adam's expression heightened in alarm. 'But that's extremely unlikely,' continued Bob, to calm Adam's fear. 'Or…' continued Bob, offering a shrug before he clutched at straws, 'they could be using some kind of mind control or powerful hypnosis?' Javed screwed his face slightly and looked awkward. The pair had discussed this, but could see no way that it could be achieved on such a scale with none of them knowing anything about it.

'Whatever causes it could also leave the body before we get to them,' suggested Javed, bringing the conversation back to the realm of the orthodox. There was a brief silence.

'So,' said Adam, 'what we're left with is needing to locate the New Philosophers to find out what they're doing.'

'Or get to one of them that's been infected before they change,' alternatively suggested Javed. Bob nodded, as did Harriet, though she wasn't sure why.

'How do we find someone who's about to change, when we know virtually nothing other than it's the New Philosophers behind it?' asked Harriet, more antagonised by their existence than what they were doing.

'Well Laura spotted one, didn't she,' said Bob.

'Adam?' said Bob, concerned by the sudden change in his appearance. Adam had his arms flat on the table, and was looking forward to the floor way beyond where it ended at the wall, his expression hinting at the startling thoughts in his mind.

'I know where we've got at least one' said Adam in a low, quiet voice. He was still as he stared at the centre of the table and then quickly looked over to Bob and said, 'They were talking about it earlier, and they're now locked up.' Adam was alluding to Kalpana, Alistair, and Ian. The earlier events that day, dominated by incompetence and swift incarceration, had somehow caused them all to overlook this far closer to home mention of the New Philosophy that they had experienced. Bob started to move as if he were about to stand, and spoke.

'We need to get to them quick.' Everyone else made similar movements then Javed offered some common sense.

'There's no point in us all going. And we're going to have to get them moved to the scientific facilities first,' he said, pausing before adding, 'safely.' He was aware that this was his area of responsibility, as well as wishing to assert his role. 'I'll go.'

'Good man!' said Adam, and everyone snapped back into their seats. Javed hurriedly left the room.

As the door clicked shut behind him, Harriet wondered aloud, 'What if they change?' No one responded.

14. The Cells

'I don't know. Do you know?'

'I don't know. I'm asking you. Do you know?'

'No I'm asking you.'

'I don't know. I just said. You must know.'

'I don't know. I just said so as well.'

'Well who knows? Someone must.'

'She knows.'

'I know she knows.'

'Ask her.'

'I did. She won't answer. You ask her.'

'I did. She won't answer me neither.'

'Then do you know?'

'No. I don't know.'

Alistair and Ian were trapped in an endless circular conversation, gibberishly churning out the same limited phrases. They were desperate to have their point answered about the New Philosophy, as their minds struggled to carry out rational acts, their lucidity gradually draining away. Little did they know that they had already received all of the information that they needed. This would soon be of little importance, as they continued to bicker oblivious to Kalpana's metamorphosis.

The three of them were sat on the wooden slats on top of the low level protruding wall at the back of the small cell they were in. Every surface was white, and there was nothing else in there apart from the occupants. Even the lighting from behind a square of shatterproof glass, flush with the centre of the ceiling, seemed to come from nowhere. The door blended similarly apart from a distinguishable frame and a head height square window, just big enough to frame whichever face would stare through it. There was no discernible smell, fully in keeping with the decor. There was nothing else in the room, not even a bed, the only signal that this was a temporary holding cell at the entrance to the main cell block; Adam's order to lock the three of them up had been unambiguous, but not particularly comprehensive.

There was a face at the window looking in. One of the guards had been conversing with the three prisoners most of the time that they had been there. 'Have you got an answer?' he asked. He was clearly a party to the ping pong debate that Alistair and Ian were engaged in. It was one of the strange features of the New Philosophy. The hunger to find out more took hold soon after hearing the first few ideas, and remained even after all the details had been passed on. However, repetition had never done any advertiser any harm.

The guard had only recently heard of the New Philosophy, unlike Alistair and Ian who had been discussing it for most of the day, Kalpana being the eager herald. The guard was getting quite irritated at the childlike chirruping of Alistair and Ian. Separated by a door, he had not been fully involved in the discussion directly, but had been able to interject just enough to ensure that he'd heard enough. This was along with everyone else on the shared intercom channel he'd patched in, having been so enthralled and wanting to share.

The sound of Ian and Alistair faded from his main focus, into a somehow suitable soundtrack to the voiceless Kalpana, who had consumed his attention. Flanked by Ian and Alistair, she was completely disengaged from them, staring straight forwards towards the cell door, but way beyond it, ignorant of the guard. She was slightly hunched forwards and breathing rapidly in short breaths, panting like a hound recovering from a long chase after having secured its quarry. Her eyes appeared rounder than before, and along with the sockets in her skull, seemed to have somehow grown bigger. They were white discs with dots of black in the middle. Saliva was dribbling along the length of her bottom lip and the sides of her mouth, forming

121

long slivers of spittle. The guard thought for a moment that it was like watching rapidly forming stalactites.

'Kalpana?' said the guard quizzically. He knew something wasn't right. 'Kalpana!' he said again, louder but not quite shouting. He was now completely tuned out to the squabbles of Ian and Alistair as they blended into the background of the room. He could hear Kalpana's panting. His eyes screwed up slightly as he stared at her, moving his face right up to the cell door glass, trying to see if he could get a better look, to make some sense of what his mind was struggling to comprehend.

Kalpana sat up slightly straighter. Suddenly, she twisted her head to the left to look at Ian, so quickly the movement was barely perceptible.

Kalpana grabbed Ian's head, shooting both of her arms round to violently grab the hair on the back of his head. She thrust his head into her face, inevitably causing trauma and damage to both of them, and then completely unperturbed by any self-inflicted harm, bit ferociously into his face, as if suddenly kissing him, like bickering characters do in movies at their realisation of mutual love, but with lots of blood.

'What are you doing Kalpana?' asked Alistair, with an air of dumbness. Kalpana turned to Alistair with the same unnatural rapid jerk, her head turning right round exorcist-fashion as she continued to grip Ian's head. Her face was bright red apart from the whites of her eyes and nicotine stained teeth.

'Oooh,' said Ian mildly with a gentle start backwards. Kalpana's fingers released their grip on the back of Ian's head whilst the rest of her body stayed rigid, her reversed head focussed on Alistair. Ian dropped, crumpling off the bench, semi-conscious from the impact of Kalpana's face thumping into his, his hands loosely moving up to his mutilated face.

In a single movement, Kalpana swung round and gave Alistair her same gory movie kiss. Although she was moving rapidly, having to turn round fully gave Alistair a split second to move slightly backwards, lessening the crushing collision of Kalpana's face into his, and allowing him to remain conscious and begin screaming. He continued his screaming along with some flailing, but to little overall effect, as Kalpana proceeded to chew away the flesh from his skull, her jaws chomping rapidly.

The guard was frozen by the scene playing out in front of him, his mind unable to make sense of what he saw. He was mesmerised by the small fountains of blood intermittently shooting out from between Alistair and Kalpana's face. There was no sign of her stopping. This one tasted good. He looked down to the floor of the cell through the tiny window and could see Ian crawling away from the bench. He was veering slightly, groggy from the attack and his vision obscured. The guard tried to see if he still had eyes but his face was too much of a mess for him to be able to tell. Blood was flowing out onto the floor, dripping down like an overflowing gutter in a torrential thunder storm.

The guard had to think quickly. He was a trained killing machine, but also trained to save lives. Ian needed help. Kalpana was absorbed in her feast, rendering Alistair an increasingly lost cause, but he could at least help Ian. There was also backup along the corridor, the other side of the door at the entrance to the cells. He began calling out frantically to the other guard as he fumbled for the key to the cell. The other guard could hear something about blood and pain, and presumed it was something medical. He needed to get in there to help his colleague.

Javed was nearing the cell block. It had taken him nearly five minutes to get there. Location Three was deceptively large, or small, it was hard to tell. The monotonous corridors of grey, gloomily illuminated by artificial lights, all seemed to be the same length, with the same number of bland doors. It was easy to feel like a rat in an experiment trying to navigate its way out. In fact, Location Three was huge, the uniformity of its layout masking the many floors and sprawling area each covered. This was without taking into account the resources beyond Location Three's walls that it commanded, making the organism that was Location Three, vast. Fortunately, there were tiny direction plates on each intersection.

Javed had decided he wanted to check on the status of the specimens straight away and could call up further support to the cells for their subsequent removal later. Javed reached the top of the steps leading down to the entrance of the cell block. The subliminal familiarity that steps to cells should lead downwards, somehow gave him some comfort in the order of things being maintained. This was no coincidence. The designer of Location Three had deliberately made the steps that way as he wanted the cells to have a dungeon feel.

As Javed reached the bottom of the steps, a corridor in the ubiquitous grey, bland house-style stretched about fifteen yards in front of him. He immediately noticed that the guard was agitated, if not on the edge of panic, trying to open the door. Javed's instincts were quick. 'What's happening?' he called out to the guard. The guard flashed a look to Javed, registering his seniority.

'Some kind of emergency, sir. I think they're hurt,' replied the guard. Javed took a second to assess the situation. It was a momentary pause of virtually no significance, but it felt like minutes to Javed. He would always wonder if the delay was the difference between the outcomes that followed or those that may have done.

'No!' shouted Javed, lunging forwards to run at the guard, as if flipping forward off a diving board. The guard looked up to him, as he turned whilst simultaneously finishing unlocking the door to the cell block. The door swung open away from them.

Javed reached the guard and pulled up from his sprint. He exhaled heavily. The guard was taken aback at first then looked into the cell block. He could see his colleague had got the cell door open and was staring in, inanimate. The hand of Ian Milton began to protrude out of the doorway at about knee height. It was bright red and quivering. The rest of Ian followed through after it, crawling. As his head appeared, a foot struck out from inside the cell, driving into the back of it and crushing his face into the floor. Ian was merely a step in Kalpana's path, bounding over him and launching herself onto the guard. Her preferred method of consumption, grabbing the head of the meal and chewing the face off, followed. The guard let out a muffled, woeful scream, falling over backwards, and failing to raise his arms to break his fall until he was half way towards the ground. He didn't reach the ground straight away, his head thudding into the wall behind him, which with Kalpana's momentum and his weight, had enough force to afford him the consolation of being knocked unconscious for the remainder of his life.

Javed's stomach churned violently, knowing he was too late and was confronted with one of the beasts he'd felt safe from in Location Three. The remaining guard staggered forward a couple of steps. Although everyone knew what was going on outside with the attacks, and had seen pictures, it was still little preparation for being confronted with the reality of a fellow human malformed into such a monster. The guard tried to regain his composure and started to ready his gun.

'Get out!' shouted Javed who'd had enough presence of mind to remain the other side of the door, 'Now!' but the guard wasn't listening. The training had kicked in and his mind had taken a path that had him acting almost hypnotically. This situation would cause most people to be torn apart and rendered useless by their emotions, but instead he was detached from his everyday self and mechanically carrying out the instructions with which he'd been programmed. Javed continued shouting at the guard, but there were no subroutines.

The guard readied his gun, taking aim at Kalpana as she knelt on the stomach of her victim, still chewing his head. She was able to distinguish the click of the gun being readied, and looked over, flying towards the guard in a single movement. He got the shot off whilst she was in the air. Her leap forward significantly reduced the target area he had to aim at as she came at him head first, arms outstretched. The shot took away her shoulder in an explosion of blood, bone and flesh. She hit the guard with enough force to knock him off his feet. The shot increased Kalpana's rage as she lost control of an arm that now flailed wildly. She let out at a shrill piercing scream towards Javed as she stood on her latest victim. Javed pulled the door shut, and felt his blood shooting round his body as his heart drummed. He couldn't move as he watched the zombie through the small glass panel in the door.

The guard was on his back. Kalpana stood over him looking down, her face stretching apart to bare her teeth in a berserk grin. She grabbed the guard's jaw and ripped it off, took a quick bite of the flesh and threw it behind her. The guard writhed and grabbed his face, trying to scream. She fell to her knees, rapidly pummelled and tore at the soldiers face, then tasted his flesh. She was now well-fed, and looked to her useless arm. It was twitching, but she had no control. She looked down at the gun and picked it up. She grabbed it with her hand as the solider had done and pulled the trigger. The recoil jolted her and the noise of the shot made Javed start.

Javed was aware of the sound of the automatic doors in the cell block and at the top of the steps, triggered by the sound of the gun shots. He went straight to the intercom to inform Adam of what had happened. As he spoke, shots rang out. He could see through the glass in the door, that Kalpana was squeezing the trigger of the gun, merely interested in the noise and jolt. There was no awareness of what it was doing, as the odd fountain of blood sprung up into sight through the door.

Javed heard a clatter, as Kalpana dropped the gun, followed by the sounds of feasting resuming. He'd finished his call, and was now trapped by the automatic doors. It made him think of the stokers on the Titanic, sacrificed below decks as the captain tried to stem the flow of water. He wondered if it was better to drown or starve to death.

15. Quarantined

The squad were silent as they observed Adam talking to the intercom handset. They could tell by his tone and his half of the conversation that something very serious was in hand, unaware that elsewhere in Location Three an alarm was sounding. There was no need for the automated alarm to inform everyone in the facility of what may just be a routine matter. It wasn't without effect though, as guards were rushing towards the locked down entrance to the cell block, ready to neutralise any threat.

The other occupants of the room, Bob and Harriet, reacted in sympathy with the jolt from Adam's head as he heard the zombie's random shots firing out. He spoke briefly some more to Javed. He thanked him. Then he replaced the receiver. He stayed standing where he was by the intercom set next to the door, briefly staring forward, and then straightened up and looked at everyone calmly.

'I'm afraid we don't have a specimen.'

'So it's nothing to do with this New Philosophy then?' said Harriet.

'Probably quite the opposite, Harriet,' replied Adam. Harriet frowned in confusion. 'We no longer have a pre-zombie, infected specimen.' Bob sat still, immediately comprehending. Harriet was beginning to understand.

'You mean…' began Bob, but Adam interceded.

'They zombified.' Adam thought for a second. 'Or at least one of them did.'

'My God!' exclaimed Harriet. 'What about Javed?'

'He's fine,' Adam paused again, 'Well, not dead and he's safe from the zombie.' Adam had an intent look on his face, as he rapidly processed the information, knowing that he needed to come up with actions quickly.

'Have they got out?' asked Bob, a tone of fear running through his voice, 'into the rest of Location Three?'

'No!' said Adam, offering some limited reassurance. 'A shot was fired and it's triggered an automatic shutdown. No one's getting in or out of there for now.'

Bob spoke. 'The zombie's isolated, but something's got in, hasn't it?' he said, with chilling realisation.

'How? Hasn't everyone in here been quarantined? The virus can't have got in!' demanded Harriet of Adam, bravely. Adam looked a little taken aback, but before he could respond, Bob spoke.

'It's in. It doesn't matter how. It's in.' He was staring straight at Adam. 'Adam. It's in,' he repeated. The message Bob was conveying hit home. Adam quickly picked up the intercom handset, made a call, and began issuing various instructions and code words. It was largely unintelligible to those in the room, but the intent was clear. Internal quarantine was being ordered. The whole of Location Three was being locked down into a patchwork of isolated chambers with movement between each impossible. Whilst Adam was speaking, those in the room became aware of a humming sound seeming to come from everywhere, gently vibrating, like the cooling cycle of a freezer turning, as the automatic internal quarantine doors around Location Three slid into space.

'How the hell's it got in?' continued Harriet to Bob, as Adam continued his call. She thought for a moment. 'If everyone in here's been quarantined, it's been released by someone in here.' She thought some more. 'It's just like the Tupelo Star. It's the girl in the cells, isn't it, the one who's just become a zombie?' Harriet was on a roll. 'She brought it in. She must have infected herself.' Harriet looked pleased at the brilliance of her hypothesis. Bob didn't answer, but was aware that what Harriet had said could possibly, hold up. Bob thought for a second then spoke.

'We can't deny the fact that the girl, Kalpana, knew something about the New Philosophers. That's the reason why

Javed…' He stumbled slightly as he briefly considered Javed's potential fate, '…why Javed was down there in the first place.' Bob paused. 'What do we do now though?' he asked rhetorically.

'What can we do?' blurted Harriet. Her transformation in the last hour was pronounced. Her perfect civil servant persona, behind which may have been hidden anything from a genius to an idiot, had slipped to betray spontaneous moments of erraticism. 'You've locked us in,' she said to Adam. 'What can we do if we can't get out of here?'

'We've still got this,' said Adam calmly, touching the handset of the intercom, placating Harriet.

'What are we meant to do with that?' came back Harriet. 'Beat the zombies to death?' Adam chose not to answer. Bob understood that Adam's position, the codes he knew and the commands he could still issue, meant that there was still considerable power in the room.

'We need more information. We need to know what we're dealing with,' said Bob to Adam as Harriet continued to gradually declare herself a sideshow. 'It doesn't matter what resources we can direct if we have no idea what to aim at.' He took a breath. 'If we don't know what we're dealing with, we're as well off doing nothing.' Harriet looked shocked. One of the golden rules she'd learnt in her career was that even if you don't know why, always do something and most people will presume you know what you're doing. She felt lost. Adam gazed up to the ceiling then looked down. 'How can we find out?' concluded Bob.

Adam picked up the handset. He issued a series of instructions, briefing the communications team. He replaced the set. 'They're looking now,' he said and cast a half angst-tinged smile at Bob. 'We should have something soon.' Bob nodded. 'Don't hold your breath though,' cautioned Adam, aware of the limitations they faced and how they had been so unaware of their enemy.

'There's the girl,' said Bob in a moment of realisation, 'We could talk to her.'

'Which girl?' came the sharp reply from Harriet.

'Laura,' said Bob, directing his reply at Adam. Adam stepped forward, and slowly pulled a chair back to sit down at the table. Bob recognised he could see the possibility.

'We don't have much else,' said Bob. Adam nodded his head twice.

'You can't mean the girl next door!' exclaimed Harriet, clearly agitated. She saw the answer to her question in Adam and Bob's expressions. 'But…' continued Harriet, looking for an objection, 'she's come from outside. She's probably infected.'

'She's isolated from us,' said Bob, putting down Harriet's objection. Harriet looked very unhappy. 'We don't really have many other choices,' said Bob. 'Laura had already made the link with the New Philosophy before any of us had realised.' There was a momentary silence.

'What if she's one of them?' exclaimed Harriet, somewhat alarmed at her own question.

Bob raised an eyebrow.

'One of them,' stammered Harriet, 'one of those New Philosophers, and we've let her into Location Three!'

Adam spoke. 'I think it's a little too late to worry about them getting in,' he said.

'What if she is one of them?' responded Harriet desperately.

'Then we really should be talking to her,' said Adam. Harriet thought about disagreeing, but Laura was really all that they had, and this about their only option. Even if she was a New Philosopher, as long as they were aware of this possibility, what could she do? Infect herself? She was isolated from them, so couldn't spread the infection. Laura's purpose in coming to Location Three was still questionable, and maybe there was still some way this could be a trap. However, this had never stopped prisoners being questioned before.

The decision was made to return to interrogating Laura, despite Harriet's objections. If nothing else, it would give them something to do. They stepped into the corridor, Adam leading the way. They were only just lucky with the internal quarantining. Immediately to their left the automatic doors had closed, creating a barrier consisting of the same grey, featureless facade as the walls. Two doors up to the right was access to the interrogation room. The corridor ran for some way to the next barrier, and there were several other rooms along the stretch containing around another forty staff or so, and thankfully, a toilet though not everyone else in Location Three was so fortunate.

The three of them entered the interrogation room. The guard was still in there. The door closed behind them and the three sat down. Adam gave an instruction and a few moments later, the screen drew back to once again reveal Laura and Simon. They were still seated side by side, facing the screen, though it was impossible to tell whether or not they had moved since they had last been revealed.

16. The Beginning

'Laura,' said Bob, anxious not to be patronising. 'When we last spoke, you mentioned the New Philosophy.' Since she'd last been interrogated, Laura had had time to ready herself, to reflect on how she might present her information. Her first reaction to Bob's comment was to think that he'd completely missed the point if he thought it was just a mention. The New Philosophy was at the heart of the matter. She restrained herself as she replied.

'I did, yes, I did mention it.' Bob recognised the pause before 'mention' and looked down briefly, then back at Laura, a vague smile across his face, as he realised he'd not succeeded.

'What's your involvement with the New Philosophers?' asked Adam. Laura's status as infiltrator or ally was of deep concern to him.

'I'm not involved,' she replied. 'I've tried to keep away from it.'

'We know you can tell if someone's infected. Do you know how they're doing it?' asked Bob, less interested in Laura's status. Although the interrogators were unconvinced, Laura's reaction had provided some reassurance that she wasn't involved. She looked puzzled.

'Well, of course,' she replied. The room was slightly taken aback at such a forthright answer.

'How are they doing it?' blurted out Harriet.

'They tell people about it, don't they?' replied Laura. Harriet appeared about to speak, but Bob, in anticipation, glanced up to her and raised his eyebrow, taking full command.

'That was what you said before,' replied Bob, 'the way you know that they're infected. We need to know about how they get infected.' Laura looked perplexed. 'Have they got a virus, a toxin? Do they inject them, put it in their food?'

'No!' said Laura, struggling to hide her irritation. 'It's what their talking about, it's the New Philosophy. That's what it is.' She was struggling to explain.

Harriet couldn't help herself. 'Look! We know this cult, the New Philosophers, is behind this. How are they doing it? Have you met the people behind it?'

'You're not listening,' said Laura through gritted teeth. 'You don't get it. It's the New Philosophy that's doing this!' Having made her point, she addressed Harriet's supplementary questions. 'And no, I haven't met them, only people going on about it. Like I said, I didn't want to get involved.' The occupants of the room were gradually releasing their suspicions of Laura's involvement, but were still struggling to make sense of what she was telling them.

Bob tried again. He drew a breath and prepared himself. 'So if you're infected, it makes you talk about the New Philosophy?' offered Bob. 'A virus that changes how you think?'

'What?' replied Laura. She was agitated at her inability to communicate her message to them. 'How could an infection make you talk about something like that?' she seemed to ridicule.

'But isn't that what you just told us?' replied Bob.

'No,' came the brief reply.

'I'm sorry if I misunderstood you,' said Bob. He was prepared to take his time. He couldn't risk upsetting this potential source of valuable information. 'I thought that what you said was that if you were infected, you'd be talking about the New Philosophy?' Bob gently began to dissect the conversation.

Laura thought for a second. 'I did,' came her hesitant reply.

'Then doesn't the infection make you talk about the New Philosophy?' proposed Bob robustly. Even though he was a man of more independent thought than most, he was still susceptible to his thinking becoming entrenched with assumptions.

'Not really,' replied Laura diplomatically. 'If you're infected, you do talk about the New Philosophy,' she confirmed.

Everyone waited.

'But it's not a symptom of the infection.'

Puzzlement.

'It is the infection,' Laura concluded. Faces in the room contorted as they tried to take in what they were hearing. Laura began to realise that what she had said was stretching beyond the limits of what the assembly could comprehend.

'Listen,' she said, quickly gaining everyone's attention. 'Have you found any kind of virus yet? Something you can photograph? Something you can see? Something you can touch? Something you can test for?' Bob and Adam looked at each other. How did she know that they hadn't? 'Something you know how to cure?' Laura added bringing real impetus to the need to listen to her.

'Laura,' Bob began, 'what do you mean, that the New Philosophy is the infection?' He paused briefly then tried to help by providing some options. 'Do you mean the people behind the New Philosophy? Are they infecting their followers? Are they telling them to do this? Is it making them infect themselves with whatever it is that turns them into… zombies?' However hard he tried, he couldn't move beyond the idea of something material. He stopped, momentarily running out of ideas, eager for Laura to furnish him with her inner thoughts and understanding.

Laura looked straight at Bob. 'I can't answer all of those questions. But what I do know, what I believe,' said Laura, taking a less firm stance, 'is it's not something you can touch, like a flu virus. It doesn't exist like that. It's the New Philosophy itself. It's the talking about it, the knowing about it that makes them…' She paused as the horror engulfing the country flickered through her mind, '…change.' She looked over

134

everyone on the other side of the screen. 'It does exist, but not as something… you can touch.'

'What do you mean?' Harriet suddenly spluttered out in frustration. Everyone paused for a second, taken unawares by this outburst. This was too much for her. 'How can it exist and not exist? How can it be real and not real?'

'I think that the slaughter out there is very real,' whispered Laura, but everyone heard. Harriet shrunk.

There was a long pause. No one knew what to think. What Laura was saying was fantastical, but she appeared lucid. They all felt trapped between wanting to believe her, and questioning her sanity. Simon felt very alone, sat next to her. He wasn't sure himself.

'How do you know?' asked Adam. A certain rationality and reason descended.

'I don't know how. I just do.' Some doubt crept back. 'I just know what I've seen. Call it a feeling. It just makes sense.' Everyone was quiet. The silence in the room seemed to intensify.

'Have you got anything that makes sense?' asked Laura softly, but strongly emphasising the 'you'. Bob realised that Laura's question really defined their position. They knew nothing about what was causing the problem, only the effects. Adam turned from his chair, swinging round to look up at Bob. He had no answer. Bob gave a half shrug that answered Laura's question.

'This is ridiculous!' exclaimed Harriet, feeling that her time was being wasted, despite their quarantine meaning there was little else for them to be doing.

'Wasn't it Schopenhaur who said that all truth passes through three stages. First, it is ridiculed. Second, it is violently opposed. Third, it is accepted as being self-evident,' said Bob.

'We don't have time to go through all of that now to see if what she says is true or not,' offered Adam pragmatically. Bob offered a word of caution.

'But remember, this doesn't mean that just because something sounds ridiculous, it's true. All truth may be ridiculed at first, but so is the ridiculous. If someone claims they're Elvis, being ridiculous doesn't make it true, just that they're a nutter.' Adam chuckled. 'The point is that we don't just dismiss this because it sounds ridiculous.' Bob smiled to Laura, who realised that this was about the best she could expect.

'Please, Laura,' began Adam, 'tell us more.' He thought a second then added, 'Tell us from the beginning.' Laura took a breath, held it for second, exhaled, and began to speak.

'I knew all of the first people who became zombies… well most of them.' Laura corrected herself as she realised that what had been a fact in her head may now not be quite so concrete after all. She suddenly wondered if she'd made too many assumptions to fit her theory. She rapidly ran over how she had reached her conclusions in her head. She continued. 'The first morning after Kate…' Laura trailed away obviously still distressed at losing a close friend. 'I got in touch with everyone. I'd not spoken to them for a few days, not since they'd got into the New Philosophy. It was all that any of them had been going on about.

'It was rubbish, but they couldn't see it. I didn't want to know about it. Neither did a couple of others, Luke and Sally. It was so annoying. Every time you saw them, they'd just go on and on about it. I know it wasn't everyone at first. It seemed to start with a smaller group of people and then suddenly it was everyone.' The interrogating group's stares enhanced, as they realised these could be the leaders of the New Philosophers.

Laura continued. 'I didn't take much notice at first. You hear all sorts of mad stuff at uni. But then came the New Philosophy. People were just taken in, and were telling others. I was thinking, 'How can you believe this stuff?' But they did. In no time, virtually everyone was talking about it. I couldn't call home, because they were all on the phones telling people about it.' Laura stopped, her emotions being driven to the surface by the rerunning of events in her mind. Bob and Adam exchanged glances, patiently waiting for Laura to regain her composure, whilst Harriet stared at her.

'Me and Kate had been really good friends,' continued Laura on a tangent, 'but that was it once she got into this New Philosophy. With it being nearly the end of term there were other things to worry about. At first, I wanted to know why she was acting like this, hanging around with this lot. I'd ask them where they'd heard it from, who was telling them this, but they just went on and on about the New Philosophy. It felt like they wanted me to believe before they'd tell me anything else.'

The interrogation room now sat transfixed, mesmerised by the tale. Laura continued.

'Anyway, term ended and I returned home. Then I heard the news; the first event,' said Laura referring to Kate. 'I started calling round everyone when I heard. At first I didn't see the connection. I spoke to Luke and he said he'd call back. When we spoke later, it was awful. Everyone except me, Luke and...' Laura paused, an emotional spike triggered. 'Luke told me Sally was dead.' Laura paused. The room waited eagerly to hear the detail. 'They'd got her. She was going to hang about at uni for a couple of days before going home. She didn't have a hope. She was stuck right in the middle of all of them.'

Laura took a second to resettle herself, and swallowed before continuing. 'The connection was obvious to me and Luke immediately.' Laura could feel surprise among her interrogators at how quickly they had jumped to their conclusion. 'We were there,' she responded. She was still suppressing her emotions as she retold her story, but was able to continue, knowing she had to.

'Luke had stayed on as well as Sally. He said that the night Kate... changed, a couple of the others at uni had as well, later on. He said that he saw some of those who hadn't yet, but they were talking nuts and going on about how great the New Philosophy was.' Laura's expression turned to one of pain and desperation. 'He was trying to tell them about what had happened... how horrific it was... but they just wanted to go on about the New Philosophy. They just didn't care.' She stopped and breathed out. 'Their friends were dead, murdered. And murderers!' Laura looked down and shook her head slowly from side to side twice, 'But they didn't care.' She paused a second or two.

'Luke said that they were getting crazier and crazier until they just made no sense. Soon after that, it just went mad. There were people changing all over, killing everywhere. It was mental.' Laura sighed. 'That's probably why no one else has realised the connection. It's just manic and anyone who knows about it, becomes part of it.' The people in the observation room, made gentle, slow nods as they acknowledged the national chaos.

Laura was beginning to talk more quickly. 'After that afternoon I couldn't get hold of Luke again.' Laura's emotions were now escaping her. Tears filled her eyes. She stopped talking.

The occupants in the observation room didn't respond. They didn't know how to. They even felt like they were struggling with basic thoughts and reasoning.

The tension was broken by a dull glow throbbing in the room, like far away lightning. The intercom was signalling. Adam stood up as it continued to flash.

'Spelling,' he spoke into the handset. Adam's expression quickly became intense, but the attention in the room was still revolving around Laura's tale. Adam said little except the odd 'hmm' as he listened to an update. It was news from the field.

17. The Canal

'Oi! Zombie!' shouted Dave. Paul, who was sat next to him, laughed aloud. The pair were both seated on the roof of their military Landrover watching to their great amusement, the zombies coming towards them. This scene had been unfolding earlier that day, away from Location Three.

'Getting colder mate,' said Paul. A cold front had moved over the country the evening before. It had already been chilly for the past few days, but the new weather had brought an extra bite. The day was entering late afternoon and they could feel the air sharpening on their cheeks. Their voices were muffled and indistinct through their bio chem suits, but they had adapted well to communicating in these new tones, just like Second World War pilots and their garbled radios competing with the thunderous Merlin engines. 'Shall we get inside?'

'Nah! Not yet,' replied Dave. 'This is a laugh.' Paul was having fun watching the zombies as they came closer, so was happy to go along with his soldier buddy. 'Shall I shoot him?' Dave asked.

'No!' replied Paul, anxious the zombie should be allowed to get closer. 'It's nearly on the ice. They're well funny when they fall in.'

In front of the Landrover, a few yards ahead, was a canal. The overnight chill had frozen the still waters. The zombies on the other side could see Dave and Paul atop of their vehicle, as they made their way towards the two soldiers. They were not running towards them, but not staggering slowly either. They moved with the occasional bound, but with no finesse, slightly hunched with arms flailing, as if they were not fully, if at all, self aware. The first ones into the canal had tried to run all of the way over.

The zombie that had just been spared being shot by Dave reached the edge of the other side of the canal. This was no act of humanity by Dave. His actions were motivated by his desire to gratify his own sense of amusement. What did he care? They may have appeared alive, but he had no sense of compassion for them. It may have been part of his soldier mentality, but it was now also the general view of the wider public towards the creatures.

The zombie, eyes fixed on Dave and Paul, stepped down onto the ice to continue walking towards them. Its foot immediately slid forward causing it to do the splits, falling sideways and rolling fully off the edge of the canal onto the ice. The slapstick type humour caused Dave and Paul to roll with laughter, like toddlers watching a clown. They had to grab hold of each other to ensure that they didn't fall from the top of the Landrover. They continued to laugh and giggle, unable to speak, as the monster tried to get to its feet, slipping further towards the centre of the canal. The overnight freeze had not been sufficient to create a solid surface across the whole of it. The centre was already broken by the earlier zombie forays, and it took only a few seconds for this one to roll and slide out enough to the centre to tumble into the icy water.

They watched it thrashing in the water. It caught the head of another one that was nearing the end of its desperate struggle, pushing it momentarily below the surface and bringing forward marginally, its final succumbing to the cold and the water. It floated back up to the surface face down, its hair, arms and most of its back visible, twitching slightly before becoming static. There were a few other similar zombie corpses in the water. The blood had been partially washed away from their faces. The change in the hue of the water was not evident, though pink streaks on the ice were. As the zombies had been overwhelmed by the water, they'd seemed almost human for a second, struggling like a normal drowning person. The new inhabitant of the canal waters continued to thrash. Even a good swimmer would die in these conditions, and the icy water would have its next victim within two minutes.

They weren't people in front of them. All Dave and Paul could see were zombies, those in the water and those on the other side of the canal, close by and in the distance coming from the direction of the village. It was part of the human condition, how quickly a fellow being could be demoted to an empty shell, once communication between two reasoning intelligences was removed. The pair would probably feel more for an animal that could convey something through its expression. The zombies' blood-covered faces making their features and expressions invisible, only furthered the dehumanisation. For some people, even the lack of a shared language, culture or experience is often enough. These zombies had once been human. They had all once been someone's son or daughter, maybe brother or mother, or just an acquaintance. However, this previous existence was now wiped away, leaving a blankness like the cold vacuum of deep space.

Dave and Paul had been playing at guessing what the zombies might have been before, another game to ridicule them for their own amusement. They were pretty well able to distinguish the things that had been male or female. They could identify children but struggled with the ages of the adults. There were none that appeared to be very old, shrunken and infirm, but it was not surprising; it was not uncommon for zombies to feed on each other. The ones in suits amused Dave and Paul's sense of juxtaposition. Maybe they'd been salesmen or lawyers. Or maybe they'd been 'the accused'. The zombie in grease stained overalls had obviously been some sort of mechanic.

They could see another three of the things, spread out from each other, coming towards the canal. Over to the right of the Landrover, about a quarter of a mile away along the canal, was a simple redbrick footbridge. It was in view to Dave and Paul, and to the zombies. It should have been easy for them to cross the canal at the bridge, but they didn't even possess the intelligence to work this out. Instead, they made a direct line from the village to the Landrover and the potential food that they could see. The four man unit had carefully positioned the Landrover so that the canal created a barrier between them and the threat.

Dave and Paul had been positioned on top of the Landrover to keep watch for. So far, they'd been successful in their task.

The zombies that were on the other side of the canal had all been turned for some time. Their faces and hair had assumed several layers of caked on blood, the fronts of their clothes and sleeves similar, finished off with various streaks of blood. Some were carrying bits of flesh that they chomped and tore at, often letting rip apparent snarls of delight as they felt the flesh tear away. Some of what they carried was unidentifiable, whilst some looked like limbs, a leg maybe, or an arm. Dave was sure he could see a hand on one of the chunks. The pair found that very funny.

'Look! He's eating a Chihuahua!' shrieked Paul. They both creased up. It was hard to be sure, being a reddened fleshy lump, but it did look a bit like it. 'I'm going to shoot it!' declared Paul, as he raised his rifle to his shoulder and looked down the barrel. Both he and Dave had been taking pot shots. The first time they tried to kill one was out of a reasonable fear. They must have dispatched at least a dozen shots into it, over half of these once it was lain on the floor as the end of its animation approached. The unit leader, Mike, had then come out to remind them why they had stopped by the canal and not to waste ammunition like that. They'd apologised, and Mike had let it go in order to avoid conflict, by convincing himself that it was good practice for the two, though really it was because he was more than happy that it would keep them amused and out of his zone of immediate perception in the cab of the vehicle.

As Dave and Paul's game had developed, the aim was to see how much of a zombie they could remove with a shot, whilst still leaving it capable of reaching the canal to provide a hilarious spectacle. They'd had various success, skimming the odd thigh, accidentally taking out half a head. But Dave so far held the honours for blasting away a whole shoulder, and leaving the beast's arm dangling, unclear whether it was attached by clothing, flesh, muscle, tendons or a combination. Paul now had a chance to even the score by blasting the meaty dog-like lump out of the zombie's hands.

Crack! Paul's shot rang out. Bingo! The lump sprung from the zombie's hands, spraying its face with a cascade of blood as the morsel hurtled over its shoulder to land on the ground behind. The zombie looked violently from side to side, not caring for the cause, as it looked for its meat. Each swing to the side gave it a wider and wider view, till it spied its food and dived on it, growling to make sure it didn't escape again.

The door of the vehicle opened as Dave and Paul once again were consumed with hysterics. Mike stepped out. He looked up at the pair contemptuously over his left shoulder, but the wall of incoming cold blocked any potential criticism, as he sympathised. 'Keeping your eyes out lads?' he asked, as he took a look around.

'Yes Sarge,' came the reply in unison as the pair belatedly also looked, pretending that was their priority.

'Hopefully the support will be here soon. I hope that bridge is wide enough for the vehicles.' Mike gave the update hoping to keep up their morale, but he knew it would soon be dark, and too dangerous to try and enter the village. They needed to check out the village for survivors, for those that had managed to barricade themselves in somewhere before an attack. There were plenty of zombies here, just like everywhere else. Survivors were being found, but not many. This was their fourth such encounter, and they hadn't found any yet. Even if they did, they weren't sure what they could do. They understood that other units who'd found survivors, given the threat of infection, limited resources and general chaos, were just leaving some supplies, giving some advice, and recording the whereabouts should things improve. They'd also take out a few zombies, a token gesture as well as a bit of fun. They also didn't want to be around too long in case they got infected. They were all still wearing their bio chem suits, but they were no guarantee of immunity, as well as inhibiting their ability to function.

They would use the bridge to reach the village, but as they couldn't risk luring zombies towards it, they hadn't been able to check out if it was wide enough for the vehicles. Mike had just hoped that it would be when he'd radioed for assistance. He hadn't been able to find anyone directly on the shared channel within his cell of the communications matrix, so their comms controller at Location Three had passed on the request, and they were informed that another unit was on its way to back them up. It was now getting late.

'Sarge! It's them!' shouted Paul, pointing back over the roof of their vehicle. In the distance, a vehicle similar to their own had just come over the brow of the hill on the road towards the canal. The distinctive sound of the engine intensified. As it approached, it left the road, pulling off to pass through the open gate that was at the point where the road turned to follow the edge of the canal towards the bridge. The Landrover carried on over the grass to pull up by the first vehicle, pointing towards the canal in a similar fashion. As it came to a halt, Rob the fourth man in the first unit got out, whilst Dave and Paul stayed atop, keeping watch for threats.

Mike and Rob where eager to get greetings over with. Although the afternoon was entering its swansong, there was well over an hour's worth of good light left, just enough time to sweep through the village and get out of there. The zombies in the canal and those approaching on the other side, were giving them serious creeps, and they were keen to get away from that place.

'Sergeant Mike Santilli,' said Mike, hand outstretched to the driver of the newly arrived vehicle who'd wasted no time in jumping out, virtually before the vehicle had stopped, and striding quickly towards Mike. He grabbed Mike's hand.

'It's great isn't it,' said the new arrival. Mike was confused. 'You must know about it?' Mike wondered if some wonder cure had been found for the zombie curse. He glanced at Rob who shrugged in complete ignorance. It had to be something major for them to seem to be completely oblivious to the canal situation, its most recent acquisition still flailing about, others approaching from the other side.

'What is it?' asked Mike. He was more than curious. The door swung open on the other side of the newly arrived Landrover, and another soldier jumped out.

144

'The New Philosophy!' the new chap shouted. 'They told us over the radio. It's brilliant. We can't stop talking about it.'

'Haven't heard a thing mate,' stated Rob in classic squaddie tone. Mike felt a bit unnerved, enhanced further by a similar emotion in Rob's tone.

'Where are your other guys?' asked Mike, trying to get back to the matter in hand. 'He knew that there should be four in the unit.

'They're in the Landy. They're fine. I reckon that they're more into this than we are,' replied the first new solider. Mike peered past him into the open door of the vehicle. He could see the other two seated inside, but something was up. The one sat furthest away was sat bolt upright, staring forwards, not moving other than a distinct tremble. The nearest one had hunched forward and his whole upper body was lifting up and down with his heavy breathing. A growling coming from him was distinctly audibly, even through his bio chem suit. Mike shuddered.

'Bloody hell! What's with him?' he asked loudly, taking half a step back to point past the soldier at the growling thing.

'Listen,' said the soldier, 'I've got to tell you about the New Philosophy…' continued the solider, increasingly oblivious to any external stimulus other than the opportunity to engage in discourse about the New Philosophy.

'Look out!' screamed Mike jumping back. He tried to pull the newly arrived man with him, but his total consumption in starting to explain the New Philosophy rendered him too slow and sluggish to move in time. The growling soldier was on his back having made it straight from the vehicle in one bound off the ground. His target had been Mike, his awareness somehow bypassing his colleague, maybe being more enticed by the image of a face rather than the back of a head. As Mike tried to pull the soldier describing the New Philosophy to safety, his inability to make any movement to help himself caused him to stumble over between Mike and the zombie bounding towards him. The zombie hit the back of the stumbling soldier, shaking off its bio chem hood as it did so, and becoming fully aware of this alternative body in its way. The soldier fell forward, the wind knocked out of him as he landed face down in the cold grass, barely moving his arms to save himself. The zombie had slowed a little, but added to its remaining forward momentum with a lunge down onto the back of the man on the floor. It ripped through the bio chem suit as if it were tissue paper, and then buried its head deep into the back of the neck of its victim, drawing screams and blood.

Mike and Rob were momentarily frozen. Rob reacted first. He stepped forward ready to kick the creature hard in the side. 'No!' shouted Mike, stepping in front of him and pushing him back with both hands on his chest. 'It won't work. He's a zombie!' Mike was trying to make sense quickly. He looked up at Dave and Paul who'd both stood up, inertly holding their guns pointing down. 'Shoot it!' he screamed at them both. They weren't sure what to do. They could see a zombie, but it was a fellow solider, and underneath that, another colleague. Mike looked down at the feasting on the floor, waiting for the shots. Nothing happened. It lifted its blood stained head, clenching the body below it by the shoulders. It saw Mike and hissed. Even if Mike wasn't sure that the soldier below was dead, though the bone from the top his spine visible through the shredded flesh strongly indicated he was, he would have still given the order again to shoot.

This time Dave and Paul sprung into life. Three rapid shots rang out from the rifle of each, half hitting the zombie's head, and the rest into its body. The shots stopped. Another two shots then hesitatingly followed to make sure.

As the geysers of blood erupted up and umbrellaed outwards, Mike and Rob jumped back, eager not to be touched by the foul liquid, even though they were wearing their protective suits. Everyone was sure that this was how the infection spread. They'd all seen the films, or were just adapting their knowledge of other plagues. All of the soldiers repeated expletives to each other and themselves. Mike looked at Rob in realisation and stopped swearing. 'If one's got it, they all might have.' All three of his colleagues heard him, and looked over to the other vehicle and the two remaining soldiers.

The other soldier who'd got out, had a big smile on his face. He was speaking quickly, only just audible through his suit. It was something about the New Philosophy. Nothing about the carnage, the devouring and the execution that had just taken place. He began to walk round towards them past the front of his Landrover.

A screaming snarl snatched at the attention of the others. It was coming from the back of the second vehicle. The thing in the back was hungry and about to start searching for food. The door had been partially closed in the previous occurrence. It jumped straight out, oblivious to the door, and clattering straight into it with such force that it flung back hard, bending the panels and making the whole vehicle shake. Even with its inhuman strength, the force of the impact was still some deterrent to the zombie, and it bounced sideways, losing its balance and falling to the ground. Even though it didn't hesitate, its unfooting provided a little extra time, just enough for Mike to shout 'Shoot it!' Before it could get to its feet, Dave and Paul's practice paid off. Another volley of shots, and a thorough splattering of its head quickly rendered the threat neutralised, smearing the inside of its bio chem suit with a mixture of blood, brains and bone, some of it dribbling out through the bullet holes in the hood.

The adrenaline was pumping, but it wasn't over. The remaining soldier from the newly arrived unit was strolling towards them, still smiling, still talking 'New Philosophy', but most disturbingly to Mike and Rob, he seemed completely unable to connect with the events that had just taken place around him. Mike and Rob began to walk backwards away from the grinning lunatic approaching them. The extreme fear they were experiencing was momentarily rendering them deaf to his sermon. None of the original four soldiers were sure what to do. This was a fellow soldier, a colleague, and he was smiling, being friendly, ironically, making things worse. Mike glanced down and saw the corpses, the puddles of blood enlarging around them. 'Do it!' he shouted as his eyes darted up to Dave and Paul. They didn't need telling again, and dispatched yet another volley of shots which amply did their job.

Mike and Rob stopped walking backwards and looked up to Dave and Paul who were stood up, rifles slightly lowered from ready. This time there were no expletives, but silence. Paul glanced over to the side.

'Look!' he shouted, pointing at the second vehicle. The force of the second zombie hitting the door had unsettled it, and along with the handbrake not being applied when the first soldier had eagerly jumped out, had caused it to start rolling forward. They all watched as it trundled a few yards, splashing nose first into the canal, picking up just enough momentum to go right over the edge, and drift to the centre before touching the bottom.

Several zombies were gathered on the opposite side of the canal. The zombie nearest to the newly created platform was easily able to make a short jump onto it. As it prepared to make a similar short and easy jump off again onto the other side of the canal, a shot took its face out, along with its brain through the back of its skull. Its body slumped back, making a dull clanging sound on the roof of the Landrover like a gong, and then slipped off the side into the freezing waters and bobbed up and down.

Whilst this was happening, another two, then three, then four zombies were jumping onto the stranded vehicle. Another shot rang out from Dave and Paul. Another zombie taken out. Another shot, but it only managed to scrape a flesh wound. Panic was starting to upset their aim. A zombie made it over the canal. Paul and Dave brought it straight down with a volley, but this diversion only allowed more to get further over. Mike and Rob reacted quickly, and ran the few yards to get into the Land Rover, ferociously slamming the doors. There was no way for them to get Paul and Dave inside. They locked the doors. Two zombies had now made it over and were bounding towards them.

'Hold on, lads!' shouted Mike, as the Landrover's engine growled to life and then snarled violently as Mike revved it. He began reversing back. He couldn't go too quick with the lads on the roof, but the movement was upsetting their aim. Too many zombies had now got over and the shooting wasn't bringing them down quickly enough. Mike was looking backwards trying to aim the Landrover at the gate to get on the road again. He glanced forward and saw that two of the zombies had nearly caught them up. He accelerated, causing them to swerve. As the Landrover jolted, he felt an awful sickening feeling in his stomach, the kind of feeling you get after having a minor road crash, and wishing so much that you could go back a few seconds and undo the event. He looked forward as Dave bounced off the bonnet, and rolled on the ground in front. The monsters pounced. Dave screamed. Shots rapidly rang out as Paul did his best to save his friend from his fate. He got some of them, and then euthanized Dave, maybe deliberately rather than let him be conscious as the flesh was stripped from his bones, or just a stray shot. The tale he'd heard of his great, great grandfather shooting a colleague who'd begged him to do so, as he was sucked into the mud at Passchendaele, flashed through Paul's mind.

The vile incident in front had consumed Mike's attention, and the vehicle lost its way from the track, jolting violently on the bumpy ground. He instinctively hit the brakes, and more zombies bounded onto the roof of the Landrover. Mike and Rob felt a cold chill freeze their bodies, from their heads moving down to their legs. The horror was too much to bear. They just looked straight ahead, saying nothing, maybe not wanting to give any tears a chance to escape, as they accelerated away, ignoring the screams and thumping on the roof. It seemed to last for hours, their own hellish circle of suffering. In reality, it only took a few seconds for the speed and jolting of the vehicle to cause the writhing mass of zombies and various parts of their victim to fall off onto the road behind them.

When Mike and Rob were far enough away from the emotions they'd just gone through to speak, they called in the incidence to Location Three.

18. Acceptance

Adam listened intently to the call, making the occasional sound of acknowledgement. The incidence at the canal was described to Adam by a communications room officer in one sentence, a single example of what was happening to military units at numerous locations out in the field. Several units had zombified and many soldiers had been lost. Adam was not cold to the emotions rattling in him, but his focus was on his resources now being compromised. The reports coming in would have been bad enough, but coupled with the outbreak in the cells inside this supposedly secure facility, he realised that he may now be facing catastrophe. The might that lay behind, and beyond Location Three was dwindling. The unseen power it commanded and realised as the infrastructural manifestation of the state was fading, taking with it Adam's ability to enact his role as Martial Governor of the UK.

As the call had progressed, Bob and Harriet had ceased talking, Adams demeanour gave away the gravity of what he was hearing. The two of them silently watched, awaiting the moment that they could share in the enthralling communication. Laura and Simon sat quietly as the focus on them shifted away. They exchanged a couple of glances and stared through the screen at the interrogators.

Adam allowed the phone to lower down away from his ear, the earpiece still level with his chin, as the call ended. He was taking a few moments to prepare himself. He regained his composure and hung up. Bob caught his attention, but Adam said nothing. Neither did Bob, who shrugged and moved his hands apart with a roll of his forearms. Adam glanced up at Laura. Obviously, he was not going to reveal what he'd just heard in front of prisoners, was he?

Adam was a unique soldier who could sometimes think beyond protocol and training if the circumstances were extraordinary enough. He judged that the extraordinary box was ticked.

He thought about the whole situation. Location Three was infected and under internal quarantine. They may be able to control it, but as they had no idea how or when it had got in, there was every likelihood that they couldn't. The rest of their resources were now succumbing to the infection. The situation was desperate. He would be Martial Governor in name only, but he still had a duty to do what he could. Standard procedure had got them to where they were now, and they were failing. As Einstein said, madness is doing the same thing again and again and hoping for a different result.

Laura and Simon were being treated as prisoners, but she had come to them, and Simon was a soldier. He only found himself in this interrogation by chance. The vast resources of science that Location Three had at their disposal had provided them with nothing. Only Laura seemed to have any idea of what was going on. At least she'd been where it had started and knew something about the New Philosophers. Adam thought back to what she'd been saying. He wasn't sure he fully understood. Was it that the idea of the New Philosophy, simply knowing about it, was what made people zombies? It was fantastical. Maybe he'd got it wrong. The whole game had changed dramatically in under an hour. He could easily have the separating screen slide back into place while he told his colleagues what had happened. However, they could just be wasting time if they needed Laura. In any case she wasn't going anywhere. Adam began to explain the call, Laura and Simon able to listen in.

'I've just received…' he began, but Harriet interrupted.

'You're not going to tell us in front of them?' she quipped, pointing. Adam closed his eyes took a breath and continued.

'I've just received,' he started again, and proceeded to explain about the infected army units. He concluded with, 'The opportunity we have to make a difference is diminishing and may soon be negligible.'

Bob turned his head nearly one hundred and eighty degrees, to look through the screen at Laura. He had understood what she had been saying, and did not share Adam's doubts. He had not been immediately convinced, but they had nothing else. When there is no other hope, straws are clutched at, and contemplating that Laura could be right was one step better than praying.

Adam took his seat again at the table. 'Adam,' Bob asked, 'what was the infection control like in the units?'

'Everything recommended,' he replied.

'What if it was something airborne, and highly infectious?' asked Bob. 'Were all of the units that zombified in full bio chem protection?' Bob had recognised that Simon had been apparently easily exposed to Laura. Adam saw the problem.

'They were,' replied Adam. Although Simon had been in a lower grade of protective suit, his exposure had been virtually a one-off among the various units, and the controller in the communications room had already checked to see if this could explain the spread. Traditional explanations for the infection were looking unlikely. Even if they could explain the outbreaks in the field, that still left the cells. Laura's hypothesis was sounding less and less crazy.

'We can't explain how this virus has spread, but she can,' stated Bob, nodding his head to Laura.

'Really?' asked Harriet, highly sceptical. There was a pause.

'Let's see if we can find out,' replied Adam, moving to action. He picked up the handset of the intercom. He needed live information from the field. Adam quickly made enquiries about survivors from any of the infections. The operator was pessimistic, but said he'd look into it. Adam kept the phone to his ear whilst he waited.

'What do you want to find out?' asked Harriet.

'I don't know yet,' replied Adam.

Adam held up a finger, as a voice sounded in the intercom handset. It was good news, at least relatively so. They could patch Adam through to Mike and Rob, the soldiers involved in the canal incident. The dialogue began with the usual military formalities. Adam asked what had happened. Mike was still in shock, and began by describing in detail the atrocities they'd witnessed. Adam was patient. Once he had heard the descriptions of gore, he pressed some more.

'You say they changed after they arrived,' he delved. 'Was their behaviour normal before this?' There was no response, and Adam wondered for a second if the connection had been lost, then heard the reassuring growl of the Landrover. Adam waited.

'No!' exclaimed Mike as he suddenly recollected the moments before the attacks. 'It wasn't. It wasn't normal at all.' He continued to describe the arrival of his comrades and the seconds before the attacks. The occupants of the interrogation room could only guess at what Adam was hearing. After a few moments he thanked Mike and replaced the receiver.

'Well?' asked Harriet as he sat back down.

'He said that two of them just wanted to talk about the New Philosophy, one of them continuing even after the attacks had started. He said it was like he was completely cut off from everything that was happening, and all he cared about was the New Philosophy.' There was shock in the room. Laura could have said something, but didn't as respect for her in the room grew.

'Looks like we should be listening more to you,' said Bob, by way of apology, though still not fully at ease with the proposed concept. Adam nodded as he rejoined the table. 'Looks like they've all been in contact on the radio,' hypothesised Bob.

Harriet suddenly looked exasperated, and raised her hand to her mouth. She was startled by the fright from the shock of what she had just realised. 'You mean it travels over radio waves!' she exclaimed, on the edge of panic, 'and down wires!'

Bob calmly replied. 'I guess you could put it that way.'

'But you've just been connected to infected people,' she pleaded to Bob, distancing herself a little from Adam. 'The germs might be on that handset!' Bob looked a little confused.

Adam observed Bob's reaction. 'They might be on you!' she said to Adam edging herself towards total terror.

The penny dropped for Bob. 'She thinks we're still saying that it's a physical virus,' offered Bob to Adam, ignoring Harriet. 'I guess she thinks that it must teleport somehow. Like Star Trek I suppose.'

'Yes, that's what it is, isn't it!' stammered Harriet mistakenly seeing an ally. Bob chuckled a little, lowering his head into his hands failing to disguise it. 'What!!' she screamed. 'We're in danger! We could all be about to be infected!' Bob gathered himself to answer.

'Harriet,' he began reassuringly, 'it's not like that at all. Trust us. It can't,' he thought for a moment, 'teleport through the radio. We're quite safe in here.' He took Harriet's trembling hand and gave it a light squeeze to reassure her. He reflected on the fact that, if they subscribed to Laura's theory, what he had just said wasn't entirely true.

Behind the interrogation screen, Laura could be seen to be jiggling on her chair as she tried to suppress her mirth. Bob noticed, his face lit up for a second, and then he laughed out loud. This continued for a few seconds, as Laura's face broke into a broad smile. 'I'm sorry,' said Bob and composed himself. Harriet, still suffering from the trauma of her delusion of teleporting bugs, was unable to say anything. Bob needed to reaffirm his professionalism.

'We've got a theory here,' he said. 'I'm not saying that I believe it, but it's holding up.' He saw that Adam was happy for him to lead the way. 'If this thing, this New Philosophy, has been spread by communication, can we check out who the infected people, the units, have been communicating with?'

'Makes sense,' said Adam as he stood up and reached for the intercom handset. 'Don't forget the cells,' Bob added, a crucial part of the jigsaw.

Adam made the call, and waited after issuing instructions to see what came back. After receiving a response, he replaced the handset and sat back down to reveal the news.

'They're going to look further,' he said, 'but they'd already been looking into patterns around the infection.' The gathered group awaited the news with anticipation. Laura and Simon, although separated by the screen, were now becoming a part of the inquiry.

'Most of the infected units were part of purple patch,' said Adam. Everyone looked confused at the jargon. 'There are too many units to be controlled by one operator. We rely on verbal communication,' Adam digressed, 'though we are looking at ways that computers could do all of this for us at some point.' No one looked convinced by these hopes for the technology, although they could see the power if it were to happen. 'Simply put, most of the affected units have been talking to the same operator. The purple patch operator.'

'It's a start…' began Bob.

'…but not enough,' concluded Harriet.

'There's more,' continued Adam. 'They've been having problems in communications today. Messages weren't getting through to purple patch.' His tone was ominous. 'It turned out that it was because the operator had kept the channel open, and was ignoring commands he was receiving.' It was clear where Adam was going. 'He'd been patching through a feed of someone talking about the New Philosophy. It was coming from the cells.' The room was silent. Laura's felt her position becoming stronger.

'What's happened to the operator?' asked Bob, already guessing at the answer.

'He's off duty,' replied Adam. 'The Chief of Comms would have brought him in, but we're in internal quarantine.' They could all guess at the operator's fate.

'Hang on,' said Harriet. 'You said most units. What about the others?'

'We've had a few go in Orange patch as well,' said Adam.

'Well that proves it's something else,' replied Harriet.

'Or just that they got it from somewhere else,' said Bob.

'Sir!' came a voice, transmitted from behind the screen. It was Simon. The interrogators looked over towards him and Laura. The two of them had been silent, Simon the compliant soldier, Laura observing.

'Go ahead,' said Adam.

'The helicopter that brought us in was from orange patch,' said Simon. The implication of the incident with the doorman was obvious.

'But how did he get it?' asked Harriet.

'It doesn't matter,' replied Bob sharply. 'The point is that he was talking about the New Philosophy. He could have heard it anywhere. They've passed it between a few of them within the patch. It's still the New Philosophy wherever there are zombies. That's what matters.'

Laura had heard it all. As her theory had continued to hold up, her status had risen. Bob saw her expression. 'Laura. Are you okay?' he asked, the tone of his voice manifesting their increasing acceptance of herself and what she was saying.

'It's everywhere,' she replied, a desolate ring to her words. 'Everything's lost.' Bob felt that she was right. He and Adam were beginning to fully comprehend.

'I don't understand. What are you trying to say?' interrupted Harriet, shattering the moment. Bob took the opportunity to recap what Laura was saying, and to see if it was possible to get Harriet to understand.

'Can I clarify Laura,' Bob asked with humility. She nodded. 'Instead of getting infected with something 'real,' like a toxin or a virus, you're saying that it's the New Philosophy that's the infection,' inquired Bob.

'Yes,' said Laura.

'Zombies haven't been infected by something else that then makes them talk about the New Philosophy, it's just the New Philosophy?'

'Yes,' said Laura.

156

'And to get infected, I guess they just have to hear it then?'

'Yes,' said Laura. She remained expressionless for a second then continued. 'Maybe they could read it as well, I'm not sure, and I should think they need to take it in, you know, understand?' She was still developing her own thinking aloud around her core idea. Bob swung round to look at Adam, who he could see now fully got it.

'How did the New Philosophers get hold of it?' asked Bob.

'No idea,' replied Laura. 'But they have done,' she concluded.

Harriet was struggling. She was very agitated. 'So you're saying that the new philosophy is like some kind of spirit, like a demon, like they're possessed.' Harriet still couldn't make sense of what Laura was saying.

'No not at all,' said Laura. The conversation continued between the pair.

'But it has to be something that is causing it to happen.'

'It is. The New Philosophy is causing it to happen.'

'But you just said that it doesn't exist. You've said it's not a real thing, and it's not some kind of spirit either.'

'I didn't say that it doesn't exist. But it's none of those things. It's not a spirit or a ghost, or a magical force… or any of that kind of mumbo jumbo gullible people are manipulated with.' Bob smiled at Laura, as Harriet missed the insult. Harriet responded.

'What is it then?'

'It's the idea.'

'How can an idea do this? It's a just a load of words.'

'Aren't ideas real?'

'Well of course ideas are real, but not in this way. They can't do this!'

Harriet's expression had been transforming. 'This is ridiculous,' she exclaimed. 'I've never heard anything so stupid.

Why are we listening to this moronic little girl? I'm a senior civil servant.' She was fuming. Bob and Adam were calm. They had listened to Harriet, but Laura's idea still held up.

'If you're so certain you're right that I'm wrong,' said Laura in a slow, firm voice, 'then how could you object to us just discussing what I'm suggesting?' Harriet was eager to blurt out a rebuttal. She was used to being able to quash anything that didn't fit her view, the correct and proper one. But she was in an alien situation, and had been deftly sidelined. She breathed heavily, fuming. Adam and Bob were content that they could continue with their exploration.

'Laura,' asked Bob, 'do you really think that an idea could have this effect on people? Could an idea have really caused all of these things to have happened?'

'Yes,' she replied.

'Why?' asked Bob. He knew that there was evidence, but he thought he may as well see if Laura had any kind of explanation for her theory. He didn't, but he also hadn't come up with the theory in the first place. Laura had, so what else was she capable of. She relaxed, a smile tugging at the edges of her mouth, as she realised she'd come through the first battle.

19. Ideas

Laura now had the stage. Despite Harriet's objections, she was going to be listened to and had a chance to make her case. She wasn't sure where to begin. She went for the obvious. 'Take her for example,' she said pointing to Harriet. 'I've watched her change over the last few minutes. She's now far angrier than she was a few moments ago, just because I've suggested an idea that she doesn't agree with. ' There was hidden amusement in the room at Laura's observation, except from Harriet. It was still a long stretch to go.

'Look,' continued Laura, 'ideas, the things we hear, the words we read, the TV we watch, can all have an effect on people, and change the way they behave and act, and people are real. We can all see ideas causing real changes. Maybe for something to be real, it just has to cause a physical change.' Laura's delving into the world of realism resonated with Bob. She continued.

'Ideas can make people happy, sad, angry or all manner of emotions, and they change the way people act. People might see a starving child on telly and donate to a charity, or suddenly kiss somebody while watching a sunset.'

'I understand what you're saying, Laura,' said Bob, 'but we're talking about killing here.'

'People have killed for ideas,' said Laura. 'Soldiers kill.'

'That's completely different. It's their job,' retorted Harriet, whose actions had caused her fair share of suffering during her career. 'They're doing it for the country. We need them.'

'Those reasons are just ideas,' replied Laura. 'They're ways to describe things, or may even be made up. They only feel real, because they affect so many things.

'We have a Government, we pay taxes, the army has military equipment, all real things. But they're built on nothing more than ideas. If you didn't know about them, a soldier killing someone is just a killing. We all believe it's okay, because of the ideas.

'Wars have killed millions of people. They may be based on valid reasons, but they don't have to be. They could have resulted from a mistake. Then there aren't even valid causes.' Harriet looked at Laura with subtle contempt.

'It's even possible that a powerful enough person, a Prime Minister or a President, could start a war based on information that they know is wrong, so it's not even a mistake, but a war intentionally started on the basis of lies!'

Harriet scoffed audibly, and assumed her contempt for Laura's rantings would be accepted. The other interrogators were not yet fully convinced, but lacked Harriet's cynicism. Bob articulated their feelings. 'It's quite a stretch to accept that the ideas that motivate a soldier aren't real. You might not be able to feel the concept of a country or state, but they're so embedded in our thinking, it's hard to accept that they're not real.' Bob considered what he had just said, and then added, 'though you may be right of course,' bolstering Laura's argument.

'What about Father Christmas then?' replied Laura.

'Now you're just being childish,' said Harriet irritably.

'Not at all,' said Laura, 'and your response makes the point. You think Father Christmas is something childish and something made up. I take it you don't really believe in him then?'

'Of course not!' Harriet snapped.

'So he's not real, but he still affects little children,' continued Laura calmly. 'They get excited, they feel happy. But it's more than this. This made up myth changes children's behaviour. They know that they have to be good to get presents. He's not just a made up idea and happens to change children's behaviour, it exactly why he was made up!'

160

'They're just children!' said an exasperated Harriet. 'We're talking about adults.'

Laura continued. 'What about mobs and riots then?' Bob shifted a little as his interest increased. 'They can act like savages. Why is it that a group of people can kick a man to death? What is it that links them? It's the culture and ideas that they've been exposed to, and what makes them what they are. It's nothing more than ideas, some ordered information that causes them to turn, not into an animal, but into something far worse. A crazed beast fuelled by its own savagery and violence.

'The triggers can be virtually nothing, like the way one person looks at another. But the result can be horrific. Something changes and that rush of power causes people to turn into something inhuman. Mobs savagely kicking someone's head in, or hanging another because they're the wrong colour. But you ask virtually anybody who hasn't been involved in something like this if they'd do it, and they find the suggestion abhorrent. So where do the mobs come from?

Everyone believes that they're above it, but most have a trigger. Imagine a massive terrorist attack killing thousands of people. If such a terrible thing were to happen, I bet you could get away with virtually anything. You could lock up and torture anyone you wanted, and no one would stop it happening.'

'Ridiculous!' cried Harriet. Laura continued.

'Whatever initial emotional response people may have towards an idea, if they're given time they can rationalise to see if it makes sense. But if they all receive a message at the same time, mobs can easily form. Imagine if everybody had something in their pockets say, that allowed them to share ideas with everyone else instantly. You could end up with riots on the streets all over the country from a simple desire, greed say. Isn't that what we see with looting?'

'Now you're sounding absurd. Something like that is never going to be possible,' said Harriet.

'Look at witch hunts,' continued Laura, unperturbed. 'People believing a crazy idea that someone's a witch. We know that

161

witches aren't real, but that idea created murderers. Witch hunts and lynch mobs. They're just a couple of examples of people acting violently because of beliefs and ideas.' Laura paused a second.

'Once the mob believes that someone is a paedophile, or a grass, or whatever other reason they believe justifies them, they can change. They may have got it wrong, they may be targeting an innocent person. Look at the Corporal Killings a few years ago in Northern Ireland. We all watched a mob on television, but carry out a sadistic beating and execution. But why did the mob do it? Because they thought the soldiers were from an opposing group. Their reason was wrong, but they still changed.'

'But that's just some groups of people!' Harriet said with an air of aloofness.

'Really?' said Bob. 'You are aware of the Milgram experiment?' Harriet looked confused. 'It showed that the majority of people will administer a lethal electric shock to someone if they're given the idea that it's part of an official experiment.' Harriet was none the wiser.

'You're talking about groups of people. These zombies are individuals,' said Harriet, believing she'd found the flaw.

'A group is just a bunch of individuals,' replied Laura.' They just have something in common.'

'But they're not all together,' said Harriet. Laura answered.

'What about shootings carried out by lone gunmen then? Like the student who walks into his school and starts shooting people. They often act alone. They act violently. And they act based on ideas. It might be ideas about how people are treating them, but sometimes it's ideas that don't directly touch them at all; conspiracy theories, religion, cults or even patriotism. All nothing more than ideas.'

'They're one offs!' Harriet exclaimed, her attempts at rebuttal struggling.

'Maybe just one at a time,' said Laura, 'but it's happened more than once. And there's only one zombie at a time.'

'What you're saying is making sense Laura,' said Bob. 'I think we see that ideas can change how people feel and act, even violently. But aren't these isolated examples? This is affecting virtually everyone, almost an ideology.'

'Exactly,' said Laura, 'and don't ideologies have the power to change people?'

'What do you mean?' asked Bob. Laura continued.

'Look at religion? Whether it's the Bible, Koran, Torah, Vedas, Guru Granth Sahib or The Book of the Dead, it's the ideas they contain that change people. It's not the paper they're written on. If the ink and paper were destroyed, the ideas would still carry on having an effect if they'd been passed on.

'And you can see the massive effect of religions as far back as history goes. Whole societies and cultures are based around them.

'But people have also committed violence because of religion. The Spanish Inquisition, Fatwa's against writers, terrorist movements, occupations, land grabs, Jihad, the Crusades. All from religious ideas.'

'So you're saying that all of the bad in the world is because of religion, then?' said Harriet, attempting to ridicule.

'Of course I'm not!' replied Laura. 'Just that violence can result from religion. Religion's do a lot of good, maybe even more good than bad. To say all religion is bad because it causes some bad acts is ridiculous.' Laura decided to expand her point. 'If man is ultimately a selfish, self-interested being, as say George Price claimed, then how did we manage to evolve to live in complex societies, dependent upon all sorts of altruistic acts, co-operation and trust? Maybe it couldn't have happened without religion. Without it, we might still be living in tribes.'

'But religions are just there,' replied Harriet. 'They're far more than just ideas. They're whole ways of life that have been around for thousands of years. This New Philosophy has only just appeared.' Bob and Adam watched as Harriet provided support to Laura's arguments.

'So what about political ideology then? That's just ideas made up by people.'

'It's hardly the same,' said Harriet, still resisting any encouragement to rationalise, 'creating different ways for running states. They've got to be run in some way. It's not violence and murder.'

'Really?' said Laura, as Harriet flinched. 'What about the Second World War? Millions of soldiers and civilians killed in fighting, fifteen million exterminated in concentration camps, all because of Nazi ideology.'

'That's a one off,' came Harriet's dismissal. 'That's as much down to Hitler being a psychopath.'

'Still relies on ideas though.' Laura paused.

'What about Marxism? That's arguably had a greater effect on the twentieth century than anything else. Those initial ideas of Marx and Engels led to an evolution of other ideas, and went on to shape events in most of the world. The creation of political parties, revolution in Russia, the Eastern Bloc, China, Cuba, the Vietnam War, the Cold War, McCarthyism. Plenty of violence there. Stalin killed millions in the name of ideology, maybe more than sixty million. But we don't hear about that so often.' Everyone was transfixed on what Laura was saying.

'The thing with Marxism is that the people who started it just came up with some ideas. Once they'd shared them, they just carried on.'

Harriet said nothing. She had nowhere to go. Bob and Adam were still taking it in. She'd made her point, but could it really explain the zombie outbreak.

'Do you really think all this explains the extremes we're now seeing?' said Bob. He wanted to believe. She responded.

'If you look at different examples, the time for changes to occur can be very different. A lynch mob may take a few hours or less. Marxism took decades. The violence can also vary. Some people just get angry, whereas some become a frenzied mob barely aware of what they're doing.

'If the level of violence and the time taken for it to happen can vary, what if you had an idea that was able to concentrate this into something that makes people extremely violent, very quickly.'

'You'd have something like we have now,' said Bob, as it sunk in.

'You'd have the New Philosophy,' said Laura.

'But why are people listening to it?' said Harriet, almost pleading. 'It's so bad!' said Harriet.

'It may only become bad,' said Bob. 'Like many things that start out with good intentions.'

'You sound like you believe her,' said Harriet. They all looked over to her. She was prepared. 'We know that the New Philosophers are involved in this, and it looks like they're recruiting. That's all this idea, is used for. Once someone's lured in, they must just give them the virus to spread. That would explain the Tupelo Star, wouldn't it?'

Bob and Adam exchanged a look. Harriet's theory was on the surface convincing, though a ring of sophistry chimed. The way people changed, how they were speaking, how it had spread, the failure to identify any sort of virus, all resonated far more with Laura's explanations, however outlandish.

They might not fully accept her theory yet, but their minds were open. Adam was conflicted.

Harriet looked up, her face mildly lightened. 'If you're right, why doesn't it affect everyone then? Why doesn't it affect you? Or Bob?'

Laura answered. 'Even with all of those examples I've given you, there's still always been some people who aren't convinced or carried along with the mob. But they tend to be the minority. I guess Bob and me can see the New Philosophy for what it really is.'

Adam raised his head to speak. He had more than the validity of Laura's claims on his mind. 'So if this is spread by communication and not by physical contact, quarantine may have made things worse. If people can't get out, they're going to be looking for any information that they can get, radio, television, telephone.' A look of despair wiped over Adam's face.

They all sat silently. They'd been at it for over an hour. The lull gave them some space to think.

The silent cloak was ruptured by the intercom buzzing. Adam took the call, aware how critical and fast moving things were. He made various 'ahem' sounds as he listened to the information being imparted. 'Right. Hold on,' he said lowering the handset. He informed everyone that the team he'd directed to look into the New Philosophy had some early reports. They'd confirmed that people were talking about it, but it seemed virtually impossible to find anyone who could give them any detail. Either no one was being told anymore, or those who had heard were no longer available. Laura said nothing.

Adam continued the briefing. 'They've got some stuff on the Tupelo Star communications. As part of this new electronic messaging they were testing, they also saved most of it. The New Philosophy is mentioned in the written messages, but not in detail.' Bob looked frustrated. 'They do tell us that Mike Cotton was planning to call his friend to discuss the New Philosophy… just before he turned into a zombie.' Bob sighed and looked at Adam forlornly, presuming the opportunity was lost. Adam didn't share his look.

'What is it?' asked Bob.

'It was a video call,' replied Adam.

'And that means…' said Bob.

'They've got a recording!' concluded Adam.

'Can we see it!' Harriet almost shrieked. Adam calmly turned his head to her.

'They can relay it straight into here now,' he replied, nodding to a screen that was so flush with the wall its blank appearance had gone completely unnoticed.

'What are we waiting for?' stammered Harriet. 'This must be the instructions to Cotton to release the virus or whatever.' The room was agog.

'Wait!' came a call. It was Laura. She spoke with authority. 'If you watch this, you're going to be turned,' she prophesised.

'Good God!' exclaimed Harriet, 'You seriously don't think we're not going to watch it?'

Laura looked to Bob. There was fear in his face as Laura's prediction sent cold chills through his chest.

'Adam,' said Bob, capturing the initiative, 'have they viewed the message in Comms?' Adam put the phone straight to his ear to retrieve the answer.

'No,' came the reply. 'They thought I should be told as soon as they found out about it.' Laura tried to hide her lack of surprise.

'What are we waiting for?' demanded Harriet. Laura's concern and all she'd said, had failed to trouble Harriet. Adam looked to Bob. He looked indecisive, unsure how to react.

'Can you really take the risk if there's the slightest chance that I might be right?' asked Laura. She found herself in a confrontation with Harriet trying to win over minds, but the urge in their hearts to partake in the forbidden was always going to be stronger.

'It's quite a risk,' said Bob.

'She wasn't affected,' replied Harriet pointing at Laura, 'Nor were you'. Adam's expression changed as he nodded. Adam considered how Laura and Simon, as well as Bob, hadn't been affected, and his and Harriet's positions. It was like the first time heroin user convincing herself that she wouldn't get addicted.

'We know what it's about already,' said Harriet as a clincher. 'It's just a sales pitch to lure people into this cult.' Adam looked ready to make a decision.

'Are you sure about this?' asked Bob.

'What else can we do?' replied Adam, aware the situation was rapidly deteriorating. 'Play it,' he said into the handset and sat down at the table.

'What if,' began Bob, emphasizing the last word, 'what if she's right?' Adam looked straight into Bob's face. What might happen was a terrifying prospect, but he was reassured that Bob had been unaffected by the New Philosophy. He reached down to his side, unclipped a holster and removed a hand gun. He held it up in front of his face and glanced it over, looked to Bob, and slid it across the table where it came to rest in Bob's hands. Bob gave a couple of knowing nods, and gently lifted the gun, placing it on his lap whilst keeping hold tightly. Adam asked the guard to leave the room.

20. The Video

They all stared at the blank monitor screen blended into the wall, gripped by anticipation. Laura and Simon were viewing it at an awkward angle being stuck behind the transparent wall that was still separating them from the others, so they could only see a narrow image, disrupted by rogue reflections on the barrier separating them. They could have got up and moved to get a better view, but they could hear clearly. Nothing happening. Adam, Harriet and Bob's heads turned to each other and back to the screen.

The monitor screen came to life, and everyone's heads jerked round to fix their gazes on it. There was no static or snow on the screen to precede the appearance of the image. It was a youngish man. He had one of those beards that men invariably grow when appearance is rendered pointless. He was leaning forward, his arms outstretched so that his hands were beyond the edges of the sides of the screen, as he adjusted the camera that was shooting his image. He appeared to be in some kind of ship's cabin, a cramped affair with a bunk behind him just above head height. He was gently swaying side to side, but the fixtures were static. He leant back in his chair, shuffled slightly, and an anticipatory smile lifted his cheeks, ending with his eyebrows hopping up for a second. His hand stretched forward towards the screen, vanishing just below it as he operated something somewhere below the camera.

He sat back and waited, still smiling. There was some text on the screen at the bottom, the type that appears on photos that have the date and time automatically added, but duller and blurred. It was possible to make out among the various lettering the name, 'Mike Cotton'. This man was now dead, a zombie lost in the Atlantic. A few seconds passed as Mike continued beaming from the screen.

A small box appeared in the bottom right of the image. It was the face of a woman that filled virtually the whole box, making it impossible to tell where she might be. She had dark hair in big waves just long enough to be considered long. Her hair along with her large round glasses dominated her face. She was aged somewhere in her late twenties to early thirties. She was also smiling, but more ecstatically than Mike. Her eyes seemed unnaturally large, but it wasn't possible to tell if this was because of her exuberant grinning or the thick glasses she was wearing. It was probably a mixture of the two.

'Mike, I can't wait to tell you about this New Philosophy.' She was speaking rapidly, almost blabbering but not quite enough so as to be unintelligible. She was eager to tell him everything she knew about the New Philosophy, and before Mike had time to say anything, she began relating the ideas.

***

[THE FOLLOWING SECTION HAS BEEN CENSORED AND REMOVED]

***

After about ten minutes, the woman had finished, and then stopped talking, reverting to her grin, which seemed even more intense as her appearance started to enter maniacal clown territory. Mike's face was motionless, his mouth slightly open, his expression one of awe etched upon a foundation of delight. A few seconds passed as the two unnatural visages projected out from the screen into the room at Location Three.

'Wow,' said Mike before returning to his trance like gaze. The woman's smile suddenly stretched her grin even tighter and she let out a hysterical cry of pleasure. She brought both her hands to her mouth, covering it with her clenched fists, laughing over-excitedly mixed with hyperventilation. She continued as Mike, his expression remaining fixed, leant forward and pressed a button out of shot. The monitor screen in Location Three returned to blank. The viewers had heard all that they needed to.

'Told you it was a load of rubbish,' said Bob. He had a look round at the others. First he looked over to Laura. She was nodding in agreement with him. Simon appeared more contemplative, but was shaking his head slightly in dismissive fashion. Bob looked around the table.

'Play it again! Play it again!' squealed Harriet excitedly.

Bob felt as if his blood had solidified in his veins as Harriet repeated several more times, 'Play it again!' The stark realisation that Laura was right hit him like a punch in the face, as he stared at this terrifying confirmation.

The Zombie Plague was the result of an idea that could mutate the mind. Throughout history, ideas had evolved and spread from person to person, just like a virus, resulting in all sorts of changes. History is littered with the corpses of religious and political ideologies. The levels of violence and the time taken to have an effect were various. Was it so impossible that an idea could have such an extreme effect within days, or hours even? The clues were all there. Only Laura had had the ability to put it all together.

'Adam!' shouted Bob. Adam turned slowly to look at Bob. He appeared to be straining through his contemplation. His eyes appealed to Bob, as if he were being dragged away by savages for ritual sacrifice. 'Adam!' shouted Bob again. He just looked back. Bob jumped to his feet, rushed round, and shook him shouting his name. Adam responded as if woken from a hypnotic trance. 'Adam. Can you hear me?' asked Bob.

'Sorry Bob. I was miles away,' replied Adam. He looked into Bob's face and continued speaking, but more slowly. 'This New Philosophy, it's...' The words tailed off as he sunk back into contemplation. Bob looked to Harriet, his hand still on Adam's shoulders as he stooped over him.

'The soldier!' Bob said loudly, as Harriet continued her parroting of 'Play it again!' He looked through the transparent screen, and felt a couple of massive thuds of his heart. He already knew Laura would not be affected. But they didn't know about Simon, the soldier who had ignored protocol and risked the wrath of his colleagues to save Laura. The heartbeats were of relief, as he saw Simon responding intelligibly to Laura. He

171

was not unscathed. His head was lowered and Laura had her hand on his back, her head turned and looking down slightly to him, as if she was comforting a traumatised survivor of a road traffic accident on the kerbside. There was enough communication though, to signal lucidity.

Bob felt momentary relief, lifted a little by Harriet's irritating repetition subsiding. But she was not silent. She was involved in a dialogue with herself. She was repeating the ideas of the New Philosophy, sometimes questioning them, but always arriving at exactly the same ideas and words she'd heard moments before. It was remarkable. From just one hearing, Harriet was able to reconstruct the entire New Philosophy. It interacted with her mind to provide a self-replicating logic, maintaining the core components without any deviation. Each element flowed on, reinforcing what had gone before, providing its own contribution, and showing a pathway to what was to come next. The proposals and resolutions seemed to be attaching onto the end of each other, creating a chain of mutually complementary counterparts, just like the double helix of a DNA molecule.

Bob looked at the gun in his hand. He knew he had to try something, anything, before it was too late. 'Harriet!' shouted Bob. 'Harriet!' he shouted even louder. Bob let go of Adam's shoulder.

'Harriet!' He moved his face closer to hers shouting as loud as he could so that his breath would have warmed her cheeks and nose. 'Harriet!' She just carried on with her fascinating recitation. Bob slapped Harriet hard round the face and shouted her name again. She paused for a second, looked at Bob, and then started to tell him directly about the New Philosophy, ignoring the aggressive intent he'd just displayed.

The way she was beginning to talk was almost like chanting. It was reminiscent of what they had just seen related on the monitor screen, but Harriet seemed to have been influenced far more deeply, and far more quickly. Her chanting took on a beat and rhythm that invoked a memory in Bob of the call to prayer that had pleasantly awoken him each morning whilst on holiday in Luxor, along with the Gregorian chants he'd heard created in churches and cathedrals. Or maybe it was like the recitation of magic spells and hexes that people once were, and in some places still are, so fearful of. Bob slapped Harriet again. There was a momentary pause, and then she continued with her rantings.

Bob hit her again. Same response. He hit her again, harder. Same again. He carried on several times, hitting harder and harder. Harriet's face was stingingly red, and the blood from the splits inside her cheeks was reddening her teeth and escaping out of the side of her mouth. There was almost a frenzy to Bob's actions.

'Stop!' bellowed Laura. He stopped suddenly in a flash of realisation. Harriet carried on talking. She was less intelligible now, partly because of the mania setting in, partly because of the damage to her face.

Bob took a step backward. He had shocked himself, but felt justified by the fear of zombies that was now present. Harriet was babbling. Bob turned away from her and took a few steps, but she stood up and followed him, still talking about the New Philosophy. Bob stopped and peered over his shoulder, just enough to see Harriet stood directly behind him. He turned and shoved her hard on the chest. 'Get lost, Harriet!' he shouted in frustration. She stumbled backwards, losing her footing, and fell awkwardly onto a chair. She got straight back to her feet, still talking, whilst walking up to Bob, eyes fixated on him. Bob took a couple of steps back, his arms outstretched to keep Harriet away, but she remained at his fingertips. He looked down to his side, to see Adam still seated at the table in a daze. There was no question in his mind about the extremity of the situation.

Bob looked at the gun that he was still holding. He'd used firearms before. He checked it was ready to go, and pointed it at Harriet.

She was very close. The gun was a finger's length from her chest. The blood from her mouth had now found its way out of both corners of her mouth, and was trickling down her chin onto her throat. She was still chanting about the New Philosophy. Her eyes were sparkling, and her countenance was embracing the euphoria. If there were any doubts in Bob's mind, Harriet's demonic appearance quickly allayed them.

He pointed the gun down and shot to his right, taking out Harriet's kneecap. Her balance had gone, but before she could keel right over, Bob pointed to the other side and took out the other one. The blood that burst from her legs somehow complemented the blood on her face and neck, producing a finality to her appearance. She tumbled over and the chanting stopped, unable to prevent her gasps and utterances of pain. Her arms reached out to Bob as she tumbled backwards. As she lay on the floor she squirmed, unable to move her legs properly, but this didn't seem to be her main priority. Her face was a mixed contortion of smiles and pain.

She was trying to say something. The pain she was experiencing was making it difficult for her to talk, but Bob could just make it out. She was still trying to tell him about the New Philosophy. He was mortified as he realised the rapid and extreme effect of the infection. It seemed from what little they knew about zombification, no one had turned quite as thoroughly as Harriet in such a short time.

The intercom buzzed. Bob went to answer it, having to go right round the other side of the table in order to avoid the blood soaked wretch, blabbering on the floor. There was a message for Adam. He offered to take it. The operator gave a code and requested a response. Bob didn't know it. In all of Adam's previous dialogues on the intercom, it had gone unnoticed that he'd always given a response code. It may even have been that he'd hidden it from them, maybe speaking quietly and turning away. 'Hold on,' said Bob. He went over to Adam, who'd remained unmoved by the kneecapping of Harriet. Adam appeared in a daze and was mumbling. Bob felt the wrench of pessimism erupt in his stomach, like the feeling of receiving a rejection letter for a job you were sure you'd get.

'Adam!' called Bob.

'Uh?' replied Adam. There was no response. This was more encouraging than the previous encounter with Harriet. Despite Adam's increasing stupor, at least some communication appeared possible. The infection affected people in different ways, though the final outcome for those who were susceptible was inevitably the same.

'Adam!' shouted Bob repeatedly whilst shaking him.

'Bob,' said Adam. He looked into Bob's face, his conscious being breaking through. 'This New Philosophy…' he began.

'Forget that!' ordered Bob, a serious kick of aggression in his voice. Adam was startled, and more of his sentient being seemed to appear. 'I need a response code. This is really serious.' Adam took a second to look around. He was aware something must be up due to his own state, but he also knew of his great responsibility. These codes should never leave him. These simple words carried immense power. Bob realised he had to convince Adam. 'Look!' he said pointing to Harriet who was still trying to rant whilst writhing on the floor. Adam looked back at Bob. 'You know you can trust me Adam,' said Bob. He briefly explained that the New Philosophy was real, and what was happening. He looked deeply into Adam's face as he explained. As the memory of their long friendship stirred, it felt as if their souls touched. Adam strained a nod. Bob repeated what he'd heard on the intercom and Adam provided him with the response code.

Bob returned to the intercom, and responded. Bob was now in effect, Martial Governor of the UK. The operator explained that they were experiencing increasing outbreaks among the external resources. This was no surprise to Bob. Bob was about to thank the operator and hang up, then realised how important this communication line was. Once he hung up, he would no longer be recognised as acting for Adam. He ordered the operator to keep the line open. He looked over to Laura who had something urgent to say. The only separation between them was the screen.

'What if they were watching the video from the Tupelo Star in the communications room?' called Laura. Bob lifted the handset to ask the question.

'He's gone to find out,' said Bob. 'Apparently that broadcast came from another comms room.' Bob lifted the receiver to his ear to await the response. 'Yes?' he said as the operator came back on the line. Bob was silent for far longer than expected. Something else was going on. 'Ok,' said Bob, lowering the receiver. He took a deep breath and looked over to Laura, who knew.

'They did watch it,' said Bob. 'The operator on this line didn't see it. He said that they're all talking about the New Philosophy in the other room and rerunning the Tupelo Star video.'

Bob heard a voice on the intercom. The news was becoming grimmer and grimmer. Zombie outbreaks were being reported across Location Three. Bob had to think ahead quickly.

'Operator,' asked Bob. 'Can you seal your room?' The reply was affirmative, and Bob ordered it be done. Bob and Laura now had to come up with a plan. He took a chair, placed it in front of the transparent screen and sat down.

'Looks like you were right,' said Bob. Laura acknowledged with a gentle smile. Harriet could be heard jabbering to herself from the puddle of blood she was writhing in behind them, whilst Adam sat motionless at the table, sinking further into his own corrupted mind. 'Any ideas?' asked Bob, deferring to Laura.

'I guess we should let everyone know what's causing it. Tell everyone not to listen to the New Philosophy, and if they do, to be aware what it can do to them if they're not prepared.' Bob nodded and smiled. It was obvious. 'Do it now,' said Laura in a quiet low voice. Bob got up quickly to return to the intercom. He gave instructions to the operator to issue a warning to all Location Three resources and then through what remained of the wider media. He dictated careful wording for the warning, explicitly describing the threat and the need to avoid it. Anyone who heard this would be in no doubt that listening to the New Philosophy would turn them into zombies.

Bob's attention was diverted to noise coming from the corridor. It sounded almost like a party, not the kind of noise that would be expected in Location Three. Bob went to the door. He opened it slightly ajar and peeped through the gap of no more than a hand's width. It only took him a few seconds to assimilate what was happening. He closed the door slowly, carefully lifting the catch with the handle then gently shutting it down, and returned to his seat. He leant forward slightly before he spoke.

'There are people coming out of the rooms onto the corridor,' he said. 'They're all talking about the New Philosophy.' This was bad news. Even though the whole of the facility was under internal quarantine in sections isolated from each other, they were still exposed to the inevitability of the zombies.

'You need to seal the door,' said Laura. Bob didn't need telling twice. He rushed over, but the lock needed a key. He didn't have it. Even if the guard did, he was in the corridor and probably already indulging in New Philosophy talk. Bob looked around. He grabbed a chair to try to wedge under the handle, but it was too short and would easily give. He grabbed the long table. It was screwed into the floor. He pushed, shoved and kicked at it, and managed to release it from its anchors. He swung it round, not caring that it sent chairs flying, or caused Adam, who was leaning on it, to topple over.

The table clunked hard against the door. Bob looked to the far end of the table where there was a gap between it and the wall opposite the door. The table was not going to hold once the zombies caught the scent of food. He grabbed some chairs and wedged them hard in the space, trying them in all different ways, like some kind of oversized child's puzzle, eventually creating a tight fit. As the last chair locked into place, he exhaled the deepest sigh of relief he may have ever managed in his life.

Bob returned to the screen and sat on the floor, all of the chairs otherwise utilised. Laura and Simon looked down at Bob.

'What now?' said Bob. 'We can't get out,' he said, then after a pause added, 'and I don't think help is going to come.' He was right. He may now be safe, but they were all possibly residents of their own crypt. Adam was lying on the floor. He was mumbling to himself, his face looked tortured. His mind was in torment trying to reject the New Philosophy, but it was taking a hold. It was still possible to retrieve some lucidity from him, but after each attempt it became harder to do so again, as he slipped away further. Bob knew that it was only a matter of time before he'd be using the gun again. Harriet was still a pathetic rambling mess squirming in her own blood.

'How come virtually everyone seems to be affected, but none of us?' asked Simon. It was an interesting question, as there was an anomaly between the proportion of non-zombies in this group compared to it being so much higher among everyone else. They all thought for a moment. Laura offered a theory.

'There are people who aren't susceptible to the New Philosophy, but given the numbers we've seen changing around us, it's very few,' she said clarifying the position. 'It may be more than we think, as most non-susceptible people are likely to be killed very quickly.' She was right, but this didn't provide sufficient explanation.

'If we were a random group of people, then the chances of so many us being non-susceptible would be virtually zero, but we're not a random set. I'm here specifically because I'm non-susceptible. I made it here because of Simon's help, which I think I got because he's the same.' She paused for a moment. 'There may have been dozens or hundreds of people like me trying to do something. General Spelling's not turning like everyone else. Most people remain quite lucid while they spread it. I guess that he's only just susceptible and he's confused.' They stopped to look over to Adam. He was gradually assuming a foetal position, like a lost child.

'We're all independent thinkers. We don't go with the herd. We make our own decisions. I'm guessing that the General is as well, but he'd never have made it so far up in the army if he was entirely that way.'

'That's Adam,' confirmed Bob.

'And he chose you to come here because you're like him, only more so. You're what he wants to be like. So we're not a random selection at all. We've been pre-selected,' concluded Laura. It all made sense, just as her earlier revelations had. Bob looked round to Harriet on the floor.

'And I guess she was selected for all the opposite reasons,' said Bob. No one responded.

A scream from the corridor grabbed their attention. They sat up to listen. There was another, more continuous this time, along with snarling, followed by an assortment of further screams.

'It's starting,' said Laura.

'And we're trapped in here,' said Bob. Laura's expression gave away that something had occurred to her. Something important.

'Maybe we're not all trapped,' she said. 'We came in through a different way. The aim was to isolate us. But maybe that means we can now get out that same way?' They realised that she could be right. Bob acted without further prompting, and returned to the intercom, to check out the theory, and garner whatever other information he could that could help them. He returned to the screen.

'Right,' he began, 'you can get back out that way.' Laura felt relief, and then embarrassment remembering Bob's situation. He continued, 'You'll come back out in the barn. There are supplies as well for just such a situation as this.'

'An abandonment,' said Simon.

'Exactly,' said Bob unemotionally. 'Adam could order the ending of the internal quarantine, but the comms room are getting reports of zombies from all over the place.' Bob paused a second and tightened his lips before adding, 'It's too late for us in here now. It sounds like carnage out there.'

'Can you get us released then?' asked Simon, elation almost spilling into his voice.

'It's not as simple as that,' said Bob, almost inevitably. 'Comms have entered the instructions to release you.' He waited before delivering his 'but'. 'But Adam's code has to be entered into one of the intercom pads. It's a double check as part of the security.'

'Well you've got the code' said Simon, grasping at his route to survival.

'It's a different code to the one used before. I've got the new request code from the operator, but only Adam has the response,' said Bob.

'Can you bring him round again?' asked Simon, his insides starting to feel hollow as hope crumbled away,

'I think I can,' said Bob, adding, 'once more.' Simon and Laura felt relief, as they missed the apprehension in Bob's tone. 'But the intercom sets that can accept a code are only in the corridors. Silence drifted down. The implication was clear. To save Laura and Simon, Bob would have to open the door, and hope that he could enter the code before the inevitable. That was if they could get the code from Adam.

'Let's give it a go,' said Bob, no hesitation or pre-condition in his voice whatsoever. He added, 'You're the only hope there is to stop this New Philosophy destroying everyone.'

'But what can we do?' asked Laura. 'There's just the two of us. What can we do? It's not like we're a big organisation like this place. Surely if 'they' can't do anything about it, we can't?'

21. Preparing to Leave

Bob considered how naturally Laura had been able to refer to 'they', a reference used all the time by so many people, but without really knowing what was behind it. 'There is no 'they',' said Bob, 'only people, people like you. 'They' is, at best, the superbeing status people attribute to the State that they hope will make everything better, regardless of reality.'

'Look at this place,' continued Bob, 'It's in chaos. It's achieved nothing. Whereas you worked this all out. Sometimes a group can be better than one person, but when it's one good idea that's needed, an inspiration, a spark of genius, then a single person may be far better than any number of others.'

Bob added, 'It wouldn't matter how many morons you put together, they'd never come up with the Theory of Relativity, paint like Picasso, or write a great novel. The breakthroughs in history have always come from one or two people. Organisations can shackle thinking.'

He raised his eyebrow as he added, 'Of course, organisations are still far better at taking credit and exploiting ideas than any individual, but that's a different matter. Ideas can still need a lot of refinement. Great individuals still tend to need big organisations.

'Organisations don't really exist,' said Bob enigmatically, 'they're just lots of people working towards a common aim. Organisations don't make decisions or come up with ideas, People do. You can't punish or reward an organisation only, the people within it, and you can only change an organisation through them. If people know that they can get away with things leaving an ethereal organisation to take the blame, eventually someone will do it. Bankers failing customers and lining their pockets with bonuses, or hospital managers allowing patients to die whilst receiving massive pensions, are not going to change their behaviour because their organisations might be fined in a few years time once they're long gone.

Bob had a lot to say, in the little time left. 'The bigger the organisation, the more that people seem to think it's more real than the people within it, probably because it's easier for the incompetent or corrupt to hide amongst the confusion. 'They make sure that they get the rewards, but let the organisation shoulder any blame. Occasionally when public anger demands someone is held responsible, a scapegoat will be wheeled out. This might be someone who's taken all they can and is happy to retire. If more is required, there may even be a criminal prosecution, but it's always easy to find a patsy who's committed some petty misdemeanour to carry the can. Sometimes it's even for the 'crime' of whistle blowing on the real wrongdoers.

'And every time they get away with it, it's another step sunk further into the cesspit. Most people complain, but they really just want to be at the trough themselves. It's everywhere, and public corporations and public sector behemoths are the most infected with this cancerous behaviour. It's like a virus that exists wherever there are people. Is it any surprise that our whole society, the most complex of organisations, is being infected by this zombie virus? Like the New Philosophy says [THE FOLLOWING HAS BEEN CENSORED] ----------------
------REDACTED---------------------REDACTED-----------------
-----REDACTED---------------------REDACTED------------------
----REDACTED---------------------REDACTED------------------
---REDACTED---------------------REDACTED-------------------
--REDACTED---------------------REDACTED--------------------
-REDACTED

Laura and Simon sat stunned. They saw the truth in what they heard. How could Bob have lived with this knowledge crushing his heart every day, only to be released in the face of his imminent demise? His face was recovering from the anger that had driven his diatribe. Normally he wouldn't have off-loaded such emotional baggage, but as he had finally concluded, there was a relevance. He smiled again, his emotion dispersed like a wispy cloud in a clear blue sky.

He felt hope as he looked at Laura, the girl who'd brought them the extraordinary truth that had evaded them all. She still felt relatively powerless but understood what Bob was saying. She would try. She squeezed Simon's hand and he squeezed back. They could hear the rising cacophony from the corridor as the slaughtering encroached ever closer on Bob's fragile sanctuary.

'Enough dong dang,' said Bob who'd spent some time in Bengal, 'time to get on.' Laura realised that the invaluable intellect of this most interesting man would soon no longer be available to them.

'Is there anyone who can help us?' Bob didn't know how to answer. Laura rephrased the question. 'Adam found you Bob. Who else might he have asked?' Bob smiled. He thought for a second, and then nodded his head as the answer came to him.

'There's an old friend of ours,' Bob replied, 'who I'm sure Adam would have loved to have had in on this, but even Adam wouldn't dare bring in such a maverick here.' There was a lightness to Bob's statement. 'He doesn't take too well to authority, and authority hasn't taken to well to him. His name's Andy Vance.' Bob proceeded to explain where Andy could be found. An academic and philosopher among other things, he was also the closest thing to a modern day polymath, something that didn't fit well in a world increasingly obsessed with cramming people into ever shrinking boxes. Andy lived out in the country on his own, keeping away from other people for the most part, and Bob was sure that his natural distrust of the world would have ensured his survival. If anyone was an independent thinker likely to be untouched by the New Philosophy, Andy was.

As Bob reached the end of relating the details to Laura and Simon, along with various other useful snippets, the mood turned sombre. They'd all been momentarily lifted by Laura and Simon's opportunity to escape and the invaluable information Bob had imparted. But now they found themselves at the beginning of the next instalment. It was like sending Bob off to his own funeral and asking him to get into the crematorium furnace himself. Laura felt herself swallow hard. Bob knew it was unreasonable to wallow.

'Right. What's to be done?' he asked jauntily, as he stood up. 'I'll get the code,' he said in a workman like tone. He grabbed Adam by the front of his jacket, lifting him up from the ground. He proceeded to shout, cajole and plead with Adam. Adam's stupor was setting in harder. Adam seemed too far gone but as Bob persevered, he gradually began to respond. As he reached the boundary of ample lucidity, Bob attempted to gain the necessary code. Adam was struggling to understand, but Bob wouldn't give up. He couldn't. He looked into Adam's face, and managed to connect with his gaze, touching deep into his psyche. Adam seemed to listen to Bob. He didn't reply. Bob waited a second then Adam painfully, slowly recited the code they needed, as if a dying man's last words.

'Thank you, Adam,' said Bob as he sensed what was to come. Adam's face glazed over as he fell from his lucidity back deep into his stupor for the last time. Anguish rolled over Bob as he watched his friend vanish forever. Adam's glazed expression began to stretch into a smile.

'The New Philosophy,' he uttered as he stared into the distance. Bob let go of Adam with a start, and despite only being raised to a sitting position on the floor, he fell back hard. 'The New Philosophy,' he said again.

'I've got the code,' said Bob as he stood up, disregarding Adam while he still could. Bob went over to Laura and Simon and they came up with a plan. It was a long shot, definitely suicidal for Bob, but it could just work.

Bob dragged the mumbling Harriet over to the screen. It was not possible to tell if she'd zombified, as she'd now lost so much blood, her movements and speech were extremely weak. Even without the plan that they had come up with, she would not live much longer. Bob dragged Adam over to the screen as well. The friend had gone, but the remaining presence could still be a useful prop.

All this time, the noise outside had been increasing, the screams, the gnashing and the grisly feasting. There had been thuds at the door and against the wall. Up to this point, they had just been part of the overall melee, but now the door handle was starting to be rattled, and the bangs were getting stronger as they became attempts to break in. Even without his self-sacrifice, Bob knew that he wouldn't have much longer. The three of them quickly confirmed their plans.

The door suddenly opened, violently forcing back the table an inch or so and rattling the chairs at the other end, squeezing them tighter against the wall. Laura saw Bob's startled expression. He knew that he had to act immediately. Despite his age, he got under the table quickly. The table was jolting around him as the battering of the door continued. The chairs had wedged tight at the other end, and may have held for a while longer. Bob lay on his back, his feet towards the chairs. He rolled his head to the side to look over to Laura and Simon. Bob nodded and the pair started banging on the screen and shouting. Simon picked up a chair and was hitting it against the transparent barrier, significantly increasing the hullabaloo. He knew these screens were virtually impenetrable, even to the zombies. The battering at the door intensified as the beasts beyond realised that something was inside, something that might be tasty.

Bob turned his head to look up at the bottom of the table as he lay on his back. He noticed a couple of pieces of chewing gum that had been wedged into the edges. He wondered who might have done this, and what was occurring in the room at the time. He closed his eyes, and with an almighty thrust, kicked at one of the chairs wedged at the other end of the table. It gave way first time, flying out and spinning across the room, only stopping as it reached the screen. The release of pressure was followed instantaneously by a charge at the door forcing the table forward. It opened wide enough for a surge of zombie to enter.

Bob couldn't really feel the extreme terror that should have been engulfing him as the adrenaline inflated his veins. His neck was craning back towards the door, watching the legs of the zombies go by. Their trousers and skirts were covered in blood. He wondered if the skirts were more bloodied than the trousers, and what that might mean. He snapped out of his musings.

He looked over towards the screen. At least four zombies had reached Harriet and Adam, with more of them running across the room to join in. The diversion was working. The noise Simon and Laura were making had effortlessly seized the zombies' attention. Once they'd reached the screen, the lure of bodies on the floor had fully engrossed them. As their blood sprayed up over the screen, Bob couldn't tell whether or not Adam and Harriet had mercifully died within seconds. In any case, it was probably irrelevant, as the quirky nature of the New Philosophy had rendered them both virtually devoid of feeling. The Martial Governor was no more.

Bob diverted his eyes from the gore, sharply looking above it. He saw Laura and Simon, still fulfilling their part of the bargain, shouting and banging vigorously. The horror of the stomach churning spectacle in full view at their feet was clear on their face, but they still continued. Bob could see that Simon was waiting for him to act, and that the window of potential opportunity was closing fast.

Bob strained his head up to look towards the doorway. There was a problem. Although the door had opened wide enough for the throng of zombies to get in, it was stopped by the table from fully opening. It was only wide enough for one thing at a time. He couldn't see through to make sure there wasn't a zombie immediately in his path. He had to act quickly, and wriggled forward towards the door grabbing a leg of the table. He wrenched it sideways, taking the table with it towards the centre of the room. The door flung open. Bob had achieved the next stage of the plan, but was now completely exposed.

A lagger stumbled through the door. Bob felt a freezing chill as he anticipated the zombie looking down at him. Laura and Simon's alarm was still working though, and once the zombie had looked straight at the source of the noise, it was pulled straight towards the shambles of blood and flesh on the floor.

As it turned and rushed towards the screen Bob felt an almighty thump of his heartbeat.

The doorway was now clear. He had to go. He knew that a zombie could come through at any instant running straight into him, but this was always a risk that he was going to have to take. He went for it.

He managed to successfully get to his feet whilst rushing forward. As he approached the door he imagined the bloodstained face of a zombie appearing right in front of him. The closer he got to the doorway, the more certain he was that this zombie was going to run straight into him, until he reached the gap and closed his eyes ready for the inevitable.

It was like pushing through into another world as he stepped out of the room. He'd not bumped into anything and opened his eyes expecting the zombie to be there about to pounce. It wasn't. He'd made it. He stopped for a moment to look around. He had to find the intercom. It was better than he'd hoped for, but still horrific. The saving grace was the lack of zombies in the immediate vicinity, though there were some in the distance. It seemed that their plan was more successful than he could have hoped for, and had drawn in all of the nearby zombies. The grey walls were now daubed with a macabre graffiti of blood. At the bottom of some of these red washes were the torn remain of bodies crumpled on the floor. Other streaks continued as slithers of blood curling along the floor. Some ended in another torn body. Some branched off into narrower slithers, leading occasionally to barely recognisable human limbs, or to nothing except bloodied footsteps leading away. Most of the doors on the various rooms stretching down the corridor were open, and various screaming and frenzied feeding was emanating from them.

Bob shuddered as he saw further along a zombie knelt on all fours chewing the body of their guard. A couple of doors up, a small group of zombies were barging at a door. Some were almost using their shoulders, whilst others were running straight into it, as if into an invisible wall, smashing their faces and spraying blood everywhere as they fell back. Bob looked at the door to the room that he'd just come from. There was a roundish shape of various bloodied smudges on it at face height. He looked back down the corridor running into a door. He hadn't been noticed, yet.

Bob saw the intercom across the corridor a few yards away. He'd been fortunate. He ran over and lifted the handset, revealing the keypad. It would only take a few seconds to enter the code, but even this may be too long. He pressed the first button. He winced as the pad made a beep. He pressed the second one. A zombie staggered from the interrogation room. Its face and hair were entirely red. Even its bared teeth only afforded the occasional flash of white. The kill in the room had been nearly consumed.

The zombie didn't notice Bob until it had taken a couple of steps. It opened its mouth hissing an inhuman cry, as it ran straight towards him, arms and fingers outstretched ready to start feasting. The intercom let out a longer beep as Bob pressed the enter button on the pad. The code was accepted.

'Done it!' said Bob to himself with a mix of jubilation and resignation. He closed his eyes and watched his past life pass by, thankful for so much of it being pleasurable.

22. Released

In the interrogation room the zombies were nearing the end of their meal. Laura and Simon's view of the mess on the floor was obscured by the blood covering the screen between them and the main room, but they could still see plenty to the sides. Some of them had become aware of Laura and Simon. They couldn't smell them, but something in their ravaged minds told them that they moved as if they were tasty. Some were hammering at the screen, whilst others were repeatedly running at it and bouncing off. Laura and Simon thought that they heard Bob screaming, but could not be sure.

A whirring noise activated behind them ending with a click from the door that they had entered through. They rushed over and tried it, eager to leave behind the events of the interrogation room. Simon held the door handle for a second and looked back. They realised that if it didn't open, they'd failed. Simon braced himself, and gently twisted the handle. It did not give.

'Harder,' said Laura. Simon didn't respond, frozen by disappointment. Laura pushed him aside and gave the handle a strong twist. It was stiff, but she was able to turn it all the way. The door opened, just in time for them to see the lift that had brought them to their current set of circumstances gently coming to rest from its descent. They knew they had to be quick. It was all automatic now. They briskly made their way to the lift, closing the door behind them. The screaming became more distant, as if halfway through awakening from a nightmare.

Nothing happened as they stood in the lift. A full minute must have passed, and still nothing. Was it working? There were no controls for them to try. They were utterly powerless. Suddenly, it began to whirr, and they felt it joyously rising. The sound of the screaming grew more distance until the whirring of the lift covered it entirely, and it was gone, freeing their senses from the preceding trauma. The lift clunked to a stop. The automatic door opened. They were back in the barn.

They started breathing heavily, overcome with relief. It was still dark and gloomy, though their eyes were better adjusted having this time come from artificial light. They turned to each other, embraced, and then both started sobbing, the relief overflowing out of them. Their tears subsided and they released each other. The intensity and danger of the situation had not left them, and though they'd needed the release that they'd just shared, they also knew that it may have cost them essential seconds.

They stepped from the lift into the barn. The lights were on but the large front doors were closed. They glanced at the vehicles in the barn. There were as an estate car and a saloon. They were ramshackle and rusty. They looked like they hadn't been used for several years. They might get around in them, but a concerted zombie attack would probably succeed. Laura and Simon felt dismayed, but knew they had to carry on.

Simon went over to the wall as they'd been instructed, and looked carefully. He counted along the steel support girders from the front to the fourth one. It was an I-beam that was just able to hide a small box round the back at about knee height. It would normally be locked and the switch inside useless. Thanks to Bob, the lock had been released. As Simon flicked the switch, a large door towards the back of the barn could be seen to be sliding open, and dull but sufficient lighting sparked into life. The design of the barn intentionally created the illusion that there was nothing beyond the door that was now sliding open.

They both made their way past the straw bales towards the back. They felt that at last something was going right. The rusting vehicles at the front were just a cover. There were now two substantial four by four vehicles in front of them. They only needed one. Each was armoured and had large wheels. They were a shiny, sinister black with tinted windows, which oddly was appropriate camouflage for such a vehicle, most owners preferring this type of look. Both vehicles were open with the keys in the ignition. Inside they were luxurious; any abandonment was expected to involve General Adam Spelling. They opened the backs of the vehicles and found each full of adequate supplies; food, water, fuel, tents, maps, and assorted weaponry. Simon chose a type of handgun that he was familiar with to keep at his side.

The pair quickly loaded all of the supplies from one of the vehicles into the other. They considered taking the keys from the stripped vehicle with them, but realised that as it would be of no use to the zombies, it might help anyone else who might find it, however unlikely. They got into their vehicle. It started first time. They felt lucky, ignoring the wider circumstances in which they found themselves. They drove up to the front of the barn. The doors were still closed, but as they'd been told there would be, there was a release button in their car. Any abandonment was anticipated to be hostile, so being able to drive straight out without stopping was essential. Simon pressed the button. The doors slid open.

They squinted slightly, expecting to feel the hit of the strong daylight in their faces that had been denied them for so long. It didn't happen. It was dark outside, the middle of the night. They'd lost all track of time and clearly Location Three worked whenever it had to. They could see a dark heap in the distance. As they drove forward, they put on the lights, shooting through the blackness and illuminating the wreckage of the helicopter.

They'd not had a chance to view it on their arrival whilst running away. It was a twisted lump, the rotors scrunched and dangling like mangled, wilting flower stalks. They struggled to believe that they'd survive such a wreck. As the vehicle moved forward bumping over the rough terrain, they saw the body of the helicopter doorman, the zombie that had tried to kill them. It was not how they had left it. It was torn apart revealing flesh and bone, the ground around it darkened. It may have been animals that had done this, but they both realised that was unlikely. The threat from the zombies was ever present. They felt vulnerable. The terrain was rough and it was unnerving not knowing the ground, even though their vehicle was robust and making progress.

They could see a gate across the field. They were nearly there and so far, no zombie attack. They might just make it. As they approached, they could see that it was closed. The thought of getting out, or even opening the door to the wild world outside was too much to bear. Their vehicle was well enforced with various bull bars and bumpers. Simon put his foot down. They bumped violently as they suddenly gained speed over the rough ground, smashing into the gate.

The gate was flimsy in the face of their car, and was easily flung open, twisting and contorting in the process, tearing it from its hinges as it rattled to the ground. The vehicle hardly stuttered, skidding slightly as it turned sharply onto the road. The lights illuminated the clear road ahead far into the distance. They accelerated rapidly keen to escape the hell from whence they'd come. They didn't want to think about Location Three anymore, the soon to be dehumanised tomb.

23. The Shop

They travelled for over half an hour before they encountered any buildings, a rare occurrence travelling through the tiny land of England. They had maps and the location of Andy Vance that Bob had given them, or at least the isolated house where he lived, and had been deliberately avoiding main roads. They'd plotted out a route which meant that they should be able to reach him without encountering any substantially inhabited areas, although it was impossible to avoid such places entirely. They also wanted to avoid any army units. There was a curfew, and even though they're vehicle would be authorised to be out, it was always better to avoid any potential trouble. Furthermore, even with the instructions out warning everybody about the connection between the New Philosophy and the zombie infection, it wasn't worth risking that everyone had received it.

Laura wondered to herself what the leaders of the New Philosophy might be doing now. If they're aim had been to create a zombie plague, they'd scored a massive success. It was hard to believe that anyone would want to do this though. What kind of minds would not only to want create this havoc, but have been able to do so? It occurred to her that they must be some kind of geniuses. As many geniuses pay the price for their intellect through deep mental flaws, maybe it wasn't so surprising that anybody who could create something so incredible, could also be driven by a darker desire. She wondered if the New Philosophers' intention had been something else, and it was meant to do something quite different. She wondered if she would ever know the answers.

Laura felt the car slowing down, as they approached some buildings, less than a quarter of a mile away. Ahead of them was a settlement of about twenty houses. As they got closer, they could see that the building nearest to them was a small shop. The car stopped, still some distance away from the building.

'What are you doing?' asked Laura. Simon turned off the engine and the lights of the car went out, plunging the road ahead and everywhere around them into darkness. It was the dead of night. There was no sign yet anywhere on the horizon of dawn approaching.

'We need to take on more supplies if we can get them,' replied Simon, guided by his military training. He was right. Although they had plenty for a few days, they had no idea how long they might be relying on them, and they had room to fit in plenty more. Simon looked out into the gloom. It was virtually pitch black. There was no light in the village. The moon was just beyond new and the sky cloudless, providing what little illumination there was, but it was inadequate. Simon pressed a button that wound down one of the rear windows. He only let it open about a third of the way. A grasping hand might get through, but no more, before they'd be able to speed off.

The clear sky also ensured a crisp night, and they felt the cold air drifting into their comfortable heated space. They sat still, listening. They allowed their ears to adjust to the silence, just as one might allow their eyes to adjust to a dark room. They heard nothing. They continued to listen. Still nothing. It was absolute silence, the sort of silence that people who live in cities don't realise is real silence, until they find themselves in the countryside, quite naked without the normal ubiquitous hum of thousands of relentless vehicles. They continued to listen. They listened longer than they needed to, to be absolutely sure that there was nothing out there. They still needed to summon up the courage, or maybe stupidity, to get out of the car.

Simon opened the door, as quietly as he could. He went to the back, careful not to make a noise, partly so as not to attract any attention should there be any zombies nearby, but also to hear any impending attack against the silent soundscape. Simon heard a faint rustle. He froze. Maybe he should have rushed straight back into the safety of the car, but having chosen the freeze option, he stuck with it. The silence returned, more intensely. His ears had become so attuned that he'd heard a nocturnal animal rustling through the undergrowth some way off. He continued on his mission, more quickly, but still deftly. He retrieved from the back of the vehicle a torch and a big gun, and then quickly returned to safety.

'Ready,' he said to Laura. She nodded. He started the car. The noise was deafening after their close scrutiny of the rural still. They were sure that they were about to see zombies running at them from all directions. The lights lit up the road all the way to the shop and beyond. There was nothing there. The vehicle rolled off to travel the short distance to the shop, and pulled up outside. The engine went silent again.

They opened the doors and got out. Having committed to their course of action, they wanted to get it over with quickly. The door of the shop was wide open. The various blood smears on the buildings and ground and the occasional discarded body or limb barely registered with them now. They entered the shop. It was only small, not much bigger than someone's living room. It may even have been that once upon a time, changing as the locals' numbers had expanded, though the settlement still wasn't quite big enough to be called a village.

It was cold in the shop, the sort of cold one rarely encounters in buildings, the sort that comes from a complete lack of power and use. It was the cold of the outside, in its place there, but incongruous and strikingly evident in a manmade structure. The usual warmth of the inside, that subconscious comfort, had gone from this place.

They looked around the shelves. One set had been knocked over. There were smashed jars and dented tins randomly scattered. And blood. This was of no interest to them. They were only interested in what might be of use.

'Here,' said Simon. He was pointing at cans and plastic bottles of soft drinks and water, the ones without blood stains. There were also crisps and chocolate. Bluey, grey covers of mould could be seen enveloping the loaves of bread through their transparent plastic covers. There were some boxes of cakes, and some apples, which although beginning to wither were still edible. The apples, and some other fruits which were now rotten, were in large twee wicker baskets, carefully chosen by the owners to create a rustic feel. They were ideal for filling with the supplies to take out to the car, once the waste had been tipped onto the floor. They rapidly began filling them. They'd be able to get what they managed to scavenge from the shop back to the car in a couple of trips.

In their eagerness, they were oblivious to the obliteration of the silence, and didn't hear the danger until it was nearly upon them.

'Stop!' whispered Laura, who heard it first. The sounds of rapid footsteps and animalesque panting were blended together, and close. They looked to the window by the door of the shop and saw the familiar faceless, shadowy form flashing by to appear in the doorway. It had found meat, and didn't stop as it continued its shambling towards Laura and Simon. Laura saw its grotesque face bearing down on her. The blood was a fresh red, and the zombie lacked the encrusted covering of the older ones.

It was now only a couple of seconds away. How could they have been so stupid? They were safe in the car, but they'd chosen to walk straight into obvious danger. She felt like a character in a horror movie who'd ignored all of the signs that the audience could see. Simon's training kicked in. He lifted the big gun and a tremendous shot rang out. It was a very big gun. The zombie's head disintegrated, splashing blood across the whole shop.

'Quick!' said Simon as he picked up a basket, placing the gun on top. Laura followed him out of the shop with another basket. As they reached the car they could see in the distance, about five or six buildings, away another zombie making its way towards them, and then another one a similar distance back. Simon felt brave. 'Get the rest!' he ordered Laura. Her instinct was that this was ludicrous, but she felt unable to resist Simon's command, and ran back into the shop to get the baskets. As she picked them up, one on top of the other and made her way back out, she expected to hear the bangs of the big gun going off again, but didn't. She was apprehensive as she reached the door, fearing the worst.

Simon was loading his baskets into the car and grabbed Laura's to put them in quickly. The zombie's were nearly upon them. Simon might have been being gung-ho, or maybe he didn't want to keep signalling their whereabouts with the big gun. It was hard to tell. He shouted at Laura to get into the car, and she complied again. As she slammed the door, the momentary rush of relief was forced aside by the sight through the windscreen of a zombie now a couple of steps away.

Laura heard the back door slam as Simon shut it, then the head of the zombie ahead of her disintegrated in unison with the bang of the big gun. Spots of blood landed on the windscreen. There was a second bang, and the other zombie, several steps behind the first but close enough to prevent Simon from getting back into the vehicle, succumbed to the same fate. In the distance at least two more zombies were making their way to the car. Simon got in.

The doors were now closed and the windows shut. Safety. Simon started the engine and they sped off towards the newly arrived zombies. There was no particular point in trying to avoid them as they were trying to get in front of the vehicle. It was more than a match and easily shattered and smacked them aside. It was clear that there were still plenty more zombies to come before the warning about the New Philosophy reached the population.

24. The Child

Laura and Simon's encounter in the small shop had left them rattled. They drove for some time, on through the darkness, saying nothing. The dark edge of the horizon off to their right was beginning to turn a pale grey as the light of day began to break through. As they travelled on, the blue of the daytime sky began to break through. The bleak solid black of night was now retreating as the stars faded away. It would soon be full daylight. It was already bright enough to illuminate the greenery of the countryside, as they traversed the undulating roads.

Up ahead they saw some buildings, a similar settlement to the one where they had acquired some extra supplies back in the recent dead of night. They had passed through a couple of other such places since, but had sped straight through, fearful of what might be hidden under the cloak of night. They'd also seen zombies. Some were just stalking, black shadows, glimpsed through their side windows. They couldn't be sure, but their guess was probably right. Occasionally, a shadow would stumble into the glare of their headlights, flashing up the now familiar blood soaked and encrusted wretch eager to eat them. A quick swerve and no hesitation was ample to avoid these encounters.

Now as they approached this newly encountered place, the world seemed to have changed. It felt altogether more hospitable in the cleansing light of dawn, though the danger was only partially mitigated. The illusion of safety the light afforded caused Simon to slow down as they approached.

As they slowed and no attack came, Simon felt confident to slow further until they were just rumbling along. The place appeared deserted. There were plenty of signs of carnage, the ubiquitous blood smears and limbs, along with crashed vehicles. The doors on most houses were open. Some looked as though they may have been left ajar while the householder was doing some early morning gardening, a not uncommon occurrence in quaint villages. Others showed various signs of chaos, from the odd broken window pane or dent, through to being ripped from hinges and smattered with blood. The place seemed lifeless, but they knew the zombies were around, ready to flock to the hum of the vehicle passing through. Laura wondered if anyone else had survived, or if there was enough humanity left for them to try and save. She gazed over the apocalyptic landscape, trying to ignore the devastation whilst scouring for any sign that could provide the slightest speck of hope.

'Look,' she suddenly said, her voice eager, but not raised. She pointed to a building ahead on the left of the street. Simon didn't stop immediately, but slowed a little more as they approached. He leant over the steering wheel of the car, his face so close to the windscreen that his breath was starting to fog on it as he tried to make out what Laura was looking at.

'That window there,' she said, realising that Simon was struggling to identify the cause of her excitement. As Simon saw what she was pointing at, he couldn't help but bring the car to a stop just outside of the building. They were both now staring up at a window. They could see a young child, a girl of around seven years of age. Her head was peeping over the sill just enough for her eyes to see over, and her waving hands were only just visible. The child was down so low, not because she was small, but because she was trying to get their attention without attracting anything else.

'What do we do?' asked Simon. They were overwhelmed by their natural desire to help, to get the child and save her, a part of their nature that had got them this far. They looked at the door of the building. It had been smashed in. They had no way of telling what might be inside, and once within, they could be trapped by zombies within an instant. If the girl was to try and come down through the house herself, she would face exactly the same danger, such a slight thing becoming an instant meal. Although it would be a most heroic act to attempt to get the child out, it would be suicidal. They would be no match for the inevitable zombie army. In the distance they could hear a shriek.

'She's safe in there if she's survived this long,' said Laura, confirming what they were both thinking, struggling to alleviate her conscience. They looked up again. The girl had a dirty face. She was pale, and was pointing at her mouth. They couldn't just go without doing anything.

'You get ready to drive,' said Simon, as he opened the door and jumped out into the realm of extreme danger. He ran to the back of vehicle and got out some supplies that they'd acquired that night. He signalled to the girl to open the window. She tried to, but it was stiff, and she was only small. It wasn't budging. Simon held up a plastic bottle of fizzy pop and waved it at her. Her face lit up, and she yanked hard at the window, wrenching it open. It made a high pitched squeaking sound that rang out though the buildings, the echo seeming to take forever to fade as it chased around. Simon's face cringed as the signal went out. He threw the bottle at the window and hit the wall. He was a skilled, but needed to calibrate. The bottle bounced back and off the bonnet of the car, sending out another signal as the clang echoed. He threw another bottle and this one was on target. Then another and another. The girl vanished from view, desperate to sate her thirst. Simon carried on throwing whatever he could, chocolate, apples, a box of cereal.

'They're here,' came a matter of fact call from Laura, almost in a sing song. Simon looked and saw the zombies appearing at the end of the road. It had taken them well under a minute to arrive, and confirmed their fear that an attempted rescue would have claimed their lives. The zombies were a way off, but more could just as easily appear from the sides at any moment, seconds away. Simon thought for a second whether he had time to throw up anything else to the girl, but knew it could cost him his life. He slammed the back door shut and leapt into the passenger side of the vehicle. The bottle that had bounced from the wall was on the floor right by the door. He dare not even stop to take the split second to pick it up, but once he was sat inside and could see how far away the zombies still were, he leant down and scooped up the bottle. He was only a slam of the passenger door away from safety. He took hold of the door handle to slam and Laura revved the engine. It seemed to make the zombies move faster towards them. Just as he was about pull the door, he glanced up at the window. He looked at the bottle in his hand and with a skilful flick of his wrist, dispatched it straight through the window to the girl.

'Go!' said Simon before he'd even shut the door. The wheels spun, the car surged forward and the door slammed. They were safe and had probably saved the girl. They now had greater reason than ever to try and do something to stop this plague, if they could. Their mission had all seemed unreal up to that point, trying to save the whole of the human race, but now it was about this single child that they had encountered and looked into the face of. It was now more real.

As they accelerated forward, the zombies gravitated directly into their path. Each and every one of them was a threat to the young girl, and Laura made no efforts to avoid them, even swerving to clip those that hadn't managed to quite get themselves into the unforgiving path of the vehicle. Simon watched Laura with surprise. Only a few zombies had come out so far, and as Laura passed the last, she looked at the rear view mirror to survey the damage she had inflicted on them. She could see that one was writhing on the floor, severely damaged by its encounter with the car.

Simon's head thumped on the dashboard. Laura had slammed on the brakes before he'd attached his seatbelt. 'What the…' began Simon.

'Look,' said Laura, pointing backwards between the two of them through the rear windscreen. A group of zombies were gathering at the house of the little girl and beginning to enter. Their act of salvation had alerted the zombies. They may have even heard the girl eagerly guzzling the first food and drink that she'd probably had in days. She was now going to be the food. She must have barricaded herself in somehow to have survived this long, but there were so many zombies, and they seemed to be getting hungrier and more persistent in their quest for food.

Laura and Simon were mortified. How could their attempt to help have had such a grotesque opposite effect? Laura looked ahead and changed gear. The wheels spun, screeching as she reversed, far faster than they had previously proceeded forward. The wheels crunched over the body of the writhing zombie, completing the job. As the car reached the front of the house, she slammed on the brakes, skidding to a halt, but not before she thumped into a couple of the closest zombies, sending them hurtling into the group. Simon gasped in sudden fear as he thought they may overshoot, damaging the vehicle and rendering them stranded. Laura had deliberately stopped well before this.

'The doors are locked?' she asked Simon. He looked around as she did also to double check and nodded, a pointless but comforting precaution. Laura hit the horn. The piercing hoot rang out. Almost immediately the car vibrated to the thud of zombies attacking it, like wasps on an unfortunate rambler falling into their nest. Some jumped on top. One started face butting the passenger window as it ran at it. All of the zombies that had entered the house now came out to join in the assault on the vehicle, diverted from their speculative quest for food to this more definite one. Laura knew that they were safe in any vehicle supplied for the Martial Governor. She engaged the controls and the vehicle began to crawl forward. She kept it at a steady speed, ensuring that all of the zombies kept up, following the bait away from the house. The numbers were increasing. The windows were now becoming obscured by the zombies that had climbed onto the bonnet and were hanging off the roof. Even though the vehicle was more than capable of handling the onslaught, Laura and Simon couldn't help but feel the creeping onset of fear that it may be breached. Not being able to see, though, was a real threat.

They crawled on until they were a good few hundred yards away from the house of the little girl and had the full attention of every zombie within range. They correctly assumed that the zombies had little short term memory. Laura accelerated a little more. Within a couple of seconds, there was a bump. They were sure it was the body of a zombie crunching under the wheels, but they knew they could quite easily be off the road at any moment. Laura gave the steering wheel a couple of rapid turns from side to side, flicking the vehicle to dislodge the zombies just enough from the bonnet for her to see ahead. Plenty were still holding on, and some of those that had fallen off were still trying to follow. She carried on, not much faster, allowing the zombies to carry themselves away from the little girl, with the occasional flick to clear her view. The number of zombies on the vehicle gradually decreased as each lost its grip. After about five minutes, the last one fell off. Laura operated the washer and wipers to remove the bloody smears from the windscreen, and sped up.

They were back on their way to try to find Andy Vance. Their encounter had given them much to think about, and hope. Not only were there survivors, but even very young children had managed to survive, and possibly, not be affected by the New Philosophy. They were encouraged that there was still plenty of humanity left to save.

25. The Unit

They watched the buildings shrinking in the wing mirrors of their car, until they slid out of sight as they took a bend, then carried on down the road descending ahead of them. Laura and Simon had mixed feelings. They felt partly jubilant that they had stopped a zombie attack on the little girl in the house, and reduced the size of the threat. This was more than overwhelmed though, by the shroud of guilt they felt at not having embarked on a futile attempt to rescue her that would have inevitably ended with their destruction.

Dawn had fully arrived now. The sun had climbed well above the horizon, though still some way off its lowly winter pinnacle. They were making good progress and had travelled well over a hundred miles since leaving Location Three. They could expect to arrive at Andy Vance's place sometime that afternoon. They were still keeping to the quieter roads, but they knew that there could still be further encounters.

Even though they were aware that there were possibly many survivors, virtually all of them were surviving on the basis of being barricaded away and off the streets. They'd be hoping that the authorities would bring relief or an end to the plague before their supplies had run out. Those who'd only managed to squirrel away a few supplies may already be starting to succumb to hunger or thirst. If they knew what Laura and Simon knew of the fate of Location Three, they wouldn't be quite so hopeful.

As they came out of a sharp bend, they could see an army Landrover stopped by the side of the road around half a mile ahead. Their pulses thumped as they anticipated what may come next. They slowed slightly. If need be, they would probably have been able to make a quick u-turn and speed away before even reaching the vehicle. The only real threat they were likely to face now was zombies, as the warning about the New Philosophy should have reached the army units. Their vehicle had authorisation and Simon was still in his military fatigues, though they were showing plenty of signs of their recent adventures. As they got closer, they could see a couple of soldiers stood outside the vehicle, leaning against the doors. Their movements were resonant of happily chatting, salient human beings. Laura and Simon continued to approach.

They knew it would be odd if they sped straight through, so as they got closer they prepared to stop to exchange a few words, and Simon lowered his window in anticipation. The men ahead were out of their bio chem suits, no longer worried that the plague was caused by a virus. At last, hope.

'Hi Guys,' said Simon through the passenger window as they approached. He couldn't see the faces of the soldiers who were chatting on the other side of the road as Laura and Simon came to a halt. It seemed a little odd to him, that a vehicle being out should warrant so little attention from the unit. He realised that it was probably because of their vehicle's authorisation, and the unit didn't want to seem to be questioning the very important people they would expect it to be carrying.

'Hi Guys,' called Simon again, this time louder. They turned their heads, and looked pleased to see him. As they strolled over to the window, they appeared fairly happy given the circumstances. In fact they were very happy, smiling broadly. Laura felt a chill.

'Don't get out,' she said to Simon, and kept the engine running. Simon already had no intentions of leaving their sanctuary. As the two soldiers reached the car, one leant on the door through the open passenger window.

'Nice,' he said. It was odd behaviour, given that he should have expected to be addressing a senior officer. He grinned at Laura, as if her somewhat bedraggled appearance was entirely normal for a driver. 'Have you heard about this New Philosophy thing,' said the soldier. The familiar mantra sent a shockwave of dread through Simon and Laura. The soldier continued, 'you know, this thing that they say is causing the zombie plague.'

The relief nearly caused Laura to burst into tears. They'd got the warning. The message was getting through. The nightmare may soon be over. No wonder the soldiers were so happy and relaxed.

'You heard?' asked Simon to reinforce his relief.

'Yes, of course we did, hours ago,' came the reply. It looked like Bob's last few acts had saved them all. The soldier turned away from Simon and carried on talking to his colleague. Laura wasn't sure exactly what they were saying, but she thought that she could make out something. She strained to listen, leaning over towards the passenger door window to hear better. Simon could hear. He was expressionless.

'They're still talking about the New Philosophy,' said Laura.

'I know,' said Simon.

'And how great it is.'

'I know,' replied Simon again. The soldiers carried on talking as Simon prepared to enter the situation cautiously.

'Guys, how did you find out what the New Philosophy is about?' asked Simon. The soldier leaning on his door turned to him. He grinned enthusiastically, pleased that Simon wanted to know more about it.

'Well, when they warned us about it over comms, we wondered what it was exactly and wanted to find out more. We knew it would be okay to listen to it, because we'd been warned,' replied the soldier.

'Yes?' came the drawn out response from Simon.

'Well, everyone else had thought the same. We got onto comms and there'd been a few people who knew about it and were telling everyone. Soon we all knew about it.' The soldier finished with a big grin, happy to have explained how he'd joined in with the mass conversation. Simon and Laura realised that the warnings from Location Three about the New Philosophy had ensured that it had spread quicker than ever. Even though everyone had been told that listening to it would change them, they had presumed that they would be safe as long as they were aware of the danger. No one could accept that they were just like everybody else, susceptible and possessing human weaknesses. Each of them was now being led over the cliff of self-destruction, by their egos convincing them that they were the special ones. After all, it was only words, and they all so wanted to know what it said.

'Come and join in,' said the soldier still grinning.

'What do you mean?' asked Simon. Laura leant back into the driver's seat, pulled there by her apprehension. She gripped the steering wheel and held her foot over the accelerator, wrought by grisly foreboding.

'We've been talking about it all morning. It's great. You've got to listen. All four of us love it,' said the soldier beginning to confirm Laura and Simon's worst fears. Simon looked at the soldier who'd been speaking and then the others. There were only three of them. He moved his head to look round the soldier at the window into the Landrover. He could see a fourth seated in the back. Simon could make out a beaming face with a broad grin, made incongruous by the dribble and spittle dripping from his lower lip. He was slightly hunched and appeared to be hyperventilating. Horror washed over Simon repeatedly. He had to hold it together.

'You know that the warning said that listening to the New Philosophy is what turns people into zombies?' Simon asked the soldier as calmly as he could, but his voice was quivering.

'Yeah, course. But forget that. It's brilliant. Come on. Get out. Let us tell you all about it.' The soldier grabbed the handle of the passenger door and opened it. Simon quickly grabbed the interior handle and pulled the door back. The soldier was startled. His face was only a few inches from Simon's and increasingly manic. Simon needed to find the right words very quickly.

'Ok. Just let us park up a second, and we'll be over,' said Simon deceitfully. The soldier grinned more as if his face might split, and let go of the door. Simon turned to Laura. His face was terror itself. Before she could even turn and look forward fully, she'd floored the accelerator and they were speeding away. The other soldiers remained in the road chatting. If they knew about the impending turn awaiting their colleague in the Landrover, they may not have been quite so carefree, but given their absorption in the New Philosophy, it may have made no difference.

Simon and Laura were breathing rapidly as their bodies responded to the adrenaline release. Another escape.

'You know what this means?' said Simon.

'Yes,' said Laura.

The warnings hadn't worked. People still wanted to listen to New Philosophy. Knowing it was a bad idea was no protection, and once they were warned, they'd all been desperate to hear about it, to taste the forbidden fruit.

26. Meeting

Laura and Simon continued on their journey to find Andy Vance. They didn't intend to stop unless they had to, helped by their extra large fuel tank. There was a kind of solace, a safety in their own tiny world within the car, made all the more intense by their failed attempt to stem the zombie plague. If anything, it seemed that they had made it worse, causing people to seek it out, having acquired little, if any, resistance. Laura and Simon were beginning to feel that their efforts may be futile, and that it was only a matter of time before they fell victim to ravenous zombies; their supplies would not last indefinitely.

Their only hope was vested in their last moments at Location Three. Bob had sacrificed himself to save them, a spirit of humanity from the depths of the most savage hell that might just signal a way through. If Andy Vance could live up to Bob's promise, maybe, just maybe, along with Laura and Simon's knowledge of the New Philosophy, there may be a chance.

As the car droned along the empty roads towards the tiny hope they still clung to, they ignored the occasional zombies they saw, as they became a part of the everyday landscape. They had little time to react as the vehicle whizzed past, or were easily avoided by a shallow swerve.

It was well beyond midday as they neared Andy Vance's place. The road acquired trees and thick hedges to either side, providing a virtual canopy and restricting the winter light to create a gloom, even though the sky was visible beyond the foliage and the sun was just beyond its apex. The road had been cut through the vegetation, creating a lower channel for its course. This was not an uncommon type of road and they hadn't seen a zombie for some time, but it still filled them with a sense of claustrophobia. It matched the description that Bob had given them, but instead of slowing down to look for the entrance to Andy Vance's place, they sped up slightly.

'There!' shouted Simon. Laura hit the brakes and they came to a halt. Being stationary for the first time in a long while sent a bolt of fear through them. 'Back up,' said Simon, as if panicked by a legion of zombies ahead of them. Laura, already in the process of doing so, reversed. They had to travel back some eighty yards, travelling at speed to create a sense of safety, but occasionally clipping the edges of the narrow lane. Every strike made them catch their breaths, fearful of incapacitation. They reached the gap at the side of the road with only superficial damage to the car's paintwork.

It was easy to miss as the trees either side leant over it continuing the canopy. It was plenty wide enough for their vehicle, and stone walls, about hip height to the average person, led back about ten yards where the opening cut in. It was exactly as Bob had described.

They turned in and slowly proceeded. They quickly passed beyond the end of the walls, and then past the trees, before emerging into the sunshine. The brightness made them squint, but it was a pleasurable feeling, heralding a sense of triumph. They were high up and the landscape ahead of them sloped off for some way before rising again in the far distance. A beautiful, sparkling river cut through the landscape, about a quarter of a mile away. There were various clumps of trees along the river's edge, along with banks that opened directly onto grassy fields, undulating up and away.

If this was sanctuary, it couldn't have looked more fitting, except for, or even including, no sign of human existence. It was how Bob had described, a place he had happy memories of visiting, portraying it wistfully in the minutes during which the end of his life at the mercy of the despicable zombies hurtled towards him. They continued down the road, dipping towards the river fairly steeply, towards a clump of trees, followed the road through them, and emerged out of the other side on the same level with the river.

They pulled to a halt. In front of them was a larger than normal, but not too large, modernist house atop a platform. It was white, with plenty of glass, comprising mainly square and straight-lines, as if the architect had designed it by piecing together various cardboard boxes. The platform was just high enough to be impossible to jump up and reach. Grass ran right up to the edges of the platform's struts, and continued all the way down to the river's edge. A couple of vehicles were parked beneath the under it. They looked up to the front of the house, and leaning on the railings that surrounded the edge of the platform creating an all-round balcony, was a man.

He looked extremely relaxed, smiling slightly, and confident, looking down from the platform. He was leaning with one elbow on the railing beneath which was frosted glass, but it was possible to see that down by his side he was holding a crossbow. He looked in his mid fifties, but very good for it, slim and tall, with dark hair not yet receding.

Simon and Laura knew who this was. And he wasn't a zombie. They both felt immense smiles fill their faces, and each laughed a little with relief despite the crossbow. They jumped out of the vehicle and went round to the front. They almost subconsciously took hold of each other's hands and squeezed.

'Andy?' shouted Laura.

'Hello!' called back Andy with a big smile, as if delivering a fop's line from a Noel Coward play despite having very little of the look of Terry Thomas. This was a little out of character for Andy, but he was relieved at the novelty of meeting people who weren't zombies.

'Bob Davis sent us?' shouted Laura. Andy smiled more and his demeanour lifted as he heard this name.

'Well, you'd better come up then.' He walked round to the side of the platform, and gestured them to follow with a big arm movement. As Simon and Laura reached the side, they saw a set of steps that were built into the platform and hinged at the top, lowering down from their horizontal position. As the pair reached them, the bottom settled on the ground, and they both strolled up. They were beginning to feel relaxed, then Andy said, 'Quickly now,' taking on the anxious persona of a defender, scanning round the edges of the grass that surrounded the house, the crossbow raised slightly. Despite appearances, it seemed nowhere was entirely safe.

Laura and Simon quickly ran the last few steps to the top, and as their feet touched the platform, Andy immediately raised the steps. They all stood for a second facing each other. They were complete strangers, but knew they were more bonded than many people who've known each other lifetimes. Andy stuck his hand out.

'Pleased to meet you,' he said with real passion. Simon shook his hand and Andy responded heartily, and then he shook Laura's. 'Let's get inside,' said Andy and he strolled along, leading the way through a glass door, which he closed as Laura and Simon passed in behind him. He showed them to a seat, and then as he made them all a nice cup of tea, Laura and Simon spent the next half hour explaining everything that had happened to them.

They reached the end of the explanation, and although they'd told Andy all that they knew, it had been quite garbled. Andy was quite frustrated at how hard it had been to absorb the badly related information, as was his manner in such instances, but on this occasion, he was able to make the effort to hide the feelings he usually struggled with, keeping relations more than pleasant. His elbow rested on his knee as he sat and finished the last, cold mouthful of his drink. He leant his head over, resting his forehead on his outstretched fingers. He was taking time to understand before asking anything else.

'Is anyone else here?' asked Simon as the silence seemed to prolong. Andy looked up, and gave a pained, smile.

'I'm alone now,' said Andy, then seemed to tense his face, especially round his eyes. It was not possible to say whether or not recent events had left him alone, or something else back in time, but no more was to be said on the matter. An almost imperceptible glaze flashed in Andy's eyes as he took in the appearance of his guests properly.

'You both look very tired,' he said, stating the obvious, 'and I should think you'd like to freshen up.' Simon and Laura looked to each other, realising they'd missed at least a night's sleep and that their adventures had left them dishevelled and grubby. They were also variously speckled with darkening splatters of blood. 'Why don't you get a shower and have some rest. We can talk later,' said Andy sympathetically as he rose and led the way, the discussion over for now. Laura and Simon wondered for a second if they really should be relaxing in the circumstances. However, they were still only human, unlike so many others, and the adrenaline that had kept them going beyond the cycle of needing a nightly sleep would soon be subsiding as the secure feeling of Andy's place started to take its effect and their ravaged bodies demanded respite. They had also barely been making sense as it was to Andy, and this was only going to get worse.

They both followed Andy who showed them showers and places to sleep. He gave them options as their arrangements were of no concern to him. Something was forming between Laura and Simon, but at this particular moment they were overwhelmed by their need to rest. Dusk was setting in by the time Laura and Simon were asleep. Whether or not they had meant to recharge themselves with a quick nap or sleep through the night was not of their choosing. They would sleep deeply, right through to late the next morning.

Once both of his guests had fallen far into their slumber, Andy took their clothes to launder. It gave him something to do whilst he contemplated what he'd heard. After he'd returned the fresh clothes ready for Laura and Simon to find in the morning, he searched for some books and papers, reading late into the night. At some point close to midnight, he went outside and stood on his balcony. There was little animal life disturbing the stark silence at this time of year. He felt a fleeting joy, being safe where he was and having company. He looked up to the sky. He remembered looking out like this as a child, wondering if any of the stars were Father Christmas. Often he'd spot one slowly tracking between the bright pinpoints, and was sure he'd seen the real thing, oblivious at that age to the existence of satellites.

The warm nostalgic flush of that ingrained childhood memory fleetingly lifted him. Even now he could still be powerfully moved by that imaginary man.

27. Next Morning

Morning had fully arrived by the time Laura and Simon emerged. Andy had left them clean toothbrushes, and they felt so refreshed that they might even have believed that the previous days' events were just a dream, or a nightmare. They were after all, gone and in the past, their only existence being memories.

'Morning,' said Andy, merrily. He was putting up Christmas decorations. Laura and Simon were both startled to a halt by the incongruous scene. It made them wonder even more strongly for a second whether they'd imagined the previous days' events. Was Andy insane? It took them a second to remember that they were approaching Christmas, so it wasn't the kind of insanity of putting up decorations in the middle of summer. It just seemed to be a bit odd.

'Come and help,' said Andy invitingly. The pair didn't move. Andy was fully aware what they must be thinking, but he was the sane one. He knew he should maintain his own identity, and not become a slave of circumstances. He knew that Simon was a soldier. 'You celebrate Christmas Day in war zones, don't you?' said Andy. Simon smiled and walked over to help. Andy was stood on a chair hanging tinsel. There was a large cardboard box full of it, and Simon took some out to hand to Andy. It was still unnerving for Laura.

'Do you mind if I just watch,' she said awkwardly.

'Of course not,' said Andy, and the tension ebbed completely. Laura sat on a sofa with a coffee table in front of it. There was various reading matter there that Andy had been looking at the night before. Laura shuffled through it. She found an article that bore Andy's name.

Bob hadn't had long too tell them much about Andy. They knew that he was a part time academic, dabbling in natural and social sciences, just one manifestation of his maverick tendencies. Andy's career had been varied, but he grew bored too quickly to ever really establish himself in any one field. He'd had enough success to build the house in which they now found themselves, was largely self-sufficient, and chose his social world carefully. His natural distrust of the course that the world was going down had driven him here, and he'd spent a few days feeling a certain amount of vindication, in no way mitigating his despair at the current horror.

As Simon and Andy put up tinsel, Laura picked up a magazine with an article's title circled in red pen. It wasn't an academic magazine, but also not a weekly tittle tattle digest, more a monthly for the thinking person with a dose of humour. The article was by Andy Vance. It was not a long article, and Laura was keen to find out a little more about their host. She looked up to Andy who had already noted her interest.

'Go ahead,' he said with a smile. Laura leant back on the sofa.

Doing the Impossible: How to Trigger a Butterfly Effect, by Andy Vance

The Butterfly Effect, a phenomena described by Lorenz in the early sixties, has captured the public imagination to become a well known modern scientific principle. This idea, that tiny actions can have huge effects, such as the beat of a butterfly's wings in Brazil triggering a tornado in India, has entered our everyday language and culture. There's a popular film that bears the title whilst others, such as Sliding Doors, are also based on the same concept. Even though the concept was developed from a study of physical phenomena, namely meteorology, it's such a powerful idea that it has effortlessly transgressed into describing social situations.

The Butterfly Effect tells us that very small forces can trigger substantially larger ones, but because they happen at chaotic boundaries, it's virtually impossible to calculate the small force required to create a specific large change. In other words, a tornado in India cannot be created on demand by flapping a butterfly's wings in Brazil. Our common sense supports this. However, there are ways to achieve effects akin to this impossible feat.

216

To do this, we need to first consider what is being described by the Butterfly Effect. It is a very tiny force disrupting a complex system to create a massive force and movement. Mathematicians and physicists will know that to model and calculate this for something like a butterfly's wings, a tornado and the global weather system is impossible. However, we can consider any other systems with similar forces involved to create similar effects. By choosing an appropriate system, we can then model it not physically, but informationally, or put another way, socially. Importantly though, the physical model can be substituted at any point, the key points for these purposes being the beginning and end. This can be demonstrated by example.

Let's consider a system that starts with a switch that is part of a centralised control system for a national railway company. The movement of that switch may involve a very tiny force, the flap of the butterfly's wings. When triggered, it notifies a change of platform for a train coming into a station hundreds or even thousands of miles away. This information is displayed on a map in the central control location, and is then passed on by people as instructions, talking face to face, over telephones, and by inputting this information into other control systems. Eventually this leads to local staff at the station where the platform change is happening, making an announcement over a tannoy system. Hundreds of passengers hear this and then all start moving on mass between platforms. These movements of passengers involve far greater forces and physical movements than the original flicking of the switch, but have been entirely predictable, and getting these passengers to move was the intention when the original switch was flicked.

This cause and effect would have been impossible to predict by modelling the forces involved. Even though parts of the system are closed, something maths and physics can cope far better with, the passing on of instructions and announcements, sound creating tiny vibrations in the air as does a butterfly's wings, can only be made sense of as social phenomena.

Though the passengers' movements might not possess the same energy as a tornado, the principle is the same, and could be applied to all sorts of other examples such as ship movements, mining operations or the release of nuclear bombs. A result has been predicted that is impossible with a purely physical analysis, but relatively simple with an informational one, whilst highlighting that either approach applies to exactly the same things. It is *simply our choice that we choose to describe them in physical or informational terms. On a further point as previously alluded to, the films that are based on the butterfly effect tend to apply it to a social or informational world, whilst the theory was developed to describe the physical world. Whether or not the butterfly effect can be used in this way is a matter for further discussion, though it does make for good entertainment.*

The article continued with a more detailed ontological discussion, but Laura had read enough to understand the key points. She put it down on her lap. Andy particularly liked this article, having gained a certain amount of popular recognition and influence without the effort of scholarly publishing. He'd just wanted to share the idea. He stepped down from the chair and spoke.

'What do you think?' he asked.

'I'm not sure I understand,' replied Laura. Despite her reply, and the confused retelling of recent events from the previous evening, Andy already recognised that Laura was sharper than most people. He was keen to engage her in discussion, feeling a certain resonance.

'Do you see any similarities with the New Philosophy that you were telling me about last night?' he asked. He'd not managed to glean much from their explanations, but had understood the basic concept of the zombies being created by nothing more than an idea. Andy left the Christmas decorations to sit down on an armchair just to the side of the sofa where Laura sat, whilst Simon continued decorating.

'I think so,' said Laura. She strained in thought for a second. 'Our world is a world of information things and physical things, but they are both interlinked, so that everything is physical and information at the same time. They're just ways we choose to describe it. Changing either affects both, so that information affects real things and I guess it works the other way round?' she suggested.

'That'll do,' said Andy. He'd been highly sceptical of the New Philosophy theory initially. It was just so fantastical and divorced from the conventional world that we imagine. He'd understood the thrust of the proposal, that it was simply knowing the idea of the New Philosophy that turned people into zombies, and that is was backed up by what had happened at Location Three. He'd thought on this late into the evening, and had increasingly felt similarities with his own ideas.

He asked Laura to go over it again. Refreshed by sleep, Laura was now more succinct and clear, and Andy having had time to ponder on her previous night's ramblings, was able to ask the pertinent questions and glean the necessary facts. He heard about Laura's experiences at university, the helicopter journey and the doorman, the zombies in the cells at Location Three, the Tupelo Star incident, and how Harriet changing after watching the video had finally removed any doubt.

28. Two Worlds

'I'm still struggling to believe it myself,' concluded Laura, 'that nothing more than an idea could cause all of.' Andy waited for a second. He had enjoyed listening to her, hearing such an inquiring, curious and sharp mind come to its own decisions based on facts. Her youth was unsurprisingly, no barrier to her intellect, only to her experience and knowledge. She was rare in being able to set aside the pressure of received wisdom and normalised ideas that directs the vast majority of people into a prescribed existence. She could see what lay beyond appearances, and articulate her own thoughts into a deeper insight. Andy had thought that he may never have the pleasure of engaging in face-to-face human discourse again, let alone like this. It was all too rare an occurrence even before.

'It may be hard to take in,' said Andy, 'but it's a far more reasonable and realistic proposition than you might think.' He awaited the flicker of curiosity in Laura's face. Simon was still putting up the decorations, but could hear what was being said. Andy got his cue, and smiled as he began to explain.

'We live in a world of physical things and of ideas, or you could describe it as matter and information. They're not the same thing, but they are not independent of each other. Each can be considered a phenomenon of the other.

'The physical world only exists to us as information. You might say that a mountain is a physical thing, but why not say it is a lot of rocks, or aren't those rocks a lot of silicon compounds or aren't they a lot of molecules, or atoms, or leptons and so on. They're all ideas we ascribe, and are the only way we can know the mountain, or anything physical. Ideas may relate to a specific physical thing, but we only ever know that idea. We can't know the actual thing. It can't go into our minds, only an idea of it.

'Likewise, information can only exist through matter. If we take a basic piece of information, say the letter 'A', it can only ever exist as something physical, say as ink on a piece of paper, or the lighting up of a TV screen to create the image. That's the only way you can know it. That letter, that piece of information, isn't the matter though. It's not the piece of paper or images. They just represent the information. If I write something on a piece of paper and then make copies, the information still exists if I destroy the original piece of paper. The information isn't the thing that represents it, but exists as long as there is something representing it. I can also make as many copies of that piece of information as I want, but it's still only one piece of information. If I write a book that is printed thousands of times, I've still only written one book.'

'What about if I spoke the letter 'A'?' asked Laura.

'It's still physical. It's the movement of sound waves vibrating molecules of air, which move your eardrum, and creates signals in your brain,' replied Andy. She understood.

'So, information isn't matter, but it only exists through it, whilst every piece of matter conveys information, from a message to an aesthetic, to just what the thing is, like a rock. This means that whenever information is created, something physical has to change as well. It's not just that information can affect real things. It always does.

'So there are two worlds, or realms, for describing things, the informational and physical. Each can be considered independently, but they are linked. Each can be explained entirely in its own right, and vice versa. But they will always be in perfect harmony, so that at any point, each is a perfect reflection of the other. It's not that information does its thing over in the informational world and then comes over and changes the physical world.

'Our informational and physical worlds follow their own unique path, but each continually provides an insight into the other as a phenomenon of itself. They are not interfering with each other. Physical laws will always stay intact and anything that appears to contravene the laws of physics is probably a mistake. It cannot be explained by the informational world interfering. There are no poltergeist, no 'superphysical', no 'supernatural'. The two worlds are phenomena of each other, not controllers.

'Therefore, the world we live in can be described by the two realms at the same time, the physical and informational. If you want, we exist in a physical world, and live in an informational one. These may even be individual imagined worlds to each of us, but we can interact because that information is based on the same physical world.

'We can model the world in either physical or informational terms and use either to predict what will happen. Each will give the same results, but in their own terms, which can be translated to the other if you want to. The only limitation is, how accurately this can be one.

'Think of an example such as asking someone to raise their hand. This can be understood in terms of information, the words used, the person's character, the setting they're in, the various relationships and so on. We could explain, or even predict that they would raise their hand using this informational model. We can also do the same as a physical one. The shape of the sound waves from the instructions, the vibrations of the air and eardrums, the firing of neurons in the brain, the impulses sent to the muscles, the chemical reactions moving the hand.

'Even with this simple example, we can see the problems of complexity. We can't fully describe every detail of a brain at the molecular level, but we can and group together physical elements, such as neurons and brain centres, just as words and their meanings are groups of many smaller bits of information.

'Complexity limits a lot of what we can do. Imagine trying to understand how information can change whole societies, but by modelling the physical effects of the information and how people think. It's beyond any imaginable form of computation. But we do have the option to choose whichever is the most suitable method of analysis, and then convert the results to the other type if we need to. So it becomes possible do something that should be impossible, like triggering a physical effect that is similar in scale to causing a tornado by moving a butterfly's wings, by analysing it in informational terms, and re-interpreting it into physical ones.

'Neither realm takes preference. Either may be the only real one, or both may exist, or even neither may exist, just being phenomena of each other ad infinitum!

'People struggle with the idea that information has real effects but isn't something physical. Anything that has an effect they naturally want to attach to something physical that they have given the power to make things happen. They create a superphysical or supernatural, a physical entity that they believe is as real as any other physical entity, but is not yet known in the same way as the physical things we already know. Things like ghosts and spirits and gods.

'We may believe that one day we will be able to understand most, and maybe all, physical processes, but will we ever be able to use that to explain and understand the world we experience? Being able to see a landscape, a face, a building or anything, presents me with a wholeness of that experience that is never going to mean anything by describing it as individual specks of light. Or a song we hear, a fruit we taste or any of the things that we sense as tiny impulses, but come together as a single experience in our consciousness. That feeling, that wholeness, that 'qalia'.

'It may even be that consciousness, the one thing that is immediately obvious to all of us, entirely unexplainable and that we presume is the same for others, is where these two worlds collide. Consciousness may just be the interaction between physical and informational worlds, where there is so much exchange taking place that the separation becomes fuzzier and fuzzier until there is just the one thing sitting above all of it. Maybe that's the real beauty of a brain.'

Andy stopped. He realised that he'd become completely self-absorbed. He'd just enjoyed being able to explain his ideas to someone who was so interested. He was like a man finding an oasis and not being able to stop drinking after being lost in the desert for days.

Simon had stopped decorating, and had sat on the chair that he'd been stood on, absorbed by what Andy was saying. Laura was agog. There was a stillness after Andy finished. He leant back in his chair to allow Laura and Simon to feed on the cognitive nourishment. The pair had managed to take in some of it, but it was a struggle. They felt their brains aching as if they'd been trying to complete a difficult cryptic crossword for far too long. They could not make full sense of it straight away. They would have to go over it again and again, maybe ask Andy for clarification and restatement. But they would come to understand it, and it would change how they thought about things.

'Tea, anyone?' asked Andy, standing up with vigour. He made his way over to the kitchen area right by where they were seated, separated by a low unit of cupboards providing a table top, but otherwise fully exposed to the large open living area. Laura and Simon were slow to respond to Andy's offer, just giving slight affirmative nods, as their minds remained tied up with the endeavour of making sense of what he had just related to them.

Andy made them all a cup of tea, brought it over and sat back down. Laura and Simon each took a sip, and began to feel more able to engage in conversation.

'I think I get it,' said Simon, 'but what's it all got to do with the zombies and the New Philosophy?' he asked, getting straight to the heart of the matter. It could have brought Andy down to earth with a crash if he'd just been freestyling and waxing lyrical on various ideas close to his heart without any real relevance to the matter in hand. He hadn't.

'Absolutely,' said Andy. 'I think it's fair to presume that something is being triggered in people's mind to cause this to happen. Laura has already made a strong case for the power of ideas, how they change people and how they can cause things to happen. But there will be some people who will say that there is still some kind of physical change in the mind.' Laura and Simon were intrigued.

'Well, if there is a change in the brain, it could theoretically be traced back, as a physical process, possibly to a particular part of the brain. We've established that information can, and always does include a physical change. As the brain is directly affected by information, it's possible that the physical change could also be understood as something informational. An informational trigger could then be created.' Laura and Simon were struggling with this. Andy gave them a moment to go over it again in their minds, until he saw in their expressions the first shards of dawning realisation.

'If you can work that out,' he continued, 'it would be possible to create the change by administering that information.' Andy stopped, his eyes locked together with Laura and Simon's. 'Or put another way, by telling people an idea.'

'Maybe,' said Laura hypothesising, 'that's how the idea was created by the New Philosophers. They worked out the physical changes in the brain needed, and exactly where an idea would have to act.' Andy smiled slightly, feeling enthused.

What Laura had just proposed, merely extending Andy's explanation, sounded fantastical. It would take an awesomely powerful intellect to do this using current knowledge, if it were even to be possible, or the development of techniques way beyond anything within the scope of current human knowledge. This explanation was truly awesome, but it did all hold together. It was possibly the only explanation they had.

Where would this intelligence have come from? Could the New Philosophers have come from elsewhere? Could the New Philosophers possess an almost godlike cognitive ability and knowledge that enabled them to create the idea that was the New Philosophy, and to effortlessly manipulate a whole species? Was it something from beyond human ability, maybe another planet? Andy and Laura were thinking the same thoughts, whilst Simon who had a basic grasp of what he had heard, was still consolidating the concept in his mind. Laura and Andy grimaced slightly. They were both great minds, and they both realised that they were in danger of resorting to default explanations of Gods and extra-terrestrials for something that was beyond the scope of human understanding. Alien worlds and pleromas had always served this purpose. But if not, what?

29. The Recording

Laura, Andy and Simon pondered a little longer. It was a lot to take in. They already knew that nothing more than an idea was ravaging the whole of humanity. Anything could be happening out in the rest of the world, away from their sanctuary. It was easy for Laura, Simon and Andy to believe that they were the last remaining humans.

'Do you think there are many more like us?' Laura asked Andy.

'Of course!' replied Andy instantly. Laura and Simon were both a bit taken aback by the robustness of his reply.

'How can you be so sure?' asked Simon. Andy smiled.

'Well, firstly, I think the chances of us being the last three people alive and then finding each other would defy any odds.' It was an obvious point, but reassuring for all of them to hear it. Andy had more though. 'And then there are the people I'm in touch with.'

'What?' stammered Laura and Simon together. They were aware that infrastructure had been rapidly collapsing since the outbreak. Phones had ceased to work. There were some emergency radio and television broadcasts, but even these may have stopped by now, and were unlikely to be anything more than loops played out by a machine. Andy was still smiling, enjoying the air of enigma he'd been able to create, but saw no further point in prolonging the suspense.

'Amateur radio enthusiasts,' he said, 'or radio hams.'

'Of course,' said Simon, chuckling with Andy. Laura was none the wiser.

'There's a whole network of amateur radio enthusiasts around the world,' said Andy. 'I dabble occasionally. It only seemed sensible living out here.' Andy went on to explain how a whole community of hobbyists and enthusiasts used amateur radios to communicate with each other around the world. Most of the time they were operating almost invisibly, but in times of crisis they were sometimes the only source of communication. It might be when an earthquake had sent its ripples through hundreds of miles of landscape, effortlessly ripping apart the modern world, or letting everyone know the details of a totalitarian government crackdown which had strangled existing mainstream media into silence. In this late twentieth century world, where the vast majority of communication was controlled by the most powerful and best resourced interests, this meagre last line of free communication still had the ability to show what the power of information meant. Many of the radio hams dreamed of a world with freedom of information. They also realised that as well as being a massive liberator, it could also be exploited for less pleasant purposes, feeding the darker sides that exist within most people, exposing them to even more manipulation and control than current mass communication allowed.

The radio hams were largely left to their own devices for most of the time though. Often viewed as oddballs, most were creative and adaptive, easily able to rig up their own power source when the world around them had collapsed, or spot a threat coming from the rest of society that they tended to avoid, hiding themselves away securely while the storm raged. Most importantly, they also tended to think for themselves. Maybe all of these reasons were why there still seemed to be so many of them in communication through their rag-tag network.

'So there are other people out there?' said Laura.

'Yes,' said Andy. 'We can talk to them if you like,' he offered.

'What have they been saying?' asked Laura, cautious at the exchange of any information.

'There are still people out there,' said Andy, 'not just the radio hams. There are people who have managed to barricade themselves away, but I'm told that some of these are still turning, often shortly after they've made contact with others.'

The mood cooled. The New Philosophy was still potent. It just took one in a group to turn, and that would be all of them lost.

'But we now know what's causing it,' said Simon, excitedly, 'We must be able to help them.' Laura and Andy were less enthusiastic and looked at each other.

'Don't you remember the army unit?' said Laura.

'It's a difficult one,' said Andy. He scrunched his face slightly as a thought occurred to him. 'You know what,' he said, 'I don't know what this New Philosophy is. I think I'd like to hear it.' He knew that he was confirming the danger of warning people about it. 'Can you remember it?' he asked Laura and Simon, turning to each of them in turn. They were both startled. Laura whitened at the terrifying thought that Andy may be stepping onto the inevitable path to zombiedom. Andy awaited a reply, despite seeing their anxiety.

'I don't think that's a good idea,' said Laura, bravely rebutting their host.

'Can you remember it,' asked Andy, undeterred.

'Bits,' said Laura. 'It seems to flow once you start going through it, but I lost track. I just wasn't interested.' Laura's natural desire to engage in rational debate prevented her from being smart enough to pretend she couldn't remember it at all. Her failure to remember it all though, was probably a symptom of her immunity.

'Me neither,' confirmed Simon.

'That's no good, is it?' said Andy. Laura and Simon were momentarily relieved. 'Wait!' exclaimed Andy. 'I know where we can get it.' The wave of fear crashed over Laura and Simon again, like the swell of the sea that had receded from a rocky sanctuary, only to crash back over more ferociously than before. 'There's a radio ham, Clive Hill. I remember now. He mentioned it to me a few days ago, and how ridiculous it was. He was intrigued by how people were getting so engrossed by it. He made a recording, but thought it was so laughable he never actually played it to me.'

Andy was smiling. He had his access to the New Philosophy. Laura and Simon were mortified.

'Please don't,' whimpered Simon.

'No, please,' came a similar plea from Laura. Their experience in Location Three with Harriet and Adam was still all too fresh in their minds. Andy had not tasted this experience firsthand.

'What's the problem? I'm not going to let it change me,' he said with excited confusion. He was getting up, ready to make his way to his radio set, but stopped dead in his tracks. He wasn't sure if he'd ever seen two more frightened individuals than those he was now looking at. His playful vigour drained away from him in an instant. Although Bob had suggested Laura and Simon seek out Andy as someone who was unlikely to have been affected by the New Philosophy, now that they realised he'd not been exposed to it, those reassurances disintegrated.

'Come with me,' said Andy calmly as he walked to a door and entered a small study. Laura and Simon followed and stood in the doorway looking in as he entered. There were bookshelves and a desk. Although there were a multitude of papers and books, it appeared relatively well organised; it didn't quite have the feel that one over exuberant sneeze could bring everything crashing down. There was a comfortable black executive chair at the desk at the end of the study, and a window affording a view of tree tops and green fields. The river could just be glimpsed through some of the branches and hedges. Along the wall to the right was a small settee.

'Please,' said Andy, a hint of begging in his voice, as he gestured to the settee. Laura and Simon entered and sat down. Laura gave Simon a stern look, her strength coming through. Simon was in no doubt that he was expected to act if called upon. The exchange didn't escape Andy, but he felt no criticism. He understood their fear. He took from a shelf half way up the wall, the crossbow that he'd been carrying the day before.

'Here,' he said handing it to Simon, still bearing various indicators of his soldiering. Simon gripped it ready to fire, but chose to hold it across his chest, aiming up to his left away from Andy. Simon would be able to turn it on the intended target quickly enough. He took in a deep breath, and turned to Laura to give a nod of reassurance as he exhaled. Andy missed this, already putting on the headphones and twiddling knobs on a box in the corner.

'Hello?' Andy began repeating into a microphone he had positioned in front of himself on the desk as he continued twiddling. Laura and Simon were not privy to the sounds in Andy's headphones, and merely had to gauge progress based on Andy's reactions. The twiddling and 'hellos' continued for some minutes.

'Clive!' said Andy eventually. 'I've got hold of him,' said Andy in an aside whisper to Laura and Simon. They jostled uncomfortably. Simon gripped the crossbow tighter. Laura felt her heart thundering at the thought of yet another zombie confrontation. She drew closer to Simon feeling warmth and comfort from his tensed bicep.

Andy proceeded to converse with Clive. He related the tale of Laura and Simon, and that it was just knowing the idea of the New Philosophy that was causing people to turn into zombies. It took a long, long time as Clive, like everyone else, began sceptical, but he seemed to understand and be responding to all of the various arguments. It wasn't essential that he believed them. His current role was merely to replay the recording of the New Philosophy to Andy.

They discussed whether or not they should spread the news of the cause via radio hams, quickly dismissed by the already established fact that it would just make matters worse. The psychological effect would also be extremely damaging, telling people that this horror was just words, but they couldn't stop them having an effect. It was like American soldiers not being told about kamikaze pilots during the Second World War.

Laura and Simon sat and listened to it all. At this point, their only solace was that Clive, the radio ham, apparently hadn't been affected.

'Ok then. Let's hear it,' Andy eventually said. He looked over to Laura and Simon, not saying anything, but straining a smile, unable to ignore the crossbow. It had protected him well up to now, he thought ironically. The playback began and Andy listened.

The room was virtually silent allowing the tinny sounds from the headphones to penetrate through, though with far from enough clarity to make any sense to Laura and Simon. Andy could hear every word as he listened intently. The memory of watching the Tupelo Star video jangled hard against Laura and Simon's emotions. The atmosphere reeked of familiarity, like a juggernaut hurtling towards the back of a traffic jam with no sign of stopping. Andy seemed to be detaching from the room as he continued to listen. Laura and Simon tried to edge closer together, their arms pressing hard into each other. The tip of the crossbow had crept around a little towards Andy, the neutralising bolt readied.

The seconds and minutes dragged by, but having watched the video at Location Three, Laura and Simon knew that it must nearly be finished. The tinny noises stopped coming from the headphones. Andy was motionless and looking into the distance somewhere towards the floor.

'Thanks Clive. I'll be in touch,' said Andy, in a slow drawl. As he stretched his arm over to turn off the radio, almost as if in slow motion, Simon couldn't help but let the crossbow swing itself round more, so that it was virtually pointing at the target. Simon's finger tensed on the trigger. Andy was still not focussed on the room, as he moved his arm back and sat slumped in his chair. His manner possessed reminisces of Adam and of Harriet after their viewing. It triggered churns in Laura's stomach and she wondered if she might vomit. She leant back more into the settee, eager to get further away from Andy, only managing a few millimetres.

Simon was now fully aiming the crossbow at Andy's head which was beginning to lift slowly, his gaze sharpening on Laura. The sides of his mouth began to lift. He was starting to smile. Was it just a smile though, or the start of a manic grin, the signal of mind-warped euphoria embracing Andy's mind and beginning him on the march towards zombification? Laura grabbed at Simon's arm, and squeezed it hard. She was terrified, a terror that she'd only become acquainted with in recent days. Simon was ready to fire. He couldn't decide. A moment's indecision now could be fatal. He tensed his finger some more and felt the trigger move back slightly. He stopped a fraction before the bolt was released. He knew it took time for the New Philosophy to turn people into full zombies. He released the trigger slightly, but then tensed again as Andy began to speak.

'What a load of rubbish!' said Andy, laughing as he did so, and throwing his head back. Laura and Simon were overwhelmed by relief and began breathing rapidly. Simon let the crossbow drop down onto the settee to his side releasing his grip. Andy continued laughing, and then after about half a minute, Laura began to laugh as well, and then Simon. All three of them kept laughing, along with some tears of relief. When they'd finished, they returned to the living area, and Andy made them a drink. They chatted about the absurdity of the New Philosophy's claims, as if deriding a dreadful film that they'd all just watched, not a sinister mind control mechanism that was wiping out the human race. After a while, the humour, essential to them coping, subsided.

'What do we do now?' asked Simon after some time.

'We need a weapon,' said Andy.

'We need our own New Philosophy,' said Laura.

30. A New Weapon

Laura and Simon's experience with the army units on their way to see Andy, along with the turning of Harriet and Adam in the interrogation room at Location Three, had made it clear that just telling people that the New Philosophy was what was turning them into zombies was no defence, even with such horrific and manifest effects. The New Philosophy was a weapon that they had no idea how to defend against. Hoping to protect people by telling them that it was listening to it that changed them, was like hoping people could survive standing in front of a machine gun, because they'd been told that it was the bullets that would kill them. Worse still, once warned they were desperate to put themselves in the firing line.

Laura's comment, 'We need our own New Philosophy,' had got them all thinking. There was some truth in the adage, 'fight fire with fire'. The question was where to start?

'What about looking at the New Philosophy itself?' suggested Simon. The only military brain among them, it seemed the obvious thing to do. Laura and Andy did not respond. They were taking in what Simon had suggested, not ignoring his idea, but he didn't know this and backed it up with, 'If we understand how the New Philosophy works better, then maybe we can use it to come up with something ourselves?' Laura and Andy looked to each other, more convinced, but still not speaking. 'That's how military technology works,' Simon concluded.

'Can you remember it?' Laura asked Andy, aware that she and Simon had been unable to relate it accurately to Andy.

'No,' said Andy. Disappointment tightened the chests of Laura and Simon, but it was a short lived deflation. Andy smiled at them. 'I don't need to,' he continued, 'I taped the whole conversation from the radio.' Elation at this tiny breakthrough lifted the mood. They were a long way from defeating the zombie menace, but at least they had a starting place. Even if their efforts were ultimately unsuccessful, the activity they could now engage in would at least give them a sense of contribution.

Andy, Laura and Simon set to work. Andy was the de facto leader, but he displayed a deference to Laura's abilities. His experience as a researcher and writer, along with his organisational skills, enabled them to quickly progress, and Laura and Simon were happy to have him leading the way. Simon did not possess quite the other two's aptitude, but was still a rarely found critical thinker, and his occasional insights were often enlightening and key to progressing beyond logjams and cul-de-sacs that Andy and Laura could occasionally wander into.

Their first task was to transcribe what they had on the tape recording. As they put the words down, Laura and Simon read it back to themselves with astonishment. Andy felt a flicker of anxiety kindling inside as he watched them becoming absorbed. They hadn't yet established whether immunity to the New Philosophy was lasting or could fail at any time. It was not unreasonable to believe that repeated exposure may break down resistance leading to eventual infection.

Andy watched the pair reading through, now almost oblivious to him. They were all working at a table in the main living area. Andy stood up, unnoticed. He took a few steps towards the door of the study where they had communicated with Clive Hill, the radio ham. He was now a couple of steps away and could see through the door the handle of the crossbow. It would only take him a second to rush in and grab it.

'Everything okay?' Andy asked Laura and Simon. They didn't hear. They were absorbed in the transcript they were assembling. 'Guys!' called Andy loudly. Laura and Simon were snapped back to the shared reality of Andy's house. They looked around as if they'd been suddenly awoken from a deep sleep, and were unsure of their whereabouts. Andy waited to see what happened. Laura and Simon said nothing, but looked over to Andy. It was a fair enough response to his call.

'Something interesting?' asked Andy. Laura and Simon looked to each other and instinctively knew they were thinking the same thing. They'd grown very close through the shared traumas they'd been experiencing. Laura replied to Andy for them both.

'It's just,' she began hesitantly, 'it's just… amazing.' Andy wondered if she was succumbing to the more than awe inspiring message that most people found in the New Philosophy. Andy took a furtive step towards the study, his stare locked on Laura and Simon. If they moved, he would be quicker. Laura sensed the tension. 'No, not the New Philosophy itself,' she continued, aware of Andy's nervousness, 'it's just that now we can see it written down, it's exactly word for word how we heard it at Location Three.' Andy relaxed. He saw the significance. It wasn't just the power that the New Philosophy had to change people, but that it was able to preserve and replicate itself, often only existing in the mind of a human host before rematerialising to the next without change or mutation.

They were right. The sophistication of the New Philosophy was even greater than they'd first anticipated. It seemed to follow its predefined path inexorably, each twist and turn being indicated by not just what had come immediately before, but almost everything that had come before, reinforcing itself over and over again, whilst etching itself deeper and deeper into the pliant host, through into the subconscious, the ego, and maybe even, the id.

Despite the overwhelmingly powerful influence the New Philosophy possessed, it was still difficult for the three of them to understand exactly what it meant. At first, it appeared to be a rolling prosaic, but mysteriously engaging, diatribe. Even though the three potential saviours were immune, they could still feel their emotions stirring to the suggestions filtering into their subconscious. They knew that they would need to keep their wits about them.

They read through it again and again, shared elements with each other when they thought they'd spotted something, only for their insight to be yet another vision of nothing. Translating ancient texts written in long lost archaic tongues would seem effortless compared to trying to make meaning of the script before them. They were at a loss. Dusk passed by, and the world outside turned pitch black. There was no light to speak of in the area surrounding Andy's lair, and a cloudy night prevented any moon or star light penetrating and offering the slightest hint of illumination. They had made no progress in their task, and if they were to have continued until dawn, it was unlikely that they would be any further forward than when they had first started. No one wanted to give up though. An injection of sanity was needed.

'I think we should stop,' said Andy.

'What! Give up?' responded Laura. She was tired, but there was distress in her voice. She knew that what they were doing may be the only chance of defeating the zombie plague.

'No! Of course not!' replied Andy. He felt exactly the same as Laura did about the last-chance mission they were carrying out for humanity. 'It's just that we're very tired, and I'm not sure we're getting anywhere. We need a break.' They were all sat at the table. There were various papers and books spread over it. All three leant back in the chairs, thankful to take the rest that Andy had finally suggested. 'We can start again tomorrow,' he said. Everyone's eyes felt ready to shut immediately, although their brains were still whirring behind them. It must have been way past midnight, and if they had been doing this close to the summer solstice, instead of the winter one, they may well have seen light dawning on the horizon, ready to fill the nothingness with light. As they were about to leave the table for their beds, Simon spoke.

'Have we made any progress?' he asked. No one answered, for they all knew the unwelcome answer. 'Is there any reason why we should make any more progress tomorrow? Or even after that?' Laura slumped forward on the table. She was so tired, and having had the idea of retiring implanted in her head, was desperate to leave, but knew that Simon's comment had to be addressed. They all knew that if they carried on as they were doing, it was probable that they would carry on getting nowhere. Andy summed up the situation.

'I think it was Einstein who once said something like insanity is doing the same thing, over and over again, but expecting different results.' Laura and Simon were both too young to have been exposed to this popular quote, but it was to become one they were sure to use themselves in the future, should they have one. The three crusaders felt strangely liberated by the comment. They didn't want to be seen to be quitters despite knowing that their efforts could be futile, but now the onus was on not going ahead to show they were still sane. The relief lasted a few moments, before a wave of despair gently began to flow over them.

'We can't do nothing,' said Laura. 'We're so close.' Andy had no answer. She looked to Simon, who had a knack of providing pragmatism when most needed. This was the greatest test of his character so far. Could he respond?

'We need to get more information?' he said, 'Reconnaissance.' The suggestion lifted Laura and Andy enough to hold back the gloom.

'He's right,' said Andy, who realised more research was obviously the answer.

'You know where it all started and some of the people involved, don't you Laura?' said Simon recalling their interrogation at Location Three. Laura nodded. 'Then that's where we need to go.' The mood lightened, but the tiredness returned with a vengeance, sensing a natural break in proceedings.

'We go in the morning,' said Andy decisively. 'Sleep now. We need to be ready.' No one needed telling twice. Laura made her way straight to bed. Simon hesitated as his training troubled him. He realised that although the house was protected by its elevation, it only offered glass should a zombie have scaled the platform. He shuddered at having already spent a night sleeping in such an exposed environment. As he pondered on the vulnerability they faced, he wondered whether a man as well-prepared as Andy would really leave his survival to chance. Suddenly, a low rumbling emanated throughout the house seeming to come from everywhere. Simon turned quickly from side to side, back and front, trying to identity what this new threat was. He saw all around at every window, grey steel shutters slowly coming down. Andy was true to his persona. Simon could see him with his finger on the button operating the shutters. They exchanged a smile.

31. The Source

There was still plenty of the day left as the three of them neared Chesborough. They'd managed to get away from Andy's place well before the morning was over having all managed to get a good night's rest, and had made good progress, reaching their destination in just under two hours. They'd travelled in the large four by four car that Laura and Simon had acquired at Location Three. Before they'd left, they'd taken some time to inspect the abundance of weaponry that the vehicle came with, and Simon had briefed Laura and Andy, demonstrating various guns to them. They all now had experience of holding and firing the weapons, and each had in their possession the one they felt most comfortable with. Simon still had the big gun as well as other small weapons, the de facto security man of the group.

The journey had not been without incident. They had done their best to avoid areas of dense population, but it had been impossible to avoid passing through a couple of smaller towns. Occasionally their route would be blocked by abandoned, often crashed vehicles, doors still open. They saw bodies, decaying flesh and bones. There was a stench, a foul stench, of the rotting and putrefying remains. Entering these warped places, with their sense of desolation and crushed humanity replaced with gruesome evil, gave a vague sense of the experience that liberating allied troops entering Nazi death camps may have had.

Zombies would frequently run out at them, but the few that caught up were no match for the rugged vehicle. When they had to double back to find another way round obstructions, several zombies might manage to thump themselves into the car, a couple even getting on top. Although there wasn't a total absence of fear from the occupants, there was never any real threat as it became the norm to deflect zombies with a swerve, or feel the jolts from their bodies crunching under the wheels.

They had tried to use a motorway early in their journey, but this would have involved continual zigzagging to avoid the slalom of wrecked cars or even possibly finding it entirely blocked by mechanical debris. Many of the vehicles were burnt out, but this had happened so long ago that they were now just dead black lumps of twisted metal. They could see ahead that there were zombies still crawling over the wreckage looking for nutritious pickings, like insects following the simplest of instructions that their brains could manage. Many people had become trapped in their vehicles as the mass of people trying to escape had choked the network further, until the overwhelming volume of cars and increasing number of collisions, the majority caused by zombie outbreaks, had seized it up entirely. There was nowhere to go for those who had been trapped. Those near an outbreak may have been forced to witness zombies feasting on other motorists who'd left the relative safety of their cars, whilst they locked their doors and awaited the help that would never come. This had all happened many days ago, and it was a virtual certainty that there was no one still left alive in their cars. The zombies were also getting hungrier, and more determined to get at the cadavers within. Maggot-infested stinking flesh was no deterrent, and they could just as happily feast on this as warm fresh kill.

During the journey, Laura had gone over the details she could remember about the lead up to the zombie outbreak and the people involved. She narrowed it down to three people who had appeared to be at the heart of the New Philosophy. If they could find them, they might be able to find out where the movement had come from and its intention. They may even have an antidote. Laura knew where their rooms were. Thankfully, they were all in the same halls of residence.

Eventually they reached their destination. Chesborough was a small place, smaller than the towns they'd passed through on their way there. There was similar vehicular carnage to that seen previously, the odd burnt out building and the same stench of death by mutilation. The place had a sense of being more subdued though, and as they drove along the streets to their destination they saw no zombies. As the first place to turn, it was possible that all sources of food, had been consumed and the zombies had moved on or starved to death. They had to travel for around a mile once they'd entered the town, and as they pulled up at the halls, it was still peaceful, in a macabre kind of way.

They noticed that there must have been a higher proportion of army units here, as they could just make out that some of the mutilated bodies had the remnants of bio-chem suits hanging from them. As the location of most of the initial outbreaks, the now virtually non-extant Government had sent their people there to try and find out what was going on. The carcasses were testament to the success of their investigation.

Laura turned off the engine and they waited for a second. They'd spent the journey planning what they needed to do, and knew that the longer they hung around, the more danger they were in. Simon was first to get out, and stretched to refresh himself after being cooped up for so long. The other two quickly followed, also needing to stretch.

'Let's go,' said Simon, as he began striding soldier-like towards the door of the building that he'd recognised from Laura's descriptions. He'd made her go over the layout of the building again and again, until they were all as familiar with it as if they were regular visitors. Laura, who'd been driving, locked the car, and along with Andy had to run a few steps to catch up with Simon, finding his pace difficult to keep up with. They didn't complain. He was right to make them hurry.

Simon strolled through the front doorway of the building, the door itself lying broken on the ground a few feet away. He intended to keep up his rapid pace, but suddenly pulled up as if he'd walked into a waist high swamp of thick decaying matter, choked by the intensity of the stench that met him. He tried to ignore it, but was wincing and couldn't breathe. It was the same stench that hung in the air outside, but concentrated many times over, as if into a thick black olfactory liquid clogging up his nose. He had to stop a few paces in. He turned and saw Laura and Andy catching up with him. They were breathing hard, and looked relieved as they thought Simon had stopped to wait for them. They were both confused by his pained expression, but as they completed their last couple of steps into the doorway, they realised why.

'Oh God!' said Andy, as he turned, stepped back outside and threw up. Laura stopped dead, and lifted her arm to her face, allowing some filtration of the smell through her clothes, though she could still taste its poison. Simon was still suffering, although he was more accustomed to such situations.

'There's no one alive in here,' said Laura, keen to find an excuse not to proceed.

'We need to check their rooms,' replied Simon undeterred. 'See if we can find a lead, anything that might lead us to them.' Laura and Andy realised that it was all they had, and if they didn't enter the foul halls, they had nothing. They were still hesitant as they tried to force themselves to enter the building.

'The first few breaths are the worst,' said Simon encouragingly. 'The sooner we get on, the sooner you'll get used to it.' He could see that Laura and Andy were still struggling to muster the resolve to battle the foul reek within the building. 'We need to be quick. We are seriously exposed here!' Laura and Andy knew that Simon was right. They stepped inside cautiously, Andy struggling not to retch, and the three of them continued, significantly more slowly than their initial approach.

The building was cold, dark, and stunk. They ignored the bloodstains and body parts, something they now did naturally. In any case, the smell was taking up all of their attention. They quickly identified the three room that were all on the same corridor a couple of floors up.

'Let's take one each,' suggested Laura.

'No!' said Simon, almost aggressively rebutting her. 'We'll be sitting ducks,' he explained. 'I'll keep guard out here.' The logic of Simon's proposal could not be argued with, as any second they could be discovered by a hungry zombie. 'Be careful.'

Laura and Andy withdrew their guns and held them up ready to fire, just as they'd practised with Simon that morning. Simon could have checked the rooms first, but no one realistically believed anything alive was still within these walls. Simon thought it good practice for them, but kept watch just in case. As Laura and Andy each entered a room, the doors of which were both open, Simon suddenly felt alone and isolated. He stood side on to the corridor, so that his back was to neither end. He kept turning his head rhythmically as if a pendulum, scanning both ways as it could be entered from either end. The noise coming from the rooms of Laura and Andy searching seemed indistinguishable from the noises that might be expected from an approaching zombie.

A couple of minutes passed, though it felt much longer to Simon as he increasingly expected the inevitable appearance of a zombie. Even with his big gun and skill in killing things, he was afraid. A shout made him turn cold as he anticipated contact, and flashbacks of his army encounters raced through his mind.

'Anything?' It was Andy.

'Not sure?' called Laura. 'A lot of books. Some are obviously course work, but the others aren't. Religion, political theory, cults, management policy.' There was a moment's silence.

'It's the same here,' replied Andy, who'd applied Laura's observations to the room he was investigating and found the same. They both stepped out together into the corridor. The stench was now hindering them far less, and they were able to virtually ignore the torment in their nostrils or the churning of their vomit-threatening stomachs. 'Let's try the last room,' said Andy, and the pair walked towards it.

Simon's attention was diverted to the progressing pair, suddenly jerking the muzzle of his gun over to point at Laura just before they reached the doorway of the third room. She stopped, a bolt of terror freezing her. There was horror that Simon may have changed, but also something else depressed her heart. She was staring into Simon's cold eyes, but they were cold with routine and training. He nodded down to her waist, which he was pointing at with his big gun. She looked down to see that Simon was pointing at her gun, reminding her that she needed to be prepared for anything within the room.

Andy was a step ahead, and about to open the closed door of the third room. Laura reached out and grabbed his shoulder, pulling him back. He turned to ask her what she was doing, but her other hand had already grasped her gun and was holding it at shoulder height. Laura had learnt quickly and her survival instinct was working well. Her hand remained on Andy's shoulder as she pulled herself past him. She took hold of the door handle, whilst holding the gun ready. Simon was rapidly glimpsing up and down the corridor again, but now there was this third point of danger. A closed door was a threat, and as Laura turned the handle and pushed it open, Simon swung his gun round, ready to back her up.

As it opened, slamming back against the wall, Laura stumbled back, her face stretching with shock at the sight in front of her. She lifted the gun up, straight out in front of her and grasping it with both hands. She bumped into the wall behind. She was choking on her desperate breathes. Simon realised that she might be frozen by terror, unable to shoot, and anything could be about to emerge from the room. It was a couple of bounds for him to leap to Laura's side with his gun pointing directly into the room as he arrived. He recoiled at the same horrific sight that had greeted Laura. He lowered his gun and stood alongside her staring in.

Andy had had no time to react to the drama created by the unveiling of the third room. He watched Simon's gun drift down and realised that there was no imminent threat. He stepped forward and peeked into the room in front of Laura and Simon.

'Ooo,' said Andy, as he gazed on the unpleasant site. There was a pile of assorted corpses, limbs and torsos. The generous blood decorating the walls and furniture had matured to a shade or two away from black. The flies and maggots were well-gorged and still feasting. Andy saw the last couple of rats' tails vanish, but Laura and Simon had seen far more.

'It's them!' said Laura. The faces, or more accurately, the mangled and rotten traces of facial remains, offered no clue as to the identities of the bodies, but fortunately as with many students, these three had taken to wearing the same distinctive clothes incessantly, keen to establish their new identities bearing virtually no resemblance to the ones they'd deserted in their home towns. They'd done such a good job at being consistent in their change, they provided ample definition for Laura to know who they were, even though the rest of their existence was now long gone.

Simon and Andy looked to Laura. She was still staring at the bloodied mess. Although she was sure the three protagonists that they sought were here, it was difficult to tell just how many other bodies there might, and it was no longer possible to distinguish the eaters from the eaten.

'Well I guess we've found what we were looking for,' said Andy. He was right, although it was unexpected. If these people had really been part of the New Philosophers who'd created such a monstrosity, their genius in its crafting appeared to be matched by an equivalent ineptitude in its implementation.

'Look,' said Andy, pointing to the walls. He quickly realised their hunt for the conspirators was now at an end and they should move on to what they could do and get out. The walls were covered in pieces of paper with various bits of writing and pieces of string connecting them. They were on different colours of papers, with highlighter and scribbles daubed on. As they read some of the text, they realised that some of it had a certain familiarity with the transcriptions they'd been reading of the New Philosophy. They walked slowly in, their fascination and acclimatisation overcoming their natural revulsion.

'This is where they created it' said Laura. They found a pile of books and papers like those in the other rooms. A screech echoed down the corridor. Simon bounded out of the room, ready to exercise his big gun. He looked both ways, already poised for combat, whilst Laura and Andy struggled to ready their weapons. The echoes of the screech subsided, and they strained to hear any other signs of impending attack in the silence. There was nothing, but they now knew that they were not alone.

'We need to bag everything up and take it back with us,' said Andy. The sense of danger had magnified, and the feeling that time was running out quickly consumed them all. Laura and Andy began piling the books, notepads and papers into various bags that they were able to locate. Simon kept guard in the corridor. As they loaded in the last of the books there was another screech. It was in the distance, somewhere outside, but still unsettling.

'We've got to go,' said Simon, assuming responsibility for everyone's safety.

'If we don't get it all, we've got nothing,' said Andy. Simon knew he was right, and that the whole escapade could have been a waste of time. Andy and Laura were now rapidly removing the items stuck to the wall in the third room. They couldn't avoid the bloody mess as they stepped around, but as the blood was now so dried and congealed, little of it was sticking to their shoes and lower legs. They hadn't the time to preserve the order of the wall display, but had to hope that they would be able to reconstruct it. Laura felt a tiny flash of bemusement that with all of the resources of the Government descending on Chesborough to try to establish what had happened, they'd completely missed what they should have found simply because it wasn't what they were looking for. They may have even entered this room, blind to the crucial information they needed.

'Done,' said Andy. There was a pile of bags on the floor. It was going to take all three of them to lug them out. They piled them onto their shoulders, each of them taking at least two. Laura felt the strain, but it was not the time to argue for feminine dispensation. Simon naturally led the way. He had his gun to hand as best he could, but was noticeably impeded. It was just a question of whether it would allow a hungry zombie to be successful in its hunt or not.

Although they expected a confrontation imminently, they made it to the outside door of the halls without incident. The less concentrated stench of the outside was like fresh air compared to the rank atmosphere behind them.

They all filled their lungs, but this simple pleasure was abruptly brought to a halt. Ahead of them, their car, their means of escape from this cursed, manifestation of hell, was crawling with zombies, like wasps over a melting ice cream. There must have been at least two dozen clawing at the windows and scrambling all over it. However much they tried, the zombies would never get in, but now neither could Laura, Simon or Andy. Whether or not the zombies were expecting to find food in the car was unclear. They were probably just attracted by something so different to the decaying detritus around them. It could simply have been the alternative smell the car had to the odorous fog of rotting flesh that hung so heavy in the air, or even the lack of encrusted and blackening blood plastering it.

The zombies were taking on an increasingly terrifying appearance. Their clothes were now torn rags, fully blackened by the congealed blood of their kills, which was also spattered over their bodies melding with the dirt and grime. Their hair was wild and their expressions not much more than menacing teeth and soulless eyes penetrating out from pale visages. They'd been acquiring various bruises and tears to their skins, maybe from forcing the life out of victims or attacking each other. But it wasn't just that all of the zombies had now spent several days in their crazed state. Evolution had been swinging its merciless axe, and as food supplies diminished and the competition to survive increased, the stronger, more violent, more ferocious zombies were the ones that were winning as their weaker counterparts failed to feed and became the food.

The three humans froze, and took slow steps back into the vile atmosphere of the halls of residence. It had all seemed too easy.

'What do we do?' asked Laura, her desperation more than evident. There was silence and she and Andy instinctively looked towards Simon. He was standing tall and solid. He was trained for these kinds of situations.

'We've got to get this information away from here, to try to come up with something to stop the New Philosophy,' he said, stating their objective. 'As long as at least one of us gets away, we'll have succeeded,' he said hinting at the level of required sacrifice. The realisation of what he was saying hit Laura, making the distress of seeing the zombies on the car seem negligible. Simon continued, 'I'm going to lead them away from the car, so you can get away.' Laura could only just manage to prevent tears rolling down her face as her eyes glazed. She couldn't speak.

'What about you?' asked Andy, broaching the almost unmentionable part of the plan.

'I'll be okay,' said Simon. He wasn't intending to die, but he knew he was increasing the chances of his own extinction dramatically. His expression was almost emotionless, but a glimmer of the fear he was feeling slipped out. Andy hugged him then stepped back. Simon looked down to Laura. Both of them felt the crushing desolation as all of what they had imagined might be once that they were out of this nightmare, was shattered. Simon hugged Laura, and she hugged him back. Laura's eyes were closed, and as Simon looked into her face, he saw her lips beckoning. Simon leant down and touched his lips against hers. Laura's lipped pouted gently in response. It lasted only a second or so, and then they stepped apart. Simon looked up to Andy.

'Whatever happens, don't wait for me,' instructed Simon. 'It's too important that you get away, to take any risks.' He was now focussed on his mission. He didn't look at either Andy or Laura again as he dropped his bags, checked his big gun and other assorted weaponry, and stepped out from the halls.

He checked out the zombies. They didn't see him. He then stealthily set off to his right, away from the car, and vanished from sight. Laura and Andy said nothing. The only sound was an enthusiastic general snarling hum coming from the zombies on the car. The stranded pair were now reliant on Simon. Nothing happened. One of the zombies got pushed back off the car by a stronger zombie and it stumbled back a step and turned, before regaining its balance. As it straightened itself, it saw Andy and Laura. Laura caught her breath as an icy shiver trembled her skin. The zombie didn't move, but locked its gaze on the pair. They knew what was going to happen next. Within an instant it would be charging towards them, quickly followed by the others. Even with their guns, and even if they had greater skills with them, they were never going to be a match for this many zombies. Laura felt pain as she considered that Simon may have deserted them.

Suddenly, there was a loud bang off to their right. It was the sound of Simon's big gun. No zombie was hit, but their attention was taken. Their heads all turned in unison, swishing their wild bedraggled locks round like tattered, frayed ropes. As quickly as they turned, they leapt from the car towards the source of the sound, like a pack of greyhounds in pursuit of a track hair zooming past their gates. And they were gone. All except one. The one staring at Laura and Andy.

As the pack vanished from site, Andy and Laura awaited the inevitable. Andy was frozen, but Laura was attempting to ready her gun. The zombie launched into a sprint towards them and was moving faster than Laura could act. The pair felt a grim realisation of inevitability engulfing them. Although Simon hadn't deserted them, he hadn't accounted for this rogue zombie. In an instant or two, what was possibly humanity's last hope was about to be destroyed by the zombie's ferocious assault.

There was another loud bang from the big gun, and a shower of blood erupted from the side of the zombie's head in front of them. It fell to the ground, twitching violently. Laura felt an elation as she realised that Simon hadn't betrayed them in any way. She stepped forward, and saw the ravenous pack of zombies disappearing into the direction that the shot had come from, running off the road towards some buildings, and then entering one. There was no sign of Simon. There was no time to dwell.

'Come on!' she shouted to Andy, as she grabbed the handles of half of the bags. They were too heavy to carry, but she was able to drag them at speed. She was making more noise than desirable and could easily have alerted a zombie. More were likely to be appearing now that Simon's big gun had gone off.

250

Andy followed suit and grabbed the remaining bags. As they reached the car, they saw a couple of zombies down the road running in their direction. They had just about enough time to get into the car, but knew that if they allowed their increasing panic to befuddle them, they may well not succeed.

A zombie threw itself onto the bonnet and started headbutting the screen, just as they slammed the car doors shut, having managed to load the bags and get inside within the tiny window for survival. They locked the doors, and breathed hard sighs of relief. There was a bang as another zombie hit the side of the car. Then another, and another. They were coming fast, and they could feel the it rocking and sinking under the weight. The vehicle was solid, but Laura and Andy didn't want to wait to see how many zombies it might support or be able to drive through. Laura started the engine, and accelerated forward. The windscreen cleared slightly as the zombies began to fall away, and the vehicle jolted to the now familiar sensation of zombie under wheels. As they gathered speed, Laura swung hard on the steering wheel, sharply skidding the car into a turn flinging off the remaining zombies. She corrected their course and sped up, but only fast enough to prevent any zombies from clambering onto the vehicle.

She was hoping that they may see Simon. There was no sign of him, and the pack of pursuing zombies was gone. Through the thudding sounds of zombies bouncing off the car, Laura thought she may have heard the occasional crack of Simon's big gun, but it was impossible to tell where it was coming from, or even if it really was him. She gripped the wheel, as she forced herself to drive away. It was the hardest thing she'd experienced throughout her entire ordeal since the start of the zombie plague. The tears were now rolling down her face as she failed to hold them back any longer. She kept looking forward, concentrating on getting them away safely, blinking to clear the glaze obscuring her vision. Andy sensed Laura's soul numbing torment, and said nothing.

32. The Creation

It was getting dark as they pulled up on the grass in front of Andy's house. The oncoming gloom would not normally have tainted the feeling of relief that the sight of their sanctuary produced, but the day's events meant that a solemnity pervaded. There was an unspoken agreement not to mention what had happened to Simon. It may have been that the distance from such a subject that is normally only reached through an expanse of time was somehow acquired more quickly due to the extremity and demands of their circumstances. Either that, or they knew that to talk about it and experience it all over again was more than they could bear.

They got out of the car, and stood for a second to enjoy the sensation of the fresh country air filling their lungs and their whole being. For a second, zombies were forgotten. There was a rustle in a bush, and their alertness returned. They stepped back to the open car doors, ready to jump in if need be, staring towards the bush. A fox ran out, an early riser, and then vanished off towards the river and out of sight.

They hadn't spoken on the journey back, and they still didn't exchange any words as they gathered their hoard together and transported it into the house. Laura was keen to wash her face as soon as possible, the tear stains clearly visible streamed down her cheeks. She knew there was still work to be completed. Despite there being no guarantee that zombies couldn't reach them there, they could afford to take it a little easier, and made several trips to get everything back inside. As they closed the door of the house behind them, they finally felt some sense of safety. Laura vanished into the bathroom, returning a few minutes later and slumping into a settee. The loss was still very raw for both of them.

'Tea?' asked Andy, as was becoming expected. Laura nodded, and smiled ever so gently, but her sadness overwhelmed her spirit. Andy made the tea and brought over something to eat. They both sat on the settee, the large coffee table in front of them with the various bags strewn around just within reach.

'Shall we make a start?' asked Andy. Laura nodded. It was the least they could manage after Simon's sacrifice. They began randomly taking out books, looking at the titles, flicking through papers and notebooks. They kept the handwritten stuff to one side, the direct thoughts of the New Philosophers. They laid out the parts of the wall display on the floor, and made a pretty good job of recreating what they had viewed in its original grisly setting. They worked on into the dead of night, occasionally flashing something of interest at the other, before continuing in their task. Eventually, everything was unpacked, and even displaying the beginnings of what might develop into some kind of order. They sat back as the last bag was emptied.

'What do you make of it?' asked Andy. Laura scanned over the pile.

'They were definitely involved with the New Philosophy,' said Laura, the 'they' referring to the mangled bodies that they'd found at the halls of residence. 'But I don't get any sense that they were leaders or in charge in any way, or even part of any groups. The stuff that they were writing is obviously earlier drafts of it, but there's stuff from other people there as well. It's almost as if they were just a bunch of friends and these three were the only ones who bothered with taking any notes, kind of like self appointed scribes to chaos.' Andy nodded.

'The books and texts they've got are an interesting mix, don't you think?' said Andy. They were. There were books on religions, cults, political ideologies, unions, bureaucracies, a couple of copies of the Prison Notebooks, organisational culture, management manuals, corporate rule books and a good representation of the psychology of persuasion. They seemed to cover a whole range of groups, from formal organisations to informal movements, the sort of things that turn people into drones every day to a greater or lesser extent, guiding their actions and hiding them from the reality that their lives are ebbing away.

Having spent the previous day meticulously scrutinising the text of the New Philosophy, there was a ring of familiarity. They appeared to be closing in on the backbone of the demonic sermon.

'Look!' said Andy, waving a tattered piece of paper in his hand. 'Some of these books are listed here, and a description of what they were looking for.' Laura shuffled up next to Andy and they both read it through. The ideas were still confused, but it indicated that the New Philosophy had begun with the notion that society is dominated not by people, but groups and structures, which are based on ideas that people join up with and subscribe to. They'd identified that understanding how these groups work, and how they change people, could be used to change and bring about a better society.

It was a simple idea really, and hardly unique. Every new movement, from religious and political to commercial, is trying to bring people together to achieve what they think is better, or at least the organisation's aims. It was starting to appear though, that the New Philosophy had emerged from starting with everything relevant that had gone before and building on it.

'What I don't understand,' began Laura, 'is why the people who were involved in creating the New Philosophy were killed by the zombies.' The pair realised that it could well have been that they had suicidal intents, but to subject oneself to that kind of death at the hands of zombies, or even to have become zombies themselves, was hard to believe. Laura and Andy began scrabbling through more of the hand written notes, scanning their detail. At first they did so rapidly, handing anything of interest to the other and amassing a small pile of the most salient writings. Eventually they stopped and looked at each other confused. They had both come to the same conclusion, but it was unsatisfactory, and still left the same holes in their explanations.

'They just seemed to be trying to come up with something to make the world a better place, almost randomly,' said Laura.

'I agree,' said Andy. 'It's like they thought that if they took all of the best bits of ideas that influenced people and brought them together, they might be able to come up with something that could do some real good. Like a code for living together that everyone wants to share and benefit from.'

'Didn't work very well, did it?' said Laura dryly. Andy couldn't help but chuckle.

'It's not been ineffective though,' he replied. They paused a second.

'What's missing,' said Laura, 'is how they went from an idea to do some good, to creating an army of zombies.' She thought for a second looking for an answer to her own rhetoric. 'Maybe it was hijacked by someone else?' This sounded like a possibility to Andy. He looked down at the notes they'd amassed and shuffled them with his hands, moving them into a line. He looked at what he had created, held his hand to his mouth and screwed up his eyes as he considered deeply what was before him, then shook his head.

'I don't think so,' finally came his reply. 'I don't think it could have been hijacked'. 'Look. I've put their ideas into an order. You can see it developing, from scribbling based on what they've been reading, suggestions from other people, all the way through to virtually the New Philosophy that they ended up with. It's the same the whole way through. There's no sudden takeover.'

'Then why did they do it?' asked Laura, her perplexity now causing her agitation. Andy leant back and looked upwards slightly. He could feel the sensations of what could be a crucial insight coming to him. Laura just looked at him and said nothing. She could virtually see Andy's mind working out his thoughts before sharing what might be a breakthrough, and she didn't want to disturb the process. After sometime, Andy spoke.

'Maybe what they ended up with didn't really come from them,' he said.

255

'So who created it?'

'What do you mean?'

'Well it didn't write itself!'

'They still wrote it, but the idea that emerged happened in spite of them.'

'I still don't understand?'

'I guess that the idea evolved.'

'But it was still made up by people, by the New Philosophers.'

'Yes and no! It was created by people, but 'made up' suggests that it's something that they intended to do. But ideas can evolve, and maybe their direction has some independence, regardless of people. People are needed to make the evolution happen but the ideas are always going to go in the same direction. Do you think someone sat down and created something as complicated as language?' said Andy.

'I'm not sure?'

'It got added to bit by bit, by a lot of different people. Even then you can't say who created a particular part, and no one person could stop it happening. Sometimes language changes at random and then it changes again in the way people use it. This has happened independently in many different cultures. The fine detail of different languages may be different, but fundamentally they are the same thing. Language is an idea that will evolve eventually, wherever there are people. It's not about specific people. It's about the idea.'

'I'm still not sure it's the same thing. This is a specific idea like a story, a song, or a poem. Those things are made up by people.' Laura was trying to catch up with Andy's thoughts.

'What about urban myths?'

'Aren't they made up though?'

'They are, but similar ones emerge independently. They start off as a simple story that then evolves as they are passed around. Things like babysitters and clown statues, or dead bodies under beds. Everyone who goes to university hears the same story about a famous woman who used to go there, and had sex with the whole rugby team on the pool table. The amount of people who've heard this, and very often with exactly the same details seems endless. It really would be quite a coincidence if that happened to every single famous woman who had been to university.'

Laura smiled, for she had heard her own university's take on this particular tale, and had failed to question it. As she considered what Andy had suggested, she shared one of her initial thoughts.

'So what you're saying, is that ideas have an independent existence, parasitically manifesting in whatever medium is first to respond?' Andy hadn't even thought of this yet.

'Kind of, but the ideas would never exist without people. It's more that they are an inevitable consequence of how people are,' added Andy.

They looked again through the prototypes of the ideas. They could see that numerous changes had been made to the text and structure. They didn't have the full documentation, as some had inevitably been lost, but what remained still told the story. The changes often appeared almost randomly and blindly applied. The annotations showed that the three core members were really only recording the information. They didn't see themselves as a formal group, as the New Philosophers. That name only emerged towards the final incarnation of the idea, and only ever as its name, 'The New Philosophy'. Lots of people had been involved in commenting on it and never saw themselves as part of any kind of group. The most real part of the whole enterprise was the idea itself, bouncing from person to person, like a rumour going round a hysterical crowd, facilitating the inevitable emergence of a gruesome Frankenstein.

The New Philosophy could easily have been mistaken for a chimera of the texts and concepts that had gone before, but very little had won through. What was left was an amalgam of the winners in this competition for survival, the weaker parts dying becoming extinct. Laura stopped looking at the papers.

'Can ideas evolve?' she asked Andy. It was one of those questions that should be obvious, but is rarely, if ever, asked. Andy looked to Laura for clarification. 'Evolution was originally all about living things. We're talking about ideas here. I know we talk about all sorts of things evolving all of the time, as a kind of de facto law of everything, but is it right?' Andy understood Laura, and she was completely right.

'Generalised Darwinism is used to explain all sorts of things such as society and economies, but it's not a rigorous approach in its own right,' said Andy. 'It's really just the power of Darwin's original ideas that drives through its use. I guess that with all of the things we've accepted about the New Philosophy, it's not really that difficult to accept ideas can evolve. I guess it's really just common sense that in any system where there is any form of competition, the fittest service.' Laura trusted Andy.

As they looked further, it remained apparent to them that there was no mention of zombies or anything remotely like the gory acts and massacres that had been taking place. There was no agenda for what finally resulted. In fact, it was all quite the opposite.

'Why do you think this has happened?' asked Laura.

'I could only guess,' replied Andy. 'Maybe it's an evolutionary response to intelligence, and is needed to wipe out the weaker intellects who are a threat to the survival of the whole species? Maybe there's something in our subconscious that is aware of what we're doing to the planet, how it's over populated whilst resources are running out and no one's doing enough to stop it getting any worse? The New Philosophy could just be down to the ruthless efficiency of nature. It may be that this is going to be ultimately good for our species, weeding out the minds that follow and perpetuate the worst kinds of cultures that wreak havoc and mayhem on society.' Laura nodded slowly. She could see the sense in what he was saying. She then offered her own thoughts.

'Maybe it's the inherent evil in people coming out,' she said. 'We're an evil species. Like all survivors, we're self-interested, otherwise we'd die out. We've simply managed to develop an intellect to fool ourselves into thinking that we can work together when really all we want to do is exploit others. It's a fragile deal. It wouldn't take much to break it. It might just be the inescapable subtext of 'morality', and we're just seeing an extreme manifestation.'

Neither responded to their gloomy theories. Andy perked up and looked to Laura.

'The thing about evolution though,' he said, 'is that although it may get to its results by a completely random process, the eventual results can be explained by rational thinking, by how effective they are at exploiting a particular niche.' Laura was intrigued. 'The New Philosophy may have come from chaos, but that doesn't mean there isn't order to it. In fact there has to be. We just have to find it, and then we can use it.'

33. Making Sense

It was late the next day that they made a breakthrough. It would still take until late into the night for them to start coming up with anything that made sense.

They had made an early start with their new found insight gained from their expedition to the source of the New Philosophy. Initially it still seemed impenetrable, but gradually, order and patterns of meaning began to emerge. They could see that there were various sections to the New Philosophy, though not always following on from each other, that ideas were repeated, and that there were concepts within statements. Occasionally a meaning would appear blatant, but then more depth would emerge beyond.

The structure was mind blowing, containing all sorts of mechanisms and tricks to enable ideas to be transferred to the recipient more powerfully than ever imaginable. It was a mentally draining exercise for the pair, as they each realised that their conscious and subconscious minds were engaged in continual resistance to the New Philosophy trying to implant its warped views into their psyche. The ideas were complexly embedded, using figurative language, metaphor, parable, subtle suggestion, but underlying it all, clear, discrete messages were gradually found to exist within.

For every element deciphered, there appeared to be yet another hidden layer peeking out at them. The New Philosophy had to be finite, it was a set number of words, but as its sophistication continued to astonish them, they felt that they couldn't dismiss the idea that somehow it would take them round in circles forever, continually creating new meaning. They knew though in their hearts that it couldn't continue without end. To affect the human mind it had to be something that the mind could cope with, even if only subconsciously.

Eventually, their tiny breakthroughs began to amass. They grouped them together and found even greater understanding. They could see the New Philosophy for what it was; a highly sophisticated framework embedded with a set of specific ideas, ideas that turned people into zombies. They created a list of them that [THE FOLLOWING HAS BEEN CENSORED] ---
------------------REDACTED---------------------REDACTED----
-----------------REDACTED---------------------REDACTED-----
----------------REDACTED---------------------REDACTED------
--------------REDACTED---------------------REDACTED-------
-------------REDACTED---------------------REDACTED-------
-------------REDACTED---------------------REDACTED---------
------------REDACTED---------------------REDACTED---------
------------REDACTED.

After many hours, they had succeeded in decanting the ramblings of the New Philosophy into its core messages. Laid out bare in this way, they could clearly see why people were taken in and would change in the way that they had.

As they analysed the meaning, they realised that the New Philosophy didn't just force its own message. A whole series of caveats, defences and pre-emptive arguments were entwined within to prevent it being discredited, or even any seed of doubt being sown in the mind of the potential zombie. They could now see why their initial attempts to warn people were so utterly futile. It was like a bow and arrow against an Apache helicopter. If anything, attempts to warn against it would make it stronger and more virulent. Their earlier pathetic efforts had made things worse, preparing the ground for the New Philosophy's assault. One of the particular mechanisms, that they'd never seen anything like before was [THE FOLLOWING HAS BEEN CENSORED] ----------------------REDACTED---------------------
-REDACTED---------------------REDACTED---------------------
REDACTED---------------------REDACTED---------------------
REDACTED---------------------REDACTED---------------------
REDACTED---------------------REDACTED---------------------
REDACTED---------------------REDACTED---------------------
REDACTED---------------------REDACTED---------------------
REDACTED

It was now obvious why the New Philosophy could not be stopped by telling people it was a bad idea.

'Well, that's it,' said Andy. He and Laura were stood looking down at the large table where they had assembled the culmination of their efforts. They were each sipping a hot drink that they had made themselves as a reward for the conclusion of this stage of their labours. On the table was a patchwork of pieces of paper with the concepts the New Philosophy revealed. They were now logically structured to flow from each other within a totality of meaning. Just as Watson and Crick had rationalised the chaotic chemicals of DNA, they had brought meaning to the maelstrom of words that were the New Philosophy.

'What do we do now?' asked Andy. Though they were exhausted, he'd enjoyed the journey he'd just completed with Laura, and had come to respect her intellect even more. Laura had already been trying to think of an answer to this very question.

'We know that just telling people that it's a bad idea doesn't work. If they don't understand that, they're never going to take this in.' Andy nodded in agreement, and Laura sipped her drink. A thought was niggling at her. She knew there was something about the reification of the New Philosophy that must give them a clue. It may just be information and words, but an analogous approach with the physical world had got them this far. The fog cleared as the irritable thought came into focus, a glorious moment of clarity.

'Before we knew what was causing the zombies,' she began, 'we talked about a virus. The New Philosophy has acted exactly like a virus.' Andy was feeling the hook. 'We should still treat it like one.' Andy was beginning to anticipate what Laura was about to say, but looked straight at her taking a swig of his tea wanting her to deliver her conclusion. 'We can use what we have here to create an anti-virus, a vaccine that increases natural immunity.' Andy smiled. 'We use the same structure, but attach a defence to it instead. Then when people are infected with it, they will build up their own defence. We can inoculate them against the New Philosophy.' Andy was impressed. Laura put down her drink.

'Look!' she said as she began moving round the table and pointing at specific words and phrases. 'This bit here represents [REDACTED]. The opposite of that is [REDACTED].' She moved around to another part. 'And this bit here. This is [REDACTED] which we can change to [REDACTED].' Laura speeded up, flitting around the table, now effortlessly highlighting the concepts represented and their antithesis. She was on a roll. Her insight and enthusiasm gave the weary pair newfound energy. Andy put down his drink and grabbed a pen and some paper, scribing for Laura and adding his own contributions.

For well over an hour they buzzed around the table, addressing every word and phrase that they had decanted from the New Philosophy and its meaning, improving on some earlier efforts, debating which competing categories to go with and what might be the opposite of some of the concepts.

Eventually they were done. They stood back from the table and looked over their work, taking in the culmination of the gargantuan effort that they had pulled off in the last couple of days. Just as the Manhattan project may never have marshalled the resources and resolve to create the first atomic bomb had it not been for the ultimately false belief that the Nazis were close to developing their own, without the encroaching terror of the zombie plague they may never have accomplished their challenge.

In front of them was laid bare the New Philosophy, and alongside it, its mirror companion, its potential nemesis that could defeat the warped ideology and hate that it had been spreading so effectively. It wasn't in its final form, and would see improvement after a good night's rest, but the essential work was complete, and they had their prize.

They had a good idea.

34. First Trial

Clive Hill sat in the armchair trying not to show his nervousness, but unable to hide his continued glances around looking for a chance to escape. It should be relatively easy for him to do so, but he wanted to be sure that he could make it away when the moment to act came. In front of him within arm's reach, was sat his captor, Frank Bunner. Frank would have not thought of himself as a captor or anything even nearing that description. After all, he was just continuing the conversation that Clive had begun with him an hour or so earlier. Frank was sat on a wooden chair elevating him higher than Clive's position, so that he was bearing down on Clive making him feel pinned to his seat. Clive knew that there was always a risk that this was going to happen, but he had not really prepared himself for the reality of confronting it when he'd agreed to the plan with Laura and Andy. Frank grinned at Clive, a big grin stretching his face wide apart to ensure that it was accommodated.

'I'm so pleased you came round and played me that recording of it,' said Frank, his beaming giving Clive decidedly unpleasant coulrophobic sensations. Frank continued to engage in a one-sided discussion on the virtues of the New Philosophy. Clive barely managed to maintain feigned attention while awaiting his moment. 'It's far better than that other rubbish you told me about,' said Frank, momentarily and possibly for the last time diverting his conversation to a subject other than the New Philosophy, before continuing with his eulogising.

Clive knew that he'd brought this on himself and had agreed to do it in full knowledge of what might happen. Earlier that day, he'd been back on his amateur radio talking to Laura and Andy. They'd explained to Clive what they'd been up to since they'd last spoken, how they'd travelled to Chesborough to the source of the New Philosophy, how they'd collected up the information that had been used to create it, how Simon had sacrificed himself so that they could get away, and how they had analysed the New Philosophy to create their own good idea.

The triumvirate had discussed long and hard what to do next. The warnings that Location Three had issued to all of its resources about the New Philosophy, comprising virtually all of the military and Government people available, had ensured that their subsequent efforts to find out about the New Philosophy had now rendered them an obsolete organisation. Those who had been nonsusceptible and had not been devoured by their colleagues, were now disconnected from any larger body that they may have previously been part of, lost in the pandemonium of zombie land. It was up to Laura, Andy and Clive to act.

The obvious first choice to release the vaccine, the antivirus that they had created, to everyone, would be foolhardy. The radio hams still possessed something of a network, and given that television and radio broadcasts had by now collapsed or were merely churning out repeated automated messages, the hams were the closest thing to any sort of national infrastructure. They could get the good idea out, but if it didn't work, they may just achieve the effect of alerting even more people to the existence of the New Philosophy. It could finalise the swift destruction of the last remnants of the human race and threads of hope; the radio hams had already established that the New Philosophy had wrought similar effects around the globe.

Having rejected immediate and full dispersal of the good idea, they were left with the option of testing. The only way they could do this would be to try out the good idea on selected subjects, and then expose them to the New Philosophy. This ethical predicament may well have defeated, as it often does, a lesser group of people. This didn't mean that they weren't faced with the same deeply ingrained cultural desires to distance oneself from selecting and condemning an individual to a potential death. These kinds of ethical constraints, vital for the day-to-day functioning of society, could be like a set of concrete shoes for a drowning man, when faced with decisions pertinent to the potential complete breakdown of humanity.

This was a circumstance where leadership was needed. Real leadership is always about making choices no one else would ever want to make, the choices that the majority of people defer to others then actively attack for the decisions that they have made, but would complain even more strongly if they weren't. Real leadership is for the few and is rarely rewarding, unlike the mock leadership found all too often in a gluttonous society, a leadership practised by a self-interested and self-protecting cabal who exploit their power for their own ends, whilst never having to answer for their incompetence and effects.

Andy and Clive were strong men, but it was Laura that had finally stood up, made the decision, and then convinced them both to follow. Through an argument of the greatest good for the greatest number, and that they would only be bringing forward the inevitable demise of the experimentees should they not act, a consensus, however distasteful, was reached. As nonsusceptibles to the New Philosophy, they were always going to be the types who could do the right thing, however difficult.

Having reached their decision, it was no simple matter putting it into practice. The uncomfortable role of playing God and having to choose the guinea pigs, was mitigated to some extent by a lottery. Clive, barricaded into his terraced house for most of the time, had managed to ascertain the whereabouts of several other survivors. He'd done this through a mixture of ad hoc communication methods and occasional forays for supplies beyond his sanctuary. Clive was the only one in a position to carry out the test, and he had a list of the potential guinea pigs he could get to. Those most likely to be susceptible were identified by a quickly concocted objective method, which whether or not effective, had ensured its main purpose of removing any sense of subjective decision making. A mixture of rationality and chance had led to the names being on this list, and the use of a simple lottery to decide the order in which to try out the tests deferred decision making to chance.

The plan had been to carry out one test at a time and see how it went. There was always the chance that the subjects might not have turned after hearing the good idea as they were already non-susceptible. As it happened, Frank Bunner was the first person on the list and was enamoured with the New Philosophy within a few minutes of Clive playing it to him. He'd not seemed particularly taken with the good idea, the vaccine, its starkly stated rationality finding little resonance with the simple mind of Frank. It was a different matter though when he heard the recording of the New Philosophy. He'd immediately wanted it played again. Clive had had little alternative but to comply, before coming up with the ruse that the power had gone on his playback machine. It wouldn't have mattered either way. One hearing was enough for Frank to absorb it all and relate it back to Clive, syllable perfect, as he went through ritual repetition and consideration that characterised the infection taking its full hold before the final zombification.

Based on what Laura and Andy had gleaned and shared with Clive, Frank seemed a fairly typical changeling. His ranting was going to last a few hours, and if he'd have been able to tell anyone else, he would have eagerly shared the foul message with whomever he could. As it was, this was limited to Clive, and part of the New Philosophy's warped genius was to ensure Frank did all he could to make sure Clive stayed with him.

Clive knew that he could probably physically overcome Frank. He was at the early end of his sixties, but had declined since taking early retirement. Now a target for the local kids, he remained in his tiny home as much as he could, having turned it into a virtual fortress. In many ways, not too much had changed for Frank; before the zombie plague he'd been the target of kids believing vile rumours that were peddled about his sexual preferences, whereas now he was the target of zombies created by the New Philosophy. In both cases, he was at the mercy of the unthinking mainstream populace embracing any idea that justified their inner evil. It was this isolation, a feature of the daily torture he normally faced that had saved him.

Frank was wearing several layers of clothing and a balaclava, and could have been mistaken for a pile of rags on a table at a jumble sale from a distance. He was of sufficient means, but had chosen to scrimp to ensure that he had plenty set aside for a rainy day, and so rarely used his heating; he'd hardly noticed a difference since the power had gone off. Despite knowing that he may have been physically superior to Frank, Clive was not sufficiently confident that he could overcome him unscathed, and could well have to run out of the house to escape without any checks being made first. If he were carrying injuries that prevented his swift flight, any waiting zombies would soon take advantage. Furthermore, it was impossible to tell just what weaponry a chap living the life of Frank may have close to hand.

Clive knew that he was not in immediate danger. From what Laura and Andy had already told him, he knew that there would probably be a period during which Frank would become catatonic. However, Clive was in the middle of zombie country, and had chosen his time carefully to visit Frank. He'd observed the zombies' movements over the previous days, and had identified that even these savages seemed to already be forming group habits. There were highs and lows in zombie activity in the locality. It was as if despite their savagery, the zombies had all trained together towards a common purpose, and now unleashed, were exemplary at spreading their particular flavour of vile mayhem, intent on their own selfish gratification. There could never be a guarantee that there would be no zombies present, or that an unexpected incident might bring them all running, but it was better than being out when they could be expected to be present in large numbers.

The window of escape was now closing. Clive knew that very soon there would be increased zombie activity in the area, and his chances of getting home, back to his own sanctuary, would be diminished greatly. Frank was still rapidly bumbling away. Clive had an idea.

'You know what, Frank,' said Clive, 'I've just remembered that there is more.' Frank stopped for a second, still grinning.

'I'm not sure we need it now,' said Frank, an increasing slur evident, 'I really think I understand exactly what the New Philosophy is about.' Clive had to think fast.

'But you do need it Frank,' said Clive standing up whilst stretching out to Frank to prevent him from getting up, 'the other stuff is so important. You wouldn't believe it.'

'Really?' said Frank, Clive's mollification having some effect. Frank was conflicted. The New Philosophy was trying to make him keep Clive there, but if there was something else that could increase this feeling of elation he had, better than any narcotic, he wanted it. Frank's moment of indecision gave Clive his chance. He quickly reached the door, checked outside and was away, just as Frank said, 'No wait!' and stumbled after him. The door was closed before he could reach it.

As Clive made his escape, he looked back and saw Frank's door open. Frank stood in the doorway shouting, 'Clive, come back!' but Clive had shut his mind off to Frank now. He felt sickening regret at the impending death he'd condemned him to, although Frank had taken into his own hands the manner in which his life would end. Clive couldn't help but think that if Frank had to die, he may as well as draw the attention of the zombies away from him. Clive carried on as Frank's calls became more distant, eventually masked by the sound of shrieking zombies as they swarmed towards Frank's shouts.

35. Presentation

Laura and Andy were both staring at the table. It still contained the good idea that they had created the day before, set out alongside their analysis of the New Philosophy. They said nothing. They were pondering the news that they'd just received back from Clive. They had failed. The New Philosophy couldn't be stopped. It was going to carry on spreading, converting most of its listeners into zombies, leaving the tiny group of non-susceptible people struggling to avoid being the key participant in a zombie slaughter, or else starving to death as their precious resources dwindled away.

It was impossible for the pair not to feel demoralised. It wasn't just the impending fate that was now looming upon most survivors that brought them down, or their own potential demise. Andy's place was relatively safe, and they had resources; a river with fish, country game and Andy grew sufficient vegetables upon the roof of his house to keep them fed indefinitely. He also had his own power source. The likelihood was that once the spread of the New Philosophy had reached saturation point, they would never see another human being again. They knew that they were rapidly reaching the point of no return, when there would no longer be enough survivors to rebuild society, even if the zombies could be defeated. But even this wasn't what depressed them so much at this particular moment. It was that having believed they'd cracked the puzzle of the New Philosophy and created a counter solution, they had failed.

They were both struggling to rise above the despondency, but the death of Frank hung heavy on their consciences. In the greater scheme of things, the death of Frank Bunner caused by their experiment on him to see if the vaccine for the New Philosophy really worked, was of little significance. Not least because it was unlikely Frank would have survived much longer anyway. However, Frank wasn't just a meaningless statistic, or one of a total number of casualties so large that the total loses its impact. The death of Frank was significant to them. They knew his name, the details of how his fate was sealed, and most importantly, that they had been a part of his demise. However much they rationalised their actions and came to the inescapable conclusion that they acted correctly, their emotions refused to free them from the torment they were feeling.

They were not going to talk about Frank. If they were to have any chance of survival, there was every possibility that they may be involved in making many more decisions like this, or worse. If this first ethical skirmish were to shred their resolve, they would have no hope. At one point, Andy did look up to Laura, the forlorn look in his countenance betraying the distress in his soul, and moved to speak. Laura, anticipating what Andy was about to say, strengthened, and his lost puppy overtures were demolished as they met cold steel. There would be no further attempts to talk about Frank.

'Why didn't it work?' said Andy eventually, unable to bear the silence any longer and his inescapable inner conversations. It was as much a question to himself. She shrugged without averting her gaze from the table where their work was laid out. 'I was sure that it was going to,' he said. 'We'd established that you can't stop people listening to and believing a bad idea by telling them it's a bad idea.' Laura nodded firmly. This was so true. 'And we put our good idea together on exactly the same basis as the bad idea.'

Andy stopped speaking. Laura made a sound of vague agreement, but he wasn't sure how much she was really listening. She was leaning over the table, her arms outstretched. Her long black hair had fallen down by the sides of her head, not far from touching the table and hiding her face. He noticed how feminine the curve of her body was in this posture. He considered for a second that if the task of re-establishing the human race fell to him and Laura that he wouldn't be adverse to the proposition. His attention shifted and he could see that Laura was thinking. A tiny flicker of hope ignited in his

271

stomach. He was as enthralled by her intellect as anything else, and although he was at a loss to see what they could do, he knew that Laura may not be so stymied.

'It isn't the same, is it?' said Laura after a few moments. Andy had become so entranced staring at Laura anticipating any revelation, he didn't react. She turned her head to look at him with a flick to move the hair that obstructed her vision. Andy came to.

'What isn't?' he asked.

'Our good idea isn't the same as the New Philosophy,' she said. Andy was perplexed.

'But we've based it on the same structure,' he replied. He thought he'd understood what Laura was saying. 'Have we made a mistake in our analysis? Have we got the structure wrong?' Andy moved round to Laura's side so that he could see their handiwork from her viewpoint, hoping he'd gain the same insight that was now sparking in her mind if he observed from the same position.

He looked over the layout, their notes, their annotations, and their categorisation of the concepts. He was looking hard for the mistake that Laura had spotted, but found none. They had been rigorous in the first place, checked and double-checked before finalising the good idea, and had both gone over it again that day. All the time, Laura remained leaning forward over the table staring, not at any particular element, but at the whole thing. Andy just couldn't work it out, and began to shake his head.

'I…,' he began. Laura interrupted his coming admission of defeat.

'The structure's fine,' she said. 'You know we've more than made sure.' Andy was now confused.

'Do you think the New Philosophy would have the effect it has had if we just took the information in front of us and told people that?' she asked.

'I'm not sure,' said Andy, still struggling.

'Do you think the words would be repeated exactly the same, those words that took us so long to decipher, but that stimulated such emotions and feelings?' Andy was beginning to see Laura's point as she continued. 'If the New Philosophy was just those raw facts, banal data, nobody would have any time for it.' Andy was nodding slowly as Laura's words created the relief of sense coming together in his head. 'But that's what our good idea is. So it's not the same as the New Philosophy.'

'You mean it's not just what we say, but how we say,' he said.

It was an obvious error, but almost inevitable by people who value content over presentation. The flowery language of the New Philosophy had just appeared to be an over indulgence to them. It may even have been this dismissal that caused them not to succumb to its power. But the message was almost of no significance compared to the wording, the images and feelings they conjured up, the emotions that were harnessed. Laura and Andy's good idea had the right substance, but it was nothing without the right spin. It may as well have not have existed unless it was dressed in the right clothes. People would buy the rancid scrapings of animal remnants if they were packaged in a glitzy wrapper claiming that they were a sumptuous ready meal whilst ignoring premium steak at a lower price if it was wrapped in a dreary brown paper bag.

They both smiled a little for the first time that day. Their joy was severely limited though now, having grown accustomed to false dawns only heralding continuing darkness.

'So what do we do, Andy?'

'We need to create the good idea in the same kind of language as the New Philosophy.' Laura looked weary. She knew that they couldn't just change the odd word. Whole phrases would have to be changed with their own unique imagery and use of language to create exactly the required counter emotion to the New Philosophy. It would take a highly skilled wordsmith.

'I can't do that,' said Laura. She'd taken a few seconds to consider whether or not admitting that this task was beyond her was giving up, but it was simply a case of not having the right skill. It would be like asking someone who could only play chopsticks on the piano to perform Beethoven's Sonata No 8 Pathetique Second Movement. And the cost of failure was too much as the spectre of the Frank Bunner's sacrifice kicked her in her conscience.

'Neither can I,' said Andy immediately, having thought the same,

'We need to find someone who can then,' said Laura.

36. The Writer

The large black four by four vehicle pulled up at Andy's place having completed its mission. There were three occupants. Laura driving, Andy in the back and sat in the front passenger seat, the reason for their outing. The new addition was Stuart Grams, the sort of person who always got the front seat, either through exploitation of politeness, contempt for meek protestations or any other method that got him what he wanted.

Stuart was their writer for their second attempt at creating a good idea, a version that they hoped would take the raw facts and dress them in the most beautiful garb of flowing language required to make it an effective vaccine. They had been fortunate in being able to locate Stuart so quickly, having only reached the conclusion that they needed a writer the day before. They'd once again used the amateur radio network, the radio hams. Although the hams were only a tiny fraction of the population, limited to crackly audio transmissions reliant on each operator being on air at the same time, this democratised information and media network had proved its societal impact way beyond what could ever have been predicted. Laura and Andy had fantasised how great it would be if there was some kind of facility that allowed this for everyone, but this seemed almost more farfetched than the zombie plague.

Once the message had gone out to the hams that they needed a writer, a list of suggestions was quickly compiled. From this, it wasn't just a case of crossing out those they knew to dead, but identifying those that they knew the whereabouts of. It was this final criteria that made Stuart Grams the front runner by far. Had there been any other viable choices, it was likely that they would all have been ahead of Stuart, as although a talented writer, Stuart's reputation was less desirable. Without Stuart though, they may have had a long list of none, and as it was presumed that he was in relatively close proximity to Laura and Andy, that turned out to be correct, no time was lost in finding him.

When Laura and Andy reached him, Stuart was barely hanging on within his makeshift sanctuary. He had been planning to move before the zombie catastrophe, as it already felt to him like he was living in a slum of such undesirability that the addition of rampaging zombies had barely made a difference.

Stuart wondered at first whether the sight of the four by four specifically seeking him out was a hallucination. He'd stayed hidden at first, wondering if it might be some kind of zombie mind trick. It was only a mix of Laura and Andy's tenacity and lack of any other plan that finally led to them locating Stuart. He was picked up and they travelled back without any significant zombie encounters, other than the obligatory ramming of assailants making fruitless charges. The relative abundance of food and drink that Laura and Andy had with them had been enough to convince Stuart to go with them.

One of the hams had suggested Stuart as a potential writer having become aware of his work as a scriptwriter for a late night adult television channel, though the ham chose to refer to his later work. Stuart had started his career by writing erotic short stories for a late night adult channel, voiced by a range of glamorous female wannabes in various states of undress and self-pleasuring. The most difficult aspect of this particular engagement for Stuart proved to be ensuring his use of language and multi-syllabic words was not too taxing for the beauties, whose intellect and acting ability seemed to be as small as their breasts were large. This was to prove perfect training for the task he now faced. He had excelled in this engagement, being able to write from the viewpoint of a young girl in an amazingly convincing manner.

From these colourful beginnings, Stuart had risen rapidly to become a successful screenwriter working on several feature films, and further expanded his broadcasting credentials with a stint making television documentaries. Unfortunately his world collapsed after he was arrested for engaging in an indecent act in public, an outburst that exposed the drug and prostitute problem he'd acquired from his enthusiastic attendance at the adult channel's regular parties. The incident could have been worse, but Stuart was able to convince all concerned that it was a misunderstanding, and it was soon, almost inexplicably, forgotten. It was an early demonstration of his svengali-esque abilities.

Having set aside his indulgences, Stuart had begun working his way back up having secured a position on a lower rung of the ladder. He'd found himself having to be content with a role as an assistant script editor for a daytime soap, though his arrogance and disdain for his colleagues would have suggested something much higher. As only perceptions and their manipulation mattered to Stuart, his imagined newfound success was already a reality.

His explosive storylines had just started to make their impact prior to the onset of the zombie apocalypse, suitably raising his profile, whilst not yet improving his modest accommodation. The ham who recommended Stuart had met him, leaving an indelible mark of the man. Fortunately the ham had the ability to put aside all personal feelings following his belittling at the mercy of Stuart, an objectivity he would have probably been capable of even if a lesser prize than the future of mankind were at stake. The ham had recognised not only a gifted writer in Stuart, but a man who could magically create any truth he wanted in defiance of any facts to the contrary. This was a man whose imagined world did seem to project more strongly than the real one. Those who'd seen him captivate his listeners could easily imagine him bringing a whole morgue of corpses back to life simply by insisting that they were alive. This was the ideal man to create the good idea.

The conversation in the car from Stuart's place to Andy's, subsequently continuing in the house, confirmed any preconceptions that they may have had as to the character of Stuart that the ham had shared with them. Laura and Andy's growing caution of Stuart, which would normally have kept them well away from such a character if he'd ever have actually lowered himself to stumble into their company, was only matched by the weighty matter to hand.

In the same way that Laura and Andy were not susceptible to the New Philosophy, they were not duped by Stuart's charm. However the pair of them were equally afflicted by the double-edged sword of being hopeless at hiding their feelings. They had both regularly missed out on opportunities available to the more socially adept, either at best, through their own failure to ingratiate themselves before pushing their own abilities, or alternatively falling foul of the subtle attacks delivered by their more charming competition. Unfortunately, raw honesty is rarely a pleasing behaviour to others, despite ubiquitous platitudes to the contrary. To a social genius such as Stuart, this was all too apparent. Ordinarily, a pair such as this would vanish from his awareness instantly, offering no contribution to his own rise, but on this occasion, even Stuart knew the world needed saving before he could continue with his plans to exploit and conquer it as best he could.

Although Stuart had still been in the process of scrabbling out of his current life and career low, there was something about him, something unnerving, something of the puppet master, something suggestive of an unhealthy amount of power destined to be in his hands despite everyone knowing that such a thing should never be allowed to happen. It may well have been this illusion of 'what may be some day' that tricked people into giving him far more credit and time than he should ever have been let loose with, and enabled him to continue up the ladders of success with such ease, only sliding down the occasional snake due to his own misfooting.

He was the epitome of the charming dictator syndrome, whereby those who had met the likes of Hitler or Idi Amin, would be astonished at how lovely the particular despot was, as if they expected them to be devouring babies before their eyes. Everyone knew of Stuart's more unsavoury deeds and rightly judged him on these, only to be overwhelmed by their own misguided ego on meeting the man, swivelling their opinion one hundred and eighty degrees to declare what a lovely man he was.

As is always the undoing of those who are exploited the most, the greater their belief in being a good judge of character, the less they actually possess this ability. Once drawn into the web of this charmer, the danger would only be noticed once escape was impossible. The only hope left would be to go along with the charade in the hope that attacks would be aimed at others, and to encourage this diversion.

Stuart's rumoured political aspirations sent cold chills through those who knew the true Stuart Grams. Ironically, this made them keen to stay even closer and more subservient to him than ever. Once again paradoxically, this seemed to ensure his rise. If politics was his aspiration, it had probably resulted from his experience as a young teenager when he was chosen to represent his school at an international youth conference. In order to make the event as real as possible, the organisers had ensured that the delegates were treated with all the due deference that any senior politician would expect to receive. On returning home, this was the only thing that Stuart talked about for several weeks, informing everyone of his importance. This taste of power left a lasting impression on Stuart.

Sat in the spacious and safe, living area of Andy's abode, the three unlikely comrades were able to engage in surprisingly easy chit-chat. Andy over the years had become aware of his social deficiencies, and although only a novice in the social arts, he even managed the occasional laugh as they exchanged stories, though it would never fool a virtuoso such as Stuart. Laura smiled whenever she could, her discomfort barely hidden. To an observer, it would appear that Stuart was conversing with two of his closest friends, even though unable to exert his usual charismatic control was an alien situation to him. Laura and Andy were happy to believe that Stuart was putting the existence of the human race above all his other desires, which to some extent he was, as skin saving was the first skill of any delightful rogue.

As they chatted, Laura and Andy explained the story so far behind the New Philosophy. They were fully aware of the difficulties in trying to get anybody to believe that the zombies were created by nothing more than an idea, the New Philosophy, but they were pleasantly surprised at how open Stuart was to this. He didn't just get the concept, he really believed that it was possible, almost to the point of surprise that it had never been done before.

'Amazing,' said Stuart, 'That's the power of ideas for you.' He was nodding his head. Laura and Andy smiled at each other. They'd expected this part to be far harder.

'Do you think you can do it?' asked Laura, her pragmatism knowing no restraint.

'I have to, don't I,' said Stuart, warming the relationship despite misgivings. It was getting late and they were all tired.

'Shall we get some sleep then, and you can make a start tomorrow?' suggested Andy. Stuart yawned. He was about to speak, but yawned again, lifting his hand to his mouth.

'Sorry about that,' he said looking tired. He waited a second and Laura and Andy looked at him sympathetically. 'This can't wait until tomorrow,' said Stuart. Laura and Andy looked quite shocked, for they were all truly worn out. 'I'm going to start on it right now.'

'But…' began Andy, looking to remove any pressure that their guest might feel.

'No, I insist,' said Stuart. Laura and Andy shrugged then nodded approval. Stuart arose and walked to the table ready to start work. Laura and Andy stood up to retire. As Stuart took hold of a chair at the table to pull it out, he stopped and turned.

'I was wondering,' he began, 'what's going to happen when I've done this?'

'We're going to trial it again, like we did the first attempt, and then get it out as far as we can if it works. All of the hams will be involved, and we hope it will start going mainstream soon after that,' answered Andy. Stuart nodded approval.

'If I can get on with this quickly, we don't want any delay,' said Stuart. 'Before you go to bed, let's talk to this radio guy you mentioned, Clive Hill, and show me how the radio works.' Andy felt a little astonished by Stuart's enthusiasm, but given the gravity of the situation it was quite understandable. Andy took Stuart into the room with the radio, and spent half an hour showing him how it worked, introducing him to Clive. Everything was set up. Andy and Laura went to bed to sleep deeply, while Stuart worked into the night.

37. Salvation...

'Merry Christmas!' exclaimed Stuart as Andy entered the living space. Andy had only awoken a few minutes earlier and had got straight up.

'What?!' said Andy. Stuart laughed. He was in the kitchen area making some toast and tea.

'It's Christmas Day!' said Stuart, as if stating the obvious. Andy wondered whether or not Stuart was being metaphorical, then suddenly realised that it literally was Christmas Day.

'Laura! Get up! It's Christmas Day!' shouted Andy. He laughed with Stuart and joined him in the kitchen. Laura appeared a few minutes later.

'How'd you get on last night?' she asked Stuart cutting to the chase, oblivious to the Christmas dawn. The decorations that they'd put up a few days earlier seemed to twinkle more brightly. Stuart laughed.

'All done,' said Stuart. Laura and Andy both did a double take.

'What?!' said Andy, wondering if Stuart had really managed to get it written so quickly.

'All done,' repeated Andy.

'You've finished writing it?' said Laura, amazed at Stuart's potential adeptness. He nodded whilst rotating his hand by the wrist, indicating there was more.

'And it's out to test said Laura!' Stuart's hand continued rotating. 'You tested it!' Stuart's hand continued rotating. 'It works!' exclaimed Laura, heavily tinged with disbelief. Stuart's hand continued rotating. 'You've distributed it!' Stuart's hand stopped rotating and he nodded strongly. Andy and Laura were staring incredulously, open mouthed. They were absolutely dumbfounded. It seemed beyond belief that this whole nightmare could suddenly, and in an instant, be over. They were bewildered.

'My God! How?' asked Andy.

'It took me a few hours to write, but you'd done the hard stuff. Dressing it up was pretty straight forward. As soon as I'd finished, I got straight onto Clive. He was ready to go and was straight out testing. You know, when he turned up they must have thought it was Father Christmas coming. I guess he was delivering the best present they could have.' Stuart emphasised the 'was' and laughed at his joke. Laura and Andy might have too, if they were still not in awe of Stuart's extraordinary feat. 'Clive said the results were instant. The stooge had no interest in the New Philosophy whatsoever after hearing our idea. The effect was so quick, he was able to go straight to the next two to test it in next to no time, all with the same result.'

Laura had by now managed to seat herself at the table. She was looking down at hers and Andy's work in front of her. 'Distribution?' asked Laura.

'Started about an hour ago,' said Andy. 'Clive was convinced of the results and insisted we start as soon as possible,' he claimed. It was taking time for the good news of this miracle to sink in for Laura and Andy. They'd scored the big goal! This was it. The zombie plague was going to be defeated.

The realisation hit home. Laura and Andy began laughing and screaming. Andy grabbed a bottle of champagne and they popped the cork, spraying the fizz everywhere. Laura and Andy did feel a slight tinge that they would have liked to have been part of that night's events and to have seen the good idea before it went out, but they would have plenty of time to do that now, and such negative traces were completely swamped by their elation. There were still niggling, annoying doubts that they may be hoping too soon and that at any moment the news would come in that it had failed, but throughout the morning the reports from the hams kept on confirming that the good idea was working. What a Christmas!

As the morning moved into early afternoon, the news kept arriving from the jubilant hams, often in the form of an improvised carol or other festive song. Everyone who heard the good idea was unaffected by the New Philosophy. The hams were having a busy Christmas day, and as the whole story was shared that the zombie plague was caused by the New Philosophy, the vaccine administered first though, others were joining in with spreading the message. Now everybody would be hearing it soon, and although it meant that they still wanted to hear the New Philosophy, it would take an act of immeasurable lunacy not to listen to the good idea first. The zombie threat was still present for the time being, but its spread was finally being halted, and over the next few months, as Stuart's work would be translated into other languages and spread globally, the tiny group of remaining humans, their demise curtailed just in time, would rebuild the world as the remaining zombies naturally, and with human assistance, declined.

Andy prepared a Christmas dinner for the three of them that they sat down to a couple of hours later, the joy of the day overwhelming their feelings. Although others were out working hard at spreading the good news, they felt entitled to a day's respite, and were far away from where they could be of use in any case. As they raised their glasses to a new future, Andy's emotions resonated with the tinge of sadness that he saw in Laura's eyes.

'What's that?' said Andy. Laura and Stuart shook their heads oblivious to whatever had caught Andy's attention, their hearing far less attuned to the background sounds of rural isolation than Andy's. Andy got up and went outside onto the balcony. Laura and Stuart followed, both still holding their champagne glasses. As they stood outside on the balcony overlooking the countryside, they could all now hear something. It was coming from the direction of the approach road that meandered down towards Andy's place, the view obscured by trees. As they realised what it was, a car appeared on the road emerging through the trees, pulling up in front of the house. It was a saloon, not very big and may have once been white beneath the liberal daubs of grime and blood that now obscured its original appearance. There were numerous dents, and the windscreen had a spider's web smash obscuring the driver's vision and sight of who was inside.

'Who on earth's that?' said Andy. Stuart shrugged. They could at least be sure that it wouldn't be a zombie driving. Laura's heart pounded with excitement. She knew of only one person that was aware of Andy's place. Could it really be? She dropped her glass not caring that it shattered on the floor, and ran along the balcony. She scrambled over the railings at the end and lowered herself down from the platform to drop the last couple of feet to the ground, falling over to roll on the ground just as the door of the car opened and a man stepped out. He was bedraggled, obviously exhausted, but stood astride firmly holding his big gun, a smile effortlessly materialising through his weariness as Laura threw her arms around him. They embraced and kissed, holding each other tightly, not wanting to let go.

Andy simply couldn't believe what he was seeing and caught off guard, he couldn't prevent a couple of tears of joy from escaping.

'Simon?' asked Stuart, having heard all about him the previous night. Andy nodded, whilst tying to keep his face turned away from Stuart. As Simon and Laura's embrace continued, snowflakes began to fall, its timing creating raptures of pleasure that easily masked any bitter undercurrents from the chilly air. Laura and Simon swung each other around in a circle, gripping each other's hands tightly as Laura's swishing hair captured flakes of the seasonal surprise, whilst Andy and Stuart raised their glasses whooping with cheers and laughter.

Their joy that afternoon was unlimited as they caught up on past events amidst much drinking and eating. Laura and Simon could not leave each other's grasp, their feelings for each other now declared, as Simon described how he'd spent several days in hiding in Chesborough, scavenging for scraps, then making his escape using various vehicles he'd acquired along the way. He was absolutely insistent that he knew he would survive and return, and that his heroic diversion allowing Laura and Andy to escape had never been suicidal. His rewriting of events almost managed to spare the feelings of the pair.

As is always the way on Christmas Day, darkness descended early catching everyone unawares, but the celebrations continued. It was a beautiful night, and Laura decided to take a minute out on the balcony to take in the rare pleasure of a star spattered sky untainted by ground light. As she stepped out and looked up, she became aware that Stuart was stood to her side, leaning on the balcony looking out. Her misgivings were gone, buried beneath her awareness of Stuart's gargantuan efforts to write the good idea the night before, a day of revelry and the reunion with Simon.

A thin layer of snow now covered the ground and frost was setting in, making the already beautiful view even more appealing. The moon and star light was reflecting off the white expanse, illuminating the countryside, with the beautiful and eerie glow that only comes from freshly fallen snow, and sparkles of frost were glinting across the vista, as if handfuls of diamonds had been thrown down from the heavens.

'I really look forward to reading what you've written,' said Laura.

'Yes, you must,' replied Stuart.

'I've had a quick look, and the language is every bit as effective as the New Philosophy,' said Laura. 'If I didn't know what the real meaning was, I could never tell.' Stuart chuckled. His reaction made Laura think for a second. 'I hope we've done the right thing,' she said as a realisation came over her. She turned and looked to Stuart, but he continued to look at the sky. He appeared to be taking in the infinity of the universe, as if he were its master not intimidated in anyway by its unimaginable vastness, the stars timidly twinkly in deference.

'I mean, we've stopped the New Philosophy, but we had to replace it with something didn't we.' She awaited a response from Stuart but there was none. Laura tried to stimulate one. 'I guess there's no such thing as a neutral idea is there? We had to put some ideas into the good idea?'

'Free choice is an illusion. A myth,' said Stuart philosophically, continuing to take in the eternity of the stars. 'We all desire the freedom to make choices more than anything else, but every part of every choice we make is influenced by whatever experience and ideas we've been exposed to.' Laura was listening intently. 'A person born today would make completely different choices, have completely different ideas and ambitions, than if they'd been born a hundred years ago, a thousand, or even just ten.' Laura's thoughts coalesced.

'So we've created something that will change how people are,' she pondered. 'Maybe we've created the start of a better society.' Stuart was unmoved as he continued to absorb the enormity before him. A coldness came over Laura penetrating through the warmth of the wine.

'You realise,' she said, 'that this new viral structure for information could have the power to completely control humanity. Someone could get hold of this and do anything they want.'

Stuart turned his head towards Laura, his grin triggering pangs of terror throughout her. He erupted into laughter, at the world he knew before and the one he now stood in front of. He began to walk around. Stuart Grams circled laughing. Laura saw the truth within.

Made in the USA
Charleston, SC
18 September 2013